T0354869

WRECK ON THE
HIGHWAY

WRECK ON THE
HIGHWAY

LOGAN ST. MICHAEL

WRECK ON THE HIGHWAY

iUniverse books may be ordered through booksellers or by contacting:

iUniverse
1663 Liberty Drive
Bloomington, IN 47403
www.iuniverse.com
844-349-9409

ISBN: 978-1-6632-6302-5 (sc)
ISBN: 978-1-6632-6303-2 (e)

Library of Congress Control Number: 2024909967

Print information available on the last page.

iUniverse rev. date: 06/20/2024

PART ONE

DRIVERS! START YOUR ENGINES!

Last night I was out driving,
Coming home at the end of the working day,
I was riding alone through the drizzling rain,
On a deserted stretch of a county two lane
When I came upon a wreck on the highway . . .

-Bruce Springsteen

PART ONE

DRIVERS! START
YOUR ENGINES!

Time rushing past. Pushing through, pushing through.
The sun, blinding. The one in front, a quick turn, left. Legal?
Moving. The roar of an engine.
A face, behind reflective shades, goes slack with surprise.
An oath, yelled.
Impact.
Glass shatters, flying, reflecting the setting
sun dully like uncut gems.
Metal and plastic, bending, groaning, snapping loose and free.
Then the scream.

CHAPTER 1

Ari jerked awake, but refused to open his eyes to the sun tapping on his lids. Hours of sleep, but no rest. He peered through the slit of one lid to read the digital clock on his bureau. 9:30.

His face burrowed itself deeper into the pillows. Twenty minutes went by with him thinking, but not thinking. A dull ache in his crotch tugged at him. Despite being outnumbered by roughly every other cell in his body, the bladder won, forcing him to his feet as he made those long steps to the bathroom.

He felt the tingling release in his back muscles as he relieved himself, which brought an involuntary smile of contentment to his mouth. *Most pleasure I've had in the past eighteen hours,* he thought.

The hot water felt good on his face as he filled the sink. He stared in the mirror and made the daily mental tally of the flaws of his face. The ultra-kinky hair (*Jew-Fro!,* he said to himself), the way-too-big nose (*practically needs a builders permit*), the confused mixture of olive and sallow in his complexion (*at least there aren't any major zits happening*), the too- feminine mouth (*you got a real purty mouth, boy*).

About the only thing he found worthwhile (and that only because he had been complemented on them) were his eyes. At least they were a nice, warm shade of brown, if a bit intense and piercing. They made the rest of his face seem almost interesting, like an owl peering out of a dead tree.

He closed them. And that was a mistake. In his mind he sees it played back again, the video rental from hell. Trying to make that left hand turn and almost making it. Then comes the biker out of nowhere. Like a photo still: the weathered face with reflecting sunglasses perched on the nose, the tangled frizz of orange hair shooting behind like flames from a match head, the sudden O of surprise the mouth forms when the rider realizes collision is inevitable.

Then the crash itself, and the film speeds up slightly. After his scream of Holy fuck!, Ari's two side windows shatter. The car is rocked, and Ari hears the screech of his tires as they protest being taken off course. He reflexively pulls back, but it is unnecessary: he is miraculously spared from any shards of flying glass. The biker mysteriously, seems to have disappeared.

A gap in memory; the film is shut off. He supposes he got out of the car then, but can't remember if he did it under his own power, or with the help of the elderly lady who comforted him on the sidewalk. She talked to him soothingly, gently caressing his back; he remembers nothing of what she said.

He chanced to look over at the biker, huddled over the glass littering the blacktop like cast-off gemstones, cradling his (her?) left arm, but seemingly otherwise unhurt. Then the motorcyclist rose and, like a stagnant rain, drops of blood fell and joined the glass, flattened rubies amongst fake diamonds. Ari saw the tensing of solid sinew in the back of the legs and chanced to look up at a blood-streaked face as it surveyed the damage before it.

Amazingly, the glasses were still in place, if askew. But the lenses were streaked red From the gash in the biker's forehead. Ari couldn't really tell if the biker was looking at him, but he didn't think so. Instead, the figure seemed much more involved with what lay at its feet.

The tailpipe (*big, bulky, like the business end of a small bazooka*) had popped off and lay at the biker's feet. The front wheel lay a few more feet down the road, most of the spokes broken, still attached to the handlebars. The gas tank had cracked and the seat lay soaking in gasoline, a broken toy tossed aside by a careless child.

Ari felt it coming before he actually heard it. He saw the muscles in the back of the legs tense; big, meaty hamstrings poised like a taunt rubber band. It rippled up the lower back, to the coils of the trapezium underneath the dingy-grey, cut-off T-shirt, to the veins that bulged like malignant worms under the flesh of the neck.

The scream the apparition let loose froze Ari's blood. Even the elderly woman comforting him stiffened underneath the moth-ball smell of her shawl. Harsh and guttural it came, starting small, growing in volume. A barely human roar of hate, rage and pain. Louder and louder it came, eclipsing the piercing wail of the approaching sirens. Loud enough to swallow the whole fucking world . .

Ari doubled over, stumbled, and dry-heaved into the toilet, feeling his pulse thud behind his eyes. When it became evident to him that nothing was coming up, he pressed his throbbing brow to the cool porcelain. He massaged his temples with the heels of his hands, trying to ease a headache that was not quite there, trying to block the scream as it continued its unholy echo in his mind's ear.

The sink was full, and Ari plunged his entire head underneath the soapy tide, feeling tension drain from him like the oil from his pores. *How good it would feel,* he thought, *to stay this way, to just let everything drain away.* How good that would be. How easy that would be. How-

Ari jerked upright as he pulled his head free of the watery pull, gasping for air in harsh, racking breaths. His back slammed into the wall behind him. He stood there a moment, then felt his knees buckle, sliding into a squat. His gasps dissolved into sobs as he buried his face in his hands and felt the dark tide once again wash over him.

When he managed to get himself under control, he returned to his bedroom, hoping to catch a few minutes more of rest; the haze of weariness chomped at his edges.

Collapsing back on the bed, he spent several minutes gazing up at the ceiling, tracing the path of a small crack over in the corner. *Damn old house,* he thought. *All the money we're supposed to have and we live in the cheapest house in the neighborhood.* He had just let out a sigh when a knock came at the door. "Ari?" came his mom's high-pitched whine. "Ari? Are you up?"

No, Ma, I'm not, he thought. *Like that damn old lady in that stupid commercial, I've fallen and I can't get up. And I'm not even sure I want to.*

He sighed again, shutting his eyes. *Maybe if I just keep quiet . .*

The door opened and his mother entered. Ari resignedly opened his eyes again, regarding the small, aging woman with a spirit as faded as the red rinse of her hair and the blue of her bedclothes she rarely changed out of anymore. He studied the perpetual glazed-over look in her eyes and noted, with no small relief (a relief he hated himself for having), that at least the pupils were normal sized, something guaranteed to change as the day wore on.

He slapped that thought away as his mother sat on his bed beside him. "I heard a noise, she said. "I was worried you might've hurt yourself."

"I'm okay, Ma. Just feeling down."

"It's gonna be okay, Ari," she replied. "Your car-"

"-is totaled, Ma! I know! God, I know! Don't tell me any different!"

"We don't know that for sure. You haven't even gone to have it assessed yet."

"Oh, come on, Mom! I am not stupid! You didn't see what it looked like afterwards. The whole thing is smashed, wrecked, totaled!"

"You don't know that yet."

"I know, Ma. Believe me, I know!"

She sighed, and Ari could smell the first beer of the day on her breath. "Just like your father", she said.

"Don't say that. You know I hate it when you say that."

"Well, it's true", she retorted as she rose from the bed. "I don't know how I put up with you two sometimes."

I know how you do, Ari thought. Out loud, he said, "Ma? Don't go, okay? Please? Just sitdown with me here for a few minutes. Okay?"

She did as told. "Are you getting up soon?"

"Yeah, but don't go, okay? Please? Just sit with me awhile."

And that's when it hit: the most profound sense of helplessness and hopelessness he had ever felt in his twenty years on the planet. Whatever front he had put up for his mother cracked wide open, and

4

he felt the familiar sting in his nasal passages that always precludes a good cry.

Seeing this, his mother took him in her arms and held him close as all the pressures of the preceding day flowed out of him, bit by bit, tear by tear. They sat that way for a long time.

CHAPTER 2

Terry popped the top of her Zippo with her good hand, flicked it, thrust the end of her cigarette into the flame and inhaled deeply, letting the soothing power of the tobacco fumes flow into her as she slouched back in the hospital bed.

The TV was on, showing some stupid game show where the only thing dumber than the contestants were the prizes. Mostly she was lost in her own head; a good smoke always helped her think straight. Fuck the rules. The present situation required her to do some real thinking.

The clock on the wall said 9:30, but she had been up for the past hour or so, when the damn kitchen crew had shown up carrying a tray of crap they labeled "breakfast". Terry had never actually eaten shit before (not literally, at least), but she figured what they gave her was pretty damn close: two cracker-thin slices of bread, as brown as spoiled milk, a couple strips of lard that must have come off a pig that died of a heart-attack, and a heaping yellow pile of pus that had as much relation to a chicken as she had to a nigger. Even less, if that was possible. On the TV, some yuppie bitch was getting all hot and bothered over winning a goddamn all-expense-paid trip to Florida. What the fuck was in Florida? Just old people, spics and Jews.

Terry's faded-sky blue eyes narrowed. If that little fuck she'd run into yesterday wasn't a kike himself, she'd kiss somebody's ass. With that nose and skin tone? Maryland was full of them, especially this part. Rich-ass Montgomery County. The voice of her father spoke up in her head, unbidden, a rare moment of humor on the old turd's part: *Goddamn Montgom'ry County, Terry,* he snorted between swigs from one of the many bottles of hooch that became his only friends after Mama died. *People so rich there, they don't get crabs. They get the LOBSTERS!!*

Terry felt the hairs on the back of her neck rise, felt the familiar rage that always washed through her like a boiling tide when she thought of her father. The fact that he was six years dead did nothing to soothe her anger; the fact that she helped make him so consoled her only a little.

She grabbed the remote off the side table, pulling a little on her elevated, cement- encrusted left arm as she did so, causing a sharp bolt of pain to go coursing through her body. She barely noticed in her effort to flick channels.

Another game show. Some talk show where everybody felt all their emotions while wanting to feel each other up. The news, carrying some interview with that wrinkled old movie actor some conspiracy somewhere elected president years back. Terry knew about conspiracies; didn't her father fill her head with enough about them when he was still farting around on this planet? If it wasn't the "comuniss", it was "the niggers". If it wasn't "the niggers", it was the "Ay-rabs". If it wasn't the "Ay-rabs", it was the "Heebs", who were all a bunch of "comuniss" anyway, and so on and so forth.

Whether the old fuck was right about all them was still open; what Terry knew for sure was that there was at least an unspoken, loose-knit conspiracy of people who liked to keep people like her on a constant diet of shit sandwiches and fuck-you tea.

Until now.

The ends of her pale, bloodless lips turned upward in a smile as she contemplated the possibilities: the piles of cold, hard cash that was sure to come her way after this little setback. She knew her brother had kept up the insurance payments on her bike (or at least he said he had, and there'd be hell to pay if he didn't) and if she added onto that the money from the lawsuit she was considering slapping on the little twat who'd pulled in front of her at the last minute, she could be in hog heaven. Maybe even be able to give up the "courier service" that was her main source of income.

In her mind's eye, she can still see it: the little punk huddled over on the sidewalk next to that old lady, digging his face in her dried up old tits like the world's oldest (and ugliest) baby. Sure, she got a little mad when she saw what shape her bike was in, but who could blame her for that? Hell, once she was done bleeding the little cocksucker dry (or more likely, his rich daddy), there'd be more than enough loot to get it all fixed up. Or even get a new one. Or two. *Yeah*, she thought as she flicked an ash onto the floor. *Maybe things're finally lookin' up.*

She had just sucked down another deep drag on her cancer-stick when trouble arrived in a uniform and sensible shoes. The chief nurse, a fat, ugly, sixty-years-old-if-a-day crone barked, "Miss Scranton! How many times have I had to tell you?! You are not allowed to smoke while you are in the hospital!"

"Dunno", she responded. "Ain't been keepin' track."

"Put that out before I have an orderly come and put it out for you!"

Terry regarded the old bat for a moment under heavy-lidded eyes, then exhaled a cloud of smoke directly into the woman's face. She dropped the butt on the floor, snaked a hard, muscular leg out from under her hospital gown (while also giving the nurse a wide-eyed view of her heavily-scarred privates), and crushed the burning ember with her bare foot.

Once the cigarette was out, the nurse allowed a hint of a smile to play about her wet, rubbery mouth. "I just came to tell you," she said with obscene cheer. "That you have a visitor."

"Do I have a choice?", Terry asked.

"No," the nurse said. "Right this way, Detective."

In walked a large, heavy-set Negro in a cheap suit and a fedora, carrying a large, manila envelope under his arm and a smug expression on his face. For Terry, it was hate at first sight. "Will there be anything else, Detective?"

"No, thank you, ma'am. You can go. Miss Scranton and I need to speak in private."

"I'm sure," the nurse said, smiling as she left.

The black cop flopped his bulk in a chair next to the bed and took of his checkered hat, placing it on top of the bureau next to the hospital bed. "Hello, Terry", he said.

"Do I know ya?"

"No, but I know you." He reached into his jacket pocket, pulling out a long, plastic tube with a hard-rubber screw top, then slapped it down on the tray table in front of Terry. She didn't bat an eye, or even bother to look at it. Instead, she kept a hard, steady gaze at the cop's eyes. "Whassat?, she said.

"Why don't you tell me? I mean, seeing how it was sitting in the gas tank of your motorcycle and everything."

"Sometimes I loan my bike out. Prolly somebody else put it there."

"Bull. You don't have that good a friend anywhere in the whole world. It's yours, Terry."

"I ain't sayin' it is, I ain't sayin' it ain't. But so what? It ain't against the law to carry a tube in yer tank."

"It is if its carrying illegal contraband. Don't play dumb with me, lady, even if you're a natural at it. You know what it's used for."

"Pretend I don't."

"What're we gonna find when we run some tests on it, huh? Maybe some coke residue? Crack? Nah. That's too sophisticated for a piece of trash like you. Maybe some of the cheap stuff? How 'bout some home-cooked methamphetamine?"

"Who the fuck are you, and what the fuck do you want?"

The cop pulled a badge from his jacket pocket and flipped it open. "Detective Bernard Jones of the Maryland State Police, Vice Division. But that's enough about me. Let's go on to you," he responded. He then opened the manila envelope and pulled out a thick file with Terry's name typed out on the top flap. The detective flipped it open and began to read out loud. "Name: Terrencia Scranton. Born twenty-five years ago in Wheeling, West Virginia, on April 20th, 1965."

The cop gave a low whistle. "Wow. West Virginia. Bit out of your element being here, ain'tcha, Terry? Do they even have hospitals in West Virginia, or do y'all go see the local witch doctor? Or vet?"

Terry said nothing, so he went on. "Arrested for the first time at twelve for breaking and entering at your local grocery store. Nice little mom and pop kinda place? Hmm. They don't play around in ole W-V-A, do they? Got your ass sent right to the local house of juvenile detention! Damn, girl! Not even into puberty yet, and already into hard time!"

"How'd you get that? My lawyer told me that shit is sealed."

"C'mon, Terry, you think it's impossible to unseal a record, once you've proved just cause? Especially for a little lady like you, who started so early? Hell, we in the poh-lice do it all the time!"

Jones flipped to the next page, skimmed in, and decided with a mixture of compassion and calculation to hold back its contents. For now. "Well, that's all ancient history, ain't it, Terry?," he said. "Why don't we move on to the here and now?"

"Do we have a choice?"

Jones slapped a photo down flat in front of her, his thin film of humor stripped away like a scab on not-yet formed skin. "No, you don't. Not on what we have."

It'd be so fuckin' easy, Terry thought, staring deep into the red-rimmed eyes of the nigger cop. *So fuckin' easy to jam my finger right into the eye socket, hear the scream, feel the blood squirt onto my overgrown plastic diaper, never minding it, feeling my finger go deeper, till I popped through the skull and ripped right into his brain. How would it feel? Could I make it all the way, before the orderlies got here? Could I just take one of these self-satisfied fucks down with me? No, hold up*, a calmer, sterner voice answered in tones she would never admit to in the haunted backwaters of memory as sounding much like her father's. *Wait it out. See what else this uppity spade's got. Cool it down and ride it out*.

One deep breath later, the wild impulse was flushed away; dismissed, if not forgotten. And when she picked up the photo, her hand was almost steady.

The photo showed a cleared out patch of wilderness centered by a ramshackle wooden structure one-story high, but a thousand feet long. In another time (and by another race), the place would be called a juke joint, but to call it that now would be giving it an undeserved credit. Several super-sized motorbikes were seen parked out front, but that didn't interest Terry. She had seen them all, many times, up close and personal. It was the two figures seen arguing in front of the structure and the bikes that Terry assumed this public dick was all in a huff about.

The first had her back to the camera, so at least she still had that going for her. Still, with the same outfit on in the picture that was now in the hospital rooms closet, it was pretty tough case to argue. That, and the bright, carroty-orange hair she had tried to dye out with Clorox one evening, with less-than-positive results.

The other, facing out in full view, was a pockmarked, diminutive, long-haired Hispanic male with a huge bushy mustache and a perpetual scowl on his face. *Fuckin' Nesto,* Terry thought. *Just had to be a prick that day, start with an argument. Well, maybe I can still pull yer wetback ass out of the deep fry. Since I like ya so damn much.*

The cop was talking. "Not the best angle, but I think we can safely assume that's you, Terry?"

"Maybe. Maybe not. Lotsa people look like me up there."

"Yeah, I heard that about West Virginia. Everything's relative up there."

"Huh?"

"Never mind. Just explain why you're there with the biggest drug kingpin outside the D.C. area."

"Who?"

"Oh, gimme a fuckin' break, lady!", Jones snapped back. "You're caught red-handed, dead-to-rights, in the parking lot of the Demon Heads clubhouse, with the Head Demon himself, and you're still gonna play the babe-in-the-woods routine? How stupid are you?!"

Terry said nothing, just stared. Then she smiled. And Detective Bernard Jones of the Maryland State Police, twenty-five year veteran of the force and countless drug busts, a man who believed he had seen every form of human depravity and evil on record, in every possible state of existence, froze at the sight of that one grin. It was the smile of the most terrifying sort of person imaginable, from a cop to the everyday civilian on the street: the smile of someone with nothing to lose.

"You know how you catch a racoon, Detective?," Terry began. "Nah, 'course you don't. Yer such a sophisticated sonuvabitch, you dunno nuthin' 'bout tryin' t'catch food out in the country, where I grew up. You got it all laid out for you in some store somewhere, all nice 'n' neat. Well, where I come from, where there ain't much money, either cuz there's no work or cuz yer shitter of an old man drunk it all up the night before, you try n' make do."

"When catchin' a coon, you slip something bright and yellow at the bottom of a short barrel, and leave only one opening on top, just big enough for the coon's paw to get in. Now this hole is surrounded by nails, so when the coon tries to pull up the shiny stuff on the bottom, he gets his fist caught and can't pull out."

"Now, yer thinkin' what I was first thinkin' when I was first told this: what's to keep the coon from opening his hand, dropping that thing he wants, and high-tailin' it outta there? Nothin' 'cept the coon's own stubborn ass. Couple times, I didn't even have t'kill the stupid thing; it ripped its goddamn arm up and bled to death. And it was still holdin' on!"

Terry smirked even more broadly. "Guess that's why they call you niggers 'coons', Detective Jones. Y'all'd rather kill yerself over something that looks like it might be gold."

"Why you goddamn-"

"Shaddup!!," Terry roared. "You're on *my* fuckin' time now! The only reason you're still here is cuz there ain't nuthin' good on the TV right now. But I'm gettin' to the point where I'd rather sit though a day's worth of your homegirl Oprah's touchy-feely shit than have t'listen to you flappin' yer fat lips."

"You realize how miserable I could make your life, girl?"

"You realize how quick I could have an orderly throw you out? Or maybe you ain't got no choice, huh, cop? I mean, since you like to dig around people's lives, why don't we see whassup wit' *you*?

12

How old are you, forty? Fifty? More? And how long you been a cop? Prolly over half yer life. Being a cop makes you proud, kinda. But sometimes it's tough. Tough on you, tough on yer family. How many divorces you been through? More than one, prolly. Maybe it's not even the late nights away from home. Hell, most marriages I know of, the only reason people stay together is cuz they ain't around each other much. Naw, I can tell what it is jus' from lookin' at ya. From *smellin'* ya. Livin' mosta yer life with a rummy, you can see one comin' a mile away. How many you had this morning, Detective Jones?"

Now it was the detective's turn to be silent, so Terry eagerly continued. "And comin' all this way just to talk to a 'red-neck bitch' like me? Sounds likes yer desperate. My guess is yer bosses been yankin' yer chain lately, so yer gonna grab fer whatever straw there is, no matter what, just to prove they're wrong 'bout you. Even if you bleed to death, just like that *coooon*."

Jones said nothing for a time, and Terry just continued to smile.

Finally, Jones broke the silence with a voice low and steady. "You're pretty good with your mouth, girl," he said. "Real good. Your daddy like it when you used that mouth on him?"

The color drained from Terry's face, then returned in shades of red and purple. Her smile had disappeared faster than mourners around a corpse with gas. "You . . .motherfucker," she croaked. "You son of a goddamn-"

"Tell me something, Terry," Jones broke in. "Something I've always wondered, but it's not exactly something I can ask real people, y'know? Somebody might take offense, report me to those same bosses who're always 'yankin' my chain, as you put it, and get me in trouble. But since you know me so well, and I, you, I think I can ask you this question."

Jones paused, as if uncertain, then continued. "All those times when a girl gets molested by her father, violated in every single way by him, does she ever reach a point when she starts to *enjoy it?* Where she actually starts to look forward to Daddy sticking his meat into her every crack? I mean, the cracks that can actually fit it in, though

I suspect Daddy didn't exactly get too choosy with you, did he? He probably slipped it in those places with the hope that someday it *would* fit."

Terry's eyes had become twin beacons of blue fire, her square jaw flexing back and forth, the teeth grinding together with a force that could crack Brazil nuts. Jones shrugged as if he didn't notice the live wire sparking before him. "Ah, well. Never mind, he said. "Forget I said anything, Terry. All of it. You can go down with Gonzaga if you want. I don't give a shit. Just another piece of slime we don't have to scrape off the sidewalk later."

He rose, picking up his hat. "Keep the pics, Terry. I got plenty back at the station. Pin it up in your outhouse or something. Maybe you can use them if you run out of toilet paper."

The cop was just about out the door when he turned for a final glance over his shoulder. "Too bad Daddy can't see you now, Terry," he said, giving her his own smirk. "He'd be really impressed how his little girl grew up."

He left without another word.

Terry was silent for a few moments more, her eyes and jaw the only betrayals of the emotions seething within. Then she rose, letting forth a heart-stopping scream and overturning the TV tray, sending everything flying: food, tray, pictures and all.

The first orderly had his ribs taped, the second received a concussion, the third lost two teeth before she was subdued.

CHAPTER 3

"This is pretty damn serious", Mr. Sussman said out loud.

Thank you for that piece of input, Oh master of the fucking obvious, his son rejoined in his mind. The three of them sat around the dinner table, a big, bulky, no-nonsense oak affair situated in the Sussman kitchen, and the scene of many 'family discussions'. Or if you asked Ari, Maury Sussman's personal soapbox where he gassed off about anything that was on what passed for his mind.

But, of all the dealings he had with his father, here was the example of the very bottom rung of Ari's personal ladder: the occasion of his "fucking up" and his father taking on the stern-but-loving parent role, which he probably got out of a book somewhere (or, considering his father's lack-of-reading habits, more likely taken it from watching too many 50s-style family sit- coms).

His mother sat on his left, making a cursory attempt at paying attention, but Ari had counted the beer cans sitting in the trash: six of them, on top of the usual two capsules of Xanax she took every evening like clockwork. That she hadn't passed out already spoke more of the tolerance she had built up over the years rather than any application of strong will and/or faith.

"Yeah, pretty damn serious," Ari's father repeated in the same thoughtful-verging-on- patronizing tone, the one that decided a long time ago what was to be done, but was going to at least look like contained an open mind on the subject.

"Yeah, I know, Dad," Ari said, trying to push the hostility he felt down through force of sheer will. They had just come back from getting the car out of the impound lot, where his father had already made the uncensored form of his feelings known. *Jesus Christ!*, his father had exclaimed while making the gravel beneath his feet crunch a little as he started in amazement. *You really beat the shit outta this thing!*

Ari, for one, didn't really think the car looked all that bad, considering. Sure, the windows were broken and part of the door was caved in (not to mention the piece of decorative stripe that had been knocked loose and dragged on the ground), but the wheels weren't interfered with when it was driven, and, God knows, the damn thing's engine still ran.

Maury Sussman said nothing after that initial exclamation, his mind automatically calculating on how "beat to shit" would translate into actual dollars and cents. Pretty damn high, Ari could see from watching his father's face. "The frame's not bent or anything, I don't think," Mr. Sussman was continuing in the kitchen. "Hard to tell with so much damage to the outside body. Better not be. You can kiss the whole damn thing goodbye if the frame's even slightly bent."

"Yeah, Dad. I know."

"Yeah, *what* do you know? Do you know how much its gonna cost to get that thing fixed?"

"I don't know! Seven hundred bucks, maybe."

Mr. Sussman snorted. "Try a grand! Easy!"

"Maury, you don't know that," Mrs. Sussman said. "You haven"t even taken it for an estimate-"

"Oh, believe me, I know! You don't know anything! I'm the one out there working my ass off while the two of you live in your own goddamn-"

"Yeah, here we go again!," Ari spat. "Another speech on how you've got it so damn rough out there, while we just sit here and don't appreciate it! Here, let me recite it for you, save you the trouble."

"Ari, stop it!", Mrs. Sussman cried.

"If I'd said that to my old man when I was your age, he'd have smacked the shit out of me! And I'd deserve it!", Mr. Sussman exclaimed, then gave out another disgusted snort. "Oughta just let you pay for it yourself."

"Well, why not then?," Ari replied. "I got some money saved up."

Now Mr. Sussman out-and-out *laughed.* "What money? From that 'summer job' of yours?"

"Yeah."

"You call that a job? Some place where you move boxes for a few hours a day and they don't pay you shit? Try spending twelve hours a day in a damn sweatshop in the garment district where the AC only half works because your old man's trying to save a few bucks so the business don't go under!"

"Oh, for Chrissake-!"

"And in the winter-"

"Yeah, in the winter, you nearly froze all your fingers off 'cause there was no heat at all. I told you I can finish the whole speech for you. And you know what? It doesn't get any more interesting in the re-telling."

Ari's dad shook his head. "I can't believe I've gotta kid like you."

Ari felt the usual pangs of guilt blossom in his stomach, feelings that were much more difficult for him to hold down than the flares of hostility. He had worked his ass off during the summer. He had! Everyone had said so, from his boss to his co-workers. The whole reason he'd even got into this damn wreck was because he was doing a favor for his boss, checking out a new restaurant where the company wanted to go for an end-of-summer celebration. So why couldn't he say as much to his old man?

Because you know what he'd do, Ari thought. *Grunt like a pig again and say how we must not be working too hard if we have time to celebrate. Some outcomes are too predictable to be even tried.*

But he knew the value of hard work, the benefits of a job well done. So why was his father able to play this guilt-card so successfully?

"Ari, honey," his mother broke into his thoughts. "You can't take anything out of the money you've earned this summer. It has to pay for everything and last you till the end of the term."

"I could get by," Ari responded weakly.

"Damn, you're hard-headed!," his father exclaimed. "Haven't you been listening to a single thing I told you? Didn't I just tell you it wasn't enough?

"Y' know what? I think I'd rather take the hit financially than to have to listen to you deride my accomplishments-"

"We are not 'deriding your accomplishments'", Mrs. Sussman retorted, the first hint of steel edging into her voice. "God! Honestly, you always act like you're so goddamn put upon all the time! Haven't you once thought about how all this affects *me?* You could've been killed! And where would I have been? How would I have suffered? Haven't you thought in the least about that?"

Ari felt like he was choking, like all the oxygen around him had suddenly turned into syrup mixed with molasses. Before he knew what he was doing, he stood up. "Where are you going?," he heard his mother say from a distance.

"Out," he responded. "Somewhere. I don't know where yet, but just out." "How're you gonna get there, smart guy?," his father sneered. "You forget already you don't have a car?"

But Ari wasn't listening; all he could think of was getting out the front door. He vaguely heard his mother shouting something about being back in time for dinner before he slammed the door shut behind him.

The open air revived him, almost made him feel giddy. Outside, he could breathe. He staggered onto the gravel of the Sussman driveway, but already it felt as though a great weight had lifted from his chest once he got out of the house and the stagnant, cloying atmosphere his parents had built around themselves all their lives.

Gradually, as his vision cleared and his heart rate reduced to normal, he noticed he was crouched down next to the ruin of his car. His father had thrown a canvas tarp over the shattered half, safe from prying eyes as they passed on the adjacent street. Still, covered or not, the damage was significant enough that one could see from the outline that something was seriously wrong. Ari ran his hand over the twists and crimps of the concealed section, tracing every broken and bent nuance, every dent, every ping. He mused to himself on how vital a place in his thoughts this hunk of junk had become in the last twenty-four hours. Before all this, he considered a car just a tool, a service vehicle that took you from point A to B, and needed some occasional tinkering in between to make it run right. He supposed he had gotten this attitude from his parents, one of the less mentally/ emotionally taxing of their legacies. Growing up, "the car" and all its makes, shapes and models never had much hold over him; in this, he felt different from most boys his age. The thought of an automobile as being a living breathing thing, much less an extension of his own self, seemed ludicrous.

His first car had been a used Volkswagen Beetle, or, as some of his less-than-kind classmates had called it (the ones that usually drove Alfa Romeros, Trans-Ams and Corvettes to school) a "Bug". Ari, for one, thought it was being too complementary by comparing it to an animal, even an insect. Privately, he thought the semi-circular vehicle looked more like a pregnant roller-skate.

Still, it ran. For a while, at least. Yes, the utilitarian automobile that Mr. Sussman thought would be such a great character builder for his son one day started billowing smoke out its tail end while driving down the highway. Ari, as scared and angry as he was when he started producing his own fogbank down the Beltway, ultimately felt great relief when his father decided to trash the moving disaster area rather than repair it so it could implode another day.

And now this. Rather than buy a new car, his father had chosen to give him another hand me down: a silver-colored Honda Accord. Still very utilitarian, but at least it looked like a car, not like the Nazis' last joke on the world. And yet, reflecting on the past day's events, Ari couldn't exactly argue with his dad's choice. The expenses of a near-totaled Accord was chicken feed compared to the price of restoring a near-totaled Ferarri. Perhaps there was good fortune in owning a near-anonymous auto.

Yeah, lucky fucking me, Ari thought as he regarded the two-ton metal and plastic hulk that now carried the most negative of distinctions a car could carry, one that reflected back on the owner, marking him as a careless idiot, a moron who zigged when he should have zagged.

Ari could imagine all the stares in his direction as he took his wreck into town for the estimates. He could anticipate the blankly shocked looks on the faces of the body-shop workers as he showed them the damage, could see them shake their heads ruefully, snicker behind his back at his stupidity. Here was a prime fool for the taking, someone who carried the vehicular form of the Scarlet Letter. A stupid owner, and a terrible driver.

Ari moaned softly to himself as he placed his head on the still-cooling hood of his car. How could things fall to shit so quickly? School was starting in less than a week; another lengthy vacation from his parents was about to begin anew. He should be taking this time to get his school supplies together, not dragging his ass around town trying to find the one who'd rob him the least while simultaneously laughing at him behind his back the most. He should be getting his dorm in order (a much-coveted single this year) and reconnecting with friends from last year, not driving this mechanized dung heap around for the world's amusement and prying, judgmental eyes.

Ari could feel that morning's headache returning to that place behind his eyes. Brought down by a piece of machinery. The another old adage cropped up in Ari's mind: the one about not knowing what you have until it's gone. Why did mankind in the late twentieth century place so much damn importance on its cars? How did it get to be that way? Twenty years ago, owning a car was considered a luxury, a status symbol for all good social climbers everywhere. Now the tables had turned and had made humans the grasping, needy slaves to their own particular vehicular rhythm. To *not* own a car these days was socio-economic death. Without a car, you were practically a Luddite, no better than the Amish in Pennsylvania Dutch Country who cut themselves from modern ways and means. Hell, from *life itself.*

Without a car, you were nothing. A social zero. An outcast. The Thing That Should Not Be.

Ari shook his head to clear it. Too many pointless musings made his head hurt even worse. He couldn't go back inside to his parents; that would've been like rubbing a salt lick on a bleeding wound. There was only one real refuge for him now, and he desperately hoped that she would be home and be open to him. She started school a week earlier than he did, and was already swamped with work. Such was the life a Pre-Law student.

Ari skipped along the flagstones that led into the Sussman's backyard, then took the well worn path through the patch of woods that bordered their property. He didn't notice until he was halfway there that he had broken into a run.

CHAPTER 4

The phone on the other end of the line rang once. Twice. In the middle of the third ring, it was picked up. "Hello?", the voice on the other end said.

"Hey there, baby brother," the caller drawed.

"Hey . . .Terry."

"Whatsa matter, kiddo? Ain't ya glad to hear from yer big sis?"

"Frankly?"

"Whatever. Guess ya heard 'bout my little. . . fuck up."

"Yeah, insurance company called me this morning."

"Jus' like friggin' clockwork. Did they tell you how soon I'd be gettin my bike fixed?

There was silence on the other end, too long for Terry's taste. "Blake? Ya there? I asked ya when the insurance company said my bike would be ready."

Terry heard a quick intake of breath from the other end, the sound of a kid getting ready to take some nasty medicine. "They didn't," he admitted.

"Didn't what? Didn't say?"

"No, they're not gonna fix your bike."

Terry felt the pulse in her ears get louder. "What?! Why the hell not? You been keepin' up with the payments, ain't ya?" Another silence, and now Terry felt her heart sink in her chest while simultaneously treble its beat. *What the fuck did you fuck up now, you little fuck?*, she thought.

"I kept up with the payments . . .", Blake started.

"Yeah? And?" "And . . . the only thing you're covered for is liability. Nothing on yourself."

Now her vision began to cloud over, and she struggled to keep her voice even. "And why is that, Blake?", she said.

She jumped a little at the sudden explosion that came out of the receiver. "Because that's the only thing I can manage, you stupid bitch! With your record, I was damned lucky to even get that! Hell, the bike is legally mine! You don't even have a goddamn license!"

"What the fuck do I need a license for? I been drivin' the damn things since I was a kid!"

"'Cuz that's the way the real world works, Terry! Get it through your thick fuckin' skull! You're not gonna get covered by any insurance company as long as you ain't got a license, and since you already got a record . . . Shit! I wouldn't get any more insurance for you even if I could, you know that?"

"Say what?"

"You heard me! It's time this shit ended, Terry. I'm sicka cleanin' up after you every time you make a mess!"

"Yeah?"

"Yeah! This one's on you, sis. You only got liability cuz that's what you are! A fuckin' liability! Well, it all ends now. You're on your own, Terry. I'll have your bike dropped off at the house, and then we're quits, all right? Fix it your damn self. Then you can fuck off. I don't want you anywhere near me or my family. You show up at my house, I'm calling the cops. Grow up and get the fuck out of my life!"

Terry said nothing, then took a deep breath of her own. "All right, baby bro. If that's the way our baby boy wants it, that's the way it'll be. But I want ya t'know three things before we break off. Number one: you don't know what a 'liability' is until ya had yer own father's cock up yer ass."

"That ain't gonna-"

"Number two: the reason y'dunno what a liability it is cuz all the times I took it up the ass for you, cuz when Daddy got drunk any crack suited him."

"It ain"t gonna work this time, Terry."

23

"An' number three, if I ever do see you or your wife, or either of your two brats in town, Jesus an' all His Apostles ridin' in on Sherman tanks ain't gonna be able to keep me from rippin' yer fuckin' guts sideways out yer asses!!"

It was a good threat, somewhat spoiled by her brother clicking off around the word "sideways". "Don't you hang up on me, you cock-sucking son of a whore!!," Terry screamed as she slammed the receiver several times against the cradle of the public pay phone until it cracked. Her jaw clenched, her eyes flared, but the most of her fury was spent. She dully stared down at the cracked receiver as it bobbed on its metal cord like a hanged man. It was a sunny day outside; the sun glinted on the exposed metal.

Terry took a deep breath and closed her eyes, willing the tension out of her. They had released her that morning from the hospital with her left arm in a cast and sling without so much as a by-as-you-leave. So much for bedside manner and compassion. She'd hopped the nearest bus to the nearest convenience store in order to make the call; now all she had was a few bucks to her name and no way to get home.

First things first, though. She entered the store and made a beeline to the front counter.

"Marlboros," she said to the clerk. "Unfiltered."

CHAPTER 5

The house before him was silent, but Ari knew that meant nothing. Rachel often locked herself away during periods of intense study. During her more cloistered moments, the Brannan household often resembled a convent, minus the laughs. Ari cautiously knocked on the door, then rang the bell, once, for good measure. After its tone subsided, Ari strained his ears and heard something positive: the faint sound of Duran Duran being played on a stereo. Despite all that had happened, he couldn't resist a smile.

He looked over at her bedroom window and saw the curtain part an inch. Duran Duran ceased and soon came the hollow pounding of approaching footsteps. The front door's lock clacked open and Rachel Brannan stood before him.

She was casually dressed in a sweat suit, but that homey touch was the only mundane thing about her. She was the same height as Ari, but there the resemblance ceased. Rachel Brannan was quite simply beautiful, and every time Ari saw her he wondered how he could've been so lucky as to have such a person in his life. Her Black Irish beauty had briefly gotten her a modeling contract when she and Ari were still in high school, but her lack of the right height and general dissatisfaction with the business stopped it before it really started. But, unlike a lot of pretty girls, Rachel refused to coast on her looks. Underneath the luxurious flow of her chocolate- brown hair, perfect alabaster skin and emerald green eyes was a fierce intellect, a kind hearted personality and a wicked sense of humor.

She smiled as soon as she saw him. "Ari!," she began. "I was going to call you tonight! How-"

Her smile turned to a frown as soon as she took full stock of her friend. "What's wrong? My God! You look terrible!"

"I feel terrible, Rache," Ari admitted.

"Well, don't just stand there! Come on in!"

She led him by the arm into the Brannan's kitchen and sat him in one of the four swivel chairs that surrounded the dinner table. "Want some coffee? I was just about to make a batch," she offered.

"This late? Won't it keep you up?"

"It's half-and-half. Just up for part of the night. Gotta finish this legal brief they assigned us. You believe this shit? Not even a week, and they're already assigning us papers. A short one, but still!"

Ari rose from his seat. "If you're busy-"

Rachel gently, but most definitely firmly, pushed him back down. "Sit," she commanded. "Like I said, it's short, only about five pages, and I'm almost halfway there already. It can wait. You don't look like you can."

She bustled over to the coffee-maker sitting on the counter and began measuring out tablespoons from the jar of coffee. "So, talk to me. What's going on?"

"Got into a car accident yesterday."

Rachel started, spilling some coffee granules on the counter. "How bad?," she asked as she wiped them into the sink.

"Motorcycle crashed into my right side. Broke both windows and crimped the door in something awful."

"Frame get bent?"

"Don't think so. Won't know till I take it in for an estimate."

"What happened?"

"I was on my lunch break at work, and my boss asked me to head on over to this restaurant he'd heard about. Wanted me to check it out. I think he wants to reserve it for an end of the summer party for the crew at the warehouse. Anyway, I was trying to rush there and get back in time. We'd had a huge shipment come in that morning and I didn't want the others guys stuck with the whole load."

"Well, that was nice of you," Rachel remarked as she ran the tap.

Ari shrugged. "So here I am, trying to hustle down Rockville Pike when I get behind this funeral procession. Do you believe that? A goddamn funeral procession! So finally I manage to get from behind it, and I go into what I think is a left-hand lane onto Shady Grove Road. At least, I see the car ahead of me make a left hand turn, so I figure I can too. But I can't see behind this van that's directly opposite me, making his own left turn. Stupid me, I figure I might as well go for broke. Stupid, stupid! Cuz all of a sudden, this biker comes outta nowhere, must've been doing at least sixty, from what I can tell from the car, and wham! Right into me!"

Ari broke out of his reverie long enough to see Rachel staring at him over her shoulder. *Whatever I got, it must be catching*, Ari thought. Rachel's jaw had dropped open and her fair skin had gone a shade paler. "Rache? You okay?", he asked.

"Yeah . . . Yeah, go on. Then what happened?"

"Well . . . I sorta lost track after that. I remember yelling 'Holy Fuck!' when I knew the biker was gonna hit me, and I think I remember pulling over to the sidewalk and getting out. But most of what I remember next was the biker."

"What about . . .him? Her?"

"You know, I don't even know. Isn't that awful? It looked a little bit like a woman, I guess, but it moved like a man. Had big sunglasses on, so I couldn't see the face that clearly. And I do remember that it was built like a brick shithouse. And the scream. I definitely remember the scream."

"The scream?"

"Yeah. When . . . it . . . saw what happened to his or her bike. It screamed. I couldn't even tell the sex from the scream! I thought its guts were going to burst out of his or her mouth!"

Rachel rushed over, placing a not-quite steady hand over Ari's more-noticeably shaking ones. "God, that's terrible!," she remarked.

"I don't think . . . 'it'. . .even looked at me once, y'know? I think if he or she had, I woulda started screaming."

"Here, let me get you something," she said, rushing over to the adjacent dining room's cabinet and pulling out a bottle.

"What's that?', Ari asked.

"Somethin' that's good fer what ails ya," Rachel answered in a pretty fair rendition of an Irish brogue. A bit o' the Walker boy, Black branch o' the family."

"I don't think-"

"Boy chick, we ain't got no Manischewicz!," she rejoined in a nasally New Yawk accent. "Take what youse c'n get!"

Ari laughed. "Why you disgustingly anti-Semitic, shiksa bitch!"

"Shut yer gob, ye Jew bastard," she retorted in the brogue. "And take yer bloody medicine!"

"Yes, ma'am."

Rachel filled his coffee cup two-thirds of the way, then poured in a liberal shot of whiskey. She then repeated the action for herself, but with a slightly more conservative shot of booze. "Thanks," Ari said as she placed the cup before him.

"No prob," she answered, flopping down in the seat next to him. "So, after this. . . person screamed, what happened?"

"It's kind of a blur. I remember this nice old lady came over and started talking to me, calmed me down a bit. Then the cops came over, and I can't remember a damn thing they said. When the ambulance finally came, they gave me the once over, and I guess they decided I was okay. Physically, at least. I was shaking like a leaf!"

"You still are. Take a sip."

Ari took a swig of coffee and winced at the taste. "Man, I could get high off the fumes!"

"One of the advantages of being born Catholic is that you have a high tolerance for alcohol. So stop complaining."

"Ha ha. Anyway, the cops took me back to work and they spent the rest of the day babying me."

"Awwwww."

"Shut up! It was embarrassing."

"I didn't say anything."

"Uh huh. Well, then I got to call home and tell my dad what happened. Trust me. All the babying ended there, that's for sure."

Rachel rolled her eyes. "I'll bet," she said. "What did his lordship say?"

"The usual shit about how irresponsible I am and how I was gonna drive him into the poorhouse, and blah blah blah, etcetera, etcetera."

"Bullshit, bullshit. Don't forget the bullshit, bullshit."

"Oh, I could never forget that. Much as I try."

"How much is it all going to cost?

"I don't know. Dad thinks a grand."

"Half empty," Rachel remarked.

"Huh?"

"The proverbial glass. He already sees it as being half empty."

"Right! You know, I'm sorry it happened! What more can I say? I offered to pay for it and he just laughed about how my so-called 'piddling little wages' couldn't possibly pay for it. If I could take it all back, I would, y' know? But I don't have that power."

"No one does. He should count his blessings, like maybe that his son's not hurt, and that the car's probably fixable. Life goes on."

"Yeah, well, try telling that to them. My mom even started getting pissed off at me for 'putting her through this'. I mean, what about *me?* I'm the one the accident happened to! It's like they'll take any opportunity they can to bring suffering onto them so they can martyr themselves. And if you have any suffering of your own, how dare you? What right do you have to complain? The old 'your life is easy compared to what I'm going through' shit. Christ! Thank God my grandfather left the old country way before the Holocaust. Can you imagine the 'glorious suffering' my parents would be going through then?"

Ari fell back into his chair, spent. "I'm sorry, Rache," he sighed. "I don't mean to burden you with all this. You got problems of your own. I shouldn't-"

"Shut up. I invited you in, didn't I?"

"Yeah, but not for this. I shouldn't lay all my shit on your doorstep."

29

"You can and you will, anytime you need to. You know that, don't you?"

Ari smiled weakly at her. "Yeah. Yeah, I know. And thank you."

"No problem. If the shoe was on the other foot-"

"I'd send 'em back for my size!"

She smacked him lightly. "Dork! You know what I mean."

"Of course I do. And I love you for it."

Rachel responded with a warm smile. "Do you really?"

There was an uncomfortable silence, at least for Ari. He felt his face flush hot.

It was Rachel who finally broke the tension. "Listen here, sugar. I want to insure that your not taking any of this shit your parents are pumping you full of to heart."

"I'm not. Really."

"So you say. And maybe on the surface, you believe it. But underneath, do you really?"

Ari gave her a numb grin. "Going to use everything you learned last year in Psychology 101 to good use, Ms. Brannan?"

"Shut up. I'm serious."

Ari sighed. "All right, Ms. Freud. Give it your best shot."

"Don't take everything your dad says to you at face value. There's some sense in the things he says, but he looks at the world through mud colored glasses. He's the pessimist's own pessimist."

"You don't have to tell me that."

"I know, but it's good to reiterate. He calls you a spoiled brat, but he's only half-right. You *are* spoiled. But both of us are. Hell, I don't see how the two of us could've grown up here in Potomac and *not* be spoiled. But you're not a brat. *We're* not brats!"

Ari gave a snort. "Yeah? Well, my father would ask, 'What's the difference?'"

"Okay, then I'll be more blunt: your father's a bitter old prick who's pissed because he thinks everybody's had it easier than him! God forgive me for saying so, but sometimes when I listen to him, I just wanna fucking slap him!"

And knowing you, you could probably get away with it with him,

30

Ari thought with amusement. Out loud, he said, "I assume you'll be coming to a point soon, you brute!"

"Or maybe I should just slap you," she responded half-jokingly. "The point is, my little Star of David, is that I think we both know the value of hard work, and that's what's kept us from being brats. I think we also happen to be pretty nice people, personally. Especially when you consider some of these rich snots we grew up around."

"Heh. No shit."

"Well in any case, I think the only reason he calls you a spoiled brat is because it somehow validates him and his whole mud-colored world view. You being on your way to becoming a fully-functioning adult, holding down a job, getting good grades, going out and experiencing the world for yourself, and it scares him a bit. It makes him jealous, because you have better tools than he had for coping. Compared to him, you do have it easier, but easier is still a far cry from easy, y'know? So it's safer for him to just write you off as a spoiled brat rather than accept the frightening possibility that you might turn out to be a better man than him."

"Whoa! That's some pretty strong words, Rache!"

"Well, it's time some strong words were used here, Ari. You're one of the best people I know and I don't even wanna even consider the possibility that you might lose heart because of this shit your parents have been telling you all your life, with so-called 'good intentions'. I won't accept that. And there's no reason why you should, either."

Ari just stared at her, stunned. Sure, Rachel and he had had intense, personal talks before, but never like this. He had come over hoping to get his ego soothed a bit, but now his cup runneth over; it was like asking for a bouquet of roses and getting a hothouse in return. "I . . .I don't know what to say, Rache," he finally admitted. "Thank you."

"I'm not just doing this for you, sugar. One of the other things we learned in 'Psychology 101' is how these patterns tend to repeat themselves in families, unless something is done to stop it. So, you could say I'm also doing it for your children, so they don't have to suffer through you acting like an ass."

"Thanks."

"You're welcome."

They sat in a comfortable silence for a time, just drinking and enjoying each others' company. Then: "Rache?"

"Hmmm?"

"Can I ask you something? When I first described the accident, you know, where it was and all, you sort of . . . I dunno . . . went blank. What was wrong?"

"I was worried, sweetie. It sounded so bad, you scared me a little."

"Y'know, that might actually wash if I hadn't known you since grade school. C'mon. What gives?"

She sighed. "You'll think I'm nuts."

"Oh, please. You're the only one whose been talking sense to me since this whole thing started."

Another long pause, then: "Ari . . . I was . . . sort of . . . *there*."

"There? What do you mean, 'there'?"

"There . . . at the accident."

"Um . . . what?!"

"More specifically, I was down the street. . . at the office supply store."

"On Shady Grove?"

"Yes".

"My God, why didn't you say something?"

"Because something freaky happened to me, too."

"What? What happened?"

Rachel sighed again. "I was pulling out of the parking lot when I saw the backup. Ordinarily, I would've just been annoyed, but for some reason, this time I wasn't. Instead, I had this thought just come out of the blue. 'I've got to call Ari. Now, I swear to you, I have no idea where the thought came from, but there it was. 'I have to call Ari and see how he's doing.'"

"You're bullshiting me."

"I swear to you I'm not! That's why I was so freaked out when you told me where your accident was. I could've just turned left, and there I was."

"Jesus. What a damn coincidence, huh?"

"Is it?"

"What do you mean?"

Another pause. Ari was about to say something when Rachel spoke. "Ari," she said haltingly. "If I tell you something, will you promise you won't think I'm a great big weirdo?"

"You mean, more than I do already?"

"I'm serious."

Ari sighed in mock frustration. "No, Rachel," he replied. "I won't think you're a great big weirdo."

"You promise?"

"Oh, for God sakes-"

"Okay, okay. I just wanted to be sure," she said as she looked into his eyes. "Have you ever wondered about us, Ari? Have you ever wondered about the two of us?"

"Wondered? About what?"

"Everything. How we met in elementary school, the second grade. How we hit off immediately, sitting next to each other? We even had the same home rooms together for five years."

"It was a small school."

"Oh, come on!"

"Hey, remember that time you lip-synched that Barbra Streisand song for the fifth grade talent show? What was it? Oh, yeah! 'The Main Event!'"

"And you remember that dork you overheard in junior high school? The one who said he wouldn't vote me class president of the seventh grade because he thought me 'immoral' for doing that song?"

"Well, fuck him. You won, didn't you?"

"I know, but still . . ."

"Well, so we've had a long history. So?"

"Well, don't you find that odd? I mean, are you friends with anyone else that you've known ever since elementary school, much less second grade?"

Ari considered it. "Hell," he replied. "I don't think I've had a friendship from elementary school that lasted into high school, much less now."

"So you see my point."

"I'm still catching up. Spell it out for me."

Rachel sighed. "I don't want to be so trite as to say we're anything like 'soul mates'. God! That sounds so yuppie, New-Ageish, but it's the only term that fits."

"Wait."

"What?"

"You know, there is something I remember. From when I was a kid."

"Yeah?"

"My parents once took me to see this play our synagogue was hosting. Think I mostly remember it because it was one of the last things we did as a family together."

Rachel gave his hand a gentle squeeze. "Well, anyway," he continued. "It was this old Jewish folk-tale play called *The Dybbyck*. It was about this rabbinical student who was drowning himself in mystical studies after the girl he had been promised to was forced by her father to marry someone else. A wealthy old merchant."

"The good old days."

"Yeah. Well, the student died during his studies and his spirit went into the girl."

"You mean, like, possessed her?"

"Yeah, but not like she would start spinning her head around puking up green shit. This is theatre, not film!"

"They had a budget."

"Right! So the chief rabbi was called in and managed to exorcize him, but since they were promised to each other, their souls were attached. She chose to join him in Heaven rather than remain on earth."

"The Jewish Romeo and Juliet?"

"Sorta."

"Well, it sounds sweet."

"I remember it being pretty good. Made my father cry. Didn't think he had it in him. Hell, maybe it was the idea of being shackled to somebody for eternity that made him cry. Who knows?"

"So if you die before me, is your spirit going to haunt me forever?"

"Only if God's got a coffee date with someone else."

She smacked him again. "Dork!",she laughed.

CHAPTER 6

"Asshole," Terry remarked under her breath as she descended the bus's steps. Behind her, unseen, the bus driver mouthed the word *cunt* in response.

The sun was quickly disappearing over the horizon, leaving a trail of rich ambers, violets and blues. Terry had made it just in time; in another half hour, things would be pitch black and she would be shit-out-of-luck. It would be impossible to find then.

She stood on the edge of the curb, her eyes darting back and forth around the intersection, measuring, calculating. Remembering. The bus pulled out behind her, the cloud of dust and exhaust enveloping her in its wake. She barely noticed, just watched as the cars drove by, crushing the shards of glass from the day before into even smaller pieces, wedging them deeper the cracks of the street's hardened tar.

There!, she thought as her eyes rested on a spot halfway through the intersection. *There's where we hit.*

She smacked the "WALK" button on the side of the traffic light pole and waited, her mind reviewing the day's events. While the convenience store clerk turned his back on her to fetch her cigarettes, Terry had pocketed a bus schedule and a cheap pair of sunglasses from the counter and into her sling, feigning coughing with her free right hand as to set up a distraction as she flipped her ill gotten gains with her left. The proprietor, a middle-aged Korean with a bad haircut and even worse skin, was none the wiser.

The traffic signal flashed its white "WALK" signal and Terry started crossing. In the middle of the crosswalk, she stopped, eliciting mixed reactions from the drivers. Her pale blue eyes darted to the other end of the street, searching.

One driver, a young high school kid with a stereo blasting Skynrd and an oversized tail-pipe blasting exhaust, placed his hand on his horn. Terry looked up at him. Their eyes met and the kid stopped and pulled his hand away.

Terry saw the crossing sign blinking red and turned her attention back to the street, feeling in her gut again the point of impact, the force that sent her sprawling over the grey Honda's roof and onto the rough scrape of the road. She winced as she felt the snap of her wrist again in her head.

The force pushing her kept going, even after she fell, pushing the item she always carried in her pocket out. An item that she realized, not long after the fact, she was lucky to lose as the paramedics and the cops swarmed around her. *Out of my pocket*, she thought. *Out of my pocket and then-*

There!

The flashing red light solidified as Terry moved, dashing over to the small, grassy mound that substituted for a sidewalk on that end. The glint of metal that greeted her when she landed confirmed her suspicions, and she smiled to herself, now certain that God (or whatever) was with her.

Her fingers embraced the cold steel of the folded straight razor like a needy lover. Quickly, before any of the passing motorists could even think to see what she was doing, Terry jammed her little tool back home into her pocket, and, for the first time since the whole miserable day began, smiled an honest smile.

CHAPTER 7

Ari ended the day just as he began it: staring up at the ceiling of his bedroom, pondering the preceding day's events. Tomorrow would begin the humiliation process: taking his damaged car to various body shops to get the best deal. He could see every part of the ordeal in his mind's eye: the other drivers slowing down to gape at him as he drew near (or drove beside) them, the proprietors of said body shops as they exploded with scatologically-based expressions of disbelief, the stare of all the passers-by and everywhere the pointing, the staring, the overwhelming sense of his shame and humiliation writ large, reflected on every face.

Ari squeezed his eyes shut, gritting his teeth as he tried to beat back the wave of defensive anger that washed over him. He knew he fucked up, why did people have to keep reiterating that fact? Did everyone really think he was that stupid?

His parents had been their usual understanding, loving selves when he finally got back in, but mentioning that he had spent the time away with Rachel seemed to placate them. His dad, at least. Dirty old bastard all but smirked, prompting Ari to sorely fantasize about smacking him one across his face.

Ari ripped the covers off himself and sat up in bed. The curtain was open and the full moon shone its beams through the window; Ari felt its gentle caress on his face as he stared out at it. Perhaps it was best for him to instead focus on the future. The past was certainly nothing to write home about (*ha, ha, ha,* he thought), and the present was even more hellish, so why not focus on things-to-come?

Yeah, the future, he thought. *The only thing you can really count on surprising you in life.*

Only a little more than a week remained before school started up again. Back to the dorms. A single for himself this year! The Ultimate! And, as it happened, rooming at school was one of the few arguments he had actually won against his parents (though, truth be told, this victory had as much to do with his mother's constant worrying out loud to his father about winter road conditions as it did to Ari's drive for independence). At any rate, it was a way from him to get away from all the relentless smothering.

Ari closed his eyes and relaxed as he further explored the future. While it was true he wasn't much of a drinker (and, after seeing how his parents had turned out, he'd rather not cross paths with that particular vice, thank you very much), he did enjoy the social aspects of college parties; the exposure to new people and situations was always exciting to him. It made him realize something he had always suspected: that life didn't begin and end in the affluent township of Potomac, Maryland, and that, far from his parents' constant admonitions to the contrary, the world was not a large, festering jungle just waiting to devour the young, foolish and pathologically naive. *Hell,* Ari thought. *In some ways, I guess I'm really just a hick. A hick with money, but still a hick. Never been more than a few miles from my hometown, never left the farm.*

An unwanted image crept into Ari's mind at that last: the shrieking form who had a close encounter of the worst kind with his car, A.K.A. the reason for all his present misery. *Why the hell did that* person, Ari finally decided. *Why did they have to come racing along out of nowhere like that? Jesus, he or she must've been doing sixty five, seventy, on a road I've been taking for months, that has a speed limit of forty, max! Christ! Why can't people be more careful?!*

Ari slumped backwards onto his bed, sighing. Back in the present again; he couldn't get away from it. *Gotta get back to the future, as Michael J. Fox would put it,* Ari thought. Must think ahead. This would be over soon. He would have his car fixed, and he could get on with his life.

Ari shifted over on his side and continued to stare at the moon. *Yeah,* he told himself. *If I can just sleep and get through this night.*

CHAPTER 8

"Hey, lady."

The voice came to Terry from the top of a deep, dark well, a well whose blackness was more comfort than cold; a place she was loath to emerge from.

"Hey, lady!" The voice, sharper now, clearer. Then she felt something touch the shoulder of her bum arm and she jolted awake, grabbing the offending object, crushing it in a steel grip. "Ahhhh!! Jesus! Let go!", a voice whined, and Terry found herself face-to-face with the bus's driver, his wrinkled puss distorted by a rictus of pain. With a degree of shock that was only slightly less than the offender's, she released his hand.

"Sorry," she stammered, her voice still slightly thickened with the effects of sleep. "Dozed off. You scared the shit out of me."

"Not as much as you did me," the man in front of her returned, massaging his fingers as Terry took him in.

He was a little guy, barely five-and-a-half feet, if that. His driver's cap was askew, showing a mess of stringy hair flowing over a rapidly retreating hairline. His light blue eyes darted back-and-forth nervously, two small animals crouched in their holes and on the lookout for predators. It made Terry jumpy just to look at them.

She murmured another half-hearted apology and slid out of the seat, not bothering to look back. At the base of the bus's exit steps, she got another bit of bad news: *Martinsburg Station* proclaimed the lettering over the entrance. *Shit!*, Terry thought. *I'm still another twenty fuckin' miles or so away from home!*

41

She felt another touch on her shoulder, making her skin crawl. Her good hand automatically jammed itself into the pocket with the razor. If the little creepazoid wanted to play touchy-feely with her again, she was going to give him a big surprise.

She paused when he said the magic words: "Ya miss yer stop, girly? I might be able to help ya!"

Terry valiantly fought back an impulse to slice open his throat then and there. Instead, she turned around as casual as if the little turd had just asked her the time. "Yeah," she replied in what she hoped sounded like a matter-of-fact tone. "Looks like I did." She yawned theatrically. "Sorry! Been a long day."

The little fucker smiled at her, showing gaps in a mealy-mouthed grin. "Oh, don't you worry none, missy. You don't haveta be formal with me!" Then he laughed, a bit too long, a bit too loud, the reek of his cigarette-and-coffee breath wafting over her. It made her want to puke.

Instead, she smiled back with what she hoped was a charming expression. "Are y'offerin' to drive me back?"

"Sure! This is the end of my shift right now, and I got my truck out here in the lot. I'll take ya where ya wanna go!"

Terry saw the oily slickness of sweat on his brow and thought sourly, *Yeah, I bet you will.* Out loud, she responded, "Well, that would be right kinda you. I live 'bout twenty miles or so offa Cooper's Gulch, just down by the river. You hearda it?"

"Sure! Lived 'round these parts all my life. Like to do a bitta fishin' over that way. Live here in Martinsburg."

"Ya mind if I go inside the station real quick n' get me some coffee?"

She saw her would-be benefactor's smile falter a bit, and thought she'd blown it, but instead he said, "Okay, but be fast, all right? Kinda tired myself."

"Ya want any?"

"Nope. Keeps me up this time a' night. Won't be able to sleep once I get home."

"Kay. I'll just be a sec."

"I'll bring my truck around. Meet ya out front inna coupla minutes."

The automatic double doors whooshed open with a pneumatic sigh as Terry made her way into the bus terminal. There weren't many people milling about, and those who were looked too tired to attend to anything but their own business. *Good,* Terry thought. *The less, the better.*

She spied what she needed at the far end of the concourse: the sign of the golden arches of a McDonald's outlet. Perfect. Luck was still with her.

The Mexican woman behind the counter looked even more out of it than everyone else in the station, barely nodding as Terry ordered her large coffee (black, no sugar) and wordlessly handed the change over.

Terry dumped the lid and sipped. Good and hot.

She exited the terminal and was greeted by the sight of a huge, dirty, rusted over Ford Bronco idling at the corner. The horn honked and the lights flashed. Terry couldn't help but smirk at the sight, but rushed over eagerly.

The man reached over, flipping the lock and opening the door so she could pile in. The smell that emanated from the man was ten times worse in the pick-up's cab, a mix of sweat and the aroma of long-ago consumed fast food. Terry carefully placed her coffee on the unsavory looking floorboards and held it steady with her feet as she settled herself in.

"Ready?", the driver asked.

"Yep. Let's hit it."

The Bronco rolled slowly out of the lot while Terry calmly, almost casually, pulled her cement-cased arm free of its sling, then reached down to pick up the coffee from the floor.

They drove for about five minutes down Route 9 before the truck began to slow. The street was deserted, dark, and quiet. The man pulled his truck up to the side of the road, situating the passenger's side next to a large tree, effectively trapping Terry in the cab.

"What're ya doin'?, she asked, purposefully raising her voice a notch in pitch. "Why're we stoppin'?"

When she looked over at her would-be helpmate, she saw him digging into his pants pocket while giving her what Terry supposed he thought was a sly look. Then, with blinding speed (again, what Terry thought he supposed), the man flicked the object he pulled out open and lurched forward. "Awright, girly-girl!," the little weasel snarled as he brandished the three-inch blade of his penknife toward her. "You jus' do what I tell ya, an' mebbe you don't get hurt too bad!"

Terry took in this all in for a moment. A penknife. The stupid son of a whore was threatening her with a *penknife.*

It was too much for her. She threw her head back and laughed, a hollow, throaty sound with the same melodiousness as rusty nails being ripped out of rotting floorboards. The man stopped short, puzzled, uncertainty creeping into his watery eyes.

Terry stopped laughing and gave him a look that made his balls shrivel. "Li'l man, she said. "You picked the wrong bitch t' fuck with today."

Then, showing the sawed-off peckerwood what *real* speed was, Terry rammed her cement encased wrist against his knife hand, pining it against the seat while simultaneously throwing steaming hot coffee in his pathetic face.

The would-be attacker screamed, high and piercing, like a little girl, recoiling backward to his side of the cab. Terry felt the rush of adrenaline as she spun her legs up and around toward him, gloating as a well-aimed kick connected with his head, catching him square in the face and knocking him through the window. There was a loud crack as the bus driver's neck broke and a spray of blood as a large shard of glass dug through the back of his head, slicing into his brain as neat as a surgeon's knife. His free arm spasmed, stiffened, then lay still on top of the dashboard.

Terry downed the last of her coffee, dropping the cup to lay amongst all the other trash on the truck's floor. Then she checked the windows. All clear outside.

Favoring her arm, she awkwardly pulled the corpse toward her.

44

There was a sickeningly squishy noise and more blood spray as she dragged it over to the passenger side of the cab. Half-stepping, half-crawling over the body, she examined the damage to the driver's side window.

Fortunately, much of the blood and brain matter had oozed inside the truck, but the window was completely shattered. Gingerly, she knocked the remaining glass fragments out with her cement-encased arm.

Perfect. Now unless someone was looking closely, they would think the window was rolled all the way down instead of being completely gone.

She popped out of the cab and slammed the door behind her to inspect it. Just few drops streaking down the side. Her luck was holding.

A quick peek in the back found her what she needed: an old, oil-stained tarp that her late, unlamented host probably used to get under the engine. She spread this out over the spilled blood and gore rapidly drying in the night's heat. No sense in making this situation worse than it was.

Terry slumped back in the seat as soon as she closed the cab's door. The adrenaline from the last few moments was quickly wearing off, and fatigue was beginning to take over. She fished in her pockets for her cigarettes, lighting one off the truck's dashboard lighter. The acrid taste of tobacco smoke flowed into her mouth, simultaneously boosting and relaxing her system as the nicotine worked its way into her.

For the next few days, at least, she had a truck. *Prolly gonna hafta slap one a' daddy's ol' plates on the back*, she thought. *Keep people from askin' too many questions.*

She glanced over at the little weasel's corpse slumped over at the far side of the cab and flicked ash on it, chuckling.

"An' you, fuckhead," she said out loud. "You can go inna river. Addin' to the pollution."

Without another glance or word, she shifted gears and drove off.

CHAPTER 9

Ari sat, staring hypnotized into a cup of coffee. The sun peeked through the kitchen window, tapping on his heavy eyelids. The house was silent, save for the ticking of the kitchen clock, the steady rhythm causing his lids to grow weightier still.

As expected, his night was fitful, causing him to jolt awake every few hours. Always he searched the face of his alarm clock, each time disappointed that more time had not passed.

Finally, he heard the alarm go off in his Dad's bedroom and the sounds of his preparing for the day. Ari sat quietly, listening. Eventually the sounds subsided, and he heard his father's own unscarred automobile rev up and drive off into the distance.

Silence reigned again, and slowly Ari stirred. Not bothering with a shower, he splashed water on his face until he felt marginally human again, then dressed himself in sweats. The effort of putting on actual clothes, even yesterday's, seeming too much to handle.

The sun moved while he sat, and now it actually was in his eyes, temporarily blinding him. Ari swore at it under his breath. *Goddamn heavenly bodies*, he thought. *First the fucking moon, now this. Why can't I get some clouds for a day like today?*

He swigged down a shot of hot coffee and grimaced as the sour taste filled his mouth.

Ordinarily, he took cream and sugar, but today he felt he naturally gravitated toward bitter and black. *And nothing's worse than this shit,* he told himself. *Instant coffee. Goddamn coffee houses springing up everywhere around town, and my old man's too fucking cheap to get a coffee-maker. So we drink fucking instant, shit you wouldn't clean your carburetor with. What a piece of work my old man is. What a piece of SHIT!*

This last flare of anger caused his hand to jolt and hot coffee to spill on his hand. He yelped and collapsed back in his chair. The frustration of it all hit him all at once, and he sobbed silently to himself, burying his face in his hands.

The kitchen clock chimed eight times as he sat like that, barely noticing that time clicked on. When his crying fit had passed, he took another sip of coffee. He vaguely entertained the notion of having something to eat before he left, but dismissed it when he realized he had no appetite. Some things are just best done on an empty stomach, he thought as he rose to pour the remainder of the coffee down the drain. Besides, if he stuck around longer, his mom might wake up (*well, not really,* he thought, *since she doesn't usually get up until around noon*) and start in on him.

He took stock of the day growing outside the window. It all looked very pleasant. Blue sky, yellow sun, with the barest hint of misty dew evaporating on the grass. Ari hated the very sight of it. Nature was not conforming to his needs. He gave out another exclamation of disgust and threw the coffee in the sink. It was time.

He slammed the door behind him and went to confront the beast under the canvas tarp he had come to loathe. Its looks hadn't improved overnight. *Well, what'd I expect? The mechanic fairy was gonna come and wave his magic wand and fix it?,* Ari thought to himself. Gritting his teeth, he started the motor.

The first stare came before he even got out of his driveway, some middle-aged blue-collar type who was passing by in a pick-up truck as Ari waited to merge into traffic. Ari couldn't see the eyes hidden behind sunglasses too small for his fat face, but he saw the mouth as it dropped open with that dull look of horror that he knew would become all-too-familiar as the day wore on.

"Take a fuckin' good look, man!," Ari screamed as the man passed by. "Get your fuckin' camera, make it last longer!"

Whether the man heard him or not, Ari didn't know, just watched his taillights vanish into the distance. He felt a hot flush of shame rush to his face. "Tell your damn grandkids what a fuckup I am," he murmured to himself as he pulled out.

CHAPTER 10

Terry dreamt, the bed sheets crumpled and soaked in her good hand. Sweat beaded on her brow, dripping on her pillow as she whipped her head from side to side. Her eyes were slightly open, but they only saw the demons of her unconscious mind.

When she was still in the living nightmare some jolly ass-wipe had termed "reform school" and had made some cursory attempts at education (at least, enough to keep the social worker off her back) Terry remembered one educational film in particular her science class had shown. Most of the bitches she was in class with just hooted and hollered at the screen, like they did with anything, but Terry, for once, sat silently, transfixed.

It was a nature film about the wildlife of South America, and it featured the ugliest birds Terry had ever seen: the Condors. These flying beasts were hideous as well as huge. They were so monstrous they fed on other birds of prey, like owls. And, knowing how damn big those hoot-owls got on the family homestead, Terry couldn't help but be impressed.

Impressed enough now to have the winged beasts intrude on her dreams. She found herself walking along a completely barren wasteland: no mountains or trees could be seen in the distance, nor behind her. The grass beneath her feet was either dead or dying and crunched as she walked on it. The sky was overcast a solid gray; she could not even make out the outline of a stray cloud. It was like the sun had blasted away whatever color or life once pulsed through this world.

These lonely and lifeless lands made Terry feel as empty inside as a whore's promise. But then came the screech from behind. Terry looked over her shoulder at the flying monstrosity swiftly approaching from behind. Not surprisingly, it was a condor, big as life and twice as ugly. She turned tail and ran, the grass underneath her feet crunching.

The screech came again, much louder this time, practically in her ear, and caught a whiff of carrion breath in her nostrils. Whatever the beast had been eating Terry didn't want to think about.

Then came the vice grips of the thing's talons tearing into her back, and she saw the lifeless earth beneath her rapidly distance itself. She trashed back and forth, but the creature held firm, this time its screech mocking her.

Almost without thinking, Terry jammed her hand into her cut-off jeans pocket. The straight razor she had with her like another limb was there, and she intended to make full use of it. The blade was out in a flash. Nearly as quick came the cut to the bird's leg, ripping through tendons and nerves like string, blood splurting as though from a freshly-popped blister. The thing screamed again, but this time with pain and anger rather than triumph. It craned its neck over to stare at Terry full in the face, fixing her with its dead, black eyes.

Terry froze as the monster gripped her even tighter. Then the beast's face changed, the jawline becoming more pronounced, and suddenly she was staring at the face of her father, silent, malignant, wanting for all the world to tear her heart from her.

Then it spoke, but the voice that issued from its twisted beak was that of the little weasel she had killed at the side of the road. *Awright, girlie!,* the slithery voice said. *You just simmer down now! Don't you move, or you'll get hurt!*

Terry gave no answer save one via cold, sharp steel. The razor sliced straight into the monster's eye, showering Terry's face with putrid, black blood. The thing screamed again and suddenly she was airborne. Or not. Terry felt herself falling, the dizzying rush of her insides pushing into her throat and head as she plummeted. Panic gripped her. She saw the dead earth rushing closer, closer- And just then a loud crash from the real world intruded, her window of sleep shattered.

Terry jolted awake just as she was about to hit the ground in her dream. "Jesus Christ!!" she screamed as she tumbled out of the hard half-cot, half day-bed she slept on.

She lay on the floor of the small, one-room trailer, her heart pounding double-time in her chest and head. Gradually, her vision came back into focus. *Just a dream*, she thought as she shut her eyes and willed her jack-hammering heart to slow itself. *Only a dream, nothing can-*

Another crash sounded just outside the trailer's window and Terry knew *that* was no dream. She muttered an oath and jumped to her feet, the bed sheets still half-draped around her sweat-matted body.

A large tow truck was pulling away down the driveway where the trailer was parked. Just a few feet away lay a scrap-heap of twisted metal and wheel parts that could only be the remains of her bike. Terry swore again and grabbed for the clothes she had thrown on the small chair beside the bed. She was still pulling her top on when she burst through the trailer door.

"Hey, fuckhead!," she shouted after the retreating truck. "You sonofabitch! Listen a' me when I'm talkin' at ya!"

She grabbed a large piece of gravel from the driveway and hurled it. The rock bounced harmlessly off a tire. Soon the truck disappeared behind a clump of trees and its rumble and whine faded off into the distance.

Terry swore again, this time silently. *And just what the fuck did you intend to do once you stopped him, girl?,* an inner voice admonished. *Invite him in for a beer? Take a shit? Both at once?*

Instead of answering, she turned to face the pile of wreckage that lay before her. Pieces of motorcycle lay everywhere, and not one part was in any way connected to the other. Her broken wrist throbbed in its cast. And no wonder, with all the excitement. A sliver of logic still existed within her to know that she would have to rest it a bit more, lest the set break and her arm take even longer to heal. Best to go into the main house and get some aspirin for it.

She rubbed her eyes with her good hand. She wanted to scream. She wanted to bash in heads. She wanted to destroy everything in her path, to go on a rampage and not stop until the entire earth was a smoking ruin.

A cool breeze blew by her, softening her edges. Terry's mind began to clear itself as it focused into more precise targets for her anger. Images flickered in her mind like stills from a lunatic slide show. Her dead father. Her soon-to-be-dead brother, if Terry had anything to say about it. The Brown cunt, the first person ever to feel the full force of her rage, all those years ago. Her slimy attacker from last night, whose body was now fish food at the bottom of the river. That last one prompted her to look over at the truck parked over behind the trailer and covered with a tarp. She still needed to scrub down the cab; it was still tacky with blood congealing in the late August sun. This was going to be a busy day for her, between the bike and all the other miscellaneous crap that kept cropping up like dandelions on the front lawn.

But first, she needed to go inside the main house and make herself a big pot of strong coffee. Maybe put on some music. Some WASP, or maybe even some Motorhead. In any case, she knew she wouldn't be able to think without some caffeine in her system.

The last (and most powerful) image came to her just as she was mounting the dilapidated structure that served as the ramshackle house's front porch: the face of that little sobbing, puking turd who got her in this situation in the first place. And, as she wrenched open the front door, she made a promise to herself, that when all was said and done, somewhere, somewhen, somehow, *somebody* was going to pay for this shitstorm that fell on her head all in one clump.

Oh, yeah. Someone was going to pay.

PART TWO

ON YOUR MARK!

There was blood and glass all over
And there was nobody there but me
As the rain tumbled down hard and cold
I seen a young man lying by the side of the road
He cried, "Mister, will you help me please?"

-Bruce Springsteen

CHAPTER 11

Ari was driving. The windows were rolled all the way down, the sun roof open. Fresh breezes blew in, providing some natural air conditioning while the car sped down the sunlit freeway. He stretched behind the wheel, feeling cramped joints popping loose and free.

It was a week later, and the light at the end of the tunnel was now a sun-kissed reality. The car was completely fixed, and it had cost a great deal (to the tune of two grand, the majority of it plundered from Ari's own bank account), but who said there was no price you pay for freedom and happiness? His parents had been said good-bye to, his bags were packed, and he was on his way to school for the new year. He had come through and survived. And now (as a recent popular song had proclaimed) the future was so bright, he had to wear shades.

Speaking of tunes, Ari thought. *Let's get some on!*

With one hand still on the wheel, he popped open in the glove compartment and scanned the selections inside. Duran Duran was passed up. So were the Thompson Twins. Then his eyes lit upon someone who epitomized the whole notion of cars, girls, and the sheer thrill of being alive.

Ari pulled out the tape box and stroked it fondly, a child with a much-loved toy. He flipped open the box and pushed the cassette into the tape deck. There was a brief pause, then came the drums, followed by some bass piano notes. An electronic synthesizer played a riff that was all over the radio stations a few years back, but for Ari, time never diminished the songs power. Then came the voice, that

Logan St. Michael

gloriously ragged voice that always sounded as if it were straining to get at the listener through the speaker:

>Born down in a dead man's town The first
>kick I took was when I hit the ground
>End up like a dog that's been beat too much
>Till you spend half your life just a-coverin' up!

Then came the chorus, which Ari sang along with: *Born in the USA! I was . . .Booooorn in the USA!* A grin spread over Ari's face, an expression he had been sorely lacking over the past week or so (*the week?! Hell, try the whole summer!!,* Ari thought). He could feel the music fuse itself into his very soul, reviving it, energizing it, making him feel as carefree as any young man just out of his teens could be. *Yep,* he thought, *I've finally turned that corner. The sky's the limit and I'm just gonna keep movin' on up, just like the Jeffersons!*

He pushed down on the gas pedal to make some time, and the newly-restored car growled its satisfaction, speeding off into the day.

CHAPTER 12

Terry backed the truck up underneath the tree, right on the edge of a heavily wooded area. She shifted into Park, then killed the engine, listening to its cooling ticks in the humid day around her.

A week later, and a busy one at that. Most of the time she had spent rebuilding the bike's engine, or going into town for parts, some of which she even paid for. Still, even with the five fingered discounts, money was running low, and that's why she was here, sitting in front of the Demon Heads's clubhouse, to get paid for her last (abbreviated) run.

Before her, a hundred yards away or so, was a shoddily constructed plywood and steel roadhouse darkly stained from excesses and time. The neon sign in the window that normally proclaimed **Open** (and advertised Pabst Blue Ribbon Beer while it was at it) was shut off, but Terry knew that was about as much true indication as a junkie's promise. She checked the side mirror. There. That was about the angle where it looked as though the picture the nigger cop had shown her was taken. She didn't see anything obvious, but she knew that meant nothing. Most pigs weren't exceptionally bright, but the ones in surveillance usually were. Still, she thought that the angle where she'd placed the truck and the tree's presence hid her enough.

She reached into the glove compartment and pulled out a .45 automatic, her daddy's old government issue from Vietnam. She had taken it from her parents's old bedroom closet, cleaned it and loaded the magazine. She didn't really expect she'd need it, but you could never be sure. She toyed with the idea of stuffing it down her pants, or even in her sling, but disregarded both as inconvenient, not to mention probably unnecessary. Her ever-trusty razor sat in her pocket, and had always worked best in close quarters. Better to have the heavy cannons out of sight but close by, if things got really hairy.

Her arm itched. It had been itching like crazy over the past few days, and was driving her a little batty. The doctors had told her it was a good sign; the more it itched, the faster the healing process, but it was still irritating as hell.

Terry stared back out at the roadhouse while half-massaging, half-scratching her arm. Only a few bikes were scattered at the far end of the parking lot, a large clearing of heavy gravel and cracking tar. She recognized Nesto's machine, a huge Harley chopper built low to the ground. *Good*, she told herself. *The Mexican midget's in. And the less dirtbags he's got with 'em, the better. We can make it short and sweet.*

She took a deep breath and emerged from the truck. The sound of the gravel crunching underneath her boots was the only thing that split the silence, and made her think vaguely upon her dream. Fortunately, there wasn't any repeats over the last few nights. *Well, this is for any condors who might be sneakin' up on me right now*, she smirked to herself. *Not to mention the pork products watchin' my ass.*

The last thing the 8am to 4pm shift saw before the figure identified as "Terry Scranton" entered in the targeted structure was said figure reaching behind her back and communicating an obscene hand gesture consisting of a single extended digit. It was duly filed in the photo log.

CHAPTER 13

Ari nudged open the door with his foot, as he was carrying a load of clothes by their hangers in one hand, and a couple of small suitcases in the other. The smile that had started on his face while driving spread even wider.

By itself, the room wasn't much. Roughly twelve by twelve feet, made up of painted white cinder blocks, the only furnishings a single bed frame with the cheapest mattress available on the market (although brand new), a plain, unpainted chest of drawers maneuvered into the far corner, and a study carrel that was supposed to function as the resident's desk. The only window was at the far end of the room, currently slapped shut against the outside world by Venetian blinds.

Ari loved every drab, spartan inch of it. It was his for the year. His domain. His kingdom. His shelter from the slings and arrows of the outrageous world beyond. No one could change this fact, unless he fucked up royally somehow. Needless to say, he had *no* intention of fucking up royally.

He dropped the suitcases at the foot of the bed, lay his clothes on top, and flopped over backwards onto the bare mattress. He lay there, enjoying the silence and the feel of the cloth on his back. Compared to the overly soft cushiness of his bed back home, this was damn near a concrete slab. Still, he saw no reason why he might not adjust.

He closed his eyes and experienced the peace of a silent dorm. The majority of the students weren't scheduled to move in for another couple of days. But Ari (well, actually his father) always believed in getting an early jump on things. *Thanks, Dad,* he thought. *One of the few times your pain-in-the-ass compulsions work to my advantage.*

He was still mulling over that bit of irony when a knock came at the door. He started up suddenly, feeling a momentary flush of guilt at enjoying himself when he thought no one was looking. The face at the open door, however, transmitted nothing even remotely guilt-inducing.

"Well, Mr. Single," the figure said, a playful grin on his face. "Hope I'm not interrupting you while you have quality time with yourself."

"Dave!", Ari exclaimed as he jumped up from the bed and gave his visitor a half-hug, half handshake in greeting.

Dave Cohen had been his roommate the year before, and if any one person could ever be an ideal roommate, Dave was it. Quiet, friendly, respectful of other people's personal space and a sly sense of humor, made him a joy to come back home to. *Plus, he gets less girls than I do*, Ari thought disingenuously. *So I don't have to put up with any macho braggart bullshit.*

"Guess you ain't havin' any trouble adjusting so far," Dave continued, a gleam in his bright blue eyes.

"Does a bear shit in the woods?"

"Only if he's got a rabbit to wipe his ass with," Dave replied. "You just get here?"

"Yup."

"Family gettin' on your nerves that much?"

"Oy!", he exalted in a mock-Yiddish accent. "Already de give me de *shpillkis!*"

"Heard that!", Dave grinned even more. "And how's Rachel?"

Ari chuckled. Every guy friend he had eventually got around to asking about Rachel. "She's good. Started school a bit earlier at Hood than they do here at U of M. She's already in the thick of things."

"Christ. Glad I'm not a law student."

"Nah, you just had to settle for some loser major like history. Dontcha know there's no future in the past, young man?"

"Better than being undecided."

"Hey! I resemble that remark! Besides, not this year!"

"Oh no? So what school of thought have you decided to honor with your enormous gifts?"

"Heh. Whuddya think? Business."

"Oh, yeah! Your just a regular fuckin' Rockefeller, I can tell!"

"Shit, it was mostly to get my old man off my back. Make him feel better that the so- called 'family fortune' might continue for another generation."

"It's gonna kill him when you finally come out of the closet."

Ari good-naturedly flipped him the bird. "You rooming with somebody, or did you luck out, too?"

"Nah. With somebody. Transfer student, sophomore. Least I won't have to put up with too much drunk-and-disorderly shit."

"So who got the other single on this floor?"

"Guess!"

"I'm no good at this guessing game shit. Just tell me."

"I'll give you a hint. He probably got it because nobody's crazy enough to room with him."

Ari considered it for a moment, then: "Aw, man! Not-"

"Yup."

"Fuckin' *Graziano!!?*"

"The same."

"Je-*sus*! Glad he's at the other end of the dorm."

Graziano. Vinnie Graziano. Mr. Black Magic Himself. Partly called that from his choice of clothing, mostly called that because of the aura he gave off. A local campus celebrity some sadistic R.A. decided to house in Ari and Dave's dorm. *Hell,* any *damn dorm would be a bad place to house him, Ariel, my friend,* he told himself. It was more than appropriate that Graziano was a theatre major, because drama was so obviously an important part of his life. A transplanted Brooklynite (*Just like my dad. Figures,* Ari thought), the guy was *New Yawk* to his core. Ari remembered one fateful evening, almost a year ago, when Ari first arrived at this happy little half- slum he expected to call his home away from home for the next four years. A group of guys sat around in the dorm's reception area, a dingy

Formica heaven last touched up during the Ford Administration. It was Friday night, a time when most of the student body took the time to chill out and decompress from the preceding week's trials and tribulations.

But not Graziano. He'd gone and locked himself in his room, studying for a midterm inconveniently scheduled for Monday. Soon he sauntered by the reception area on the way to the can. By this time, a keg of cheap beer had magically appeared around the gang in the lounge, and they intended to make the most of it.

A big, dumb, crewcut-wearing fratboy type with the unfortunate name of Hurley called out to Graziano as he went by. "Hey, Grazzy!," he said with a thick chortle. "Wanna shota some suds?"

"I'll pass," Graziano replied in his deep rasp.

"Wimp!", Hurley cried out.

There was a brief moment when the room got extremely quiet, but Graziano just smiled and continued on his way.

Half an hour went by. The room, despite the poor quality of the libations, was getting progressively soused. Then Graziano strode in, carrying a paper bag. He produced a small bottle of Jack Daniel's Kentucky Bourbon and slammed it on the table in front of Hurley. With the other hand, he extracted his set of keys and cut the seal on the bottle open. Removing the top, he put the bottle's mouth to his and tossed his head back.

One swallow. Two. Then three. Four. Which each successive swallow, his audience's mouths dropped open another quarter inch.

Five. Six. He got to seven and then pulled the bottle away from his mouth, made the sort of refreshed sound a person makes after drinking a particularly cool liquid on a particularly hot day, then slammed the bottle back down in front of Hurley. "Top that, *stu-gazz'*!, he snarled.

Taking the bottle in a shaky hand, Hurley managed three swallows before the whisky hit the cheap beer in his system and he choked. Then Hurley well, hurled. The rest of the room scattered as the sour reek of upchucked beer filled the air. Graziano just stood there and laughed, a throaty, grating chuckle. "Next time any of you charter members of the Pansy Division wanna dance, you know where to find me," he said as he turned and disappeared back into his room, not to be seen again for the rest of the night. Because of this, Ari privately wondered how much that little (admittedly impressive) display taxed Graziano's system. Only privately, though. At any rate, the point was well made: don't call the tune unless you were willing to pay this particularly psychotic piper for it. And, as far as Ari knew, no one ever did.

Of course, Graziano's reputation of being a unholy terror couldn't rest on just one incident; the campus was filled with hard-core boozers whose livers knew no bounds. But once you added his other territories of outrage, well, then the mold was set. There was the acting teacher who made Graziano dump a cup of coffee he was drinking during one of his classes. Graziano did, but who do you think showed up directly after class at the teacher's office, carrying a receipt and demanding to be paid back his eighty-nine cents? Unfortunately, posterity didn't record the teacher's initial reaction to this demand, but the end result was the same: the teacher paid, probably just so he could get some peace from this leather-jacketed lunatic.

Thinking about it now, Ari couldn't help but laugh. This was the sort of guy you wrote home about, if your family had a particularly good sense of humor. *Too bad they don't,* Ari thought, not for the first time. *But I'd probably be the only one who'd get a particular sick kick out of watching my parents try to deal with him.*

For, if nothing else, college had served to break him out, at least a little bit, from that over-protected shell Maury and Judy Sussman had chosen to encase their little boy in. *But here, I'm not 'Maury and Judy's little boy', or worse, 'the Sussman kid'. I'm just Ari, and nobody's really pinned a label on me yet. I can still be whoever I wanna be.*

"Ari?"

"Hmmmm?"

"You with me? Your eyes sorta glazed over for a second there."

"Oh. Yeah, Dave. Sorry, I was just thinking."

"You can't start thinking now! The semester hasn't even started!"

63

"Wise ass. I was wonderin', d'ya know if anything's open on campus yet?"

"Nah, not the dining halls or anything like that. You wanna grab something?"

"Yeah. Can you help me unload the resta' my shit out of the car?"

"You wanna drive?"

"Nah, weather's too good. Feel like walkin'."

"Works for me."

Fifteen minutes later, Ari and Dave exited from the dorm and made their way through the campus streets. Almost unnoticed by Ari, the last of his tension from the previous week slipped away: the slump that had taken root in his shoulders released, and the final knot in his chest unraveled. Watching from the street, the casual observer would never have guessed that anything had ever bothered him. They would just see a young man without a care in the world, with the whole future laid before him.

The shrieking demon from the street was nowhere in his mind.

CHAPTER 14

Terry kicked open the clubhouse door, slamming it against the wall. The fat man behind the bar jerked up from his nudie magazine, taking his hand off his fun gun and putting it on the real one, a sawed-off twelve-gauge he kept under the counter. When he saw who it was, he relaxed. A little.

Very little.

"Well, well. If'n it ain't the one-armed bandit!", he bellowed.

"Fuck off, Pig Meat. Y'get yer money back from those diet pills yet?"

"Up yers."

"I'd tell ya the same, but I don't think anyone's even *seen* yer asshole this year. Where's Nesto?"

"Where the fuck d'ya think? In back."

"Fuck you very much," Terry replied as she sauntered in.

The Demon Head's clubhouse was a dingy, ramshackle affair that doubled as the local biker watering hole. *Hole* was the right word for it, for it was the sort of place where even the cockroaches couldn't wait to move out. The decor was early American Neanderthal: pieces of classic motorbikes hung on the walls next to well-worn hunting trophies and advertisements for alcohol featuring women that your mother didn't even think existed, since there was nothing remotely natural about them. Terry had just passed by the advertisement with the flexible young lady giving head to a beer bottle when Pig Meat called out to her. "Hey! Don't suppose you stopped to think mebbe he don't wanna see ya?"

"Don't suppose you stopped to think if I give a shit?", Terry called back as she pounded on the big, worn oak door in front of her. There was silence for a second, then the sound of movement. It opened wide enough so Terry could see the fat, ugly face of one of the twin Samoan brothers Nesto used as his personal bodyguard. She didn't even let the man get in a questioning grunt before she slammed her shoulder into the door, pushing her way in. The door hit the giant guarding it and knocked him back a few feet. Terry saw him reach into his pants and froze, suddenly wishing she had brought in the pistol she left in the truck.

Then a familiar voice croaked: "Let 'er in, Nito. For once, I'm happy to see her."

Terry darted her gaze in the direction of the voice in the shadows. Behind a desk covered with more junk than Red Foxx ever saw in all his days on *Sandford & Son* sat Nesto, appraising her with the cool dead eyes God gave a particularly venomous tarantula.

Ernesto Gonzaga was the de facto leader of the Demon Head Motorcycle Club, an unofficial band of lowlifes held together by their mutual love of fights, bikes, booze and pussy (not necessarily in that order). But what officially held them together was the drugs, plain and simple, the dealing as well as the taking (though they did plenty of both). Terry didn't know exactly how his operation worked, or who was involved, but, given all the recent police activity, she guessed it was pretty big. And far-reaching. Most of her courier services took her to the outskirts of DC, where she dropped off either drugs (a substantial amount of home-cooked crystal meth, rocks of crack cocaine, and a new supercharged stimulant just making the rounds called "crank", or money for a bunch of spics and niggers from Anacostia or Adams Morgan (two places that even *she* gave pause to going).

Other times, she just cooked up batches of crystal methamphetamine at home in a shack out back, as she supposed did many other of his 'employees'. It was only recently that she had been promoted to courier, for which she was thankful. Cooking too much of the shit could burn your lungs out, and even with a pillowcase over her head, she often felt like she had just chain smoked five packs of cigarettes afterwards. The few times she had actually sampled her own product, she felt like a lightbulb someone had flooded with enough juice to blow a lighthouse. The upshot was she got a lot done. The downside was when she ran out of juice, she was so beat she slept for three days straight, only waking up every few hours to take a leak.

Anyway, that was neither here nor there. What was here and now was that she was broke. And that Nesto, usually punctual about payment, had been dragging his ass. And she wanted to know why. So she got to the point. "Where's my money, Nesto?", she demanded. "Ya owe me at least a grand for the last delivery."

Nesto rose from the chair, if the term *rising* could be used in his case. Nesto was very short (at five feet-two, the top of his head barely grazed the bottom of Terry's chin) and very touchy about his height, or lack thereof. Terry, for one, was always tempted to burst out laughing every time she saw this sawed-off Mexican runt, but knew it was best she didn't. What he lacked in height, he made up in ferocity: Terry had seen him once beat a man to death in the clubhouse parking lot with his bare hands when he thought he'd been cheated on a drug deal. No reason for kicking a sleeping dog if it ain't necessary.

Until they *make it* necessary.

"Pretty bad break you got there, Terry," Nesto said, a yellowing, gap-toothed smile with all the warmth of a stiletto kept in a freezer appearing under his enormous black mustache. "Hurt much?"

"Fuck you. I'll repeat myself, if only cuz ya got two ugly motherfuckers watching over you: *where is my money!?!*"

Nesto took an envelope from off his desk (*how the fuck did he find it in all that crap?*, Terry wondered) and threw it at her. Terry caught it with on hand and tore it open hungrily. A cloud appeared on her brow as she saw the contents, a cloud that threatened to become a thunder head once she'd counted. "Yer 'bout five short here, Nesto," she replied evenly.

"No, lady. *Yer* the one whose five short. I pay you to get the shit delivered without any trouble. Lemme say that again, just because you got two goddamn ears, and one of 'em may not be listenin'.

Without any trouble. Whaddya call that crash you was in? A fuckin' *date?!!* The cops was all over yer ass!"

"Jus' like the ones y'got crawling over yer ass now?", she rejoined.

"What the fuck're ya talkin' about?"

"Y'think the pigs ain't playin' peak-a-boo with you right now, lookin' down on this little shithouse a' yers?"

Nesto laughed, the sound of rusty nails on a chalkboard. "You don't think I know 'bout them, Terry? Shee- it! How dumb d'ya think I am? I knew they was up there watchin' almost to the moment they turned all their surveillance shit on! I got eyes n' ears everywhere, bitch. Hell, I knew which hospital room you was in at Shady Grove and the name a' the nurse who changed yer bedpans!" Nesto continued to laugh, and now the two mammoth bodyguards joined in too, filling the dirty room for the first time since it was slapped together with something that resembled mirth. The thunder head on Terry's brow grew even darker.

Then, as sudden as it began, the laughter stopped and the room got quiet. Nesto came from behind the desk and advanced on Terry. "Yer the one who's fucked, Terry," he said. "I suggest ya take the bone I'm givin' ya, the only bone you'll prolly *ever* get, and get the fuck outta here before I decide it ain't too much trouble to have my boys here blow out what little brains you got."

Something clicked in the back of Terry's mind. Whether it was her overriding anger that made her have this sudden flash of insight or not, she never knew. What she did know is that two and two came together and suddenly made four for her.

"You set me up," she said quietly.

"What?!"

"You fuckin' set me up. Ya made it so the cops would have a tag on me. That's why you brought me outside that time. So the cops could get my picture on file. Me talkin' to you. You fuckin' *set me up!!*"

The cold smile returned to Nesto's face. "You ain't as stupid as you look, Terry." He turned to his two fat stooges. "Hey, d'ya believe it, boys? The cunt ain't as stupid as she looks!" Then he laughed again, this time a short, harsh bark. "Yeah, I set you up, Terry. Y'wanna know why? Plenty a' reasons. Cuz I knew, way you drive, you was gonna get inna bust-up one day, and prolly while carryin' summa my shit. That's why I only sent you up there with drugs these last few times, an' no money. Cuz if you got caught with drugs, why should I give a shit? Only you'll go down, and I can always get some other asshole to send up another supply."

"An' what if I talked?"

"Then you'd be dead, if I think yer worth the trouble. Prolly not. With yer record, who'd believe ya?" The smile disappeared. "But if you got caught with my money, money that was on it's way back to me, that's fuckin' different. That's *my* money, and *nobody* fucks with that!"

The smile returned. "The other reason is, I jus' don't like ya, ya cunt. Yer unnatural. When I did that favor for ya before ya got outta the joint, sight unseen, I thought I was gettin' some fresh, young twat right outta reform school who I could spend *years* tellin' she hadn't paid up, an' all the time me thinkin' up new ways to make her pay. When *you* showed up, so fuckin' ugly I wouldn't even fuck ya with the cops's Vienna- sausage sized dicks, I wanted to be ridda you as soon as possible. I'm doin' that now. It's time to clean house, *putana*, and yer the trash that's gotta go. So get yer fuckin' ugly, redneck, inbred, white-trash ass outta here!"

Terry said nothing for a second, then smiled as she dug her good hand into her pocket. She pulled out her cigarettes and lighter, popped a cig into her mouth and lit it with the Zippo. Then she took a long drag and blew the smoke into Nesto's face. All this time, she kept the Zippo in her hand, fondling it as she spoke.

"Li'l man," she began, watching with satisfaction as the stupid smile disappeared from her ex-boss's face. "Li'l man, you have a very bad habit. A bad habit of bitin' off more'n you can chew. Clean house? You can't even clean yerself without yer momma helpin' you. Even prolly used her tongue to do it. Do me a favor, huh? Make sure yer momma gets *her* bone tonight!"

"Boys-"

"Y'think yer a big man, Nesto? Bullshit! The niggers you supply for in DC *own* you. You an' about a hunnert other wanna-bes in this area. An' they must be yankin' yer chain pretty fuckin' hard and rockin' yer brains if y'actually think they'll let ya walk their pit bulls."

"-get this bleedin' cunt-"

"That's the problem with ya damn Mexicans. You think just because you look a bit like white people, that yer as smart. But a piece a' shit like you, y'admit ya can't even get laid unless y'force some dumb cunt on her knees. That's pretty fuckin' pathetic, ya Mexican midget!"

"-outta here before I-"

"Hey, Nesto! You know what they call a Mexican Midget?!"

A beat. "A *speck!*"

"Fuck it! I'll kill 'er *myself!!*"

Nesto jumped at her, murder in his eyes. With a flick of her hand, Terry popped open the Zippo, and shoved the flame in Nesto's face, catching him under the chin. Nesto's roar turned into a howl as he threw himself backwards into his desk, knocking it over and joining the rest of the crap on the floor.

Terry heard the first Samoan behind her and ducked just as he made a grab for her. Dropping to her knees, she freed her cast from her sling and pulled out the straight razor. The big lug made another grab for her and got his hand sliced open for his pains. He screamed and drew back just in time for the other idiot behind Nesto's desk to have a go at her. This time, she kicked low, side swiping the big ox against his knee. Another satisfying howl, another crash to the ground, but now Nesto had his pecker up again and dove for Terry, who smacked her cast square in his face. He grunted as blood spurted out his nose.

She turned in time to see the behemoth she cut reach into his pants. Realizing the big lunkhead was getting out the less vulnerable of his two dicks, Terry took the hint and ran.

Terry had just opened the door when a shot rang out and part of the doorframe exploded outward, dusting her face with flying splinters. Pig Meat seemed to have disappeared; at least, Terry saw no sign of him when she ran out into the main room. Diving behind the bar, she found him, crouched on the floor. Another shot rang out overhead, and Terry heard Nesto, his voice somewhat garbled: "No shooting, you fuckin' idiot! You want the cops outside to hear?"

Terry landed on Pig Meat and he grunted. Then Terry saw the shotgun, sitting on a ledge just above his crouched figure. She grabbed it with her good hand and managed to pump a round in the chamber.

This is gonna be tricky, she thought as she cradled the stock into her good arm while bracing the pump against her cast. She wrapped her hand around the trigger, took a deep breath, and sprang up from behind the bar.

The idiot she cut was in the room, but looking back over his shoulder, his blood-tacky pistol pointed in her direction. Terry could see Nesto in the doorway, blood streaking his face. His eyes widened at the sight of Terry, and she saw his lips start to form the "look" in "Look Out!" when she squeezed the trigger.

The explosion from the gun's barrel knocked her backwards, but she stayed on her feet. The giant's head exploded like an overripe pumpkin, sending blood and brain matter flying backwards, spraying the entrance to Nesto's office. Time seemed to stand still while the rest of the bodyguard's body figured out it was dead. The bleeding hand twitched, sending a bullet to land harmlessly in the ceiling. Then the body collapsed with a meaty splat on the clubhouse's concrete floor.

Terry recovered herself and jerked back the action, pumping another round in the chamber. "Where d'ya want the next load, Nesto?," she said. "In yer greasy head?"

The Demon Head said nothing, but his eyes promised damnation and hellfire. When she saw those eyes shift behind her and she whipped the stock end of the shotgun backwards, right into Pig Meat's solar plexus. The fat Head let out a *Woof!* as the breath knocked out of him; Terry swore she felt the earth shake as he fell. "Hard to find good help these days, huh, Nesto? Just proved it in more ways n'one, didn't I?"

"Cunt, you are so fuckin' dead."

"Big words fer a runt like you. Good thing I'm in a forgiving mood right now. Otherwise I'd just blow yer ass away and leave a little tiny grease spot on the wall. Not that anybody'd notice, as fuckin' filthy it is in here."

"Then ya better not miss. I tell Piggy there to only keep two rounds in that thing. Figure that's enough to get somebody runnin'. So, even if you got the balls to take me out, yer still fucked." And for emphasis, Nesto's other goon stood behind him in the doorway, .38 Special extended, pointed right at her.

"Well, I guess what we got here is a Mexican standoff. But I don't have to tell *you* that," she cackled.

"Bitch, are you high?"

"Shut yer fuckin' hole. I'm the one callin' the shots here. Yer just along fer the ride. Now, I'm just gonna back myself up slowly, an' I don't think even you are stupid enough to stop me."

"Nah, I won't stop ya. But I will get ya, sooner or later. Maybe out onna street, maybe out around that shithole you call yer house, me an' the boys'll come by. Then yer gonna feel pain, bitch. Pain like you never felt before. Pain so bad it'll make what you got from yer daddy feel like a baby's kiss." Nesto chuckled to himself. "Hell, what them nigger girls did to ya will feel like amateurs!" Terry's eyes narrowed at that last and she felt her gorge rise. A slight tremble came into her hands, but she kept her voice steady. She grinned at Nesto, but it felt like a drawn rictus on her face. "Why, Nesto, yer so sweet! Offerin' t'show a girl a good time like that! Well, lemme make ya another offer. Make us even."

She took the chance of advancing a step, and pulled the trigger back on the shotgun, just a bit, so Nesto could see the hammer draw back. "How d'ya know, Nesto, that when ya do come an' get me, yer gonna be the one that leaves alive?"

Now the barrel was six inches from the gangleader's stony face. "How do you know," she continued, "that one day, when you get enough balls to stick yer head outta this little shithole of yers . . .that I won't be the one waitin' fer *you?*"

She paused, then winked. "Somethin' ta think about, big boy. See ya 'round."

And, without another word, she backed up until she hit the door. No one moved or breathed.

Terry smirked. "Fuckin' *speck!!*", she laughed.

Then she was out the door.

Once the door slammed behind her, she turned and hurried away. She half-expected to hear a shot ring out and a bullet from the other guard's .38 lodge itself into her back, but she knew that even Nesto wasn't stupid (or crazy) enough to commit murder in full view of the cops surveillance team, where it could be captured on film for posterity. She was momentarily worried about them getting a picture of her carrying a shotgun with there being a headless corpse just a few feet away and inside, but she knew that Nesto would take care of that, too. One piece at a time, most likely.

She pulled open the door of the pickup and placed the shotgun inside, then slid in after it behind the wheel. She slumped back into the seat, spent. *Great. Out of a job and gotta price on my head*, she thought. *Does it get any better'n this?*

She dug into her pocket for her cigs, past the five hundred she had pocketed, and realized something was missing. Her Zippo. *Fuckin' hell! Musta dropped it back there when I squashed it in Nesto's face*, she chided herself.

"Well, I got five hundred," she muttered out loud. "That oughta do fer somethin'."

Then reality set in. Every last cent of that had to go to fixing her bike. As is was, she was already tapped out. That's why she came to see Nesto in the first place. "No, not just fixin' it," she said. "Improvin' it!"

Yeah, there were a few things she wanted to add to her rebuilt bike, things she now probably needed more than ever since Nesto and she had just declared war on each other.

She pulled out of the lot with a squeal of wheels and winced. She had a mini-flashback to the accident, and that's when it hit her.

"The accident," she shouted. "That fuckin' Jewboy! That fuckin' rich Jewboy!"

Even though she had been the one who hit him, the Jewboy would be the one the pigs blamed for it, taking that left turn all of a sudden like that. And when there's blame, there's fault. When there's fault, there's negligence.

"An' when there's negligence", she said, "you can sue."

The grin on her face evaporated for a moment when she considered, at least in the short run, what this would entail. An explanation. More specifically, an explanation to a certain someone whom she was sometimes hesitant to tell the full truth to.

Terry felt her face flush, her cheeks suddenly red. *Fuck it*, she told herself. *Can't make no omelet without breakin' eggs.*

Tomorrow she would have to go see Rusty.

CHAPTER 15

Ari was dreaming. He was back at the crash, but he was alone. Very, very alone. The intersection was totally devoid of people; no other cars sped by. There was only his car, pulled over at the side of the road, a sledgehammer size dent in its side. The shops near the road were empty; not closed, just deserted, like all the world had stepped into tomorrow, leaving Ari to deal with today, and the here and now was as real as the glass and crumbling tar of the road beneath his feet.

Ari sat down heavily on the sidewalk, staring open mouthed, the shell-shocked soldier after battle. And when the buzzing came, he thought it was all in his head, a result of the calamity before him. But it grew louder, like a low-flying airplane, but the sky was as empty as the earth beneath it. Worst of all, the buzzing didn't seem to actually *come from* anywhere, but surrounded him like amber encasing a too-curious insect.

Ari stood, and the buzzing passed by him, most definitely *not* like an insect. More like a charging water buffalo. *But water buffaloes don't move that fucking fast!*, Ari thought as the breeze blew by him. *What've I got here? The world's biggest wasp?*

The buzzing faded for a second, but then returned, faster this time. And that wasn't all: this time the wasp (Ari couldn't think of what else to call it) gave him a sting. Or at least a slash. He felt a tear at his clothing, heard the *riiiip* as it went by.

Ari examined his cut, a tear along the front of his shirt. There was no blood, just a slice that extended across his belly, leaving it exposed but unscathed. A cut with a large knife. Or a razor blade.

Then came the buzz again; there was no buildup, it just appeared, like the volume on a speaker that was turned from zero to ten in an instant. But this time the sting came for his back, and Ari most definitely *felt* it. Pain shot through his system in an arc, and he felt blood dripping into the waistband of his pants and down his leg.

He was still mulling over the sensation when the buzz came again, and there was another cut, this time to his face, right below his left eye, and all the way across his cheek. Another buzz, and a cut to his leg, deeper this time. Ari felt the muscles in his leg part and the nerves fray. He fell to his knees from the shock. "Who are you?!," he screamed. "*What* are you?! What the fuck do you want from me!!?"

All he got in response was another slash, on his arm this time. He felt it go dead, and fell prone to the ground, a puppet whose strings have been cut. The blood was gathering in a pool beneath him. In fact, the whole street was rapidly becoming a crimson tide. *This is more than me,* Ari thought, his last coherent one. *No one's got this much blood in him! This is a lot more blood than I've got!! Than* anyone's *got!!*

The buzzing returned, but different this time. Slowing itself, bit by bit. Ari braced himself, certain he was about to receive the killing stroke, but nothing came. Just the infernal sound, growing louder and louder, deafening, drowning out all his other senses.

Then, in its slowing down, it became recognizable for what it was: the rumble of a superpowerful motorcycle. Slowing. Slowing.

Stopped.

"Jewboy."

The voice was harsh, guttural in his ears, devoid of any easy gender identification. Ari kept his head down, burying it in the pool of blood at his knees.

"Hey, Jewboy!"

He heard his own voice, far away, high-pitched, squeaking like a mouse in the din of a lion's roar. "Go away," it said.

Then came the crunch of feet on tar, glass and pebbles. A pair of brown leather motorcycle boots came into his view, then a pair of legs with muscles on them that bulged like steel cables, under a pair of cut-off denim shorts. He felt a hand with an unforgiving grip grab his hair, forcing him to look up.

The face that stared back at him was half-hidden by a pair of reflecting sunglasses, making the being look like more like an insect than ever. But there was no mistaking; it was the apparition that had crashed into Ari the week before. It grinned at him, the teeth sharp and white. "Didn't yer ma and dad teach ya any manners, Jewboy?", it asked. "Answer me when I talk at ya!"

Ari said nothing, just stared. Then he felt a warm sensation in his crotch. At first he thought the thing had cut him without moving, but then he saw it look down and laugh, a high pitched scrapping sound whose milk of humor had curdled into sour cream a long time ago. "Well, lookie here!" it brayed. "Jewboy here done wet himself!"

Then it pulled his face close to its own, so close Ari could smell breath of stale cigarettes and alcohol. Its eyes were still invisible behind the shades. "Well," the thing continued. "One good body fluid deserves another, don't it, Jewboy?"

It was only then that Ari noticed that it carried something. *The stinger, ohmygod, its* stinger!!, Ari screamed in his mind as the creature flicked open an old-fashioned, ivory handled straight razor. It glittered in the light, then he heard the buzzing again, swelling in his head, louder, ever louder, the razor drawn back, slicing the air as it flew toward him and he bolted upright in bed, the scream on his lips, settling into a moan. He felt damp; he thought he was bleeding, but realized it was only the sweat that had poured out of his body during the dream. But then he heard a buzzing again, and he didn't think *that* was his imagination, until he realized it was the phone ringing next to him on the night stand. He let out a breath, not realizing he'd even been holding it in. *Steady, dude,* he told himself. *Just the phone. Just someone calling me on the friggin' phone. What could be more harmless than that?*

He placed a shaky hand on it, took another deep breath, then answered. "He hello?"

"I didn't wake you, did I?"

Ari let out another sigh, this one even more relieved. "Rache! No, no. I was just getting up. What's up?"

"I just wanted to give you a call before you went in on your first day. See how you were doing."

"Okay, I guess. First class ain't till ten. English Lit in the Romantic Period."

"I thought your dad didn't want you taking any of those 'Mickey Mouse' courses."

"Yeah, that's why I decided to take 'Cartooning'."

Rachel laughed. "Glad to see you have your sense of humor back."

"Yeah, I was pretty vacant there for awhile, but I think I'm back on track. How're things with you?"

"Busy, as always. Too much damn reading at one damn time. Sometimes I don't think I get out of this damn house except to go to class."

"Any chance of getting together soon? Get yourself a breath of fresh air?"

"Oh? Do you have something in mind, Mr. Sussman?"

"Oh, nothing special," Ari replied, smiling. "Just anything you might want to do."

"Well, let me check my date book and get back to you."

"Ah, yes! What's more beautiful than love in the 1990s? "Let my schedule get back to your schedule, and we'll talk!"

Rachel laughed again. "Yeah, and when mid-terms come around, it's gonna get even worse. Why is it that we seem to get busier and busier even though we have so many time saving devices and stuff?"

"Because with all these so-called 'labor-saving devices', people expect us to do more and more. The more you can do, the more they give you to do."

"Ahhhhh. See, I hadn't thought of that. Very good, Ari. I knew you'd have the answer. A college education *hasn't* been wasted on *you.*"

"Talk is cheap. So is enlightenment."

"Yeah, you're definitely getting back into the college groove already."

"And this is just my first day. Imagine how insufferable I'll be after a few months."

"You're never insufferable. You're just you."

Ari smiled again. "Thanks. Call you in a couple of days."

"Good luck. Love ya!"

"Love ya, too."

He replaced the phone in its cradle and slumped back into bed, staring at the ceiling. *Rache did it again,* he thought. *Pulled me out of a nightmare.* Admittedly, he hadn't given the accident much thought over the past few days, the other person involved barely a thought in a week. *Wonder if this makes me a self-involved little shit. Well, they'll get plenty of settlement by my insurance,* Ari grimaced.

He had just started drifting back to sleep when the explosion came. Not a physical one, but one of sound, followed shortly by one of fury.

The sound was a musical one, or, at least, one that apparently the owner *thought* was music. The crunch of power chords and the rumble of double-bass drums drifted down the hall relentlessly, pushing forward, pushing its way into the ear canals of unwilling listeners.

Ari, at the other end of the hall from its source, was reluctantly pulled back into consciousness because of it. At first he thought it was another dream, but since there were no accompanying images, he realized this was something from the real world.

Then came the shouting. "Who the fuck is making all that fucking noise?," came one deep voice Ari didn't recognize. "Who the fuck do you think it is?", answered another.

"Graziano!!!!", screamed what sounded like an entire hallway full of people.

Then came the sound of a door opening, and the music was even louder. "Good fuckin' morning to ya, motherfuckers!!!" Graziano bellowed in what sounded like good (or at least amused) humor. "Welcome to another goddamn school year! You all get yer lazy, cracked asses outta bed!!" Then came the sound of a door being slammed, and the music became a dull roar.

"That young man has some serious problems," Ari said out loud to himself, then found his face breaking into a smile. Then he laughed, longer and louder, working out the tension that had infused itself in him since the dream. And once he got started, he couldn't stop. Peals of laughter erupted out of him so hard and so fast, Ari thought that anyone hearing him would've thought that *both* the guys who had singles this year were put there for being mentally disturbed.

He looked at the clock. 8:30. "Ah, well. Just a half hour of sleep lost," Ari said. He threw off his covers and stretched as he heard the sound of several angry fists pounding on a door, presumably Graziano's. *Yep,* Ari thought. *Looks like another typical school year.* He laughed again as he made his way down the hall and into the showers. And, by the time he got to his first class and was studying its syllabus, the bogey of his dreams had become a distant, misty memory.

CHAPTER 16

The intercom on the phone buzzed, and a manicured, callused hand reached across the desk to push the receiver button. "Yeah, Maybelle?"

"Terry's here to see you, Rusty," an elderly female voice drawled.

Rusty could feel the beginnings of a headache form behind her eyes at the receipt of that news. Automatically, her hand went to the desk drawer where she kept an economy-sized bottle of aspirin. *Probably should stop taking so many of these a day,* she thought. *Bad for my stomach.* "Send 'er on in," she said out loud. With her other hand, she massaged her left temple gently, hoping the stressor points would loosen on their own.

Clara "Rusty" Darrow was a handsome woman in her forties who received her nickname thanks to the thick crop of red hair and freckled complexion she had as a young girl. Not as young anymore, with her hair shot through with gray streaks and the freckles on her face fading, she still carried a larger-than-life vitality about her that dominated any room she was in. Despite her five foot, five inch stature, people tended to think she was much taller, a useful trait to have when one makes their living as a trial lawyer, as Rusty did. Being the top notch street lawyer she was, and her reputation as a tough cookie as secure as a Swiss vault, Rusty got a good deal of patronage, not all of them as savory as your everyday jurist might like. But Rusty didn't care; in a profession often wrought with ass-kissing, boot-licking, double-dealing suck ups, she found her mostly country-living, plain-spoken clientele refreshing, even if they were not always the most genteel of souls. *Besides,* she often told herself, *it's not like I'm too old to forget my days hauling pig slop on a jerkwater Louisiana farm.*

And so it was with Terry Scranton. Still, that didn't mean Terry couldn't (and didn't) aggravate the shit out of her sometimes (okay, *most* times) and that her headaches didn't increase in direct proportion to the amount of time spent with her. Nor did she expect this time to be any different from the others. But when Terry walked in the door with her arm in a cast dangling from a sling around her neck, all Rusty's previous expectations of aggravation flew out the window. "I need your help," Terry said as the door closed behind her.

"My God! What the hell happened?" Rusty exclaimed simultaneously as she launched herself from behind her desk.

"Aw, it don't hurt," Terry replied. "Itches mostly. The docs're tellin' me its healin' good."

"So what happened?"

"I'm comin' to that! Lemme finish!"

"You tell me the truth, girl! Did somebody do this to ya?"

"No! I got into an accident. Wiped out on my bike."

"You wearin' a helmet?"

"Uh . . ."

"What did I tell you, girl!? You gonna knock the rest a' what functions for your brains out all over the street!?"

Terry's face flushed, and she looked down at Rusty's feet, not quite able to meet her eyes. And an instinct honed after years of ferreting out the truth from witnesses and wayward clients knew, just *knew,* that there was more. A lot more. *Keep it together, Rus,* she told herself. *Don't blow your damn cool, hard as it's gonna be. And this time, I think it's gonna be a doozy.*

Out loud, she said: "Come and sit down. Want coffee?" The twinge of pain and unease in her head had by now spread to her gut, and she thought perhaps it might help compose her for what was to come.

"Yeah, I'll have some if yer havin' some," Terry replied.

Rusty went to the extra-large coffee maker she kept at the base of a bookshelf full of law books at the other end of the room and poured the two of them heaping cups of coffee in mugs so brown, plain and no-nonsense they could double as spittoons (and sometimes had, for Rusty's clients who dipped). Both ladies took it straight black. "So, talk," Rusty said as she settled in the chair opposite the one Terry had slumped down in. "What the fuck happened to you? Start from the beginning, and don't you dare leave anything out."

"I won't," Terry replied. "I was drivin' down this road in Maryland-"

"Where in Maryland?"

"Round Gaithersburg. Anyway, I was goin' a little faster'n normal, headin' up to this intersection, when I notice this funeral procession headin' toward me from the opposite direction. This was 'round Shady Grove Road."

"Wait. You was on Shady Grove?"

"Nah, Rockville Pike, I think it was. I just stopped off fer somethin' t' eat, and I just got back on Rockville Pike, and I take my eyes offa the road fer a second, seein' this funeral go by, an' right as I'm in the intersection, outta the corner a' my eye, I see this silver-colored Honda pull out in front a' me."

Terry shook her head. "I can still see that li'l fucker in my mind. We made eye contact right before the crash. Looked like a Jewboy. Hadda big goddamn nose, dark-like skin, kinky brown hair."

"Coulda been an Italian, but you're probably right. Lotta Jews there in that part of Maryland. Anyway, go on."

"So, the next thing I know, I'm flyin' ass-over-head over the fuckin' car! Tried to break part a' my fall with my arm, an' ended up snappin' my wrist. Broke the damn thing as neat as can be. Took me to this hospital that was just down the road. Doc there told me it'd take about a month t'heal. Shit! It's been a week, an' already the damn thing's drivin' me crazy with the itch!"

"It's a good sign. Tells you're healin' pretty quick. Might not take a month."

"Man, I hope not. Drivin' me outta my fuckin' mind."

"So what about your bike? Is it trashed?"

"Does a bear shit inna woods?"

"How're you getting around then?"

"Gotta pickup truck. Borrowed it from a neighbor to get down here today."

Rusty scanned Terry's face, probing her with her dark blue eyes. Once again, Terry couldn't quite look her in the face. After a moment, Rusty merely nodded, deciding not to press the issue. Probably unimportant, anyway. "You fixing it yourself, or is somebody else?", she asked.

Terry snorted. "Yeah, like I could afford it? I got no insurance, no money comin' in. Fuck, I'm lucky I got enough socked away to still eat!"

"Ain't your brother helping you out any?"

Terry's face turned bright red, then to a deep purple. "That little peckerwood!? I called him right when I got outta the hospital, and he told me to go take a flyin' fuck! Paid some tow truckin' asshole to dump my bike on the doorstep, and that was it. I'm still pickin' up all the pieces! After all I took for him growin' up an' the little sonovabitch-!"

Rusty held up her hand. "Okay, okay! So that dog ain't huntin' no more, huh?"

"Yeah, an' he'll be lucky if I don't decide to go down there an'-!"

"Terry! That's enough!!"

Terry broke off, snapping her mouth shut and slumping back in her seat. Rusty was no longer looking at her and instead stared off into the distance, lost in thought. "So," she said. "If you have no insurance, how're you gonna get some cash for yourself?" Terry said nothing, knowing that the question was not necessarily directed at her. She also knew from past experience that when Rusty got *that* look in face and *that* tone in her voice, it was best not to interrupt, lest she be distracted from some vital bit of information she'd absorbed. Better to let her take all the time she needed.

After a few minutes, Rusty's gaze cleared and focused directly on Terry again. "Did you get the guy's info?"

"Wasn't time. Cops and the ambulance whisked me off before I hadda chance to think of it."

"Doesn't matter. His name'll be in the police report, which I'll subpoena. But before I even start, I gotta ask you two questions we sorta bleeped over earlier."

Terry saw Rusty's face grow hard, and eyes become two solid chips of blue ice. Terry felt a cold sweat on her brow and an equally cold something form in the pit of her stomach. *Aw, man, here it comes!,* she told herself.

"You still haven't told me," Rusty said, "just what you were doing over there in Maryland."

Terry was silent, looking down at her feet. "The answer ain't down there on the carpet, girl," Rusty continued. "Answer my question. I need to repeat myself?"

"No," Terry replied, almost timidly. *What the fuck,* she told herself. *I already lied to her once, and I know she saw through me, but she didn't push it. She thinks I'm snowballin' her now, and she'll flip. Fuck! She's gonna flip anyway!*

"I . . . I was on my way back from DC," she said out loud. "From makin' a run. For Nesto an' the Demon Heads."

Terry knew the explosion was coming, *knew* it, but was still more than a little taken aback when it happened. Because Rusty didn't just flip, she *blew her stack.* She launched herself out of her chair and into Terry's face, her eyes now twin beacons of blue fire threatening to scorch Terry's skin. "WHAT DID I TELL YOU, GIRL!!!??", she roared, sounding like the devil himself had shot red pepper up her ass. *"WHAT DID I TELL YOU??!!!"*

Terry could say nothing; Rusty's face was now nearly as red as her hair. She felt certain Rusty was going to grab her and shake her, maybe even slap her one for good measure. *And goddamn it,* she thought morosely, *she could do it, too. I'd let her get away with it. Her, of all people, I'd let her.*

But Rusty didn't. Instead she just stood there, pinning Terry to the back of the chair with her eyes, letting the question stand. "Well . . .what the fuck do ya expect me to do, Rusty?," Terry finally answered. "I need money, fer Chrissake! What kinda honest job could I get, with my record an' all?"

"You could try waitressin' again!"

Terry gave out a single bark of a laugh in response. "An' have m' ass grabbed again? An' have to call you again to come bail me out when I clock that sonovabitch upside his head? No thanks!"

Rusty laughed in spite of herself. "Yeah, you sure as hell gave that trucker motherfucker something to chew on!"

Terry smiled grimly. "Look, Rust, I'm sorry," she said. "I know y' told me to stay away from Nesto an' his merry band a' fuckwads, but I swear to ya it won't happen again. I'm quits with 'em now. I paid off my debt, an' I made m' last run for 'em."

Rusty regarded her for a moment, then nodded. "All right, then," she replied. "If somethin' like that comes up in a deposition or something, just say you stopped off in Rockville for some food, and you were lookin' to get back on the highway. But I got another question for you, baby girl, and this one's probably even more important: you got your license back?"

Terry said nothing; it was all the answer Rusty needed. "No, of course you don't," Rusty continued. "Why would you wanna make any part of this easy for me?"

"Well, what the fuck do I need a license fer anyway?," Terry answered. "I been riding a bike since I was a kid. Hell, I ride it better'n a lotta them stunt people out in Hollywood."

"Yeah, well maybe you do," Rusty answered back. "But if you're gonna try to bring a reckless driving lawsuit against somebody, it sorta helps when you gotta *fuckin' current license yourself!!*"

Rusty had been resting her hand on some law books piled on her desk, but now she shoved them violently to the floor with a loud *thunk!,* turning her back on Terry. Terry said nothing, just sat slumped in her seat, sullenly staring into her cup of coffee.

After a few moments, Rusty spoke again, this time her voice much more even. "All right, she said. "Here's what I can do. I'll start the process of getting together a suit. I'll subpoena the Maryland police department for the accident report, get all the required information from that, then serve a process on this kid, whoever he is. Maybe, if we're lucky, he'll decide to settle immediately without any of us seeing the inside of a courtroom. But I can't promise that, girl! If he decides to call my bluff, we're fucked, because no judge in his right mind is gonna find for a plaintiff with no driver's license. Without that little document, it wouldn't matter if he mowed you down, stopped, backed over you, and ran you down again! So we better hope he folds before the game begins."

"But if we did take it to court, couldn't ya try to work anything?"

Rusty sighed. "You think too much of me, girl. I can baffle 'em with legal bullshit with the best, but I sure as hell can't work miracles."

"But yer gonna try, ain't ya?"

Rusty barely regarded her over her shoulder. "Yeah, girl. I'm gonna try."

"That's all I ask," Terry replied as she rose from her seat. She took a last sip from her mug and laid it on Rusty's desk. "Thanks, Rus," she went on. "I owe ya more n' I care t' count, but I want ya to know, I appreciate ya fer tryin'. How much do ya think we oughta try for?"

"Don't know yet. Once I find out this guy's name, I can make him disclose his finances. If it's a kid like you said, he might not have anything. Or maybe he's got some sorta trust fund. Or maybe his daddy's loaded."

"Hmpf. Awful lotta 'maybes'".

"This ain't an exact science, honey bunch. There's *always* a lotta 'maybes'. What's your financial situation right now?"

"Could be better, I guess."

"You need any money?"

"Rusty, I told ya. I owe ya too much already."

"You can pay me back out of the settlement, if there is any," Rusty replied as she pulled her purse from a large drawer at her desk. She removed her checkbook from the center compartment. "I ain't got much on me, so I'll have to write you a check made out to 'cash' for, what? Three hundred enough?"

"Anything you can spare."

Rusty wrote out the check and peeled it off, handing it to her client. "Gimme a couple of days to get things together, and I'll call you. Once I know enough, I'll file the suit. You eatin' okay?"

"Guess I am. Took yer advice about saving money and started buying mostly fruits and vegetables. Don't think I've had any real meat in six months. 'Cept that shit they gave me inna hospital."

"And? How d'ya feel?"

"Best I've felt in years."

"Good. Still exercising?"

"Well, I ain't been able to do much weight-liftin' lately, obviously, but yeah, I still am."

"Good. If an old bat like me can do it, ain't no reason why a young'un like you can't. And that cast'll be off before you know it. Just sit tight and stay outta trouble, you hear me? Let me take care of this."

"'Kay. See ya 'round. Wanna get some parts for the bike while I'm here in town. An' thanks fer the coffee," Terry said, waving at her discarded cup. She was halfway out the door when Rusty called after her. "And Terry?"

"Yeah?"

"When yer done 'borrowing' that truck, put it back where the owner can find it. Or at least where the cops might find it."

Terry's face flushed crimson. "Yes'm," she replied.

The door closed behind her, and Rusty dropped herself into her chair, spent. She massaged her temples vigorously. *Here it comes, Rus,* she said to herself. *One bloody headache leaves, and another one's there, hot on its heels.*

She looked down at her aspirin drawer, still half-open. She pulled out the bottle, regarded it, then shook out three tablets. After another moment's consideration, she shook out two more, downing a total of five pills with the remains of her coffee. *Wonder how much Terry's not telling me,* she mused. *I'm sure there are plenty of gaps to fill. I just hope they ain't too huge. Or insurmountable.*

Rusty chuckled dryly to herself. "Like yer one to talk, Rus?," she said out loud. "You've certainly kept a few things from her, ain'tcha?"

88

But instead of letting her mind continue to wander down that road, she shifted mental gears into "work" mode, punching the intercom button on her desk. "Maybelle?"

"Yes, Rusty?"

"Get me the Maryland Police Department, the station in either Rockville or Gaithersburg."

"Any specific division?"

"Auto and traffic violations."

CHAPTER 17

Another day, another phone rang in another town, and another hand reached for it. "Jones", another voice answered.

"Jonesy, you old cuss! How the fuck are ya?"

"Billy Bob! What it is?"

"It is what it is."

"Heard that. What can I do you for?"

"No, my man. It's what I can do for *you.*"

"Do tell."

"Does the name Terry Scranton ring a bell?"

Detective Bernard Jones bolted upright from behind his desk. The paperclip he was toying with flicked out of his hand, joining the piles of papers that lay before him. "Yeah, one the size of Big Fucking Ben," he replied. "Whatya got?"

"A subpoena for the report on the accident recently involving the good Miss Terrencia Scranton. Sittin' here, right in front of my face. When I checked it into the computer, I noticed that you had flagged Miss Scranton's name, saying you should be contacted immediately if anything involving her passed by the Auto Division. So what do I get for being the bearer of good news for an old friend?"

"My undying gratitude, Billy Bob. You just became an even *better* friend."

"Aw, shucks. Weren't nuthin', ma'am," Billy Bob drawled.

Jones chuckled into the phone as he reached for the file he had placed on the far corner of his desk. He flipped it open to a page he had tabbed earlier. "The lawyer who subpoenaed the information, Billy Bob. That wouldn't happen to be Clara Darrow, would it?"

"Give the man a cee-gar! I knew if you spent enough time on the job, you begin to become psycho."

This time Jones didn't laugh, just sat in silence as some pieces of information clicked together in his head. "Jonesy, you there?"

"Huh? . . .Oh! . . .Yeah, Billy Bob. Sorry. Just wool-gathering."

"So this is pretty significant. Something to do with the case you're working on, or can you tell me?"

"It sort of is. Not the main thrust of it, though. Something secondary."

"Man, I love it when you use big words like 'secondary'!"

Now Jones did laugh. "Ah, you fuckin' redneck! Maybe if you stayed in school longer, you'd be chief of police by now!"

"And give up my day-to-day duties of talking to lowlifes like you? Not a chance! So, when're we getting together with Smitty for another boys night out?"

"Soon, baby, soon. Just let my liver recover from the last shot."

"And all this time I thought you was Irish."

Jones laughed again. "Get the fuck outta here, man! I got work to do."

"See ya."

Billy Bob clicked off, leaving Jones alone with his thoughts. *Could be just a preliminary examination, not mean anything,* he thought as he absently fingered the file. *Probably looking into the possibility of bringing some kind of suit against the poor schmuck she got into an accident with.*

Jones then opened his official file on the ongoing Demon Head case, and examined the newest set of photos from the stakeout of the club house. The top photo was marked "11:07 AM" in the left hand corner and the date it was taken in the right. The photo itself showed the back view of a figure walking toward the entrance of the club house. One arm was bound in a sling, the other was arched behind the figure's back, and the middle finger extended in full view of the camera. *Ol' Terry,* Jones thought. *Giving half-a-peace sign to the crew on duty.*

The next photo was marked "11:24", and this time there was no mistaking who it was; the cock of the much-more-rapid walk would've given it away even if Jones could see the grainy outline of the face.

But when Jones did examine the face, he couldn't help but feel an icy finger touch his heart. The mouth of the figure was drawn back in an ugly rictus that showed all the teeth, a dubious expression that could only be a broad, sick sort of grin. *It's the smile of a shark*, Jones thought. *A shark that's just eaten somebody.*

Couple this grin with the fact that the wounded arm was now loose from the sling, and the good arm was carrying what could only be a sawed off shotgun, one didn't have to be a twenty-year veteran detective to guess that something significant happened behind those club house walls between the times of 11:07 and 11:24 a.m.

The next picture in the series was marked "11:31" and showed another figure emerging from the club house. *One of Gonzago's bodyguards*, Jones thought. *Carrying something under his arm. Can't quite make out what it is, but it's obviously something he wants to keep hidden, with that damn drop cloth wrapped around it.*

Jones flipped to the next photo, marked "11:37". Now Ernesto Gonzago himself was seen emerging from the club house, also carrying a drop cloth covered package under his arm. *Then he fuckin' rides off, too, and at 11:42, the bodyguard returns, emerging again at 11:45 on the dot, this time with yet another package. Then Nesto returns at 11:53, and the same old situation*, Jones thought. "This goes on for a fuckin' *hour*," Jones said to the empty office. "Just what kind of mess did Terry make in there? And why the fuck hasn't anyone found anything? Does the little wetback got some sorta elephant graveyard where he stuffs shit, or what?"

Jones flipped back to the photo of Terry carrying the shotgun again, studying it closely. He thought it a pretty safe assumption that Miss Scranton was no longer on Gonzago's list of good boys and girls anymore. *Shit, Jonsey,* he thought. *This bitch ain't* never *been on anybody's list of good boys and girls. Least not from a very early age.*

Then he chanced to look over at the file he had started compiling ever since the crazy bitch was identified off of the original photo Jones had shown her in the hospital and shuddered, the icy finger becoming an entire hand that pressed its clammy grip around his heart. *And you know how she got that way, don't you, Jones, my man? Monsters ain't born, baby, they're made. And right there is the fucking 'how-to' manual!*

Jones shook his head violently. He had to focus, focus on the case at hand. Everything else had to take a back seat to the central problem of Gonzago's band of vipers pumping their cash- only venom into the system of the Washington D.C. area. *Anything else is self-indulgence on your part. And didn't your missus already take off because she couldn't put up with a certain little 'self-indulgence' of yours?*

"Goddamnit!," Jones cried out loud. "It wasn't that! It's because some of this shit makes you wanna crawl inside a bottle and never come the fuck out!" *Shit like what's in the file on Terry Scranton,* another voice inside Jones's head whispered coldly. "Yeah," he said out loud, also in a whisper. "Shit like that."

He pulled out Terry's file's most recent entry: his own copy of the accident report recently subpoenaed by Scranton's legal rep, the good Ms. Darrow. *It's a pattern, maybe?,* he thought. *A fucking deadly sort of pattern?*

Or maybe not. All the signs were there, yes, but the circumstance was more than a little different. Jones checked the other name on the report. "Ariel Sussman", it read, and underneath listing an address just down the road in Potomac. *Probably just for the money, then,* he thought. *Nice, rich, Jewish boy from the suburbs? Mucho dinero to be had, indeed! Yeah, probably just has to do with getting some sort of cash settlement.*

It would have been a whole lot easier if he just passed what he knew on to Homicide, but one of the traits that made Jones a good cop (if not a successful one) was his inability to pass a buck, no matter how large. That, and the fundamental determination that finally resolved him to watch and wait, to keep an eye on the movements of Terry Scranton, and see where they may lead. His instincts told him he would hear of her again, even if his conscious thoughts prayed he wouldn't. *Bad pennies, they say,* Jones thought, *always have a way of turning up.*

CHAPTER 18

The elevator opened up into the dorm's common area, and Ari felt he could relax, a little, as he made his way down the hallway. *First week down,* he thought. *But don't it feel great to be back, even with a load of homework?*

But Dave, who rode the elevator up with him, was having none of it. "So would you believe this fucker, Ari? First week back, and already he's setting up a test for us on a thousand page textbook he wants to cover in *six weeks!* And that's just the damn mid-term!"

Ari just sort of nodded while he mentally sorted out his plans for the weekend. *Wonder if I have time to go home and see Rachel? I know it's way to soon to see my friggin' folks again, so-*

Ari's thoughts broke off suddenly, as did Dave's voice, as they were confronted by a sight that had to be seen to be believed. As they made their way down the hallway, they passed Graziano's room, the door wide open and displaying the occupant reclining on his bed, back against the wall. That in itself wouldn't have caused the two young men to gape so; the fact that he appeared to be naked, however, did.

Further examination also showed he was reading a large book, strategically placed, and that he was smoking a cigarette, the fumes of which made a slowly rising vapor-trail out the half opened window to the right of him. Directly behind him, Marlon Brando sneered his approval from on top of his motorbike in a poster of *The Wild One.*

Graziano said nothing for a moment, just continued to read from his book, which Ari could now see was called *Beyond Good and Evil.*

Ari had just enough time to think the title appropriate when Graziano spoke, not even bothering to look up. "Unless you boys turned faggot over the summer," he said, "either move along or come in."

Dave closed his gapping mouth with a snap. "You coming, Ari?," he inquired.

"You go on ahead. Be right with you."

Dave nodded and continued down the hall. Ari turned back to the spectacle before him. "Not very self-conscious, are you, Graziano?", he said.

Graziano put down the book, and Ari was relieved to see that he wasn't completely naked: a black pair of bikini briefs encased his privates, but still left little to the imagination "Should I be?", Graziano asked, smiling a bit.

Ari found that one hard to argue. Graziano had the thickly-muscled body of a dedicated weightlifter. His chest, legs and arms bulged from hours of bench-presses, curls and squats. Ari grudgingly admitted to himself (quite heterosexually, of course) that the guy did a good job of keeping himself in shape, no matter how unusual his other habits were. *Fucker looks like the "After" display in one of those old Charles Atlas ads they used to run in the comic books,* Ari marveled to himself. *Probably could rip that book he's reading in half without even giving off a grunt.* "Well," he began, deciding finally that discretion might be the better part of valor in this instance. "You could at least work up a little modesty for the rest of us, you know."

Graziano bored into him with eyes so dark a brown they were almost black. Then his gaze softened slightly, and he chuckled, a low, dry rasp. "All right, Sussman," he said. "If your middle class sensibilities are so offended by my efforts to get comfortable, I'll keep my door a little less open and my oh-so-buff dago bod a little less available for public consumption. Besides, doesn't do me much good if I'm on display for a hallway full of men, does it? Might attract the wrong sort of element. The sort that's kind of light in the loafers, *knowhudimean?"*

"Yeah. I guess. And thanks, too, I guess."

"Don't mention it."

"Oh. . .and, uh . . .do you think it's a good idea to . . .uh, you know . . .*smoke* . . .with the R.A. and everything?"

Now Ari saw Graziano's eyes harden into two pieces of black onyx stone. "Who's gonna turn me in?," he demanded. "You?"

"No! I just-"

"Didn't think you were a fuckin' rat, Sussman."

"I'm not! I just-"

Graziano's eyes softened, just a little. "Look," he said. "I got the friggin' window open. All the smoke's goin' in that direction. Shouldn't fuckin' bother anybody."

"Okay!," Ari stammered. "All I was saying-"

"Besides," Graziano continued. "I cut down a lot over the summer. Gone down from two to one pack a day, if that. Feel a whole lot better, too. Doubled the distance I can run."

"Well, good! That's great!"

Graziano chuckled again, this time more to himself than to Ari. "Still," he said. "I like to make sure that when I do light up, it's somewhere around Tawes, or some other place where I know there's gonna be a high concentration of theatre fags. Know why?"

Ari wasn't quite sure where this trip down the rabbit hole was heading, but he figured he had nothing to lose by following along. "Why?" he asked.

Graziano's eyes went hard again. "All last fuckin' year," he said. "When I was in voice class, the uptight guinea bitch who taught it was all over my ass about my smoking. 'You'll never have a career if you abuse your body that way. Especially your voice!'"

Graziano's voice had raised in pitch on the last in a way that was a little frightening coming from such a bulky specimen. "Now," he continued. "I don't want that bitch to actually get the idea I'm quitting on account of *her,* so whenever I know she's around, or if I know she's coming around, I always make sure I got my coffin nails and my Zippo ready!"

Graziano burst out laughing in a lusty cackle, an even darker rasp than his chuckle. "You should see the look on that bitch's face whenever I light up in front of her, Sussman! She looks so far down that big dago nose of her's at me, you'd think she needed binoculars!"

He collapsed into a rich belly laugh that made Ari more than a little uncomfortable, the reluctant eavesdropper on someone else's private joke. Uncertain of what else to do as Graziano yukked it up amongst himself, Ari furtively looked around his dorm room, and was rewarded with a familiar visage peering down at him from a poster positioned above Graziano's study carrel. "Bruce!," Ari exclaimed.

Graziano's laughter broke off. "You a Springsteen fan, Sussman? Never figgered you for the type!"

"Hell, I could say the same thing about you, man! Don't you usually listen to that metal shit?"

Graziano smirked at him. "I listen to a lotta 'shit', Sussman. My metalhead persona is just one aspect of my personality."

"Uh-huh."

"Besides, Springsteen used to be in a metal band."

"Man, get outta here!"

Graziano's smirk broadened. "'S'truth. Back before he decided to become this generation's answer to Woody Guthrie, he tried to be a Jersey answer to Eric Clapton. He was in a four-piece metal band called Steel Mill. Little Stevie was the bass player."

"Who?"

Now the smirk verged on a sneer. "Y'see the 'Glory Days' video?"

"Yeah."

"The guy who was singing with him. The one with the scarf on his head."

"Oh, yeah!"

So, what d'ya like about him?"

"Well, I like his energy. The fact that he gives it his all. The songs are all good, too. And I like all the patriotism he showed with 'Born in the USA'."

"I'm sorry, the what?"

"You know. How the guy's come back from Vietnam and everything, and he tells how proud he was to serve, even though it was rough. And no matter how bad it gets, he never forgets he's an American. You know, he's born in the USA!"

Graziano threw his head back and laughed a laugh that was even more unpleasant than the one he had used when discussing his voice teacher. "Sussman," he said between guffaws. "Have you ever *really listened* to the song?"

Ari felt his face heat up, and he imagined a brilliant blush come to his cheeks. "Well, sure," he replied. "I listen to it in my car all the time."

"I mean, have you *really* listened to it?"

"Well, I can't recite all the lyrics off the top of my head."

"I can. And I've got a different, bootleg version of it on tape."

"Aren't bootlegs illegal?"

"And your point?"

"Never mind. All right then, tell me. What do *you* think the song is about?"

"If you heard this acoustic-based version, you'd know, too. Do you know what irony is?"

"Of course."

"Uh-huh. Well, ol' Brucie uses it all over the place in this song. Here he is, describing all these shitty thing happening to him, but the well-known chorus counterpoints it ironically. As an American, he was always told he could get a piece of the well-known 'American Dream'. But he's finding, as he goes through life, that everything he was told was bullshit. He got left behind, even though he tried to do everything he was told, even fighting in a bullshit war that everyone told him was 'for his country'. If anything, he ain't celebratin', he is *pissed off!*"

Ari was stunned and said nothing, more out of embarrassment than anything else. Finally, he stammered, "You're . . .you're making this up!" "Nope," Graziano replied. "I can play it for you if you like."

"That's okay," he responded, feeling a kind of tightness in his stomach, like someone had reached down his throat and grabbed his internal organs. He gave out a nervous laugh. "You know, Reagan thought that that was what he meant, being patriotic and all that."

"Reagan?! Don't get me started, kiddo. I'm embarrassed to say that old fuck was once an actor, even though obviously not a very good one, or he wouldn't have gotten another job!"

Graziano leaned forward on the bed, as if to confide a great secret. You know what Bruce said when the old fuck got elected?", he asked.

"No. . . .what?"

"He said, 'I think what happened last night'. . .meaning the election. . .is pretty frightening.' Ha! Tell it like it is, Bruce!" he exclaimed.

Ari looked and felt like someone had slapped him. Several times. All this time, he had thought Bruce Springsteen had been on the side of everything decent in the world. But after hearing all these terrible things, and on top of that, hearing how he slandered one of the greatest presidents, he was devastated. He felt as though not only the rug had been pulled out from under him, but the entire carpet.

"You're full of shit, Graziano," he managed weakly.

Graziano jerked his head toward the bookcase behind Ari. "If I'm lyin', I'm dyin'. Check it out for yourself, if you want. Third book from the left on the third shelf. 'Born to Run' by Dave Marsh. Marsh kisses Bruce's ass pretty shamelessly throughout, but he does get a lot of good info, I'll give him that."

Ari snorted. "Next you'll be telling me he isn't Jewish."

Graziano's face broke into a grin that could only be described as pure evil. "Well . . ." he began.

"Oh, come on now! *Spring-steen?!*"

"It's a Dutch name, but his dad's a Mick. Nobody's perfect, I guess. But his mom's a gen-you-wine, top of the line, Grade A, numero uno, dago-guinea-wop-gumba-guida straight-off the boat, with the last name of Zirilli! Also, in the book. Wanna borrow it? Obviously, you gotta lot to catch up on!"

Now Ari felt his anger rise as well as his gorge. "You know," he said. "You're a real condescending motherfucker, Graziano! Your know that?"

Graziano's brow furrowed for a second, then cleared. "Does that mean you don't wanna borrow the book?", he asked with mock-innocence.

"Man, you can shove your fucking book up your fucking ass!"

Graziano took a final drag on his cigarette before extinguishing it on the makeshift ashtray he had placed on his night stand. "You know, it's not polite to tell someone that who's just making you an offer. Didn't yer mom and dad teach you that?", he said.

Ari exploded. "Lay off my mom and dad, man! Christ! No wonder nobody likes you around here! You're always fucking with people and making them feel like shit! Like you're something better? Fuck you, man! Fuck you and your fucking white trash lifestyle!"

Ari stormed out of the room and bee-lined down the hallway, half-expecting to hear Graziano barrel after him. *Let him follow me,* he thought. *I'll punch him one upside his head if he touches me. He might beat the living shit out of me, but at least I'd get a couple of good licks in.*

But when he came to his door and proceeded to unlock it, he realized he was alone in the hall. With a shaky hand, he finished unlocking the door, shoved his way inside, and slammed it behind him.

It was only when he was behind closed doors that he could take full measure of what happened. *Christ, what the hell was that all about?* he thought. *I get in this stupid little disagreement about something so damn trivial, and I act the Wild Hare himself jumped straight up my ass!*

He shook his head in an effort to clear it. *Fucking Graziano! Son of a bitch really knows how to get under your skin, playing those mind games of his. Should've just passed him by and let the R.A. catch him in all his naked, smoking glory!*

Out loud he said, "Yeah, we'd get some peace and quiet, all right. Boring-ass peace and quiet. Face it, man. You like it when he goes wild. Saves this place from being routine."

Ari blinked once, twice. Where the hell did *that* come from?

"Where the hell is right," he replied. "You just hated the fact that the guy made you look no, *feel* stupid."

He laughed morosely to himself. *Like I'm not used to that? And then, actually mentioning my parents in the same breath? That's what really hurt.*

He checked his clock radio on his night stand. 6:03, it read. He suddenly realized he was hungry and was thinking of knocking on Dave's door when he saw the light flashing on the answering machine built into his phone. *Wonder if it's Rachel, probably telling me she can't do anything this weekend,* he sighed to himself.

But at the touch of a button came the speak of an electronically-filtered devil. "Ari, it's Dad," came his father's voice, booming in the tight space of the room. "Call home, right now! You really did it this time, kid! That person you got in the accident with? She's fucking *suing us!*"

CHAPTER 19

Terry made the final adjustment with the wrench, straining with all her might against the bolt, then threw the tool to the ground with a satisfied grunt. *Fuckin' A,* she thought with a grin. *Engine's fixed. Now let's see if the little 'adjustment' I added works.*

She took the shotgun that had become her constant companion lately from the work table and lay it gently on the ground. Then she pushed to one side all the excess and building debris that had accumulated over the past two weeks and dug her keys out of her pocket. She slid the main key in the ignition, thought *Here goes nuthin'*, and turned it.

Adjusting the throttle, she made the engine roar into life. Terry's grin grew even broader. "So far, so good," she said. Now for the special feature.

She gripped the new knob she had installed on the motor and clicked it over to the right. The roar became a soft puttering as the muffler did its work, making the motorcycle engine sound for all the world like the outboard motor of a small fishing boat. "Hot damn!," Terry exclaimed. "It works!"

Then, over the throb of the muffled engine, Terry could make out another sound, one that was a lot less familiar here at Scranton Manor: the sound of the phone ringing in the main house. Terry killed the engine and vaulted over to the ramshackle porch, leaping over its two steps. The torn screen door slammed behind her as she jumped over the back of rapidly deteriorating couch in the center of the room. As her bottom connected with the caved-in middle, she simultaneously snatched up the phone sitting on a huge, stained block of wood that functioned as the coffee table. "Hello?"

"Where you been, gal? I musta rung twenty times!"

"Sorry, Rus. Was outside workin' on the bike. Whassup?"

"Well, you really hit the jackpot this time, baby girl. You know who you hit?"

"I dunno. The fuckin' chief rabbi a' Maryland?"

"Ha! Not quite, but close. You ever hear of a clothing chain called Sussman Styles?"

"Think so. Seen it advertised around there. Cheap suits n' shit."

"The same. Actually, the advertising slogan is: 'High quality clothes for low quality prices'. Hell, half the fuckin' lawyers in West Virginia gets their suits from there!"

Terry could feel the grin begin to spread again, across her face. "So you really think I'm in hog heaven here, Rus?"

"Don't go shopping for a fleet a' Harleys yet, baby girl. If anything, this means it's gonna be as hard as I thought. Wherever there's a shit load a' money, you can guarantee there's another shit load a' lawyers tryin' to keep it safe. You know how much the kid's old man's got?"

"Hit me."

"Thirteen mil. And that's his net worth, not how much he might have socked away as other assets."

Terry's mouth had dropped open when hearing the first figure, but now she snapped it shut and managed to get it working again. "Other assets? What'd'ya mean?"

"How much he has invested in his house, maybe even his other houses. Maybe he's got a boat out on the Chesapeake. Hell, with this kinda money, he might have a damn house on the French Riviera with a team a' servants standing by. Hell, *I* would!"

Terry suddenly felt light-headed, and the phone nearly tumbled from her grasp. Thirteen *million*, not even counting all the toys. *Christ, Terry*, the voice inside her head squealed. *You just caught a break. For the first time in your miserable fuckin' life, you finally caught a break!*

Rusty was still talking. "But like I said, girl, all this is academic if the old man doesn't decide to settle. Or even the son." *Oh, the little turd'll settle, Rusty, don't you worry. Cuz if he don't, Jesus, his fuckin' Apostles, Mother Mary and Father Joe the Carpenter ain't gonna be able to keep him from me.*

The thought came so suddenly, brilliantly and violently into Terry's mind, she feared she had actually spoken it aloud. She even gasped after having it, thinking she had just floated it into the air.

"Terry? You all right?"

Terry let out another breath in relief. It *had* been just a thought. "I'm okay, Rus," she said. "Just stubbed my toe. So what now?"

"I sent a copy of the lawsuit we're filing to the kid's home. It's in Potomac, by the way. Of course, huh? Anyway, I'll be calling him soon if he doesn't get back to me first. But I do intend to get back to him first, to keep him a little off balance. So, for now, sit tight. Work on your bike and stay outta trouble."

"Can I get a copy of all yer info?"

There was silence on the other end of the line, and Terry thought she had just overplayed her hand. "What do you want it for, girl?" Rusty asked, a sharpness coming into her voice.

"Well, shit, I'd like to see some of the numbers fer m'self, y'know? Even if it falls through, it'd be nice to see what thirteen mil looks like, even on paper."

Rusty bought it. Or, at least, seemed to. "All right," she said. "You wanna come get it, or should I mail it to you?"

"I gotta come inna town anyway, fer more stuff, so I guess I could drop by. Tomorrow?"

"Sure."

"What's his name?"

"Huh?"

"The kid. What's his name?"

"Terry heard the sounds of paper being shuffled, then: "Ariel. Ariel Sussman."

"Air-e-al? What the fuck kinda name is that?"

"It's a rather common Jewish name, for both men and women. Also got an auxiliary address for him out on the University of

Maryland, College Park campus. Lives in a dorm during the school year."

"Spendin' his daddy's money away one dollar atta time."

"I guess. Not much on him really here, just the father. You can see for yourself when you pick the stuff up tomorrow. How's your arm doing?"

"Not bad. Only itches ever once in awhile now. An' I can move my fingers."

"Great! It'll be off in no time, then. See you tomorrow."

"See ya."

Terry replaced the phone in its cradle and slumped backwards against the protesting couch. She stared at her surroundings, the remains of what used to be her family home. The worn out scraps of carpet that littered the floor more than covered it. The loose floor boards which time had cracked to the point where you could put your foot through if you weren't careful. The peeling yellow wallpaper, and the parts of the wall where the paint had faded to the shade of weak piss. The cobwebs that hung from the ceiling, so neglected that even the spiders who inhabited them had long ago left from greener pastures. The cracked windows that let in more weather than it kept out. The general atmosphere of filth, neglect and decay that kept its sole remaining inhabitant outside it as much as possible. *Especially at night,* Terry thought to herself as she felt the shudder work its way through her. *Fuckin'* always *at night.*

For night was when it always happened. Long ago, perhaps, but still a fresh, open, seeping wound in Terry's mind. *And always on this couch. This rotten, filthy, stinking, bloody couch.* Deep within the recesses of her mind, she could still hear him, smell him, taste him.

Fear him.

Remember the first time he took you, Terry? Of course you do, a cold, whispery voice inside her head simpered. *Blake hadn't cut the grass like he was supposed to, so the old man got pissed. So he started chasing him with a tire iron. So you threw a plate at him to make him stop. And he jumped you, forced you over to the couch, pulled your pants down, said 'I'm gonna teach you a lesson you*

105

ain't gonna forget!' and, instead of a whippin' you like you thought he would, he shoved his filthy cock up your not-even-teenaged ass. How old were you by the way? Eleven? Twelve, maybe? Hard to tell, you've blocked so much of it out just so you can get through the day. So you don't fucking explode all over the goddamn scenery and take everyone out within three miles of you.

"But its hard," she said out loud. "So fuckin' hard."

Her eyes, that had glazed over from memory, cleared and focused on the .45 automatic placed next to the phone. *One a' the few things Daddy left me, other than bad memories,* Terry thought. *His piece from 'Nam. Momma always said the Army was what changed him, but I knowthat's bullshit. He was a piece of shit before he left, and became a bigger piece when he came back. That's the way with shits, they never reduce in size. Just get bigger.*

She picked up the gun gently, almost lovingly and began to trace it with her fingers. The perpetually stiff barrel, the thick, no-nonsense grip. The trigger that could spit out a single word of death to the person unlucky enough to be on the other end. "Daddy used to say that me an' Blake was lucky," she said out loud. "Lucky that the Army didn't issue him a revolver. Otherwise he'd use his kids for Russian Roulette when they fucked up. Used to tell myself he was jokin', but I could see in his eyes that he wasn't."

She slid her fingers around the grip, placed her hand on the trigger, aimed the gun in front of her. *If Nesto comes within a hundred feet a' me, I'll blow his greasy taco brains all over the ground. That's the difference between you n' me, Daddy. You was a coward who only killed when it was safe for ya. Like when you was in the Army, and no one really checked too hard to see if the gooks you shot really was armed or not. Or when the only people who could speak out against ya was two kids you could terrify inta shuttin' up.*

The face in her head changed, from the craggy, toothless countenance of her father to a much smoother, much weaker, much younger face. "Jewboy," she said. "I gotta name fer ya now, Jewboy. Sussman. Airy- fuckin'-el Sussman. And once I get that info from Rusty, yer gonna know who the fuck *I* am."

The half-sneer, half-snarl grew wider, became something less than human, as she tucked the gun into the waist band of her pants, and pushed her way through the dilapidated screen door, out of the shaded realm of her nightmares and into the light of her possibilities.

CHAPTER 20

Ari turned his car in the driveway of the place where he had hoped to get a respite from for at least a semester, killed the engine, and stared at the single-level, brick-laden nightmare before him. He sat quietly for awhile, saying nothing, not even thinking anything in particular, then sighed and got out of the car.

He just managed to open the front door when the barrage started. "Where the hell have you been?," his father bellowed as he leapt from his "throne", the large, brown leather easy chair situated in exactly the center of the room.

"Got held up at school," Ari offered. "Had to do a few things."

"Well, nice of you to be so casual," Mr. Sussman rejoined. "Considering the fact that if we get taken to the cleaners, you'd actually have to get a real job instead of going to school."

"Maury, please," Mrs. Sussman slurred from the couch she was half-seated, half-slumped on. Ari glanced at her with well-hidden contempt and wondered darkly if it was booze or pills she was using to escape reality this time. Or both.

Mr. Sussman ignored her. "But that's okay, y'know? You'll probably end up all right. I mean, it's just the old man's hard earned money that'll be going down the crapper, not yours. Just the friggin' nest egg I'm supposed to use for my retirement."

"Jesus, Dad. It can't be that bad."

"What the hell do you know? When have you ever had to work for anything in your life?"

Ari felt the anger spark up in him and was about to protest that

108

over the summer he had worked plenty, fuck you very much, when the doorbell rang. "Who the hell is that?" Mr. Sussman roared. Ari said nothing, just went to the door and opened it. Who he saw wasn't just a sight for sore eyes, but a balm for bleeding ones.

"Hey, Ari!," Rachel said, smiling from behind the screen door. "Saw your car pull in a few minutes ago, and thought I should hurry over."

Ari returned Rachel's smile with a weak one of his own. "As always, Rache, your timing's perfect," he said as he stepped aside to let her in Ari's father's face flushed as he saw who it was. "Rachel," he said. "You're going to have to excuse us. We're discussing a private, family matter."

"Ari told me, Mr. S. He called me from his dorm."

Mr. Sussman's face turned even redder. "You let somebody who's not family know our business?", he snapped at his son.

"Mr. Sussman, please. I've been Ari's friend since we were in grade school together. If he doesn't turn to his best friend during times like these, then who?"

"His family, of course! They're the only people who ever watch out for him!"

Rachel's eyes drifted over to Mrs. Sussman's half-slumped form, but then she turned her gaze back to his father. "Mr. Sussman," she said. "I'm not here to debate what's proper family procedure, but to help. Can I see what was sent you?"

"Why? What can you do to help?"

"I'm a second year law student, Mr. Sussman," Rachel continued patiently. "I know a bit of the way around a legal writ. Have you consulted with a lawyer yet?"

Mr. Sussman's face darkened. "Those goddamn crooks! They'll bleed you-"

Rachel held up her hand. "If you're not satisfied with my amateur opinion, I can take it to the law firm I worked for last year. As a favor to me, they might look over it for free."

His father's face changed expression for the first time since Ari came through the door, and it showed an emotion that looked so out of place as to seem obscene. It was hope.

Without another word, Mr. Sussman exited the living room and went in the kitchen, presumably to fetch the document. While he was gone, Mrs. Sussman took a chance on speaking. "You really think you can help us, Rachel?", she mewled as she attempted to raise herself into a sitting position.

Rachel gave her the barest of glances, and Ari knew from her body language that she was fighting down a contempt so strong it bordered on nausea. "I'm going to try, Mrs. Sussman," was all Rachel would say out loud.

Mr. Sussman returned from the kitchen and thrust the document out eagerly to their unexpected guest. Rachel took it from him and started to read, plopping herself down squarely (and with no small amount of amusement to Ari) in "the throne".

The house was silent as Rachel examined the papers intently. She turned a page, read some more, then spoke. "It doesn't give an amount for damages. Nothing specific, at least," she said.

"No," Mr. Sussman responded. "They probably need time to go through my financial records, see how much they can get."

"I think they already have a pretty good idea," Rachel said matter-of-factly, and Ari saw his father turn whiter. *Yeah, you cheap old bastard,* he thought. *You talk a good game about family, but when it comes to money, that's where you* really *go ballistic. Fucking walking stereotype.*

But Rachel was still speaking. "No, I think why they haven't specified an amount of damages is that there's something tentative here. It's like a legal fishing expedition, so to speak. The only information they're giving you is the list of injuries to the other party." She read further down. "Which really aren't that much. Other than some superficial cuts and bruises, the woman only broke her wrist."

Now it was Ari's turn to be stunned. "That was a *woman?*, he asked in open-mouthed shock.

Rachel stopped reading and gave him an amused glance. "I guess it was kinda questionable at the time?", she asked with a chuckle.

"Well. . .yeah! You shoulda seen . . .her, Rache! Built like a brick shithouse!" Behind him, Ari's mother gave a disapproving look, but Ari ignored it and continued. "And . . .well, from what little I could see of the face . . .She was wearing a pair of big, dark glasses. . .But the way that jaw of her's jutted out, I coulda sworn it was a man!"

"Could we get back to the matter at hand, please?," Mr. Sussman interjected, his face scowling in its usual mixture of anger, arrogance, and disgust.

Rachel shot him a glance and Mr. Sussman's mouth closed with a snap. Ari hid a smile. *If she ever patents that look,* he thought, *she'll be a fucking legal genius someday.* And what was that he saw behind his father's back? His mom seemed to be smiling, too. Much more openly and broadly, as a matter of fact.

Rachel went on. "No, the person who hit you is definitely female, even if the name is kind of gender neutral. There's a check in the 'F' box under 'Gender'."

"What's the name?", Ari asked.

"Terrencia Ann Scranton, but probably goes by 'Terry' unless I miss my guess." Rachel read further down, and snorted with a mixture of humor and disgust. "Ha! She has an address in West Virginia! More'n likely some goddamn hick!"

"Well, she has a lawyer," Mr. Sussman piped up grumpily.

"Clara Anne Darrow, Esq.", Rachel read. "Hmmmmmmm. Another thing I'll have to check. When I present a copy of this to the office, I can ask around, see if anyone knows this woman, Ms. Darrow, or knows of her. Might be some legal-aid lawyer looking to make an easy buck, just as big a hick as her client."

"Well, bottom line, Rachel," Mr. Sussman demanded. "Do you think they can touch me?" Rachel said nothing for a moment, just chewed her lip, then spoke in measured tones.

"Bottom line?," she said. "Something is very, very fishy here. When did you get this?"

"Late yesterday, at my office," Mr. Sussman responded. "Around this time."

"Just as you were about to leave?"

"Yeah."

"Close of business, Friday night," Rachel murmured. "Why? And why no amount on the damages, even if they know how much money . . . ?"

Then a gleam came into her eyes. "Mr. Sussman," she said. "Did a copy of the police report on the accident come with this?"

"No, but a copy from the cops came a few days ago."

"Can I see it, please?"

Mr. Sussman went back into the kitchen. "What are you thinking, Rache?" Ari said as his father left the room.

"Not sure yet. But I want to see the police report before I make any sort of guess."

Mr. Sussman returned and held out a small ream of papers to Rachel, which she took and started reading. Her eyes widened. "Wait a minute!" she exclaimed. "Wait . . .one . . .stinkin' . . .minute." Another silence as she flipped through the report. "What? What is it?" Mr. Sussman demanded.

Rachel ignored him and held the police report out to Ari. "Ari," she said. "Look at this and tell me what you see. Or, more precisely, what you *don't* see."

Mr. Sussman snatched it out of her hand before Ari could make the move to take it. Ari opened his mouth to say something when Rachel placed a restraining hand on his arm. She shook her head when he faced her and mouthed: *Not worth it.*

Mr. Sussman skimmed the document, oblivious. "Well, I don't see anything," he grumbled. "Ari's information, his license and address, and so on. The Scranton woman's information, her address-"

Mr. Sussman broke off suddenly, a furrow creasing his brow. "Damn idiot cops!" he said. Can't they do anything right? They forgot to fill out the Scranton woman's license information!"

"I don't think they did, Mr. Sussman," Rachel replied. "The cops fill out accident reports all the time, and they never *not* put down any information that they have available. Trust me, I know. I saw a lot of accident reports when I was working at the law firm, and every single one of them was complete."

Mr. Sussman gave her a puzzled look. "So what does this mean?" he asked.

"That they didn't put down the Scranton hick's license information because there wasn't any. *She doesn't have a driver's license!*"

All of the Sussmans stared at Rachel open-mouthed, an audience stunned by a master magician's latest miraculous trick. "Now, say you're a lawyer with a loser of case along with a loser of a client," Rachel continued. "What do you do? You start by hitting the person you intend to bring suit against with all you have, suddenly and without warning. Better yet, just before the weekend, before close of business. The person being sued doesn't know how to react, and worse, they're given the weekend, a time when most people are resting, to stew about it. But you don't want to leave them stewing too long, because if they have time to think, a time to actually get their forces together, you're finished, because you know the case your bringing is no stronger than a house of cards."

"So, what? They're trying to scare me?" Mr. Sussman demanded.

"Sort of," Rachel replied. "They're trying to keep you off-balance. And I'll bet anything this Darrow woman's gonna be giving you a call first thing Monday morning in order to keep you that way. That way, you'd do something you might not do normally. Like settle before any judge or jury in their right mind would laugh this case right out of the court room."

"Sonofabitch!" Mr. Sussman yelled, throwing the papers to the floor. "Goddamn lawyers! They're always trying to screw you over!"

Ari leaned over and picked up the police report. "So, what now, Rache?" he asked.

"There's a place that makes copies in the mall. You eaten yet?"

"No, not yet. And I'm starving."

"Me, too. Let's take a trip down there, make copies of everything for me to take on Monday, and get something to eat."

"Hey, wait a minute, dammit!" Mr. Sussman howled. "What the hell am I supposed to do?"

"Like I said," Rachel explained. "If my theory's right, you'll probably be getting a phone call from the Scranton woman's lawyer on Monday. Stall her, for now, until I get a real lawyer to look over everything and see if he agrees with me. If he does, you can tell her you'll be seeing her in court. I bet that's when she folds."

Mr. Sussman's face positively gleamed with that same sickening look of hope he'd displayed before. "Damn!" he said. "Glad you came over, Rachel! Good work!"

"Well, it was really Ari's idea," she began.

Mr. Sussman waved it away. "Well, whatever," he said, handing her the copy of the suit itself. "You need money for the copies?"

"No, I think I have this one. Coming, Ari?"

"Yeah," he responded. "I think I could use some fresh air."

If his father caught on to that subtle dig, he didn't show it. Mrs. Sussman called after them as the door closed. "You kids have a good time!"

Ari just barely held it in until he and Rachel got into his car. *"Fucking asshole!!"* he screamed.

Rachel grabbed his arm. "Ari, don't," she said soothingly.

"I can't help it, Rachel! I'm sick of it! Him and his goddamn mouth! He's goddamn lucky I don't put my goddamn fist in it!"

"And what would that solve, Ari?," Rachel replied. "It might make you feel better for a short time, but it wouldn't solve anything. Just make matters worse."

"How much worse can it get, Rache? Honestly! I'm sick of it, Rachel! Sick of it! I've been putting up with it for almost twenty years now and enough is enough."

Rachel said nothing just put a comforting hand on his. Ari fell silent. "Feel better?" she asked.

Ari replied with a weak smile. "Yeah. I guess. Sorry about that."

"Don't be. There's no need to apologize."

"Yes, there is. I-"

"You know, that's the first time I've ever really seen you mad?

114

I've known you for so long, and I've seen you once get really angry. Until today. Right now. Sure, I've seen you disappointed. Even upset. But never really, really mad."

"Yeah. It's been happening a lot lately. Don't know why."

"I know. It's because you're getting older, more mature."

"Yeah, right! My dad would say-"

"Ari, *fuck* your dad," Rachel replied, her green eyes flashing. "Your father is a self- centered prick whose worst fear is happening right before his eyes."

"Yeah. Someone's trying to take his money."

"No. His son is quickly becoming a man. And worse, a better man than he could ever hope to be. And that scares him more than anything else."

It was a moment before Ari could finally speak. "What . . .what do you mean?"

"You saw the way he deflected it when I tried to complement you on your foresight for bringing me over. You saw the way he snatched that paper away from me before you had a chance to get it."

"He'd probably say I was too 'shit simple' to figure it out on my own."

"He's afraid you will figure it all out on your own. And then you won't need him Anymore, once you finally discover for yourself that the world isn't the big pile of shit he's been telling you it is since Day One." She shook her head. "It's sad, really" she said. "By acting like such an asshole to you, he's only pushing you further away, till you know you don't want him or need him around anymore."

"It's more than sad," Ari responded. "It's pathetic."

"No, pathetic is, if you don't mind my saying so, your Mom. Is it just alcohol, or does she take drugs, too?"

"Xanax, I know for sure. What else is anyone's guess."

"Any way you can convince her to get help?"

Ari gave out a snort of disgust. "Are you kidding? Nothing's wrong! She's just tired! My God, Rachel, how could you possibly think something is wrong?"

Rachel sighed. "Great. You think it's because of your Dad?"

"Y'know, my grandmother told me a story once when we were in our senior year of high school," Ari said. "It was not long after my Mom went to the hospital again for one of her periodic 'rests' and wasn't home to hear it. Just as well, too. Anyway, when I was about three years old, my grandmother said that one night my mother showed up with me in tow at her apartment. My grandmother's, that is. My granddad split on her a long time ago. Well, my mom was crying and carrying on, saying how she had enough of my dad's bullying and putting her down, and how she wanted out of the marriage, and just how everything fell to shit."

Ari gripped the steering wheel, staring at it, staring into it like it was a window into his past. "My grandmother, dammit to hell," he continued. "She convinced her to go back. For *my* sake, if you can believe that. Hell, she said I was just as upset and agitated as my mom at the time. Still, she thought it best if families stayed together, if only for the sake of the kid."

"Well, unless I miss my guess, your grandma probably grew up during the Depression. That was a common way of thinking back then."

"Well, be that as it may, my mom went back. Whatever the hell happened next, I must've blocked it out of my mind. Guess it doesn't matter, really."

"I'm sorry."

Ari smiled ruefully at Rachel. "Not half as much as I am, Rache. You know what it's like to have to come home and look at this mess and think you're the one responsible, even indirectly?"

"Do you really believe that? That you're responsible?"

"Kinda. My grandma said, before she died last year, that that was one of her biggest regrets, telling my mom to go back to Dad. Because every time she saw her from then on, it just seemed like she died a little more each time she saw her."

The last word became a sob, and Rachel reached across the gearshift to embrace him. They sat that way for a time, then Ari hugged her tighter and said, "Thank you."

"No, thank *you*, Ari. Thank you for being able to share that with me."

"Misery loves company, y'know?"

"Oh, please. It's what I'm here for, okay?"

"Yeah. I guess. Why don't we get the hell out of here, huh?"

"Sure."

Ari started the car and pulled out of the driveway. After about a mile, Rachel placed her hand on his and squeezed, then put her head on his shoulder. Ari put his arm around her shoulders and hugged back, praying silently to himself that he'd never have to let go.

CHAPTER 21

Terry took a deep drag on one of the celebratory cigarettes she bought that afternoon on her way back from Rusty's. After an equally-deep exhale, she chased her nicotine buzz with a shot from the small bottle of Jack Daniel's she had splurged on simultaneously with the pack of cigs. Thus content, she peered through the exhaled smoke at the open manila file spread out on the table before her.

Christ, Rusty was right, she thought as she traced a column of numbers with a dirty finger nail. *Fuckin' family's got money practically fallin' out their ass! Two mil in profit from last year? Jesus!*

She flipped over a page. *Goddamn Potomac. No other addresses listed though. Maybe it's the only one they got?* She looked around her, anger rising. *Hunh. Still more'n what I got!*

She burst from the chair and started pacing hurriedly around the small room that was the trailer, making it rock back and forth with every step. She was fighting the urge to hurl the whisky bottle through the window when she caught a look at her pride-and-joy outside, filtered through the slats of the Venetian blinds.

Her motorcycle was now upright, leaning on a rack so she might work on it more easily. She had accomplished a lot since Rusty's call yesterday. The engine was finished, but now it had a set of tail-pipes barreling out the back like two small bazookas. The actual frame of the bike was all but done; all she needed was to find a set of handlebars that weren't bent, and a throttle that worked. And, of course, the wheel-wells for the tires.

"Lookin' good there, Terry," she said to herself out loud, her rage abated by this view of her handiwork "Good ol' gen-you-wine, Grade-A, all-American craftsmanship. Is there anything you can't do with a Harley?"

To the side of the rack, on the worktable itself, laid her next project: the megawatt stereo tape-deck system and speakers she intended on installing tomorrow. *Hell,* she thought with a smirk. *I shouldn't be so damn selfish. Oughta share my music with everyone, like them niggers and their goddamn ghetto blasters. Might as well add some better soundin' noise pollution a' my own!*

Content now, she pulled the blinds closed, after making a last peek to make sure she remembered to turn the decoy light in her house on. She had. "Want plenty a' warnin' just in case Nesto and his merry band a' fuck-ups come by some night," she muttered to herself. "Those boys're about as quiet as a crack-whore lookin' fer a midnight fix. But not much longer now. Nope, not at all." Sitting back down, she returned to the file and flipped another page. *Jewboy's school record. Looks like a good student,* she thought, drawing her finger down the columns of A's and B's. *Better'n I ever did. But then, all them heebs is supposed to be smart.*

At the top of his transcript was his home address and his local address, which Terry assumed was a dorm on campus. *No actual street number or anything, just the name of it. Might haveta do some huntin' and peckin' along the way to find it.*

She kicked back in the cheap wooden chair, feeling the back groan slightly in the process. She took another deep drag on the cigarette, her mind going back to that morning when she dropped by Rusty's office to pick up the info. "Well, there it is," Rusty had said as she handed Terry the manila envelope. "Facts, figures, so on and so forth. Amazing the shit people compile in one lifetime, huh?"

Yeah, Rus, Terry said to herself as she took the final drag on her cigarette and extinguished it in the overflowing ashtray on the table. *Fuckin' amazin'. Amazin' how it all goes into the hands a' people who don't deserve it. Or need it. But maybe we can fix that.*

Her gaze wandered over to the booby trap she had laid at the door to the trailer, a rope tied with one end on the knob and the other to the trigger of the party favor she had taken home from her dance with the Demon Heads. *Anyone who comes through the door while I'm catchin' my Zs, they'll get both barrels in the chest,* Terry thought as she leaned forward and gave the rope a little tug to check for slack.

She downed the last shot of whisky. *And after that, a second helping a' lead from the .45 next to the bed. It'll be like havin' my own roach motel; cocksuckers'll come in, but there ain't too many of 'em comin' out!*

She chuckled to herself as she disrobed and flopped down on the bed. For a moment, she just lay there, naked, her head spinning a bit as the whisky took effect. *Damn,* she thought. *Ain't really knocked 'em back like that in a long time. Must be gettin' old.*

She burrowed her head further into the pillow, trying to find a comfortable position to nod off in. *Wonder how that fuckin' Jewboy's sleeping tonight. Hell, wonder how comfortable the whole friggin' family is, them in their feather beds, with silk sheets, thinking their Jew thoughts about how to keep their money an' how to get more later on.*

She turned over on her back. *Well, they better learn to share, or there's gonna be one pissed-off biker bitch knockin' on their door. Or visitin' their dorm.*

And, with a whisky-fueled smile still on her lips, Terry drifted off to sleep.

CHAPTER 22

Rusty looked up at the clock mounted on her office wall. It was a plain, no-nonsense affair situated right next to the door; all the better to charge clients by the hour. The hands were positioned at 10 o'clock exactly.

It was a dreary, overcast Monday morning, and the nip in the air Rusty felt during her morning run reminded her that winter was creeping up fast. *It was Fall when I left home,* Rusty remembered, as she saw a few browning leaves blow by her office window. *All them damn years ago. How many? Twenty? Nah, more'n that, Rusty, my dear. Closer to twenty-five. Just a young, dumb Louisiana farm girl who thought she knew everything she needed to know about the world, and what it took to make it.*

Rusty absently fingered the big legal notepad on which she had written the main office number for Sussman Styles. *Well, don't be so hard on yourself, Rus. Ain't like you didn't have help out the door. Fucking old man drinking up everything he could get his hands on, and what he couldn't drink, he'd beat. Wife, kids, Bowzer, our dog. Didn't fucking matter. Very equal opportunity, my old man.*

The pencil in Rusty's hand snapped in two, and she swore a mild oath under her breath. She pulled one of her fancy office pens out of her ink stand and swept the broken pieces into the wastebasket. *Yeah, you got beaten, Rus,* she thought. *Sometimes so bad you couldn't sit or lay down, the bruises were so bad on you. But does that even begin to compare to what Terry went through over the years? Not by a long chalk!*

"No, not by a fucking long chalk," she repeated aloud as her vision fogged over. She wiped away the moisture there and focused her gaze upon the phone in front of her. "Get it together, Rus," she said to herself aloud. "You got work to do. For your client."

She took the receiver from its cradle and jabbed at the buttons with the pen. The phone on the other end rang once, twice, three times as she picked up the legal pad and lay it in her lap for note taking. She marked the time "10:02" right underneath the name "Maury Sussman" emblaz- zoned on the top of the page.

On the fourth ring, the phone was picked up. "Hello?" a young, female voice answered.

Rusty jotted down on the first line of the legal pad: **Young, female secretary. Affair?**

"Maury Sussman, please," she responded.

"Who may I say is calling?"

"Clara Darrow, Attorney-at-law."

"One moment, please."

Rusty watched the clock as she was kept on hold, counting. Then the line clicked open and she wrote "63 seconds" on the pad. "Yeah?" a nasal-sounding voice with a trace of New York accent said on the other end.

"Good morning, Mr. Sussman."

"Who the hell are you and what do you want?" the voice responded. **Abrupt, rude,** wrote Rusty.

"I wanted to see if you received my communication with your office this past Friday."

"Why, yes I did," simpered Mr. Sussman. "Pretty sneaky of you, lady."

Uh oh, thought Rusty. "I'm sorry?" she asked out loud.

"Side-swiping me with a lawsuit at the end of the day? What kind of idiot do you think I am? Did you really think I wouldn't know what you were trying to do? Ha! You'll have to do better than that to put one over on me!"

Idly, Rusty wrote **Busted** on her pad, but then wrote a question mark at the end as she said out loud, "Sir, I don't know what you're talking about. The information I needed to gather for the case took a few days, and the actual creation of all the necessary documents necessitated that the soonest the suit could be sent out was late Friday. I'd thought of waiting till after the weekend, but I ultimately judged I'd be doing my client no favors by delaying action."

"Oh yes, your client," Mr. Sussman responded in a voice that dripped sarcasm. "Miss Terry Scranton, isn't it? Did she happen to tell you during your initial consultation that she doesn't have a driver's license?"

That's it, she thought. *Game, set and match.* She was about to make a tactful exit, but Sussman was still talking. "Did you really think I wouldn't have somebody look over it?" he said. "Do you really think I made all my money, built this business from a half-assed tailor shop just to roll over and let some damn shyster like you and your white-trash client to take it all away?"

"Sir," Rusty answered, scribbling furiously. "I don't think it's necessary to resort to name calling." On the pad she had written: **Anti-lawyer remark? <u>Somebody</u> to look at it? No regular legal representation? Classist?** "My client," she continued out loud, "broke her wrist in the accident, causing her to be dismissed from her job. She has no health insurance. All I'm looking for is some compensation for her medical bills and to help pay for the repairs to her motorcycle so she can start looking for another job."

"Don't insult my intelligence, lady," snarled Sussman. "You just wanna get a big fat settlement. You wanna bleed me dry, so you file a suit that we both know is bullshit. You fucking lawyers are all alike!"

Rusty turned the question mark following **Anti-lawyer remark** into an exclamation point. "Sir, once again," she said, "I must point out that slanderous statements and profanity get us nowhere. I am here to negotiate as civilly and diplomatically as possible."

"Well, how's this for diplomacy, lady? You and your client ain't gettin' a plug nickel! And as for your client's medical bills, that's tough! Just because she's too stupid to hold down a decent job is no reason for me to give a shit!"

Rusty felt her temper flare. "Now, listen here, Mr. Sussman," she snapped. "Keep going and I'll slap a slander lawsuit on you as well. My client is a young woman who is just down on her luck. Perhaps if your son had been paying attention-"

"You leave my fucking family out of this!" Sussman bellowed. "I know my son is a shit simple fuckup sometimes, but you're not gonna use that reason to get anything out of me!"

Rusty blinked once, then twice. "Well, sir," she responded evenly when she managed to find her voice again. "I can see we're not going to be getting anywhere this way. Since you seem adamantly opposed to any sort of negotiation, I take it you would rather settle this problem in an open court?"

There was silence on the other end. For a brief, shining moment, Rusty thought she had managed to break the bastard, but then the voice boomed into the receiver. "Bring it on!" it said. "I'll see you and your client in hell before I pay out a red cent!"

"I see," Rusty responded. "We'll have it your way then, sir. I will see you and your son in court." She was about to hang up when the impulse to make one final dig sprang up in her. "Oh, by the way, Mr. Sussman? I wanted to let you know something. I've also got your son's college transcript in front of me, as well as his driving record. Until this accident, it was spotless. The world would benefit if we had more, how did you put it? Oh, yes. 'Shit-simple fuckups' like him. But that's off the record."

"Why, you fucking intrusive bitch!" Sussman snarled. "How dare you-"

And suddenly, back in the recesses of Rusty's mind, all the facts seemed to gel together into a cohesive whole that produced a minor epiphany, one born from years of experience in digging facts out of reluctant witnesses and savvy legal maneuvering instincts. The constant carping about money, the almost casual way he dismissed his son. The notable lack of assets and acquisitions in his financial record. *Probably a shot in the dark, but what the hell. It's not like I'm winning any points for my diplomacy*, Rusty thought. Out loud, she asked, "Does your son even know, Mr. Sussman?"

Another silence, then: "What the hell are you talking about?"

"I think you know exactly what I'm talking about. Does your son even know how much money you have?"

"None of your goddamn business!" screamed Sussman.

"He doesn't!" Rusty laughed. "Of all the tight waded-! Does your wife even know?"

"Fuck you!" came the reply, followed immediately by the sound of the phone on the other end being slammed down into its cradle.

"I take it that's a 'no'," Rusty said as she hung up her end.

She leaned back in her chair and went over the notes she had made. After a moment's consideration, she started writing:

Spoke with Mr. Maury Sussman of Potomac, Maryland (she wrote) **at approximately 10AM, Monday morning. Call lasted five to seven minutes. The upshot? Not amenable to a settlement and is actually willing to take it to court. Professional opinion? We don't have a prayer of beating him.**

Rusty chewed on her pen, thinking. She looked back at an earlier note, then started writing again. **However,** (she continued) **Mr. Sussman said something interesting in passing. During our conversation, he stated (quote) "Did you think I wouldn't have somebody look over it?" That, coupled with several anti-lawyer remarks he made during our ex-change, leads me to speculate that he has no official legal representation, for himself, or for his business. This short-sightedness on his part might be an area to exploit.**

"All that money and no legal coverage to protect it? Fucking amazing," Rusty said out loud to her empty office. "And how the hell could someone with all these damn shortcomings make all that money in the first place? Did he fuck somebody over? Take a few kickbacks? Hmmmmm."

Back on the pad, she started writing again: **Be that as it may, and my personal feelings aside, this lawsuit ultimately doesn't have a leg to stand on. Even though this guy is a perfect ass, and obviously ripe for the picking, I don't think it's going to be by us. Although it might be of cursory amusement to watch the man make a total ass of himself, we'd look like even bigger asses bringing this lawsuit to court in the first place. All any**

reasonable judge would have to do is see that Terry has no license, and the entire issue is dead in the water. "But I warned you about that possibility, baby girl," Rusty said out loud. "I told you chances were slim from the start. Now they're dead from anorexia."

Rusty sighed, threw the pen and paper on her desk, and rubbed her eyes. Another headache? Not yet, but she wondered how bad the one knew she was going to get when she called Terry on the phone was going to be. *That girl's as ornery as you were at that age*, she told herself. *Go figure, huh?*

She pulled herself up from the chair and stretched, feeling and savoring the pop of her joints and tendons as she flexed. She picked her cup up from her desk and made her way over to the coffee maker. As she poured herself a cup, her eyes wandered to the decanter of whisky that sat in a glass cabinet nearby. *Good for what ales ya,* Rusty thought as she considered the bottle. *Wonder if I can afford a little nip? Gettin' cold out there and all.*

Then another, darker thought clouded her mind. *No!,* the voice in her head practically screamed. *What if this is a day when you start before noon and don't stop until after sundown? Or when you pass out? What then?*

"Shut up," she said out loud. "I ain't lettin' myself get to that point again."

Suddenly, she gasped as she felt a familiar constriction in her chest. Her head started to spin and she reached out a hand to steady herself, dropping her cup in the process. *Oh, Jesus*, she thought. *Not again. It's been almost a year. Not again.*

In her mouth was the stale taste of cigarettes mixed with alcohol. On top of that, smothering everything, was the thick smell of sweat and fear. In her ears, unbidden, came the years-old echo of cheers and whoops, the collective hoarse voiced sound of men having a good old time, pining her down, pushing her to the floor, ripping at her clothes, jam-packed so close to her she had no room to scream-!

When the phone rang, she barely heard it at first. It came into the realm of her senses gradually, a shrill sound drilling itself through layers of mental gauze to her ears. With supreme effort, she stumbled to her desk to answer it. "He . . .Hello?"

"Rus? . . .Is that you?"

Terry, thought Rusty. "Ain't . . .ain't it a bit early for you, girl?

"Well, I wanted to call and find out if ya talked to the Sussman shithead yet."

"Yeah. I talked to him."

"Rus, are you all right? You sound like hell."

Rusty breathed deeply, then exhaled. Gradually, her chest loosened. "You caught me on the ass end of a panic attack, Terry," she answered.

"Jesus, Rus! You all right now?"

"Gettin' there. Gimme a minute."

"Christ. After all this time," Terry marveled. "It's rough, Rus, I know. Sometimes I still see the faces of them Nigger Bitches standin' over me. In my dreams."

"Yeah, but I'm a lot older'n you, girl. And like you said, it was a long time ago."

"You ain't that old, Rus."

"Feels like it. Anyway, like I was sayin', I talked to Sussman. Just a few minutes ago, as a matter of fact."

"And?"

Rusty gave out another sigh. "It's like I said, baby girl. Motherfucker didn't blink. Called my bluff. He wouldn't settle. Said he'd see us in court."

"Shit. What're we gonna do?"

"Do? There ain't nothin' we *can* do. Son of a bitch called it. Like I said, we try to take this to court, they'll laugh us the fuck outta there.

Silence from the other end. "Terry? You there?," Rusty asked sharply.

"Yeah. I'm here. Jus' thinkin'."

"What're you thinkin'?"

"'Bout what to do next."

"Terry, I told you-"

127

"I know, Rus! I know! But don't you think. . . ." Terry's voice trailed off into silence.

Rusty began to get a little impatient. "Terry-", she began.

"Look, can you still file the suit? I mean, just make it *look* like we mean to take it all the way. Play a little chicken with this guy."

"Terry, I told you-"

"Rus, we ain't gonna take it all the way! All I'm askin' you to do is to file this suit like it just looks like we're gonna go through with it. If he don't settle the day before our court date, you can still pull out, can't ya?"

Rusty considered it. "Yeah, I can, I guess. But I'm tellin' you, girl, I ain't gonna humiliate myself-"

"You won't, Rus. I swear. I jus' wanna yank this fucker's chain a little. See what happens then."

Rusty sighed into the phone. "Okay, kiddo," she said. "We'll play it your way. For now. Have to admit, I wouldn't mind givin' this son of a whore a few more conniptions."

"Oh, yeah? He was that much of an asshole?"

"Toppa the line. Secretive motherfucker, too. Probably got more dirt on him than half the fuckin' farmers in the whole state."

"Think you might be able to dig summa that shit up?"

"Dunno. Might be hard. Shitheels like that, Terry, they keep their tracks covered pretty well. Hell, I don't think this bastard even tells his family about his business."

"Yeah?"

"Seems that way. I mentioned his family and the bastard went ballistic on me."

Now there was another long silence on the end of the line. "Terry-?!", Rusty began.

"I'm here! I'm here. Jus' thinkin' again."

"Just *what* are you thinkin', Terry?"

"Nuthin', really."

"Terry-"

"Nuthin'! I swear!"

"You swear to God?"

"You know that ain't no way to get me to promise anything, Rusty. Me and the Old Bastard ain't exactly been on speaking terms lately. And I know you ain't been, neither."

"All right, then. Promise *me*."

Another silence. "All right," Terry said finally. "I promise."

"Good. I'll send you a copy of my notes from my little talk today with Sussman. Unless you wanna come down and get it."

"Nah. I'll let you mail this batch out to me this time. I'm in the thick a' gettin' my bike together. Finally seein' the light at the end a' the tunnel."

"And your arm?"

"Still healin' up. Hope it ain't much longer now."

"It won't be. Off before you know it."

"Hope so. Anything else?"

"Nope. I'll go ahead and file this, but remember-"

"Oh, I'll remember! Christ, Rus! Mebbe you are gettin' old. Startin' t'nag like an ol' gramma."

"Smart ass. Oughta kick yer ass for that remark."

"You an' what army, ya old bat!"

"Oughta pull my ass up from my wheelchair and come bust you one right upside your head."

Terry cackled. "Yeah, ya got more spunk in ya than an entire football team looking fer pussy onna Friday night. Catch ya later, Rus. Keep me up t'date."

"Will do."

"And Rus? Just remember. You really have less reason than me to be havin' these attacks. You made sure of it, remember?"

"You think I could forget?

"No sooner'n I could."

"Guess not. See ya."

"Bye."

Rusty slumped back in her chair, her eyes wondering back over to the shelf containing the bottle of whisky, and to the coffee cup lying directly beneath it on the floor. *Oh, what the fuck,* she thought.

Maybelle ain't gonna be in until another hour or so, so it ain't like there's anybody around to give me the ol' hairy eyeball about it.

She rose from the chair, suddenly feeling all her age in her joints as she limped to the coffee maker. *That's the great thing about booze,* she thought as she spiked her coffee with a liberal shot. *Sometimes it can drown out more demons than it lets loose.*

CHAPTER 23

Ari started awake from his light doze, the ringing of the phone in his ears. He peered at the clock on his bureau; "8:13 PM", it announced. *At least it isn't eight in the morning*, he thought as he noted the darkness outside his window.

He rose from the bed, stretching and setting aside the cause for his fatigue: an otherwise harmless-looking book entitled *Intermediate Accounting Procedures*. He grimly noted he'd only managed three problems before nodding off when he picked up the phone. "Hello?"

"Your father is an *idiot!!!*," exploded the voice at the other end.

Despite wincing from the sudden outburst of sound from the receiver, Ari found it within himself to chuckle and joke, "You're just realizing this now?"

"I'm not kidding, Ari!," Rachel continued. "I just got off the phone with him. Do you know what that fucking moron did?"

"Hit me."

"First, let me ask you: did you not hear me say to him to not talk to this lawyer, this Darrow woman, until I got a professional legal opinion?"

Ari felt something cold form in the pit of his stomach. "Yeah, sure I remember. What the hell happened?"

"I didn't get the full story; your father has this tendency to ramble-"

"I repeat: you're just finding this out now?"

Rachel snorted. "I guess I didn't appreciate the full volubility of his stupidity. Anyway, it sounded like this woman called him, and then he brilliantly proceeded to get into an argument with her, exactly the thing I advised him *not* to do. Well, at least I knew she'd call first thing on Monday, huh?"

"Yeah? And then what?"

"Sorry, just thinking. Anyway, your father apparently then proceeded to antagonize her to the point where she threatened to bring several slander lawsuits on his head, as well. You know, something she might actually be able to make a real case for! Then, she threatened to bring him to court, he called her on it, and that's where it left off."

"Oh, Jesus. So what now?"

Rachel sighed into the phone. "Well, fortunately, the lawyer I talked to, Dave Dujon, agreed with me all the way. Says the woman doesn't have a chance in hell of making this case stick. Oh, and guess what? He also ran the name, 'Terrencia Scranton', through the DMV database in West Virginia. Get this: the woman who ran into you doesn't just not have a license, it's been revoked!"

"No shit! Why?"

Rachel laughed. "Why not? The computer said it was pulled almost a year and a half ago for, among other things, 'Reckless Endangerment', 'Speeding', which, in this case, means tooling around seventy-five in a thirty-five mile per hour zone! And here's the capper: 'Resisting Arrest' and 'Trying to Elude a Police Officer! I mean, Christ! This woman's a friggin' disaster area!"

Ari let out a sigh of relief. "Did you happen to tell my dad all that when you talked?"

"Of course I did. Guess what he said?"

"Couldn't even guess."

"'The kid's lucky'".

Ari drew in a breath through clenched teeth. "I know, sweetie, I know," she continued "I, for one, wanted to reach through the phone and give him a good smack."

"Why stop there? Well, anyway, did you find out anything else?"

"Yeah. Dave knows this lawyer lady, this Clara Darrow. Well, he doesn't really know her, just knows of her. She's got quite a rep over there."

"Oh, yeah? As what?"

"For being a tough, smart cookie. And she's saved a lot of people's asses, too, apparently. Brought some class action suits against some big businesses, kept a lot of family farms from being foreclosed on. She started off as a union lawyer, then went into private practice. Does more pro-bono work than anybody in the whole state."

"You think she might be a problem?"

"Dave didn't think so. Good as she is, even she can't make a dead horse get up and run in the Kentucky Derby. Dave was wondering why she's even bothering; she too sharp not to know this case is a complete wash."

"So what's the bottom line here?"

"Oooooo. I just love it when you talk like an executive. It gets me all hot. Anyway, I called your dad about fifteen minutes ago to tell him what Dave said, and that's when I found out the brilliant move he pulled. Jesus fucking wept."

"So how'd you leave it with him?"

"Well, now I guess we just wait and see what the Darrow woman does. If she does go through with this suit after your dad basically pushed her into it, it's probably still just a bluff. Dave wanted me to keep him posted, though. Said he'd give you and your dad a break on the legal fees since you all know me."

"Shit. The only 'break' my dad would like is if he waived his fee completely."

"Well, much like Ms. Darrow, Ari, I can't work miracles."

"I know, hon. You did everything you could, and that was still pretty considerable. Don't think I don't appreciate it."

"You'd better, or I'll have to smack you around."

"Promises, promises."

"Besides, look on the bright side. Maybe this'll be the last time you hear anything about it. The Darrow woman'll probably advise her client to let the whole thing just go."

"Hope so. Well, thanks for calling me and keeping me up to date.

My father wouldn't call me if it was ever good news, just if it was something to bitch about."

"That man seriously needs a hobby."

"You kiddin'? That's it! See ya."

"Love ya."

"Love ya, too."

"Night."

Ari hung up the phone and rubbed the last remnants of sleep grit out of his eyes. *Lawsuits*, he thought. *Much like VD. The gifts that keep on giving.*

He picked up the accounting textbook and the paper he was using to figure out problems with and placed them at his study desk. *Hopefully, this'll make it easier for me to keep awake,* he thought.

He had just sat down and completed another problem when the knock came at his door.

Ari dropped his pencil in frustration and called out, "Come in!"

He was startled when he saw Graziano push open his door. "Hey, Sussman," he said.

"Uh, hi. What can I do for you, uh, Graziano?"

Graziano put his hands up, palms open. "I ain't here to cause trouble, man. Just came by to talk."

"Okay. Uh . . .what about?"

There was an awkward silence as Graziano studied the floor and shuffled his feet. To Ari, he looked like a young panther nervously testing out the confines of his new cage at the zoo. "Uh, Graziano said. "Shit. I'm not very good at apologies . . ."

The tension went out of the room like air out of an overinflated tire. Ari grinned up at his unexpected visitor. "You seem to be doing okay so far. Maybe I should start first. Prime the pump."

Graziano blinked at him. "What do you have to apologize for?"

"You kidding? After the way I blew up?"

Graziano waved the comment away. "You think that's never happened to me before? Shee-it! I was grateful you didn't try to haul off and cold-cock me one."

Now it was Ari's turned to blink in surprise. "No! . . .No . . .I wasn't gonna do that. I mean . . .God. What would be the point?"

"Hell, I would think half the fuckers on this floor would've jumped at the chance."

"Well, I ain't half the fuckers on this floor."

"No, apparently not. Well, anyway, like I was sayin': Sorry I got a little bit in your face about Springsteen. A Boss fan is a Boss fan, no matter what. I just hope you ain't one of these fair-weather fans that jumps ship if and when he puts out something a bit different from what he's done before."

"Like what?"

"You ever hear the *Nebraska* album?"

"No! Is it good?"

"I'll slide it under your door sometime. It's to be heard to be believed."

"Cool. Well, look. I could sit here and jaw about the Boss all night, but I gotta get these problems done."

Graziano glanced over at the book on the desk. "Accounting?! Jee-sus! Are you trying to set yourself up for a boring life?"

Ari laughed. "Hey, we all can't be edgy artistic types, my man. Somebody's gotta do the drudge work. That's why God invented business majors."

"I guess. You're a better man than me, Gunga Din. See ya further on up the road."

He was halfway out the door when Ari called out. "And thanks for wearing clothes this time, ya damn perv!"

Graziano called back. "Ahhhh, you should look half as good naked, ya pencil necked geek!"

"Actually, I wish I did," Ari murmured before picking up his pencil again and settling in for a night of mathematical stimulation.

CHAPTER 24

"You gotta be fuckin' kiddin' me!" Terry exclaimed. "This can't be it!"

But the file's address information confirmed it: this was the Sussman house. "Christ!" she murmured. "I seen fancier houses in West Virginia. An' this is supposed to be one a' the richest neighborhoods in the country."

So she wouldn't arouse suspicions, she accelerated past the house and pulled the truck over to the side of the road, camouflaging it behind a group of trees. Once hidden from prying eyes, she turned her attention back to the house.

It wasn't that the house was so incredible; far from it. It was that the home was so remarkably ordinary: a single-level brick and wood affair with no elaboration to it whatsoever. It was like the builders of it slapped it together out of some do-it-yourself kit. And when she compared it to some of the other architectural marvels she had seen on her way in, Terry found herself almost disappointed. *This motherfucker's got thirteen million dollars?*, Terry wondered to herself. *Where the fuck is he puttin' it? Up his ass?*

Terry turned her attention to the tools she had brought with her: a small pair of wire cutters and a set of screwdrivers. *Well, I'm glad of one thing*, she said to herself as she gathered her tools together and emerged from the cab of the truck. *With only one floor, it'll be easy. Won't have as much ground to cover.*

The sun was rapidly disappearing over the horizon as she scurried quickly into the back yard, stopping every few moments to see if anyone was watching as she made her way. No sudden bursts of light or sound; the Sussmans didn't appear to have any neighbors. She hugged the wall of the house as she made her way to the first window that looked out into the back yard.

Terry peered into the window and was rewarded with her first sight of the occupants. *Well, ain't this a sore sight for eyes,* she assessed as she took in the view. The window she had chosen looked into the living room, a chamber so plain as to be practically non-existent. In the center of it stood a large, brown recliner, and reclining in it was whom Terry assumed was the Jewboy's father: a fat, balding, dark-complexioned man losing the battle of middle age.

The man was fast asleep, his mouth gaping open like a retarded fish that's forgotten how to breathe underwater and snoring so loud that Terry could hear him through the window. Before him was a square box that could only be the TV, as it flickered a sickly-blue glow that washed the entire room.

Behind him, and slightly off to the side, was a rapidly aging white couch that dust was turning grey. Slumped on the couch was an equally-faded older woman dressed in a house coat that looked not so much worn as lived in. Unlike her husband, however, the woman had not yet nodded off, but the continuous bobbing of her head told Terry she was rapidly getting there.

Christ, she thought. *Looks like a night at my house when my parents were still livin'. After they both went on a bender. And if that bitch on the couch ain't doped up on somethin', I'll kiss somebody's ass.*

She watched the two for another moment, then continued along the wall. The second window she looked into was obviously some kind of home office: a computer, desk, various books on shelves, the works.

At the third window, she found what she was looking for: a bedroom. Or, more precisely, the Jewboy's bedroom. A double-bed was pushed up against the wall on the other side of the room from the window. A small desk was pushed over to the left, and Terry could see some photo frames positioned on it along the top. Above the desk, and more prominent than anything else in the room, was a large poster of Bruce Springsteen, one Terry knew was issued around the time of the *Born in the USA* album, the one with Bruce leaping in mid-air against an American flag background, his arm cocked to strum a power-chord on his well-worn guitar. *Ol' Brucie,* Terry thought. *Never was the same after he started doin' all that patriotic shit. Used to have some pretty good songs, too. Now every fuckin' shithead in every fuckin' white-bread suburb thinks he's talkin' to them. Includin'* this *one, looks like.*

Terry shrugged to herself as she unwrapped her tools. Examining the screen, she noticed it was fastened to the window by four small latches at each of the corners. Using the wire-cutters, she cut a small slit next to each of them, then used a screwdriver to pop the fasteners free. *Good,* she thought. *I leave the cuts small enough so somebody has to really look for 'em to see 'em. That way I can get in again whenever I want.*

She laid the screen aside and looked at the window. It was fastened with one large switch in the middle, and for this, Terry took out a longer screwdriver and inserted in the small gap between the window's two halves. One push, and the switch popped open. Then she inserted the screwdriver at the base, and wedged the window up until she was able to get a finger hold and push it all the way. After one last minute peek around her, she climbed in. *Welcome home, girl,* a voice inside her head spoke up as she stood up. *First time you've done any breaking and entering in a while. Ain't it fun?*

Terry went to the closet on her right, sliding open its door. She was greeted by a row of tasteful, if not overly expensive, clothing: some designer jeans, a few suit jackets, and a couple of dress shirts. Most of the closet looked like it had been cleared out. *Prob'ly took what he really wanted to school with him,* Terry mused as she closed the door.

Next she examined the desk. Nothing spectacular there, save for the photos positioned on top of it. The one that really caught her eye was one of the Jewboy (*and it's definitely my Jewboy, no doubt 'bout that,* Terry said to herself. *I never forget a nose*) and a very attractive young woman posing together. What struck Terry the most was the contrast between the two: she looked like everything he was not. Tall for a girl (and if the photo was to be believed, an inch or so taller than him) with rich, flowing, dark brown hair that framed two bright emerald-green eyes that peered directly, almost arrogantly, into the camera, and a complexion so flawless it looked like porcelain. *The girl's pretty hot*, Terry thought. *What's she doin' with a loser like that? They look like the princess and her pet frog!*

Terry replaced the photo on the desk and went to the bedroom door, placing her ear against it. Nothing, save the sound of snoring. Two people, it sounded like. One deeper and throatier, the other high-pitched and nasal. Both down for the count.

Slowly and carefully, she opened the door, and for the first time, a wave of nausea overtook her. *No,* she thought. *You noticed the smell before, in the kid's room, but it wasn't as strong. Garlic! I hate fuckin' garlic! And something else . . .*

Terry couldn't quite place her finger on it, but beneath the smell of strong garlic (which she knew all Jews cooked with, to excess) was something older, and far worse. A smell she knew from childhood, but found hard to recognize, or even put into words. *When my parents was alive, the house smelled like this, too,* she thought. *And after Mama died, it was even worse. Rusty once told me that houses sometimes take on the personality of the people livin' in 'em. Now I think I believe her.*

It wasn't the pungent scent of a seasoning that bothered her, it was the smell of death, of hopelessness and decay. The corrupt, musty odor of those who see no good in life and secretly (and sometimes, not so secretly) want their lives to end. *Well, maybe I can give 'em a hand,* she thought as she made her way through the hall.

The two snoring hulks were slumped in their respective places while the TV droned on unheeded. Terry went to the woman on the couch first, the high-pitched drilling sound of her snores burrowing itself into Terry's head. Terry pulled out her razor and flicked it open slowly, lest the slightest noise awaken her intended victims. She carefully regarded the woman's fat, waddled throat, seeing the pulse beat underneath her doughy skin. *It'd be so easy, wouldn't it?*

she thought. In her mind's eye, she could see herself slicing through the woman's milky neck, down to the arteries that pulsed life for her, could almost taste the blood as it sprayed outward in her own face, dripping down on the bare, hard wood floors.

Then Terry's eyes flickered over to the man in the chair, his bald spot peaking out over the back. She imagined taking her cast and hitting the old man with all her might in that bald spot, caving in his skull and making his brains flow out through his ears. *Prob'ly be the best thing for these assholes,* she thought. *Goddamn overstuffed, fat-assed suburban shits. Put 'em outta their misery. Put 'em outta my misery. And it'd be so easy. So fuckin' easy . .*

Terry shook her head violently to clear it. *Get it together, girl,* she chided herself. *This is just a scouting trip. Too soon to kill anyone. Just wanna see how these fuckers live. Just in case.*

She took in deep breaths to settle herself *Time to beat it, though,* she thought. *Also just in case. Temptation's a bitch.*

Pocketing her razor again, she slipped out of the room, but not before shutting off the TV. *Give 'em somethin' to think about,* she thought with a chuckle.

She was latching up the window screen and was almost home free when the lights came on. Terry froze, her heart in her throat. When nothing else happen after a moment, she carefully peered behind her, and saw that the lights came out of the woodsy area behind the Sussman house. *So, they do have neighbors,* she thought. *Might wanna check them out, too. If only to see how far away they are and how quiet I gotta be over here.*

Terry fastened the last latch on the screen, gathered up the tools, and started making her way through the woods. As she felt her way amongst the trees and heard the crackle of dead leaves underneath her feet, she was reminded of the many times she and her brother had to hide out in the woods around her house to escape one of her father's many drunken outbursts. The open wound of Blake's betrayal seeped fresh in her mind. *All the times I spent haulin' that little shit's bacon outta the fry, and that sonovawhore's got the balls to bail on me when I need help bad. Shoulda let the old man beat him to death and kept my own hide from gettin' busted. He'll be damn lucky I don't go over there and beat him to-*

The rage in her heart and mind was suddenly cut off as she got her first glimpse of the neighbor's house. "Now, *this* is A House in Potomac!" she marveled out loud. Once again, she found herself in a back yard; however, the differences between the two were the differences between a Harley Davidson and a Jap scooter. *And I think I done found the Harley!* Terry thought.

Like the Sussman house, it was made of solid brick. Unlike it, not one but three stories commanded her view, with the same number of chimneys reaching for the sky out of the finely shingled roof. Several windows peered out at her, some in the exotic shapes that Terry automatically associated with high-class. A balcony jutted out of the top floor, with a set of glass double-doors opening out into them. *Looks like somethin' I seen in movies*, Terry said to herself. *When the high muckety-mucks come out an' speaks to the peasants.*

Terry turned her attention back to the ground floor, where all the lights emanated from. The porch lights were on, but Terry didn't think anyone was watching her creep through the yard. At least, not yet. To the left was a sliding glass door that opened up onto a patio with several pieces of pricey-looking lawn furniture. Terry half-crawled, half-walked her way over to the large picnic table that dominated the patio and squatted behind the sun-umbrella.

Peering through the glass door, she was mildly surprised to see a familiar figure seated in the well-furnished living room. *Well, whaddya know?* she thought. *It's the girl in the picture!*

Said girl was seated in an over-stuffed white couch in the center of the room. By the light of a powerful floor lamp, she read from one of the largest books Terry had ever seen outside of Rusty's office. Though the girl looked tired, there was none of the sense of doom and defeat that was so prominent in the other house.

A man walked into the room, tall and distinguished looking. He was dressed in a bathrobe, but still somehow managed to seem "high class". His ruddy, tan skin was more sun- based than racial, and his quick, blue eyes promised merriment rather than defeat. All this, and a thick crop of iron-grey hair made the man seem to pulsate with vigor and vitality. *Definitely the girl's daddy,* Terry thought. *You can see it without even lookin' 'em in the face.*

The man said something that made the young woman look up from her book. The girl replied back and the man nodded, patting her shoulder as he left. *Awwwww. Ain't that cute?* Terry thought. *Daddy's little girl. And the Jewboy fallin' in love with the girl next-door. It's enough to make ya wanna heave yer guts.*

Suddenly, the girl on the couch seemed to freeze in place. She looked up from her book and stared out through the glass door, seemingly in Terry's direction. Terry knew it was impossible to see out in the dark when the room you were in had more light to it, yet there was something about this girl's gaze that unsettled her. And when she saw the girl put down the book to the place beside her and stand up, she knew it was time to get out before the getting got too good.

Terry had just dashed into the woods when she heard the sliding glass door open behind her. She hid behind a tree and dared to look back.

She could see the girl's outline in the door by the light of the living room. She stood there silently, listening. Then, after about a minute, Terry saw her reach over and shut the door, followed by a dimming of the light as she drew the curtain closed.

Terry let out a large breath she wasn't aware of holding and sat on the ground. *Well, that's that,* she thought. *Nuthin' more I can do here tonight. So, Jewboy's girlfriend lives right next door to him. This is lookin' better all the time.*

She smiled to herself. *An' I think I know how to make use of that. But for now, I better skedaddle.*

The walk back to the truck was uneventful. As she climbed in the cab, she said out loud:

"Well, ole girl, looks like it's the end a' the line fer ya. It's been fun, but I've had ya fer a coupla weeks now, and some nosy fuck might start askin' a few questions. Nuthin' personal, y'know. Not like with yer old owner."

Terry lit herself a cig off the dashboard's lighter. She noted vaguely she was down to her last one. "But my Hellion's almost finished. Couple more days'n I'll be back onna road with it."

She looked over at the Sussman house again. "Then nuthin' ain't gonna be gettin' in my way. Though, I hope it *does!*"

She started the truck and pulled out in the road, leaving no trace of herself in the still of the night behind.

CHAPTER 25

Jones's hand shook as he poured the whisky shot into his coffee mug. Not much, but enough to worry him that the booze might spill over and make his office smell like a distillery.

Fucking hell to pay then, he thought wearily. *Good ol' asshole Chief of Detectives Brosnan, and his pet corn-holer Reed, whose own asses never met a barstool they didn't like, would just love to turn it into an excuse to get me to take mandatory retirement, with no pension to boot, the jolly prick.*

He set the bottle on top of the piles of paper and files he nicknamed "The Hobby". *Every man needs one, I guess,* he told himself. *Other guys build model boats, some people collect stamps. I, on the other hand, collect files of information on how you can make a human monster. Some assembly required.*

Jones quaffed down the spiked coffee, thought about it, then poured in another shot. "Yeah," he said out loud to his empty office. "But before Brosnan throws you out on your ass, make sure he reads a bit of this here file. He'd spend the rest of the day picking up the guts he puked up on his nice, clean, imported from Timbuck-fucking-tu carpet. And then it would be worth it."

He rubbed his red, rheumy eyes and opened the top file, the one marked "Darrow, Clara". He flipped to a page he had tabbed, a run-off of a newspaper article from three years ago. Rusty Darrow's visage headlined the article, the photo showing her in mid-speech, gesturing and speaking to an unseen audience. The headline directly beneath the photo proclaimed: **Attorney Darrow Wins Landmark Decision in WVA.**

And, in smaller type beneath that: *Coal Miners' Dispute in Union's Favor Nice looking enough woman,* Jones thought. *Looks a bit like that singer, Bonnie Raitt, but with an edge. Guess she'd have to have one to take on the big business boys.*

Jones flipped a page over the next newspaper article he had tabbed, one dated three months after the coal miners's case was settled. This article was entitled: **Local Heroine Attorney to Defend Alleged Juvenile Killer.**

Jones got out his mini-tape recorder out of the top drawer of his desk, put in the small tape with the word "Hobby" scrawled on it in pencil, pressed the "Record" button, and started speaking. His words, slurred at first, grew more clear and precise the deeper he got into his narrative. "Question," he said. "You're a lawyer looking to do some pro-bono work. What makes you take up the case of a girl accused of murdering someone in reform school? I mean, other than the obvious, of course."

He flipped through all the news clippings on Rusty he had compiled; some were as local as the *Charles Town Gazette*, and as prominent as the *Washington Post*. "The obvious, of course, being that Ms. Darrow has a long professional history of defending progressive and equal rights causes. The defense of a Planned Parenthood branch opening in her area. An equal pay amendment she tried to get passed by the West Virginia legislature. A few cases where she represented abused wives accused of murdering their husbands. In light of this, it would seem that defending a young girl who not only acting in what even I would call a justified manner, even if she didn't do it, and seems to be being railroaded by the system, would be right down Rusty's alley."

Jones stopped the tape and shook his head to disperse the liquid fog around his brain. *Starting to ramble a little bit there,* he thought. *Take a deep breath. Pull back. Start up again when you're ready.*

After a few deep breaths, he pressed the button again and continued: "Ms. Darrow seems to be a good, old-fashioned, champion of the underdog type, and it's hard to fault her for it. But she also seems to work extra hard when it has anything to do with the sisters. But still, the question remains: why *this* girl out of the dozens, maybe hundreds, she could have picked? And why does she continue to look out for this girl over the years, when professionally, she should have cut her loose as soon as she got her off and released from the reformatory? Rusty Darrow has continuously gotten Terry out of scrape after scrape over the years. And brother, have there been plenty!"

Jones picked up the file marked "Scranton, Terrencia" and opened it. It had grown considerably thicker over the past few days. Jones continued his narrative. "Does she identify with this girl?," he said. "Probably. Both come from rural backgrounds, and had abusive drunks for fathers. Both have gravitated to bikers and the biker lifestyle. But that's where the similarities end. Rusty picked herself up by her bootstraps and made herself a high-profile lawyer. Terry can't even keep a job as a drug courier. Where does it all fit?"

Jones placed the tape recorder on "Pause" while he stretched out his cramping muscles. *Bitch gettin' old,* he thought as he poured himself more liquor. *Better when you have lubrication.* After another swallow, he continued. "I know how this makes me sound, but what if there's a sexual connection between the two? Possible, but how likely? Clara Darrow hasn't ever had a serious relationship with a man in her adult life. But then, given her background, I can't say I would, either. Terry Scranton seems to be asexual, but, once again, she had help in making that decision, and not just by her father. Besides, how does that old joke go? What do two lesbians do on their second date? Move in. Rusty's address is a nice little house in rather well-off suburb, while Terry still lives at her family's old home. No, the two definitely aren't shacking up, and I don't see Rusty as being the type who enjoys the rough trade. She had enough of that shit years ago."

Jones dug into the hobby stack and pulled out a third file, much thinner than the other two. It was marked "Sussman, Ariel." The file's contents consisted of only a blow-up of his driver's license and a file of the accident report. "And where does the kid fit in, this Ariel Sussman?" he dictated. "Are Rusty and Terry trying to shake him down, or something worse? A message arrived for me this afternoon from the court house, telling me that the terrible twosome are going ahead with this joke of a lawsuit against the kid. I hate to think of him getting run over by the Rusty and Terry Express if they don't get what they want."

They actually had a chance with the judge, Jones thought as he clicked on the "Pause" button. *He was dirtier than a whorehouse floor on a Friday night. But this kid's as clean as a whistle.*

He pondered a moment more, then continued his narrative: "All right, here's the sixty- four-dollar question. Do I let the young Mr. Sussman know what potential danger he might be in? Officially, I'm not on the case. Hell, officially, there is no case. Just the lunatic investigations and ramblings of a run-down, burnt-out, alcoholic of a detective with too much fucking time on his hands."

Jones shut the recorder off and flung it on his desk, burying his face in his hands. *Maybe Brosnan has a point*, he thought. *Maybe it's time to pack it all in, get my money together, buy myself a house somewhere tropical, and find myself dying in pleasant surroundings.*

When he opened his eyes, the driver's license for the Sussman kid was staring him in the face. *Barely out of his teens*, he thought. *Just about my son's age. Or ex-son, I should say. To go along with the ex-wife.*

He stared at the photo a moment longer, then felt the muscles of his jaw tighten as he made a decision. Picking up the phone, he dialed the police operator's private line. "Hi, this is Detective Bernard Jones from the Vice Squad. I want to place a flag on a certain name."

Silence as Jones listened. "Ariel Sussman," he finally said. "First name spelled A-R-I-E-L. Last name, S-U-S-S-M-A-N. Yes, a flag of notification. If this name goes anywhere through our system in any context, I want to know about it. If he files a complaint, if he's picked up in relation to anything, or even if he's stopped for speeding, I want to know. Even if he asks a cop for the time, *I want to know! . . .*Yes, thank you."

He put the phone back in its cradle and felt some weight lift itself from his chest. Some, but not all. *Did I just do the right thing? Is my "happy medium" gonna be enough?* he thought. *God, if you're listening up there, make sure my "medium" don't turn into a big-ass mistake!*

Looking outside his office window, Jones saw that the sun had disappeared behind the horizon. He shivered to feel the coming fall.

PART THREE
GET SET!

An ambulance finally came, and took him to Riverside
I watched as they drove him away
And I thought of a girlfriend or a young wife
And a state trooper knocking in the middle of the night
To say your baby died in a wreck on the highway . . .

-Bruce Springsteen

CHAPTER 26

Crack!

Terry examined the plaster, noting with satisfaction the lines criss-crossing through it. But it still held firm around her arm. *Over three fuckin' weeks*, she thought. *Enough's enough. Time for this bitch to come off.*

With her right arm, she drew back with the small, hand-held sledgehammer and swung it over her head. She brought it squarely down upon her arm propped up on the worktable.

CAARR-RACK!!!!

Now the hammer had done its job, reducing the cement to a hardened pulp. Terry could feel her arm underneath wriggle freely beneath the shards. "Yeah!!!" she exclaimed, chipping away at the more stubborn spots that held on. More and more of the cast fell away until her arm emerged, sweaty, pale and notably smaller than the other, but healed. And free.

"Free!" she exclaimed. The doc had told her to keep the cast on for a full month, but after three weeks and as many days, Terry decided it was time to take matters in her own hand, and make her own hand a matter again.

She clenched and unclenched her left hand, enjoying its newfound mobility. Sure it was definitely weaker than her right arm, but after a few days of working the weights again, she knew it would be as good as new. *Time to start kickin' some serious ass,* she told herself. *And I know just where to start.*

She went over to the garage, where the completed bike now stood, propped up and ready to roll. The Bike. Her Bike. That Frankenstein of scrap metal she had forged with her own hands, and now it beckoned to her, ready to be revived. *The Devil's Hellion Child,* she thought, remembering a snatch of one of her favorite WASP songs. *But we ain't playin' that one when we ride. No sir. I got a new one by Blackie and the boys that'll fit like a glove.*

She snatched a tape from the worktable's boom box and went to her bike. A tingle of electricity went up her spine as she mounted it, refamiliarizing herself with the feel of its metallic bulk between her legs. She virtually shook with anticipation as she popped the tape into the bike's deck and wheeled the whole kit and caboodle into the open air, stopping when she got halfway into the driveway. *Well, here goes everythin',* she thought as she placed the key into the ignition.

The machine sputtered at first, then roared. . .no, *howled* into life. "Shit-FIIIIRE!!!!,"

Terry screamed along with it. She could feel its mighty throb up and down her legs as she turned the throttle, and the shark's grin that erupted on her face threatened to expose every tooth in her head.

Gently, lovingly, she placed on foot in the stirrup and kicked the kick stand away with the other. Revving the engine once again, she was off. Slowly at first, ten miles per hour, then twenty, then she was out of the driveway and on the dirt road that lead to it. At thirty miles per hour, she punched the *Play* button on the tape deck At forty, the sound of power chords echoed off the trees as the song began, the dirt beneath the wheels kicking up like small blazes in Terry's wake.

She made a right onto the main road, paved all the way and ready for domination. The bike went up to sixty and the drums kicked in, the perfect accompaniment to the body engine's roar. Terry leaned on the throttle harder, going faster, ever faster. The tail pipes exploded into life, rocketing her up to seventy, then eighty. Terry beamed as the wind whipped past her face, blowing her hair like the tail of a comet behind her. Her face became distorted, skull-like as she took on more and more speed.

And when Blackie Lawless's sandpaper-and-vinegar vocals blasted from her speakers, she knew she was once again rejuvenated. Revived.

Reborn.

> *A tattooed madman, I'm hell on wheels*
> *Born the wicked child, left alone in the fields*
> *My father was the wind, my mother was fire*
> *Raised by the wolves and I grew up wild*
> *A Kamikaze man, I'm hollerin' Banzai!*
> *Never crash and burn, never gonna die*
> *Cannibal is me, ya squeal and shout*
> *I'll chew ya up, and spit ya out!*

> *Storm's a c-c-coming and it's gonna be me*
> *Here comes Trouble, with a capital T!*

Then the chorus, one she knew now by heart and could scream along with:

> *Cuz I'm a mean, motherfuckin' man*
> *I gotta scream, that's what I am*
> *All the way, all, all the way*
> *Cuz I'm a mean, motherfuckin' man*
> *Ridin' the wind, and I know I'll be damned*
> *All the way, all, all the way.*

All the way. She slowed a bit as she got behind an old farmer in a pickup truck, but passed him in a split-second. The old man's mouth dropped open, so far that his bottom teeth dropped out, and he had to stop to dig around on the pickup's floor for his falsies.

Terry, without a glance backward, stormed on, pushing the bike to 110, then 120. Blackie growled back with the second verse in agreement:

> *Chewbacca in the rye, the water of fire*
> *A terror in the flesh, a killer for hire*
> *California man, a white line homer*

153

The unruly one they call the Blond Bomber
Scooter gypsy, I'm a renegade
An orphan of the road, a live hand grenade
Never gonna quit, before my time
When the moon gets high, then I'll be blind!
Mad Dog Twenty-Twenty's king
I drink that stuff, and start gettin' obscene!

And this time when the chorus hit, Terry took her hands off the handlebars, feeling the full force of the machine as it whipped through the air, enveloping her body like the lover she never knew (and never would). She was the sound and fury that signified everything. The power of the road, the Devil's Hellion Child, Ms. B-A-D, the Wild Child, the mean, motherfuckin' one that no one could stop or fuck with. The Rebel in the F.D.G.-Tormentor-Thunder Head who could crush them all, and ride the wind, forever free, all the way. All, all the way.

All the way.

CHAPTER 27

Ari couldn't believe it. He held the letter in his hand, read its contents in black and white, but still could not comprehend how it came to be.

The letter read:

Dear Mr. Ariel Sussman:

This letter is your official notice of a lawsuit filed by Ms. Terrencia Scranton of Charles Town, West Virginia on the date of September 21, 1991, and summoning you to appear at the Maryland Circuit Court in Rockville in no more than four weeks after its date of notary. Failure to comply with these strictures will subject you to the harshest penalties, on top of finding for the plaintiff and awarding them their projected annuities of two million dollars ($2,000,000) to offset medical expenses, wages lost, etc. Plaintiff is represented by Ms. Clara Darrow, and it is highly recommended that you employ legal representation to act in your behalf, as well.

Sincerely, David Jameson,
Montgomery County District Court,
State of Maryland.

Ari shook his head in disbelief as he tossed the letter on his study nook. *Jesus H. Baldheaded Christ!* he thought. *This shit keeps getting worse and worse! Two million?! Do we even have two million to give?*

Glancing at the letter again, he noted the "CC" at the top of the page, followed by his home address. *Even better, my old man gets a copy, too,* he thought. *Wonder what his reaction's gonna be?*

The phone rang. "Right on cue," Ari said aloud as he crossed the room and picked up the phone. "Hello?"

"Well, I hope you're happy, kid."

"Dad? What do you mean, 'happy'?"

"Haven't you checked your mail?"

"Of course I've checked it. I don't know why you'd think I'd be happy about it."

"Well? Did you get it, or what!?"

"Yeah! I got it! In today's mail."

"Then you know how damn screwed up everything is! I knew I shouldn't've listened to one of my idiot son's friends! Especially to a shiksa!"

Ari felt something suddenly give inside him. "Goddammit, Dad! Fuckin' bust on me all you want! Maybe I even deserve it, but don't you dare get on Rachel's case. She was just trying to help."

Mr. Sussman snorted. "Figures you'd side with somebody against your family. Your own blood, you ungrateful little shit!"

"It's my own family that always fucks me up, you stupid old bastard!",he roared into the phone. He vaguely heard his father start to say something, but ran over him. "No! No!! NO!!!" he continued. "For once in your miserable fuckin' life, you're gonna fuckin' listen to *me!* I have put up with your non-stop bullshit for my whole fuckin' life, and I'm sick of it! As I recall, Rachel told you to not say anything to that lawyer until she got a back up opinion from her old boss! But nooooooooo! You decide to go off half-cocked in that woman's face until she slaps both of us- that's right, not you, but both of us!-with a lawsuit! Well, what a big fuckin' surprise! You're a good one for assigning blame, you stupid old man. Why don't you take some for a change?! You're the one that got us into this suit, not me! I might've had the accident, but you're responsible for what happened afterwards. Because you don't know when to *shut the fuck up!!!!!"*

There was a second of silence on the line, then Ari heard his dad say, "Are you through?"

"I've barely scratched the surface."

"You got some real balls, kid. I'll give you that. There you are, all your college shit paid for, livin' on my dime, and you got balls enough to turn on your old man like that."

"You want someone who doesn't argue when you mistreat 'em? Buy a fuckin' dog."

"How'd you like me to pull everything out from under you, wise-ass? That'll teach you what it takes to earn a living, like me."

"Well, in case you haven't noticed, that's what I was doing all this past summer."

"You call working in that warehouse a job? Please!"

"Just cuz it's outside your limited experience doesn't mean it doesn't exist."

"'Limited'? I got thirty years on you, you little shit! I was-"

"Yeah, I know. Working at grandpa's sweatshop for ten hours a day, blah, blah, blah. I can recite this shit chapter and verse. But maybe if you actually watched what other people are saying and doing, you'd fucking notice."

"How dare you? How dare you say I don't listen to you?"

"Truth hurts."

"Look, goddamn it! I'm your *father-"*

"Then start acting like one, instead of acting like my worst enemy. Then maybe we'd be fine."

"I don't treat you-"

"Dad, I'm sorry. I'm tired of this conversation. It's just going in circles."

"Now you listen to me-"

"That's the problem. I've been listening to you too much. Goodbye."

Ari heard one final explosion of sound before he replaced the phone in its cradle. Apparently, his father was determined to get in the last word. *Well, fuck you,* he thought. *I've reached my saturation level for bullshit tonight.* He slumped down on the bed and rubbed his head. He considered calling Rachel, but ultimately decided against it, at least for the time being. *Maybe what I need,* he thought, *is just some damn time for myself. Some time where I can be unreachable.*

He leaned over and pulled the phone jack out of the wall and threw the wire to the floor. *Now nothing can get in or out,* he thought as he lay back in bed. *Just a couple of hours. A few hours to chill out. That's all I. . . .*

When he woke, he was surprised to see that the numbers on his digital alarm clock read "3:13 a.m." *Jesus,* he thought as rose to take his clothes off. *Later than you think, ain't it?* He briefly contemplated doing some homework, but decided to the day was already shot. *Tomorrow is another day, Miss Scarlett,* he thought as he climbed back into bed.

But outside his window, it was already too late.

CHAPTER 28

Terry cruised past the University of Maryland campus, slowly and almost silently, thanks to the muffler she had installed. She stopped at a light at the intersection of University Boulevard and Campus Drive, and noted with mild chagrin that the entrance to her right was guarded; the man on duty appeared to be checking the I.D.'s of everyone who entered. While continuing to wait, she took stock of the tree coverage. *Not much, but some,* she thought to herself. *Worst comes to worst, I can hide the machine and make it on foot.*

The light turned green and Terry drove on. She hit the turn-off toward Route 1 and made a right, finding herself in the heart of College Park. The area had plenty of eateries and chain stores for the college crowd. Soon, she came to another gated, guarded entrance, apparently the main one. She passed it and continued on.

A little further down the road, she hit her jackpot; she spotted an unguarded cement path near a row of shops and the intersection of Knox Road. She made a left near the Little Tavern Hamburger Stand and found a large, metered parking lot. Parking the bike, she took a quick look around her to get her bearings. *That path was near something called "Planet X", whatever the hell that is, she thought. Jewboy's dorm is closer to that University Boulevard entrance, but I'll take what I can get at this point. Figgered I had to do some walkin', anyway.*

She dug into her pocket for change, and came out with a buck-and-a-half's worth. She fed the meter to the two-hour limit, then checked her watch. "12:56", it proclaimed. *Means I gotta be outta here by three a.m.,* she thought. *Don't want some cocksucker to give me a ticket'n have a record I was here.*

After chaining the bike, she pulled a large tote bag from the back seat that clanked as she lay it on the ground. She adjusted the sweat pants and shirt she had bought that morning, both of them emblazoned with the University of Maryland logo: a large turtle looking angrily over its shoulder. *With this n' the bag,* she thought, *I'll fit right in with all these college pukes.* As a final touch, she pulled the shirt's hood over her head, further obscuring her identity.

She hurried quickly across Route 1 even though the streets were almost deserted. While making the cross, she familiarized herself with some of the landmarks. *Ratsie's?* she thought as she spotted the name of a local pizza joint. *Who'n the hell would eat in a place called* Ratsie's?

As she approached the shop called "Planet X", she took in all its psychedelic trappings. *Nah, if it was a real bar, it'd be open. Looks more like some kinda coffee shop. Though I get afeelin' you'd get more'n a caffeine buzz offa here.*

The cement pathway to the right of the coffee shop beckoned, stretching out into the cold darkness of the night. Terry adjusted the strings of her hood tightly as the wind picked up around her. The bag slung over her shoulder clanked again with the movement.

The walk through the campus was largely uneventful, though Terry had to stop several times along the way to consult the information maps. What few fellow pedestrians she met along the way didn't even give her a second glance. *Perfect,* she thought. *The disguise is workin'. Maybe this'll be easier'n I thought.*

She had just crossed to the other side of the stadium when she encountered what she thought might be a problem: one of the Campus Police car's cruising slowly down the street.

Shit! she thought as it went by. *Steady, girl. He's just onna reg'lar patrol. He ain't interested in you.* And sure enough, the car went by without even stopping.

Finally she came to the high, towering buildings that functioned as the campus dorms. *Looks like a damn city in itself,* Terry thought as she stared up at the stone and glass monoliths. *All the little pukes, bundled up in their beds.* As she passed each building, she peered up at the names above the main entrances. On the fourth try, she found what she was looking for. *Hot shit! This is it!, she thought. Jewboy lives up on the fifth floor here. Now, let's see where the nearest lot is.*

She hurried over to the other side and was rewarded with the sight of a large parking lot that stretched out nearly to the highway on the other side. She dug into her pocket for the paper she had written the Jewboy's license plate number on. *TYY 681. This may take some doing,* she thought.

"Some doing" took only fifteen minutes as she came across her target parked off to the side of the lot. *Gotcha!* she thought as she circled her intended victim. *Looks like whoever worked on it did a good job.*

Terry threw her bag to the ground, eliciting a far sharper clank that echoed off the cars that surrounded her. *Too bad somebody has to go and ruin it,* she thought as an oily smile spread across her features.

She pulled the zipper open and removed the first implement of destruction: the two halves of an iron bar that she fitted together into a two-foot long staff. *A few swings a' this here, she* thought as she hefted it back and forth in the air, *and it'll break open anything that ain't stone.* The next object she pulled out was a large hunting-knife she had bought that morning at an army surplus store. *First things first, though,* Terry thought as she pulled its serrated edge from its sheath.

The jabbed the point of the knife into the car's right rear tire and was rewarded with a satisfying hiss. Then she gave the knife a tug and made the tear even larger, permanently damaging the tire beyond repair. She repeated the action on the other three wheels.

Putting the knife down, she picked up the iron bar. After making a cursory glance around her to make sure no one was looking, she attacked.

Pop! came the hollow implosion as she connected with the right headlight. Smiling even wider, she hit the other with even harder force. Then she went for the tail lights. The *crack* and *pop* that followed left shards of red plastic lying and glimmering in the phosphorescence of the parking lot's overhead lights like blood drops against the purplish tar.

Still, no one came. There barely seemed a ripple in the air. *Now, I can really go to town!,* Terry thought as she hefted the bar.

With a mighty swing, she took out the driver's side window. The sound of tinkling glass spilled into the night air like atonal music. Then she smashed the windshield, making crazed spider webs crisscross the tempered glass. Next went the rear window, then the side mirrors, then the passenger's side window.

Terry stepped back and admired her handiwork. *Too bad I can't stick around to see the look on Jewboy's face,* she thought with a toothy grin. *He'll shit himself a kosher load.*

She leaned the bar against a slashed tire and retrieved the knife. Opening the door, she plunged the knife deep into the fabric of the driver's seat, slashing through cloth and foam like butter. She did the same with the passenger's seat, then crawled in the back. She stabbed with the fury of a berserker, until foam flew through the air in big, yellow clouds.

Suddenly, she froze. Something didn't feel quite right as she peered through the broken window. Though the shadows remained unshifted, Terry couldn't shake the sudden feeling she was being watched. Quickly but silently, she emerged from the car, brandishing the knife.

But still, there was nothing, sight or sound. She stood that way for a minute or two, head cocked, eyes peeled, all senses attuned to the night's rhythms, but her viewer, if he or she existed, gave nothing away.

Prolly jus' my imagination, she thought. *Still, better wrap things up. Who knows how long until some pig oinks by. But let's see if Jewboy has some goodies I c'n help m'self to.*

Hurriedly now, she rifled though all of the Honda's compartments, but was rewarded with just the usual flotsam and jetsam of life. *Registration, napkins, coupons, blah, blah, blah, bullshit, bullshit.*

Hey, wait! Whas this? she thought as she pulled out the cassette case. *Jewboy's music? Lessee what he's got. Maybe something worth liftin'.*

She was more than a little disappointed with the contents. *Jesus!* she thought. *The fuckin' Thompson Twins? The Cure?!* Duran Duran?! *Man! I oughta cut the kid's throat on principle!*

Dropping the tapes on the ground, she crushed them underneath the heel of her boot. *Fuckin' music like that ain't got no right to live,* she thought with a grin as she ripped apart plastic and spools of brown thread in clotted bundles.

On the last tape, she gave pause. *Springsteen,* she thought. *Figgers, it's the only one.*

She placed the sole survivor of her rampage into a separate compartment of her bag. As she gathered up her tools, she stood back and admired her handiwork, the sheer art of the car's destruction. *A fuckin' Honda Accord's never looked as good as this,* she thought.

She suddenly became aware through a tingling in her loins that she needed to answer a call of nature. A devious smile crossed her features. *Well, why not?* she thought. *Make it the fuckin' cherry on top.*

Terry climbed into the back seat and dropped her sweat pants around her ankles as she crouched on her haunches. Her eyes closed and her smile went dreamy as the yellow contents of her bladder streamed onto the seat. When she finished, she dried her crotch by rubbing it onto a still-dry spot on the seat. *Too bad I didn't haveta take a dump, too,* she thought as she emerged from the car.

Her bag was still out there, but so was the presence Terry had felt for the past few minutes. *What the fuck? Who the fuck?* she thought as she replaced her tools. *It ain't a cop, or they'd be in my face by now. Prolly some college puke, but most of 'em'd run away by now, lookin' for a cop. Whas the deal here?*

She listened for another moment, but there was still nothing save the dead quiet of a cold night. *Yer losin' it, Terry,* she thought finally. *Prolly nothin' out there, but might as well leave bad enough alone and skedaddle.*

And so, with everything packed away, and with one last satisfied glance at the mess she'd made, she left, walking hurriedly off into the night.

Two full minutes after Terry left, a shadow detached itself from the trees surrounding the parking lot and approached the vandalized car. It examined it for several moments, circling it twice to fully access the damage, before finally turning away and heading into the dorm.

CHAPTER 29

Ari thought the pounding in his head was the echoes from a half-remembered dream until the voice broke in between the sets of raps. "Ari, you in there?" Dave's voice called out.

Ari peered at his clock. "8:43", it read. *Tuesday*, he thought. *First class ain't till eleven. What the hell?*

Then he saw the pile of books and papers on the floor and remembered: the argument with his father, his rising in the middle of the night to undress. Ari was throwing on a pair of sweat pants lying on a chair when Dave started knocking again. "Just a sec, Dave!" he called out as he grabbed for a T-shirt. Thus adjusted, he opened the door.

On the other side, Dave looked as pale as a dead leech. "Jesus, man! What's wrong?" Ari asked.

"Ari, don't you have a Honda Accord?"

Ari felt a solid thud hit his chest. "Yeah . . .why?"

"Silver colored?"

"Yeah! Why?!"

"Cuz there's one out in the parking lot. Trashed."

Ari was glad he had kept his hand on the door knob as he felt as though his knees would buckle. "Oh, God," he gasped. "Lemme get something on my feet and I'll be right out."

He slipped on his shoes and followed Dave out into the hall. Dave was talking, but Ari only half-heard him, like someone had strapped on gauze blinders for his ears. "I was on my way to class," Dave said. "And I was cutting across the lot when I saw . . .it."

"Saw what?" Ari replied as he jabbed the elevator's down button.

"What I thought was your car," Dave responded as the elevator door opened. They climbed on and the door closed behind them as Dave continued. "It was silver-grey, and I didn't really get a good look. There was a crowd gathered around it, and all I saw was some broken glass and some foam-like stuff on the ground." "There was crowd?" Ari murmured hollowly. It was the nightmare of his car wreck, coming back to haunt him, only weeks later, all over again.

Dave snorted. "Yeah. Bunch of assholes standing around staring at it, like they got nothin' better to do. Bet nobody's even called the cops or anything."

The elevator opened out into the lobby, and Dave and Ari emerged. They turned a corner and went out the dorm's back entrance, the one that opened directly into the lot. The surreality of the moment was not lost on Ari. *The shit storm just keeps comin'*, a dark, creepy voice whispered in his head. *Yes, coming at you relentlessly, sorta like a not-too-bright fratboy after a sorority pledge. You wanted to be a fratboy at one time, didn't you, Ari?*

"Shut up," Ari murmured softly to that voice in his head. "Might not even be mine."

But he knew it was, deep in his heart-of-hearts. And when Dave led Ari in the direction where he knew he had last parked his car, he didn't think his spirits could sink any lower. But when he saw the crowd, the crowd that he also knew, in his heart-of-hearts, had not merely dissipated, but *grown,* since Dave had come to fetch him, Ari felt as though his whole world sank down through his stomach, out his feet and into the earth beneath him, a hole he wished he could drop into and pull in after him. A veritable wall separated the two young men from the object of their search. "One side!" Dave barked out to the horde of human vultures that surrounded the vandalized vehicle. "Give a guy some space, for Chrissake!"

When the last person parted and Ari was granted his first view, he went from being merely depressed to being crushed underneath a heavy stone of sadness dropped from on high. It was his car, all right; license plates tell no tales. Everything that could be broken on it was: windshield, mirrors, the works. At first, Ari was puzzled by the big tufts of yellow-brown foam that sat like small clouds on top of the debris. Then he realized, with renewed anguish, that the vandal (or vandals) had actually taken the time to get inside the car and fuck up the seats.

A small gust of wind blew a piece of thin, brown tape around his ankles. Ari knelt carefully (ever mindful of his knees buckling underneath him) to examine it. *Looks like torn pieces of cassette tape,* he thought. *But why . . ?*

And then he knew. He knew the final indignity that had been thrown upon him, to the great injury he had been dealt. Underneath his car was the shattered case where he kept all of his tapes. *And they smashed everything they found inside of it,* he thought furtively. *And what the hell FOR?! Why? WHY?! FUCK IT ALL, WHY ME!!??*

This last thought was so loud in his mind that he thought he'd shouted it out loud, and jumped when he felt a hand touch his arm. Dave stared down at him, his face wracked with concern. "It's yours, isn't it?" he said. "God, it's written all over your face."

"Yeah," Ari answered smally, distantly, like his talking from a perch on the moon. "It's mine, all right. Mine all over." Now he felt the tears come into his eyes, harsh and unbidden, and he furiously tried to blink them away, without much success.

That seemed to trigger something in Dave, and he pulled himself away from Ari's tearful gaze to shout out at the crowd, "I don't suppose any of you people saw anything?"

No one answered him. A few stared back at Dave dumbly, while others stared at the ground and shuffled their feet. Ari could see a couple of fratboy-types creep away from the back without another word.

But Dave wasn't through. "I don't suppose any of you here actually took it upon yourselves to call the cops or anything?," he said with even more acid dripping into his voice. Now none of the dozen or so people without anything better to do could meet his eye. A few even grumbled under their breath. "Didn't think so," Dave continued. Even through tear-streaked eyes, Ari could see the anger and contempt plastered on his friend's face. *Sorry, Dave,* he thought

167

to himself. *I really didn't think you had it in you. Now, it's pretty obvious you're less of a pussy than I am.*

But Dave wasn't finished. "Well, as long as you're all gathered here," he said. "Would anyone like to do the right thing and watch the car for a few minutes so we can go back in and call the cops ourselves?"

Now the crowd started looking amongst themselves. A few actually shrugged and walked away. Finally, a tall, thin, African-American youth wearing glasses and the name of his fraternity on his sweat shirt spoke up. "I'll do it, guys," he said. "My next class is some bullshit elective, anyway. I'll wait til you get the cops."

"Thanks," Dave responded. "Mr. . . . ?"

"Johnson. Raphael Johnson. Call me Rafe."

Ari had some weird flashback about an old comedian he once heard, one whose shtick was introducing himself: *You can call me Ray, or you can call me Jay, or you can call me . . . .*

"Thanks, Rafe," Dave responded for him.

"No prob. Back in my old neighborhood, this shit happens every day. Thought I'd be able to come here and get away from it. Guess not. But I hate it as much now as I did then."

"Thank you," Ari said, his voice thick with barely restrained emotion. "We'll just be a few minutes."

"Take your time, Bro. You got the next hour free. I live on the third floor, by the way."

"We're both on the fifth," Dave said. "We won't take too long."

"I'll be here."

The three shook hands, and as Dave and Ari walked away, they heard their new friend bellow, "Well? What the fuck y'all lookin' at? Ain't nuthin' to see here! Move the fuck on!"

Once they were out of earshot, Dave said, "Look, Ari, I can call the campus cops if you wanna call your family or whoever. It might help get your machine outta here all the quicker."

"Yeah, okay," Ari agreed numbly as he looked up at the dorm. A flicker of movement registered in the corner of his eye, and he turned to see Graziano staring out at the two of them from his dorm window.

He and Ari stared at each other for a moment, saying nothing, then Ari saw him slowly nod his head, and retreat back into his dorm, clamping the blinds shut behind him. Ari looked over to Dave, who was already opening the back entrance to the dorm. *He didn't see,* Ari thought as he followed Dave inside. *Graziano only wanted my attention, not Dave's. But why?* An icy finger touched his heart as he considered it. *He didn't trash my car, did he? I thought we were on good terms!*

Dave was talking again as he pushed the up button on the elevator. "I'll go to my room and call the campus cops from there," he said. "You call your parents from yours, okay?"

"Kay," Ari responded as the elevator opened. "My dad's gonna hit the fuckin' roof. Dave smiled weakly at him as they boarded. "Something new and different, huh?" he asked.

"Yeah. Same old, same old."

The two were silent as they rode the elevator up. When they got off, Dave picked up his pace, hurrying ahead of Ari down the hall. "After I'm done getting the cops, I'll meet you down in the parking lot, okay? I'll wait with Rafe awhile."

"Thanks, Dave. I appreciate it."

"It's gonna be okay, man."

"I hope," Ari murmured to himself as he followed. He passed Graziano's dorm, firmly shut against the outside. Ari briefly considered knocking, but decided against it. *First things first,* he thought as he unlocked his dorm. *Need to clock in some time being screamed at for something I* didn't *do.*

He shut the door firmly behind him and slumped down on his bed. His thoughts drifted back to Graziano. It didn't seem like his style. *Graziano's the type who'd take up a problem with you directly,* he thought. *Trashing someone's personal property, he'd see that as childish, or cowardly. Or something.*

Which, of course, left behind the inevitable question of *who else?* Ari had no idea; his thought processes were being sabotaged by the waves of inky blackness that threatened to overwhelm him. *Why the fuck do I always have to be the target of somebody else's bad day?*

he thought to himself. *From my fucking parents, to the fucking kids at school, to some asshole who probably chose me at random as somebody who could be fucked with! What, did God run out of toilet paper and decide I was The Designated Ass-Wipe For Him To Use?*

The sound of the phone ringing brought him out of his downbound train of thought. Ari vaguely considered just letting it ring and have the machine pick up, but thought better of it. *Probably Dad calling right now, ready for Round Two,* he thought. *Bet he won't be expecting this sucker-punch, though.*

"Hello?" he said into the phone out loud.

No answer. Dead silence on the line. *Great,* Ari thought. *Terrific fucking time to get a prank caller.* He hung up without another word.

Five seconds later, the phone rang again. Irritated, Ari snatched up the phone and shouted into it: "Hello!?"

Once again, no response. What possessed him to do the next, he would never know, but instead of slamming the phone down, he burst forth with: "Look, whoever the fuck this is, I ain't in the fuckin' mood! I just-"

"-had your car fucked up?" an unknown voice rasped on the other end. Then a sharp click as the line went dead.

Ari was stunned into silence. Numbly, he replaced the phone. His guts felt like someone had stuck a cold, hard fist up his ass and yanked. *Jesus,* he thought. *Maybe I am a target! But who?*

Hurrying now, he snatched up the phone and punched the numbers that connected him to his dad's office.

One ring. Then two. On the third, the line was picked up by Margie, his secretary.

"Sussman Styles. Mr. Sussman's office. How can I help you?"

"Margie? It's Ari. Can I speak to my dad, please?"

"Sure, sugar. Hold on a minute."

The pause had just become unbearable when Mr. Sussman's gruff voice erupted over the line. "Hello?"

"Dad, it's Ari. Listen-"

"No! *You* listen, kid! I-"

"Dad, shut up! I have something important to tell you! Somebody smashed the car. Vandalized it."

"What?!" Mr. Sussman roared. "Who?! What happened?!"

"I woke up this morning and found it out in the lot. All the glass is smashed, and the seats are torn up."

A long pause, then: "Sheee-iiiitttt!!! Jee-sus Car-rist! What the fuck is wrong with the security in that place? What the fuck do we pay them for every year?"

"Dad, I don't know. My friend Dave's calling the campus cops right now while I'm talking to you."

"Did you call the real cops yet?"

"No, not yet."

There was a heavy sigh on the other end. "All right, I'll do it then. You got any tests today or anything like that?

"No, nothing like that."

"Good. After I call the cops, I'll meet you down there. Where's the lot?"

"Right next to the dorm."

"All right. Maybe it's a good thing you called the campus cops. Give me a chance to ask where they get off."

Ari moaned inwardly. *Great, make yourself look like an idiot in front of everybody,* he thought. *Make the day complete.*

"Anything else?" Mr. Sussman asked.

Ari was about to speak, then stopped himself. Sould he tell him about the phone calls he'd just received? No. It could have just been a wrong number, and his hyperactive imagination was getting the better of him. *Worst of all, I might get a damn lecture on just how stupid I am, and I need that like I need a third nut right now,* Ari thought.

Out loud, he said, "No, nothing else."

"All right. See you in a couple hours."

There was a sharp click as Mr. Sussman hung up the phone. Ari hung up his own phone and slumped back in bed. He vaguely thought of calling Rachel, or at least leaving a message, but figured there was plenty of time for that later on.

171

The two phone calls he had received: what did they mean? Was it really his imagination that thought the voice had mentioned his car getting fucked up? Or was the owner of the voice just apologizing for calling a wrong number? The voice itself sounded vaguely familiar, in a way that was so deeply implanted in his mind that, try as he might, he couldn't retrieve it consciously.

Then his thoughts drifted back to Graziano: why was he so interested in making his presence known, but not enough to actually meet him and Dave out in the hallway? *That couldn't have been him on the phone, could it?*, he wondered to himself. True, the voice was kind of raspy-sounding, just like his, but still kind of hard to distinguish. He couldn't even make a safe bet on the gender.

Ari sighed. All this rampant speculation was getting him nowhere fast. Perhaps it would be better if he did chase down what shadow of a lead he did have.

Graziano's door was still firmly shut to the outside world. Ari knocked on it with a confidence he did not quite feel, and was a bit apprehensive when the occupant shouted "Come in!" from the other side.

Graziano was in the process of getting dressed when Ari entered, but hurriedly waved his visitor in. "Close it behind you," Graziano commanded as he pulled a well-worn T-shirt tightly around his solid frame. His voice brooked no argument, so Ari did as he was told.

"I was wondering if you got my hint," Graziano continued once the door was shut. "Thought I might have to come and bang on your door myself."

"Why?"

Graziano looked fixedly at Ari with intense dark eyes. "Who's after you, Sussman?" he asked.

Ari blinked. "What do you mean?" he responded.

"Just what I asked. Did you fuck someone over recently? Or a group of someones?"

"Well...no, I don't think. I mean, I'm being sued by somebody, but-"

"What for?"

"I was in an accident over the summer. In my car."

"How long ago?"

"End of the break, right before school started up again. This biker woman plowed into me at an intersection. Now she's suing me for damages."

"She have a case?"

"Hell, she doesn't even have a *license.*"

Ari saw Graziano's face suddenly turn to stone, and the fist that seemed stuck in his guts grew a few degrees colder. For a moment, Graziano said nothing, as if he were debating within himself on how to proceed. And, when he did start speaking, Ari felt the fist's temperature hit absolute zero. "Last night," Graziano began. "I was comin' back from a late rehearsal. I'm doin' crew work for this damn musical, so I was decked out all in black. That's probably why they didn't see me."

"Who?"

"Whoever it was trashed your car."

"You saw it happen?!"

"Partially. When I got to the dorm, I heard this crash out in the lot that souned like glass breaking. So I decided to check it out."

Graziano ran a hand through his dark hair. "I hid myself behind some trees nearby, till I came upon your car. Well, actually, I didn't *know* it was yours at the time. All I could see was this. . .*somebody* trashin' the hell outta it."

"Who?" Ari demanded. "What did they look like?"

Graziano shook his head. "Hard to tell. They were wearin' sweats. University of Maryland sweats. A pair of pants and a shirt with the hood pulled over the face."

"You couldn't see *anything?*"

Graziano snapped his fingers. "Wait. Yes, I did. Whoever it was, I noticed they were wearing boots. Motorcycle boots, it looked like." Now the fist in Ari's stomach crept upward to his chest. "Motorcycle boots?" he echoed hollowly.

"Yeah. Other than that, I couldn't even tell you if it was a man or a woman."

Unseen, Ari's hand began to tremble. *I thought I might actually*

173

feel better if I knew who it was, he thought. *Stupid me.* Out loud, he asked, "Did you notice anything else? Color of hair maybe?"

Graziano's face brightened with the prompt. "Yeah!" he exclaimed. "Now that you mention it! I did get one look when they got outta the car. They was carryin' this big carving knife, and I thought they was lookin' right at me when they got out! I held stock still, then underneath the lights, I see they got this strange lookin' kinda red hair. Hell, it looked almost orange, like a bad dye job or somethin'!"

Now Ari's knees did buckle underneath him, and he nearly fell. Instead, he slumped down into the only chair in the room: the one at Graziano's study carrel. "Jesus, Sussman! You all right?" Graziano exclaimed.

"Y-yeah. No. I don't know." Graziano came forward, steadying him. "Jesus. Yer shakin' like a leaf. You know this guy?"

Ari could see it all over again in his mind's eye: the light change, the punch on the accelerator, the moment when his entire widow filled up with a view of the biker. The deafening crash as shards of glass flew around his face. And the final, earth-swallowing scream of rage and pain that haunted his days (and quite a few of his nights). "Scranton," he murmured so softly that Graziano had to strain to hear. "Terry Scranton. Her name is Terry Scranton."

"Christ! That was a woman?!"

Ari gave a humorless snort. "Yeah," he said. "She is."

"God DAMN! All my money was on it bein' a guy!"

"You lose."

"Guess so."

Ari stood up shakily, keeping his hand on the back of the chair for balance. "You gotta come with me. Tell the cops everything."

"Sorry, pal. I can't."

"What'd ya mean, you can't? You're a fuckin' witness!"

"I know! But . . ."

"Yeah?!"

Graziano seemed stuck, like a fat man in a Yugo. "Sussman," he said finally. "I ain't had the best experiences with the cops. Campus or otherwise."

"So, what're you saying? Your just gonna let this woman fuck me?"

Graziano shook his head again. "Believe me, Sussman. You don't want me to come forward. It might fuck things up even more."

Ari threw up his hands. "All right, fine. You don't wanna stick your neck out, be that way. I'll tell the cops what I suspect, but your name won't come up. But let me ask you one thing."

"Yeah?"

"You're the one who got in my face last week about looking around the great big world and being accountable. So where the fuck do you get off, Graziano, in telling me that?"

And without another word, Ari strode out Graziano's door, slamming it behind him.

On his way back down in the elevator, Ari almost had his knees give out again, and he seized the railing to steady himself. I *wonder what's worse,* he thought to himself as he felt the world plunge around him. *Living not knowing who your enemy is?*

Or living in fear when you find out?

CHAPTER 30

Terry grunted as she strained against the weight, the perspiration dripping from her brow in a salt river. The tendons in her recently healed arm stretched, the muscle fibers tore, then started rejuvenating and healing themselves almost instantly, growing harder, thicker.

On the fifteenth repetition of the wrist-curl, Terry relaxed her grip and pulled the forty- five pound weight on the bench she was leaning against. Standing from her crouch, she grabbed for the towel she had earlier draped across the main barbell and briskly rubbed her forehead clear of sweat.

Fuckin' arm's nearly back to full strength, she thought as she placed the dumbbell on the floor amid a pile of smaller weights and iron plates. *Always did put on muscle quickly. Let's hear it for years of farm breeding.*

Now she placed the towel on the bench itself, protecting its vinyl surface from the sweat down her back. Laying on the bench, she placed her hands an equal distance from the center of the 145-pound barbell that hung suspended over her. On a three-count, she lifted, hiking the weight the full distance of her arms over her chest.

Gradually, she let the weight fall, almost to the point where it touched her breasts, then she extended her arms to their full length. Down again, then up. On the twelveth rep, she replaced the weight in the slots on the sides of the bench. "Finished!" she exclaimed to the room as she pulled herself up from the bench. "Now, fer a few cool-down exercises!"

Over the years since she had returned home, she gradually

turned what used to be a family room into a rudimentary home gym. Dumbbells and iron plates littered the floor, centered around a bench set where she did all the exercises she couldn't do standing. The past few weeks had played havoc with her usual routine, one that she was only now catching up. *Not much you can do with a bum arm*, she thought. *Just run, maybe. Or use the exercise bike.*

Now she went over to the doorway where she had placed a chin up bar. One leap and she grabbed it underhanded, then proceeded to pull herself up and down, feeling the strain in her upper back and biceps. *Two and a half hours straight*, she thought. *Gotta get nice'n hard again. Cuz now it's time I* really *started kickin' some ass.*

After the twentieth rep, she dropped down from the bar and looked at the clock across the hall in the kitchen. *Gettin' on five-thirty,* she noted. *Another half-hour and I'll call the Jewboy again, this time at home. That'll really get what little balls he's got inna clinch!*

Earlier that morning, after a few hours sleep, she had stopped at a nearby gas station and placed the call to his dorm. *Little punk sounded like he was gonna shit himself blind,* she laughed to herself. *Tonight I'll have him* beggin' *his dad to pay me off!*

Terry dropped to the floor and started doing push-ups, *An' I'll bet my million dollar pay off, his house is where the Jewboy's hidin' out after my little redecoration of his machine. Prolly doesn't know who hit 'em, or why. No prob. I'll give him a much bigger hint tonight. Not enough to hang myself with, just a helpful little hint from an old pal.*

After fifty, she was done. Terry slumped against the weight bench as she grabbed her water bottle off a side table, downing it. "Time fer a shower," she said to the empty room as she felt the salt lick of her sweat flowing through every pore. "Nuthin's better'n a long, hot one after a balls-to-the-wall workout."

She stood and stretched, excited by the feel of every tendon, joint and muscle pop and expand in their rightful places. *What if, the Jewboy* still *won't budge on settling? What comes next?*

Terry smiled to herself, because she knew the voice wasn't really a nagging doubt. At least, not totally. Part of it asked the question in eager anticipation, hoping that the Jewboy was even dumber than he looked, and that this level of harassment would continue. Expand, even.

"If he don't," Terry said with the smile of a tiger just released from its cage. "He ain't gonna like what I'm gonna break next."

CHAPTER 31

Mr. Sussman slammed the phone back into its cradle, making Ari jump. Ari was seated on the family room couch, right next to his nearly-sombulent mother. The elder Sussman glared down at his son. "Well, hotshot," he said. "Guess what the total bill comes to?"

Ari braced himself inwardly. "How much?"

"Over a grand."

"Christ."

"Yeah! 'Christ' is right! There goes another wad down the tubes!"

"What the hell are you getting on my case for? I wasn't the one who wrecked it!"

"That ain't the point."

"Then what is?"

"How I have to keep shelling out and you don't appreciate it!"

"What the hell are you talking about?"

There was a knock at the door. "Who the hell is that?" Mr. Sussman snapped. Ari ignored him and went to open the door. There stood Rachel on the front stoop, breathless from her run over.

"Ari, are you okay?" she asked as she stepped inside.

Mr. Sussman exploded as soon as he saw her. "Christ! Can't you keep anything a secret, kid?"

Now it was Rachel's turn to blow a fuse. "Listen here, goddamn it!" she snarled. "I came over here because I care about your son. I don't give a shit what *you* do, or how you conduct yourself behind closed doors, but Ari's my friend, and I'm gonna stick by him no matter what, like it or not!"

"Yes, I told her," Ari replied. "I just needed to talk to a friend."

"Oh, yeah? Well, she's not family! No one ever sticks by you more'n your family, and you better learn that, kid."

Ari looked over at his mother, passed out on the couch, sleeping soundly despite the high volume. *Yeah,* he said to himself. *And there it is. Exhibit-fucking-A of the results of what happens sometimes when you stick together as a family, Dad. Especially when you got an ignorant bully for a father. You have a son who can't stand you and a drooling, self-centered, drugged-out zombie for a wife. Good plan, Dad. Fucking great plan!*

But before he could even think to communicate these thoughts out loud, Rachel shot back, "Someday, maybe I *will* be part of this family, Mr. Sussman. Did you ever think of that?"

Man, this is good! Ari marveled to himself as his father was left speechless. But a look into Rachel's eyes also left Ari thus, for the flames in them added the unspoken corollary: *And you better pray to God above for help when and if I do.*

Out loud, Rachel said, "Why don't we step outside, Ari? I could use some air."

Mr. Sussman finally recovered himself with a snort. "Hunh! You probably went and told her about your paranoid idea, too, huh? That whoever trashed your car was after you? Well, I got news for you, kid: The world doesn't revolve around you!"

Ari nailed his father with some fire in his own eyes. "Oh, I know that, Dad. That's one lesson you've always taught me. Better than anyone else."

Then Ari turned and slammed the front door behind him, following Rachel off the front stoop. He went to her as she stood in front of the road, staring off into the distance. "I'm sorry, Rache," he said. "Sorry about what happened in there. I-"

She spun around to face him. "Do me a favor, Ari," she snapped. "Stop apologizing!"

"What? I-"

"What I'm saying, Ari," she continued in a gentler tone, "is that you should stop apologizing for things that aren't your fault.

I was the one who decided to come over. I was the one who went after your father. He's the one who decided to make all those snide comments about you and me. You apologize too much, hon. You've been apologizing your whole life. *For your whole life.* Your parents have been making you ashamed of who you are for your whole life, Ari, and there's no excuse for it! It's time to stop it. You're a full grown man, for God's sake!"

Ari couldn't quite meet her eyes. "I sure as hell don't feel like it," he responded.

Rachel touched his chin and made him meet her eyes. "You are, hon." Rachel gave him a warm smile, then her face turned serious as she continued. "Now, tell me why you think it was this woman, this Terry Scranton person, who trashed your car."

"I don't just think it. I know it. Somebody saw her."

"Well, great! Can't you just tell the police?"

Ari shook his head. "No. He made me promise."

"Who?"

"His name's Graziano."

"That crazy guy you keep telling me about? Why not? From what you told me, he doesn't seem to be the type to scare easily."

"He wasn't too clear on the why. He just basically told me he's had some problems with the cops in the past."

"You don't think he's mobbed up, do you?"

"Him? Nothing would surprise me. I almost wish he was."

"Crap."

"Yeah. Well, anyway, it's a dead issue."

"Well, can't you go to the police anyway? Tell them what you suspect?"

"I did, but I dunno how far that's gonna fly. They didn't find any fingerprints, so she was careful. Nothing left behind to specifically pin her to it."

"What about the phone calls?"

"You know even better than I do that'll never hold up. Even if I did recognize the voice."

"Shit. She's playing this one pretty well, I gotta give her that."

The front door to the house opened and Mr. Sussman walked out on the stoop. "There's a phone call," he called out. "Probably another one of your friends."

Rachel and Ari exchanged a glance as they headed back to the house. The phone was lying on the coffee table, placed in front of the still-sleeping Mrs. Sussman. With a shaky hand, he picked up the extension. "Hello?"

"Real shame what happened," a voice rasped on the other end.

Ari froze, but the trembling in his hand trebled. "What? Who is this?" he stammered.

"I think you know damn well who this is, kid. This ain't no time to play dumb. You bein' college boy an' all that."

"What do you want . . .Ms. Scranton, is it?"

"Pretty clever, kid. I guess we got a few listeners, huh? I'll keep it short, then. I'm just phonin' with a piece of advice. Yer choice what to do with it."

"What?"

"Pay what you owe. Think of that as a piece of financial advice between friends. You know about financial advice, doncha? You an' yer daddy?"

Ari felt a hand gently, but firmly, pull the receiver out of his hand "Listen here, you white- trash bitch!," Rachel growled into the receiver with a voice Ari barely recognized. "If I catch you anywhere near here, if I even *think* you're gonna come anywhere near, I'm gonna kick your low- rent, trailer-trash ass so far up between your shoulder blades, you're gonna look like the rest of those West Virginia, hunch-backed inbreds! You goddamn lowlife, piece-of-shit redneck *cunt!!*"

Rachel suddenly stopped her tirade. "She hung up, for some reason," she replied disingenuously as she replaced the phone.

Ari looked over at his father. "Now, do you believe me?" he said. "Now do you think I'm not just being paranoid?" Mr. Sussman got a look on his face that his son hated above all others: the pouty, sulking little-boy look that his father always wore when someone accused *him* of making a mistake. Ari was fighting back an urge to slap him across the face when the phone rang again.

"This time, Rachel picked up. *"Hello!?"* she exploded.

The expression on her face shifted. "Oh, sorry, sir. Yes, he is. Who may I say is calling?"

Ari heard the murmur on the other end, then Rachel held out the phone. "Ari, it's for you," she said. "It's the police."

Ari grabbed for the phone. "Hello?"

"Ariel Sussman?" a deep voice intoned from the other end.

"Speaking."

"I'm Detective Bernard Jones of the Maryland State Police," the man said. *Black guy*, Ari thought. *Older, but not as old as my dad.*

"What can I do for you, sir?" Ari responded.

"Actually, I think we may be able to do for each other. I saw on a report today that your car was vandalized. At your college, wasn't it?"

"Yeah! . . .Yeah, it was."

"Son, are you familiar with the name 'Terry Scranton'?

Oh, Christ, Ari thought. *This is getting too weird.* Out loud, he said: "Yes, sir. Very familiar."

Jones grunted. "Are you going back to school tomorrow?"

"No, sir. I'm not going anywhere until I get my car fixed. It's in the shop right now. Needs a new windshield, seats, everything."

"Hm. That'll set you back some."

Ari sighed. "Yeah." There was a brief pause. "Sir, I don't mean to be rude-"

"-but get to the damn point?" Jones finished with a chuckle. "Sorry, I was just thinking. Would you have time for me to drop over tomorrow? Around 2 PM, say? I've got a bit of information about our mutual problem that I think you need to hear."

"Uh, sure," Ari responded. "Two o'clock is fine."

"See you then."

Jones clicked off and Ari hung up. "That was a police detective," he said. "He wants to drop by tomorrow. To discuss my car and some other things."

"What? Didn't we give 'em enough of a statement this morning?" Mr. Sussman rejoined.

"This sounds like something different, Dad. This guy specifically wants to talk about the woman. Terry Scranton."

"*What* about her?" Rachel asked.

"Dunno. I got the feeling he wants to tell me about something else. Something that involves her."

"What!? You don't know?" Mr. Sussman said. "Jesus Christ, kid! You gotta ask these questions! Next thing you know, *you'll* be the one locked up, not her!"

"Oh for God's sake, Dad-"

"Okay, fine! Don't listen to the old man! I'm thirty years older'n you, kid! You think I don't know shit, and you know everything? Fine! Call me an idiot behind my back. I know how these friggin' cops operate. They don't care who they have to arrest, and the more they lock up, the better it looks for them."

"Now who's being paranoid, Dad?"

"Hey, y'know, fuck it! Don't listen to me! Do whatever the hell you want. Goddamn, you're hard-headed!"

Mr. Sussman stalked off down the hallway to his bedroom, calling after him one final time, "You're gonna miss the old man when he's gone!"

Then came a door slam, and the house was silent.

Ari spoke aloud to himself, just under his breath. "Why dontcha do us both a favor then, and kick some night? So I don't haveta listen to any more mouth!"

Rachel laughed behind him, and Ari blushed. Maybe he wasn't as quiet as he thought. "And another chapter in *The World According to Maury Sussman* comes to an end," Rachel said. "Tune in tomorrow, for another poisonous pontification. Damn, Ari. You must be winning. I think this is the first time *he* left the room first. Told ya he'd back down."

Ari heard a high-pitched snore from behind him. He was both disgusted and amused to see his mother hadn't stirred. If anything, she had fallen even deeper into her drugged slumber.

He shook his head ruefully. "Whole fuckin' world falls down around her, but she sleeps on."

A warm hand interlocked with his. "You blame her?" Rachel said softly. "It's probably the one thing that's kept her going through all these years of being married to that asshole. Drugs and sleep are some people's only escape."

"Yeah, I guess. And some people jump into action when you least expect it. *'Goddamn lowlife piece of shit redneck cunt'?* Jesus, Rache! You kiss your mom with that mouth?"

Rachel giggled. "Sorry, hon, but I wasn't gonna let her off the phone till I had a piece of her."

"I thought you were encouraging me to stick up for *myself*?"

Rachel shrugged. "Old habits die hard, I suppose."

"Do they?"

Rachel glanced at the clock over the fireplace. "Jeez! Look at the time! And I got a few briefs to look over tonight."

"Don't make me make the obvious joke here, Rache."

She smacked him lightly. "Dork! That's not what I meant!"

"You wanna look at mine?"

"All right, the humor in this room has hit an all-time low," she said. "Time for me to leave."

Ari saw her to the door and just about saw her fade into the distance when he spoke up again. "Hey, Rache?"

"Yeah, hon?" she called back.

What could he say? There was something about how the night had closed around her that made him apprehensive. Was he just being paranoid again? Or was it the fact that, at that moment, it seemed as though a large chasm had just opened into the pit of his stomach, reached up, and left a void in his chest? That made him feel even more disconnected to the world? *What would it be like to lose her, Ari?,* a slithery voice whispered in his mind. *Could you go on? Would you even want to? Or would you just shut down that part of yourself that allows you to feel? That makes you think there's something worthwhile in your miserable little life? What would you do, Ari? What would you do?*

"Look after yourself, Rache," he called out. "Please."

She smiled at him. "Always do, hon. You can count on that."

And off she went into the darkness, fading from her best friend's vision.

Ari shivered in spite of the late summer warmth. He tried pushing the unreasonable sense of loss to the back of his mind, but it wouldn't budge. *She's right*, he told himself. *I've got to get some control over myself. My life. Show some strength instead of being weak all the time.*

A thought popped into his mind, a positive one. There *was* a way to gain strength and control, and someone who could help him get it.

And that someone was now in his debt.

He ran over to his book bag and retrieved the number he had written down that morning.

With renewed sense of purpose, he grabbed the phone and started punching out the number sequence he hoped would change his life.

Graziano picked up on the third ring. "Yeah?"

"Graziano! It's Sussman."

"Hey, whassup?"

"Too much. You weren't busy, were you?"

"Nah. Just trying to make my way through a German Romantic play. You gotta hand it to those Romantics. Why use one word when a hundred can do the same job?"

"I think you'll survive, boss." He paused a second before continuing. "Listen, the whole thing about my car-"

"Yer still keepin' my name out of it, aintcha?"

"Sure. So far. But I need something in return."

Graziano sighed. "The old 'Godfather' thing, huh?"

"What?"

"Never mind. What d'ya need?"

"Train me."

"Huh?"

"You heard me. Train me. When I get back to school. When you go to the gym, I wanna go with you. Show me what to do. I wanna build myself up a bit."

Graziano said nothing for a second. "This wouldn't have anything to do with our 'friend' out in the parking lot, would it?", he said finally.

"Yes. And no. I mean, not entirely. I had a police detective call me a little bit earlier. Said he wanted to discuss her with me. Sounds like he's got something on her."

Graziano snorted. "Shit, man! I coulda toldja that! If that bitch hasn't done some hard time in her life, I'll kiss yer ass in the middle of the mall for everybody to see."

"So will you do it?"

Graziano sighed. "Guess I really got no choice. All right. What's yer goal? Strength or endurance?"

"Both, probably."

"Yeah. I think so, too. I'll get you on the weights and get you do some light cardio to start with. Think you can handle it?"

"Won't know until I try."

"Good man. That's what I like to hear. I'll see ya further on up the road."

"See ya."

Ari hung up, feeling as though a great weight had been removed. *No, that's not entirely true,* he thought. *A lot of weight's about to go on me, and I'm gonna enjoy it. Like the old Charles Atlas ads say, you can't go around having sand kicked in your face forever. Because if you do, in the end, you're not the only one who gets hurt.*

CHAPTER 32

Terry was just taking a swig of her RC Cola when the unexpected voice came on the line. "Listen here, you white trash bitch!", it snarled.

Terry nearly choked in surprise, spraying soda from her mouth onto the parking lot outside Pop's Bait and Tackle. The bottle itself jumped out her hand and shattered on the hardened tar.

The voice continued: "If I catch you anywhere near here, if I even think you're gonna come anywhere near, I'm gonna kick your low-rent, trailer-trash ass so far up between your shoulder blades, your gonna look like the rest of those West Virginia, hunch-backed inbreds! You goddamn, low-life, piece-of-shit redneck *cunt!!*"

Terry slammed the pay phone back in its cradle, more out of shock than fear. One minute, the Jewboy was there, stammering all the way, as expected. Then came the voice. The *unexpected* voice. A tough voice, full of steel resolve.

"It was that girl!," Terry exclaimed into the humid, early-evening air. "That girl in the picture!" For, although unexpected, the voice was still recognizable as a female's. "An' it sure wasn't his moms!", Terry said out loud. "Not by a long shot!"

Terry's eyes wandered over to the remains of her soda bottle and the familiar anger returned. *Bitch made me drop my drink!,* she said to herself. *May notta been a bottle a' Jack Black, but that shit cost money!*

"Bitch next door has guts, I'll give her that," Terry continued out loud, her mind flashing back to the night she crept through her and the Jewboy's yards, checking her memory for any probable entrances and exits. "An' if she's willin' to get herself in the line a' fire, I got no problem with that," she continued as she ran her fingers against the cool steel of the pocketed razor. "Death should be like shoes. It should always come in pairs."

CHAPTER 33

Jones pulled his old, battered Ford in to the Sussman driveway, stopping almost directly in front of the door. He raised a mental not of the house's plainness in contrast to the more opulent surroundings, but pushed such thoughts into the back of his mind. *You ain't here for the sights, Jonesy,* he told himself. *You're here to deliver a shit load of bad news. Not quite like when you were a patrolman, telling some family that their kid just got his brains splattered all over the highway, but close enough.*

The detective shook his head to clear it. *No time for these inner dialogues, my friend,* he thought. *Work to do.*

He popped the lock on the door and pushed it open, wincing at the creaking of the rusty hinge. For the umpteenth time, he made a note to himself to take a can of WD-40 to it, then promptly pushed the thought into the back of his mind again as he gathered up the file resting on the passenger seat.

The day outside was bright and sunny, with no hint of the approaching fall. Jones checked his watch. Five minutes after two. *Just about on time,* he thought to himself as he mounted the front stoop.

He pulled open the screen door and rapped his knuckles against the heavy wood of the door. There was a brief silence, then the sound of voices and the feel of footsteps approaching. The door opened on a bleary-eyed older woman wearing a faded house-coat, whose dazed expression did little to mask the suspicion pulsing out from her gaze.

Jones smiled at her and doffed his hat. "Afternoon, ma'am," he said. "I'm Detective Bernard Jones, Maryland State P.D. I'm here to see Mr. Ariel Sussman. He's your . . . son, I believe?"

"Yes," the woman answered, staring out at the large, African-American man on her doorstep. "Ari mentioned something about some policeman coming over."

Then an uncomfortable silence fell, neither of them speaking, just staring. Jones began to feel uncomfortable, not to mention a little annoyed. He was just about to clear his throat to say something else when a voice rang out behind the woman. "Who is it, Mom?" it said.

The woman didn't even glance around. "A man who says he's from the police," she replied in that same thick voice.

"Well, let him in, for God's sake."

"I dunno, Ari-"

"Mom!"

The sharpness in the tone seemed to surprise the woman, and she jumped as if goosed. She moved out of the doorway and a young man with warm brown eyes and pleasant, if somewhat, soft, features took her place. "Detective Jones?" the young man inquired.

"Yes," Jones replied, replacing his hat and pulling out his identification. "Detective Bernard Jones, Maryland State Police, Vice Division. He placed his badge in the young man's left hand and shook his right. "Are you Ariel Sussman?"

"Yes. Ari, please."

"Okay if I come in?"

"Sure," Ari replied as he stepped aside and gave the I.D. a once-over. Jones stepped inside a rather shabbily decorated living room dominated by an aging, off-white couch and a large brown recliner placed exactly in the center. In this recliner sat a short, squat, balding man who glared at Jones with naked suspicion and hostility. *Shit,* Jones thought. *At least the lady was trying to hide it. What crawled up these peoples' asses and died?*

Undaunted, he extended a hand out to the seated figure. "Hi," he said. "I'm Detective Jones. You're Mr. Sussman?

"Do I need a lawyer, Detective?" the man snapped in reply.

Jones blinked once, but otherwise kept his cool. "I don't think so, sir," he replied with a thoughtful frown. "I'm not here in any official capacity. I'm just here to discuss with your son certain aspects of a case I'm working on."

"So, my son can actually be of use to you?"

"Well . . .yes."

The man gave out a snort. "Hunh. Imagine that."

Jones dislike for the man, already nascent, blossomed into full adulthood. He turned to Ari. "Ariel? Perhaps we need to speak in private?"

"Ari, please" the younger man replied. "We can go to my room."

"Don't say nothin'', Ari!" the man in the chair snarled. "Not without him readin' you your rights!"

Jones regarded Mr. Sussman coldly, like a scientist examining a malignant virus he had just discovered. "Ari? Can I have my badge, please?" he said.

"Um . . . sure, Detective Jones."

Ari placed the silver coated star and identification document in the detective's hand. Without missing a beat, Jones slapped it down on the arm of Mr. Sussman's chair. "There you are, sir. My badge."

Mr. Sussman was momentarily stunned into silence. Then: "What the hell is this?"

"I told you, sir," Jones replied. "I'm not here on official business. I just came to have a friendly chat. Perhaps you would feel safer if you had my shield in your possession?"

"Uh . . .?"

Jones reached into his suit. "Would you like my gun as well?"

"No! . . .Um, I don't think that will be necessary. Do . . .whatever you want . . . with my son."

"Thank you." Jones turned to Ari, wide-eyed and transfixed by the scene before him. "Can you show me to your room, Ari?"

"Uh . . .yeah! Right this way!"

After he had closed the door behind him, Ari spoke again. "Sorry about all that back there. My dad's a little. . .well, my parents really have a tendency to be . . . overprotective."

Jones waved the statement away. "Nothing for you to apologize for. Not like I've never been given a hostile reception before."

"I guess not. Why don't you have a seat at my desk? Sorry if it's a bit cluttered."

Jones chuckled as he placed the files he was carrying on the desk in order to sort them. "This? Hell, I *dream* of days when my workspace is this clear."

Ari placed himself on his bed, directly across from the detective. "What is it exactly that you do, Detective Jones? You said you work in the Vice Squad?"

"Yup. Detective Sergeant Jones at your service, sir. But you probably knew that while you were looking at my badge."

Ari grinned. "Better make sure you get that back. My dad has a tendency to lose things."

"Then I'm glad he didn't take my gun." The detective's face turned serious. "Um, the reason I came, Ari, is because certain . . .aspects of a case I'm working on . . .sort of involve you. Someone you've recently had the . . . pleasure . . . of talking to."

"You mean Terry Scranton."

"The same. I actually knew of Miss Scranton long before I actually made her acquaintance." Jones reached into one of the files and produced the photo of her and Nesto arguing in front of the club house. "The man our mutual friend is with," the detective continued, is one Ernesto Gonzaga, leader of the Demon Heads Motorcycle Club. He's also one of the biggest drug pushers in the tri-state area, operating a small empire from that shithole of a club house you see in the background."

"What's Terry to him?"

"Right now, I would assume they're on the outs. What she was was one of his couriers, taking illegal contraband from Charles Town, West Virginia to Washington, DC. As a matter of fact, we believe Terry was on her way back from a drop-off when she literally ran into you."

Ari's stomach suddenly felt a bit queasy. "Was there anything on her?" he asked.

"Nothing that would hold up in court. Some transporting materials like a sealed tube in her gas tank, ideal for transporting cocaine, or more likely, crystal meth. But we found no residue or anything in it, and, last time I checked, it's not exactly illegal to carry a plastic tube in your tank. No money on her, either. No, whatever else this lady is, she's one clever bitch."

"'Whatever else?'"

"Mmm?"

"You said, 'whatever else' she is. I'm guessing there's more to come."

Jones gave Ari a tight smile. "That there is, son. A lot more. Enough to concern me for your safety and to make this trip."

He dug into the file and brought out a small, official looking document. "What's this?" Ari asked as he took it.

"I like starting at the beginning, so that's where we're gonna go," Jones replied. "The very beginning. That's Ms. Terry Scranton's birth certificate."

So it was. Ari skimmed it, reading the **Wheeling Memorial Hospital** title at the top, followed by a less bold *Certificate of Birth* underneath. He had just enough time to view his antagonist's full name (Terrencia Ann Scranton) and marvel that her birthday was less than a month after Rachel's when Jones's voice cut through his thoughts. "Pretty good forgery, huh?"

Ari looked up. "Forgery?"

"Yes sir! A gen-yoo-ine, one-hundred per cent, all-American forged document. Even the seal looks real. But I called Wheeling Memorial-there really is a hospital by that name, in western West Virginia-and they have no accompanying original, or even a record of Ms. Scranton being born there. Not in 1965, or any other time."

"Then what-? Who-?"

"Dunno. At least, not for sure. I have some suspicions, but I don't wanna get ahead of myself. The long and the short of it is, we've got a mystery about our friend from the very beginning. When, where, or even *how*, was she born, and why is someone going to the trouble to make that document, in order to cover up those facts?"

Jones shook his head. "But let's not get off track, shall we? Let's jump ahead a few years. The Scranton clan was pretty well-known around that podunk little hometown of theirs. The family patriarch, Conroy Wayne Scranton, was a notorious drunk, a hell-raiser even before the law gave him a choice between jail-time or the military. This was right around when that national tragedy known as Vietnam began heating up."

"And her mom?"

Jones frowned to himself as he perused the file. "Nothing special about her, unfortunately. Name was Roberta Jean Prather. Clean record, no trouble with the law. Probably one of those women, and there was a lot of them at this time, and not just in rural areas, whose greatest ambition in life was to marry the first guy she dated for more than a month in high school and have kids. She pretty much stays under the radar until Terry turned twelve. Then she hits it in a big way."

"How?"

Jones handed him two pages from the file. "Read the top on first, then go on to the next underneath."

Ari did as he was told. The former sheet was a document of Conroy Scranton's induction record, dated July 16, 1967. He noted the man's date of birth (in 1940, like his own parents) that his marital status (married), number of children-

Ari raised his eyebrows. The check mark in the box was right next to the "None" option. He looked again at the date of the document. 1967. And Terry's birth certificate said-

"You've found it, haven't you?" Jones said softly. "If Terry's birth certificate says she was born in 1965, why does her father's induction record of 1967 list him as having no kids?"

"This is what lead you to believe her certificate was phony?"

Jones nodded. "Now, look at the other sheet."

This proved to be Scranton's discharge papers. Ari wasn't surprised to see it was a dishonorable discharge; what *was* shocking (and not a little nauseating) was the circumstances. Ari paled as he read the writing at the bottom of the page.

195

The doctors' findings aside, the slaughter of children during wartime is always reprehensible. It is my personal opinion that Cpl. Conroy Scranton should be sentenced to the maximum penalty of life imprisonment in Fort Levenworth for his crimes, but given the current popular dissatisfaction with the Vietnam operation, making this case public would only serve to fan the flames already licking a potential tinder-box. It is hereby requested that Cpl. Scranton be dishonorably discharged from the United States Army and sent back to whatever rock he crawled out from under.

And, typed neatly under a scrawled signature: *Capt. David Malcolm, 33rd Infantry.*

"My God," Ari said. "What the . . .what the fuck did he do?"

"In a nutshell . . .when his unit secured a certain village, he was ordered to take all the children they had found during the raid and lead them somewhere safe. He took them out of sight and then started slaughtering them wholesale."

"Oh . . . Christ!" "Fourteen kids were killed altogether. The youngest was a toddler of two, the oldest eight. He wouldn't stop firing his M-16 into them until a private had the decency to cold-cock him upside the head with the butt of his rifle."

"But why? What the hell possessed him to-"

"When they questioned him afterwards, he said he was 'killing commies before they had a chance to grow'."

Ari let the paper fall to the floor. "So why the hell . . .why the hell didn't they lock the bastard up?"

"You read it yourself. Bad public opinion. The tide was turning against the war. The returning vets were already being called 'baby killers'. How would it have looked if they actually *had* one?"

"So they just let him go?"

"The army docs deemed him insane. Cracked under battle stress. All the military wanted was for this to go away as quickly and quietly as possible, even if it meant letting Conroy Scranton slither away." Jones picked the paper off the floor and placed it back in the file. "Now let's flash forward a few years. Somehow, Terry comes on the scene as Conroy and Bobbie Jean's daughter. In 1968, we have a birth that actually does look legit, that of Terry's younger brother, Blake. So now it's the four of them, sitting out on a small, ramshackle farmhouse in a little shithole town called Cooper's Gulch. Or I should say the three of them, maybe. Ol' Conroy was back to his old tricks, public drunkenness, vagrancy, minor assaults. Yep, he was a constant, if minor nuisance to the local sheriff's department. His employment history's as spotty as his record. Never held down a job more than year. The only reason the family didn't starve to death was because of Bobbie Jean's stint as a waitress at a local diner. But all good things come to an end, eventually."

"What happened?"

The detective's face was stone. "What do you *think* happened?"

A pit of sickness formed in Ari's stomach, like someone had reached up and given his nuts a healthy twist. "She died" Ari responded hollowly.

"Yes," Jones said, then began reading aloud from a page in the file-of-horrors. "At approximately 10:45 pm on July 16th, 1977, a 911 call came in. Whoever dialed it didn't say anything, but the operator on the other end heard plenty of screaming and sounds like, her words, 'somebody was throwing heavy pots and pans'. After tracing the call to, surprise!, the Scranton's happy little hovel, the operator called dispatch. Two hours later, the local cops finally got around to answering the call and paying a visit."

"God! Why so long?"

Jones smiled wanly. "You ever listen to Public Enemy, son?"

"The rap group?"

"Yeah. My son likes them."

"No, rap isn't really my thing."

"Mine neither. But they have this one song called '911 Is A Joke', about how the authorities are reluctant to pursue calls coming in from the ghetto. It looks like this here's the rural white-trash version of that."

"So what happened then?"

"The two sheriff's deputies found Conroy Scranton passed out drunk on the lawn. They tried to roust him, but ended up carrying him to the house. That's when they noticed the blood on him. They opened the front door, and I quote, 'two of the dirtiest-looking, skinniest ragamuffins popped out the door, bawling their heads off. The oldest, a girl of about twelve, kept screaming the foulest language and tried to fight [them]. The boy, on the other hand, just collapsed in a pile on the front lawn and kept saying something about his mama. Upon closer inspection of the premises, a woman was found in the basement, dead upon arrival."

"Oh, man."

"'The woman, later identified as Roberta Jean Scranton, looked [as though] she had suffered a terrible beating, but the official cause of death was surmised to be a broken neck, experienced when she tumbled down the basement stairs."

"I'll bet she had help."

"Oh, you're probably right, Ari. But that's not how the authorities saw it."

Ari's jaw dropped open. "Wha-? You're kidding!"

"Wish I was. The coroner officially declared it a 'death by misadventure', and the judge in the case officially placed Terry and Blake back in the loving arms of their father."

"But that's outrageous! How could they?"

"It was a different time, son. A different place, too. Nobody really wanted to think a man would murder his wife even after years of abuse. And besides, as the feminists are wont to say, and with some justification: back then, it wasn't called 'wife-beating'; it was called *life*. And even more so in a backwoods area where everyone was expected to mind their own business and keep themselves to themselves." Ari slumped back down in his chair; he suspected the detective was just getting started. "You all right, Ari?" Jones inquired.

"Yeah . . . I just . . ."

Jones placed a comforting hand on the younger man's shoulder. "I know, son," he said softly. "It can be pretty damn overwhelming. No need to be ashamed. Nearly twenty-five years working in Vice, I still get the shakes, sometimes. And this is definitely one of those times. But, bear with me, huh? Some of this stuff I think you need to hear. You need to know what you're dealing with." Ari managed a weak smile. "I'll be okay, Detective Jones."

"Barney, please. This is supposed to be an 'informal chat', so I don't see why we can't use our first names, y'know?"

"Barney, then."

"Good."

"It's just that . . . well. . .you think it would be obvious to everyone involved what the hell happened, but everyone just bought into it."

"Maybe it was, maybe it wasn't. Couldn't tell you. I wasn't there. But realize something else, too. This wasn't the cream of society we're talkin' about here. Nope, this was a bunch of hicks from Appalachia, and if they killed each other off, who really the fuck cared? As long as it wasn't too obvious. Then the paperwork might actually get messy."

"Small town values," Ari muttered.

Jones let out a cynical bark of a laugh. "Yeah, you could say that. More like goddamn William Fucking Faulkner than Mark Fucking Twain. Well, early Twain, before life smacked him around a bit."

"Huck Finn never rode a motorcycle. Or wrecked people's cars, for that matter."

"No, he didn't, did he? Nor did he stab a classmate in the ass with a pencil, either."

Ari winced. "Terry did that?"

"Sure did. It's what got her thrown out of school. Stabbed a classmate right in his buttocks with a pencil during an altercation. She was lucky the kid's parents didn't file assault charges. Still, this little altercation did count against her when she committed her next crime."

Ari made a face. "Which was?"

"Oh, just a simple 'breaking and entering'. But, in light of her record and everything, it was the proverbial straw on the camel's back. Never mind that she was breaking into a grocery store because, in her words, she was 'trying to get something for her and her brother to eat'."

"Jesus."

"Yeah, got the report from Social Services right here. Subjects, a girl, 14, and a boy, 10, are severely malnourished. Both children also show signs of sexual abuse. Girl has considerable vaginal tearing, and the boy's anal cavity is extremely dilated. When questioned, both children admit to being repeatedly raped by their father."

"Oh, dear God."

"He sure as hell wasn't in attendance there, Ari. We have two kids, half-starved, repeatedly raped by their drunk of a father who in all likelihood also murdered their mother. And there, my friend, is a recipe for disaster straight out of a fuckin' cookbook."

"So what the hell did Social Services finally do with them? Please tell me they finally got off their asses and got involved."

"Well, they had to this time, didn't they? Couldn't have a couple of hick kids victimizing decent citizens by breaking into stores for something to eat now, could they? Still, at least they got it half-right."

"What do you mean?"

"Placed Blake in a foster home. By all accounts, they were good people, too. And once Blake had a stable environment, it looks as though he thrived. Honors student, no brushes with the law. He, at least, achieved a measure of happiness."

"But not Terry."

Jones sighed a sigh that made Ari tired just to hear it. "No. Not Terry. Maybe she could have, with the right sort of help, gone on to become a productive citizen. But it didn't turn out that way. No, sir. The judge involved decided it would be best if our Miss Terry pay through the nose for her crimes."

Jones pulled out a paper from the file and began to read. "'It is the opinion of this court that, given the defendant's age and previous record, that the interests of the State of West Virginia should be best served by placing her in a reformatory for no less a time than when she reaches the age of eighteen.'"

"So, for a breaking and entering charge, she gets sent to a reformatory? For trying to get food for her and her brother? For just trying to survive?"

"That's right. In other words, let's send Terry to jail, do not pass Go, do not collect $200. But hey, her brother's doing okay now. Got a wife and kid in Charles Town. Works in a bank. From what I can tell, they only have very little contact these days. Like when Terry needs to make bail."

"Man, no wonder she's pissed."

The detective looked gravely at the young man before him. "Oh, she's more than just pissed, Ari. Don't minimize what she is by just calling her 'pissed'. This woman's got a hard-on for the world and is not particularly choosy about whom she fucks with it. And you'd best remember that."

Jones took out a photo, and handed it over after studying it for a moment. "Like this shining example of humanity, for instance," he remarked.

The photo was a mug shot, with a full front and side profile of a young African-American woman with big, bulging features that seemed disproportionally large for the face that contained them. The eyes, however, were small yet piercing, glaring back at the viewer in an effort to intimidate. Worst of all was the small smile that played about the thick, rubbery lips. *All this is a big fucking joke*, the smile seemed to say. *But I'm the only motherfucker cool enough to get it.*

"Meet Tamara Brown," Jones said. "Locked up on an assault charge at fifteen. More like assault with intent to kill. She slammed a girl's head into a locker at school, then proceeded to repeatedly slam the locker door shut on her head. The girl is now a vegetable."

"Jesus."

"Tammy's explanation? 'The bitch was gettin' uppity'. Well, she certainly showed her, didn't she? Got her a trip to the reformatory. Once again, do not pass Go, etcetera."

"I'm guessing she didn't exactly get 'reformed' there."

Jones snorted. "Not likely. That's the thing about 'reformatories'. Precious few actually get 'reformed' there. At least eighty per-cent of the hard-cases I've busted got their start there. Oh, there are a few success stories; kids 'scared straight' from the experience. But, more likely than not, you'll find either the kids use the place as a finishing school for a career in crime, making contacts and whatnot, or they've turned so mean and hard from the time there that prison is the *only* place they'll belong."

"And Tammy?"

The detective shook his head. "She thrived there. Had her own little gang. They called themselves 'The Nigga Bitches'. From what I can gather from the guards and several members of the administration, she virtually ruled the reformatory. Everyone was scared shitless of her. Hell, at six feet, two-hundred pounds, you would be too."

"So how does this involve Terry? She get on Tammy's bad side?"

Jones smiled grimly. "That would be assuming Tammy had a good one to begin with, but yeah. They had a run-in with each other. Big time. I guess it was inevitable, if you think about it.

An already-racist redneck like Terry verses the biggest, blackest bitch on the block? The only surprise for me was that the officials *didn't* see this one coming."

Jones took back the photo from Ari and pulled out another sheet. "This is the transcript/write-up from the incident that started it all. I interviewed the monitor personally, too. It happened about six weeks after Terry first joined their happy little extended family. Apparently, our Terry was making quite a name for herself in the joint as a real hard case. The other girls gave her a pretty wide berth, and Tammy didn't like that."

"Only room for one, huh?"

"Right. Tammy didn't like the fact that there was now competition in the intimidation sweepstakes. Even worse, the newcomer didn't seemed to be in the least bit frightened of her, Tammy. Now *that* was unacceptable. And somebody needed to be taught what's what."

Jones started reading from the page. "This is from the lunch monitor, Lynn Compton: 'It was time for the midday meal. The cafeteria was packed. Most of the girls sat in their usual spots, as there was no assigned seating.' I guess they mean 'usual' in the sense of they sat by clique, or gang."

"Sort of like high school, but with guards."

Jones chuckled. "Yeah, sorta like that. 'Miss Scranton was carrying a tray of food and deciding where to sit. I couldn't help but notice, on earlier occasions, that wherever Miss Scranton sat, the table would soon be vacated. It made me feel sorry for her, but she didn't seem to mind, even seemed to prefer it that way'."

"'On this occasion, Miss Scranton passed by the table occupied by Tamara Brown and her group of followers. I assume it was Tammy that tripped her; I actually did not witness the confrontation. All I know is that I suddenly heard a loud clatter, and turned to see Miss Scranton pitched forward face-first into her tray of food.'"

Ari grimaced inwardly. How many times had he seen that little scenario play out in high school? *Thank Christ it never happened to me,* Ari thought. *That was one indignity I was spared.*

"'Predictably, the entire room burst into laughter'," Jones continued, giving voice to Ari's thoughts. "'I went to help Miss Scranton up, and to admonish Miss Brown, but Tammy's group blocked my way. I ordered them to stand down, but they did not listen. I blew my whistle to get more monitors on deck to help defuse the situation, but it was not in time to prevent what happened next.'"

"'I saw Miss Brown standing over Miss Scranton. She was speaking in a high-pitched, babyish voice. She said, "Awwwww. Did the little white girl have herself a *ass-i-dent?"* Miss Scranton said nothing, just remained hunched over her tray. I yelled at Miss Brown to step away from her, to back off, but she ignored me.'"

"'Then, she started singing. Singing to the tune of that famous song from the musical *Evita.* I heard her sing: *Don't cry, little white girl,* then BAM! I didn't even see it, it was so fast! And the next thing I know, Tammy's knocked down and Terry's standing over her, holding her tray.'"

"Holy shit!" Ari exclaimed, laughing in spite of himself.

"'The whole cafeteria fell silent then,'" the detective continued to read. "'Dead silent. Like somebody just set off a bomb. In a way, I guess someone had. But just then, more guards had appeared on the floor to assist me, just in time to get in front of Tammy, who had just then picked herself up off the floor. I saw blood all smeared down her face, streaming out her nose. Terry had really clocked her a good one.'"

"'I heard Tammy snarl out to Terry, "I'm gonna kick yer little honky bitch ass for that, you shit-kicker cunt."

"'Terry, bless her heart, didn't back down an inch. She shot back, "Bring it on, you goddamn big-lipped nigger, motherfuckin', spearchuckin' *cooze!!*"'"

"'The whole place just exploded after that. Big time. On one hand you had Tammy and her group jumping up, trying to get at Terry, and on the other hand you had Terry, giving it back to them all she was worth. It took a whole dozen of us to pull them apart. Both Tammy and Terry were then sent into solitary detention. I heard that Tammy, however, first went to the infirmary to have her nose set, as it was broken.'"

Jones stopped reading and looked at Ari. There was a moment of silence.

"Go, Terry," the younger man blurted out.

Jones laughed. "Yeah, if nuthin' else, the girl had spunk, didn't she? But also, as you can imagine, she was in a world of trouble. She was Number One with a bullet, as far as the Nigga Bitches were concerned. Took only a month after their little lunch date before they finally caught up her. That night, Terry didn't show up for head count." Jones replaced one page in the file and pulled out another. "They started a search. An hour later, they found her."

Jones paused. "Or what was still left of her. They found her in the showers, stark naked., lying semi-conscious on the floor. The attending doc said it was quite possibly the worst beating he had ever seen where the patient was still alive."

"What . . .what did they do to her?"

Jones read from the page. "'Patient has a broken nose and jaw, eyes swollen shut, three cracked ribs, one broken arm, both legs, and enough bruising on torso to suggest internal injury.'"

"Holy Christ."

"Yeah, but that wasn't the worst."

The detective fell silent, his gaze suddenly distant. Ari almost spoke after an uncomfortable silence to prompt the older man, when out of nowhere came a surprise request. "Ari, do you mind if I smoke?"

Ari blinked. The force of Jones gaze as it focused on him was enough to convince him of the seriousness of the question. "Sure," he replied. "Just let me open a window. My parents are pretty militant about not smoking around here."

"What they don't know won't hurt them. Trust me."

Can you say the same for me? Ari wanted to ask, but didn't. Instead, he rose from his chair and went to the window at the far end of his room.

The window was stubborn; it took Ari several lurches before he managed to jack it up all the way. Then he realized why it was so difficult. *It's not the window, it's me,* he thought as he examined his shaking hands. *Maybe I need to be the one who asks for a smoke break.*

By the time Ari reseated himself, the detective was puffing greedily on a large, brown cigar. A measure of calm passed onto the older man's face as he surrounded it with cigar smoke. "Thanks," Jones said. "Let me know if it bothers you. It's a nasty habit, I know. Maybe I'll give it up when I retire."

Ari said nothing, just offered a weak smile. "So, yeah," Jones continued. "Terry was beaten pretty bad. She was lying in a pool of blood, which confused the docs, because there didn't appear to be any stab wounds as such on her. Then they took a closer look." Jones rubbed his eyes and sighed heavily. "Do you read the news, Ari?"

Ari shrugged at this seeming non-sequitur. "Uh, when I get the chance, Detective Jones. When I have the time."

"Unfortunately, I don't have that luxury. Part of my job requires it. Never know when some little 'factoid' might have bearing on some present, past, or future case. Anyway, I've been looking at the world news lately. Particularly what's been going on in Africa. There's a certain . .practice going on out there that the U.N. has been trying to call attention to. To make it stop."

"What is it?

"In certain backwaters out there, this practice, or ritual, or custom . . .Hell, I don't know what to call it other than an abomination. When females in these villages come of age, right around when puberty hits, the sick bastards mutilate their genitals.

"What?!"

"The women of the village hold the girl down while a village elder, some fuckin' old turd with a knife, slices off her clitoris and sews shut her vagina."

"For God's sake, why?!"

"To make her a better prospect for marriage. Why else?"

"But that's-!"

And then Ari got it; he made the final, horrible connection in his mind. "You mean that-," he began.

"Yeah, that what those sadistic cunts did to Terry. They pinned her down and sliced her clit off with a home-made knife. That's where all the blood was coming from."

Ari clearly saw spots in front of his eyes. But the detective wasn't done yet. "Then, to top it off, they heated up a curling iron . . .and stuffed it up her snatch. Gave her second degree burns on her vaginal walls so bad they had keep her under sedation for three days straight because otherwise, she'd be screaming. And to top it off, they caused so much damage that Terry had to have an emergency hysterectomy. They fucked her over ten ways to sundown."

Jones started massaging his temples again, perhaps in an effort to physically wipe away the horrors in his mind's eye. "Y'know, Ari. I'm a black man, and I make no apologies for that. And I've also been called a 'nigger' more times than I can count. Including by Miss Terry. But when I saw and read what those fucking animals did to her, I can understand a little bit why. Because I was ashamed to be the same race as those girls. Make no mistake: Tammy was pure evil, and I have to say she deserved what she had coming to her."

Jones pulled his hands away from his face and regarded the young man before him. "But know something else, too: I can maybe understand, but I don't condone it, either. Ari, are you okay? Christ, boy! You're absolutely green!"

No shit, Sherlock, Ari wanted to say, but dared not. Not because he was afraid to speak because of any words he might say, but because he was afraid his voice might be accompanied by something more tangible. He swallowed hard, feeling the clump of food that had actually settled in his esophagus relocate itself into the stomach where it belonged. "I'm okay, Detective Jones," he finally answered. "Really. Go on. You were saying?"

"Maybe we better stop."

"No!" Ari exclaimed, much louder than he intended. "I'm alright. Really. And I think I need to hear this."

"Okay," Jones responded slowly, the uncertainty stamped on his face like a brand. "But what I've got next won't exactly ease your mind."

Why am I not surprised? Ari said to himself. But something also told him that it was important for him to take in every drop of this particular medicine, even if it was as bitter as rotten lemons. He gave Jones another smile, a stronger one this time, and bore down on the queasy feeling in his gut. "I'm okay," he said out loud.

Jones nodded, still viewing his young charge with concern. "Well," he said. "As fucked up as Terry was, she didn't die. Wouldn't talk, neither. The guards and the headmaster questioned her for hours, but she wouldn't budge. I guess she had other plans cooking up in her devious little mind. Or what was still left of it, after that brutal fucking over. I've often wondered what she thought, how she decided on her plan of attack back there in the infirmary, when the lights went out and she lay alone in the dark with only her thoughts for company. I think that's when she really lost it, when she snapped, deciding it was only she who could take the appropriate steps to see that Tammy was punished. In the way that she wanted. And it was definitely the Nigga Bitches work, no doubt about that. Some of Tammy's group had injuries of their own. Some bad bruises, a sprung rib, a couple of jammed fingers. She fought hard, our Terry did. But on Tammy? Not a scratch. Apparently, she wasn't *that* stupid. I figure she sent her Bitches in first, to soften her up. And then, when the danger was over and the big, bad white girl was subdued, Tammy took her pound of flesh. So to speak."

"None of the people at the reformatory tried to make them talk?"

"Sure. And they all said that their injuries were the result of some horseplay, that they all were just 'wrestling around' when they got hurt. All the girls vouched for each other, so they had airtight alibis. Said they were nowhere near Terry when she had her 'accident'. That's a direct quote, too. They called it an 'accident".

"Jesus."

"Nope, not hardly. So with no one coming forward and everyone having alibis, the reformatory's administration decided to drop it. Wash their hands of the whole thing."

"Holy shit."

"Yeah, that's more like it. But save your tears, m'man. Don't forget who the Bitches were dealing with."

"Terry".

"Yes, indeed. The road back for her was pretty hard; she was in the hospital for several months, crawling her way back into health. And when she was placed back in the general population nearly six months later, still she waited. Kept more to herself than ever before, too. However, she did work out a lot in the gym when she got out. Told the guards it was part of her physical therapy. She also picked up quite a skill. It was part of the rehabilitation process that the girls all learned themselves a trade, whether it was home economics, or accountancy, or taxidermy, for that matter. Terry went the untraditional route, as you might imagine. She turned herself into quite the mechanic."

"Mechanic? You mean like auto shop?"

"Exactly. While all the other girls were learning to be the perfect secretary, our Miss Terry decided to be the next Mr. Goodwrench. Or *Miss* Goodwrench, as it were." Jones glanced at another page in the file. "She was good, too," he remarked. "The teacher, Mr. Goode, said he was the best student he ever had, male or female."

A dark cloud crossed the detective's face. "That recommendation came in handy after what happened next. In hindsight, it was pretty obvious. Terry bided her time, working out like a demon in the gym. The Bitches pretty much left her alone after that torture session in the showers. Didn't want to make it too obvious, lest the authorities re-open the case. Besides, Terry was now properly broken. When the Bitches came through, she scurried out of the way like the rest of them. There was no reason at all for them feel she was a danger to them."

Jones pulled a photo from the file, grimaced, then handed it over. "Until this happened," he replied.

It was unspeakable.

Ari thought back to high school, when he had a friendly acquaintance whose hobby was true crime stories. One day, he was showing Ari some photos taken during the infamous Jack the Ripper killings from Victorian England. Ari had done all right until shown the last one (*Her name was Mary Kelly*, Ari thought. *That's been burned into my mind.*) "Ripped" was a far from adequate description of what had been done to her. "Butchered", "Torn to shreds", were far better. Body parts were strewn about in such a manner to make the remains barely recognizable as human. "Jesus Christ, Ari," the kid, named Howard, had said at the time. "The son of a bitch must've been absolutely *insane* to do all that. Imagine what the police at the time must've thought. They weren't anywhere near as used to violence as today. They must've been hysterical, or even fucking catatonic, by the time they got home that night."

Examining the picture at hand, Ari now had a pretty good idea of how those Bobbies of the nineteenth century felt. From the image of clean tile on the outskirts of the photo, Ari could guess that it was taken in a bathroom area. The next instant, he knew exactly where it was: the same shower area where Terry had been brutalized the year before.

The body that was the photo's subject could be still discerned as human, but it took some effort. The face (what was left of it) stared upward into oblivion. No more would it carry the smirk on it that laughed at the world for being so uncool. Blood was everywhere, the result of many separate stab wounds that screamed like hell-mouths stuck for eternity in their private inferno. The body seemed to have been completely disemboweled, with chunks of organs standing off to the sidelines like witnesses to the horror before it.

Worst of all were the long bloody trails that emanated from the corpse's abdomen. *That isn't what I think it is*, Ari's mind raced. *Please don't tell me that is what I think it is.*

"Meet the ex-Tamara Brown, ex-leader of the Nigga Bitches, ex-post facto," Jones intoned. "Terry did get her's back. In spades, so to speak."

"What . . .what happened?," Ari asked, his gorge re-rising.

"Ol' Tammy had a month to go before she turned eighteen and was released upon a unsuspecting world. Terry knew the time had to be soon. Tammy had complained of feeling sick to her stomach during gym, and told the teacher she was going to the bathroom. She got the go ahead, but when she didn't come out after twenty minutes, the teacher went in. This is what she found. She turned in her resignation the same day."

"Twenty minutes!? Terry did . . .all that . . in *twenty minutes?*"

"It would've had to have been even less, because they found no sign of the assailant. Somehow, Terry managed to get in, do Tammy, then get out again with nobody seeing her. The punch line? Nobody heard a fucking thing. And the total damage? The coroner estimated that from the beating alone Tammy would've been dead. Half the bones in her body were broken, head was caved in, they counted over fifty separate stab wounds done with a home-made knife. But that wasn't what ultimately killed her."

Jones started massaging his temples again. "Tammy was sliced open, from the base of her sternum to the pelvic area. The killer strangled her to death with her own intestines."

Ari rose, along with the bile in his throat. This was no false alarm; he really felt he was going to puke. He bolted from his room, ignoring the sound of Jones saying his name behind him.

He plunged into the bathroom and was one millisecond late to get the lid open on the toilet before his digestive system exploded, spewing for his breakfast, and probably a good portion of the previous night's dinner, as well.

When the last retch in his body subsided, he placed his head against the cool edge of the commode. He felt a warm hand press upon his temple. Slowly drowning out the voice inside his head was the voice of Jones, a soothing voice, an apologetic one that brought him back to a desperately needed center.

Then the moment was broken as a much more shrill voice pierced the metal gauze in his head. "Detective!" it cried. "What the hell did you do to my kid?"

Good ol' Dad, Ari thought sourly. *Always knows the right thing to say at the right time.*

Before the detective had a chance to speak, Ari broke in out loud. "It's all right, Dad," he said. "Just feeling a little sick, is all."

Mr. Sussman loomed in the doorway, adding to the claustrophobia. "Look here, Jones," he continued. "I've taken down your badge number. You'll be lucky if I don't sue the entire department!"

"Dad, that's enough! I told you everything's okay."

"And I'll name you personally, Jones!" Mr. Sussman went on. "You'll be lucky if they still let you walk a beat-!"

Ari forced himself between Jones and his father, placing his face up to the latter's to make sure he was heard this time. "Goddamnit, Dad! *Get out!!*"

Mr. Sussman's jaw snapped shut in mid-threat. In shock, he backed away from his son, then turned and stalked down the hall. "Sorry about that, Detective," Ari continued. "My dad has a tendency to be a bit . . .overbearing."

"Think nothing of it. I've been snarled at by leaders of drug cartels. On the whole, I'd give your father a five."

"On the Richter scale?"

Jones smiled. "Yeah, on that."

Back in Ari's room, the two replaced themselves into their seats. "Sorry about my puking," Ari said. "I guess it was . . .a little much."

Jones waved it away. "Think nothing of it. I should probably be the one to apologize. I'm so used to dealing with other cops, maybe I'm not as sensitive to civilians as I should be. But there's nothing to be ashamed of. I've got over twenty years in, and some of this shit still took my breath away."

"So where were we?"

Jones leaned over to pick up the photo of Tammy Brown's corpse, glanced at it, then placed it back into the file. "When Tammy turned up dead," he said, "The administration had a pretty good idea on who to look at first. Add to that the fact that no one could vouch for Terry's whereabouts during the time in question, and you could pretty much gather that the authorities felt they had enough to make an arrest. And arrest they did. Terry was put in the hole just on suspicion."

"Did they find anything?"

"Nope. But after that butchering that went down, you can understand them wanting to make the necessary precautions. They didn't wanna have to clean any more girls up off the bathroom floor."

Jones pulled another paper out of his seemingly endless file. "But, y'know, a funny thing happened," he said. "With Tammy dead, the Nigga Bitches kinda broke rank. Well, one of them did, anyway. One of Tammy's friends, a girl by the name of Alisha Green, came forward. She gave it all up; the whole story of what they did to Terry the year before. This was how they knew that while the other Bitches held her down, good ole Tammy performed the dirty deeds. First the clitorectomy, then the rape with the hot curling iron. She really sang like a bird, too. Named the names of all the girls involved."

"So why'd she talk? Wouldn't that get her in trouble?"

Jones gave a chuckle without amusement. "In her own words: 'Don't let that crazy honky bitch get near me!'"

"Oh."

"Well, that's all they needed. With Miss Green's testimony, the powers that be charged Terrencia Ann Scranton with Murder One. She was placed in lock down at a real prison to await trial. Alisha was also placed in solitary for her own protection while the authorities rounded up the rest of the Nigga Bitches for the initial assault that started this whole sorry mess."

Jones put the page back into the file and pulled out another photo. "Now, here's where things get real interesting, Ari. Since Terry couldn't afford a lawyer, the state supplied her with one. And this is when Terry, for the first time in her miserable, fucked up life, caught herself a break. A big one. The state assigned her Rusty Darrow."

The photo Jones passed Ari was that of a handsome woman with copper colored hair just beginning to show some grey. It was obviously not a posed photo; the subject seemed to be caught in mid-speech, holding a finger in the air while looking of to her left. "Rusty is one of the best lawyers in the whole of West Virginia. I admit that's sort of like being the best quarterback in Alaska, but-" "Wait a sec. Rusty Darrow?"

"Yeah."

"As in *Clara* Darrow?"

"Right. That's her real name."

"Detective Jones . . .Barney. . .This is the same woman who's suing me on Terry's behalf."

"Not surprised. Two of them are as thick as thieves, so to speak. Kind of surprised she'd bring a suit against you personally. Individual lawsuits aren't really her thing. She likes taking on the big boys, entire corporations, where the pay outs are more lucrative. You remember the coal miners strike a while back, the one about black lung disease? That was Rusty. Bled the coal companies to the tune of fifty mil for the miners. Set up medical benefits for them and the families. She was also instrumental in negotiating a settlement for an entire town whose water system got all fucked up thanks to industrial waste. That was last year."

"Wow. So why is she after me and my dad? We don't exactly have that kind of money."

"For Terry, of course. She's bent over backwards for that girl from the start. But maybe this explains why."

Jones passed him another page. "These are notes I've taken from interviews I've read, plus some other background digging I've done. Clara Ann Darrow, born in 1945 in Baton Rogue, Louisiana. Left home at fifteen to escape an abusive father and drunken mother. Made her way westward by hanging with a splinter group of the Hell's Angels. Eventually she got to San Francisco just in time for the Summer of Love."

"The what?"

"Oh, c'mon, Ari. You know how old you just made me feel?"

"Sorry."

"Anyway, it was 1967. That was also, allegedly, the when and where of her being raped. Don't it sound familiar? I checked with the Frisco police and they have nothing officially on record for her. However, San Francisco General Hospital does have a record for treating a Clara Darrow in the Summer of '67 for injuries sustained during what appeared to be a very bad beating. The statement she gave the attending nurse was that she was sexually assaulted as well, but apparently she split before anyone could check into it."

"Did the hospital call the police?"

Jones nodded. "But by the time they got there, she was long gone. The docs patched her up as best they could, gave her a shot of penicillin in case of V.D. and then she slipped off into the night."

"But why?"

Jones shrugged. "It was a different time. Maybe she was too ashamed. This was also back when a raped woman had to prove her own innocence to the police before they did anything. Maybe she just didn't think it was worth the hassle. A little hippie girl on the road with some bikers? How much sympathy do think the cops at that time would've had for her? Anyway, Ms. Darrow virtually disappeared from the world for a about a year. Then she resurfaces as student in a GED class in Wheeling, West Virginia. She aces that, then goes right into undergraduate work at the University of West Virginia, as pre-law. Got herself a scholarship and everything. Supported herself as a waitress in the meantime, so she gets, as she put it in one interview, 'an education in people'. She gets her degree, gets accepted at law school, passes the bar on the first try, and the rest, as they say, is history."

"How did she meet Terry?"

"She applied for some pro bono work, and Terry lands with both feet on her desktop. And now the rest is mystery. Because why the hell would a prominent attorney be involved with a mess like Terry? I mean, other than the obvious reasons. When she got Terry's story, she probably couldn't help but identify. The parallels are too clear; shitty parents, the rape, etcetera. But since then? I would've thought Rusty

214

would know when to cut bait. Instead she's pulled Terry's bacon out of the fry so many times I'm surprised she isn't darker than she is."

"So, she got Terry off on the Tammy thing?"

"And then some. I talked to some of her colleagues, and they said she was a woman possessed. Not only did she provide defense, she also slapped a lawsuit on the reformatory for not protecting her from Tammy in the first place. She even went after the judge who sentenced Terry to that hell-hole. Tried to get him disbarred and off the bench. She's nothing if not thorough. But I have to admit she outdid herself here. This was no legal maneuvering; this was a fucking scorched earth policy."

Jones glanced at one of the documents. "From one of the interviews I did on the phone to a guard who was on duty when Terry first met with Rusty. He wasn't allowed to listen to the actual conversation. But he couldn't help but notice the reactions. Said Rusty looked highly agitated after about twenty minutes of talking with Terry. And that by the end of the interview, Rusty needed to stop by the ladies' room. Nothing odd about that in itself, except that she was in there for ten minutes, bawling her head off. But why? Setting aside the 'identification with' factor, why continue with her? It just doesn't add up."

"Is Rusty married? Have a boyfriend?"

"No," Jones responded a little too quickly. "I checked. She doesn't seem to have ever had a steady relationship with any man."

"Do you think she and Terry . . .well . . ."

"No!" Jones said sharply. "Uh, no. I don't think she and Terry are having any sort of lesbian relationship, if that's what you're implying. No, her friends and colleagues say Rusty firmly plays for the home team. So strike that."

I think that's what you'd like to believe, Detective Jones, Ari thought, smiling to himself. *I think you have a little crush on Rusty Darrow. Maybe you two can sort this mess out over drinks or something.*

Out loud, he responded: "Maybe that's all this is, then. Maybe she just sees Terry as a younger version of herself, and wants to set her on the right track?"

"Well, she did her job right, at least in the legal sense. Punched more holes in the state's case than a jackhammer. For right or wrong, she got the grand jury to see the entire thing as circumstantial. Alisha Green, the member of the Nigga Bitches who came forward, she tore apart on the stand. Called her, and I quote 'an habitual liar who is trying to railroad my client in an attempt in rape her further'. Alisha was in tears by the time Rusty was done. No mean feat, when you consider Ms. Green was in for manslaughter."

"So did anything happen to her? Did they end her protection after that?"

"Funny you should ask that. No, there was no question of taking Alisha back to the reformatory. She'd already been made as a rat. So they sent her to the women's wing of the local penitentiary. Some deal she got, huh? Anyway, can you guess how this story ends?"

"Someone caught up with her?"

"Maybe. But what I was talking about was the *how*. Because she was found stabbed to death. With a home-made knife. In the showers."

"Terry?"

Jones shook his head. "Impossible. She was nowhere near the prison when it happened. As a matter of fact, by that time, she was free on the outside again, thanks to Rusty. But that doesn't mean she couldn't have somehow arranged it. Had some sort of in at the jail."

"Well, where did she go when she went free? Did Rusty put her up?"

"Nope. She went back home."

"With her dad? You gotta be kidding."

"No, not with her dad. He was conveniently dead by then. The old fuck was found murdered. Two days before Terry got out, the Scranton house was apparently robbed. I say 'apparently' because it was a very curious robbery. The house was trashed, everything that wasn't nailed down was taken. And the old drunk himself was found dead in his own gravel driveway. Someone first beat the hell out of him, then shoved a gun in his mouth and blew his pickled brains out. And, once again, she had herself a rock solid alibi. Nothing more rock solid than being behind bars, eh?"

"So, who cleaned up for her? Rusty?"

Jones frowned. "Don't think so. Seems a little too ruthless for her. Who knows? Maybe it just was a random breaking and entering gone wrong. Weirder things have happened, but I don't always believe in coincidence. Not in this case."

The detective dug into the file again. "And not in this case, either. Those lawsuits Rusty filed on behalf of Terry? A mixed bag, at best. She managed to get a couple grand out of the state for the hell Terry went through at the reformatory, but the lawsuit against the less-than-honorable Justice Donald Frost was stonewalled by the old boy network in the WVA courts. No way they were gonna censure and remove one of their own. The motion to have him removed for malfeasance and questionable rulings was denied. Dismissed outright. They all claimed there was a 'studied lack of evidence', despite the fact that Rusty had put together a whole string of examples of questionable rulings and practices for over twenty years."

Ari smiled grimly at the detective. "Why do I have a bad feeling about where this is going?"

"Because I'm here, and telling you all this. Yes, sure enough, not long after the dismissal of the suit against him, the not-very-Honorable Donald Frost was found dead in his car, the victim of an apparent robbery. I say apparent not because his wallet was missing, but because of the extremely gruesome nature in which the judge was actually finished off."

Ari gave a wry look. "Don't tell me someone cut his clit off?"

"Close. Official cause of death was asphyxiation from his own genitalia."

Ari paled. "You mean-"

"-that someone cut his dick off and forced it down his throat until he choked on it. He was found lying across the front seat of his car with it still in his mouth."

"And Terry?"

"Wouldn't you know? Another airtight alibi. But this is interesting. The ones who vouched for her were apparently some new friends she'd made. The new 'friends' were the Demon Heads Motorcycle Club."

Jones slumped back in his chair, giving out a tired sigh. "So, this is how I think it all fits in. Admittedly, there are a few pieces missing from the puzzle. I think Terry somehow made contact with the Demon Heads when she was in the hole. Maybe one of the club had a little sister there who was serving time. Maybe she got info out via Rusty. I don't know. Either way, she reaches out twice. Once to get at Alisha in the women's prison, then again to clean house with her old man before she comes home. After she gets out, she waits to see what Rusty can do legally with the judge. Failing that, she goes for some street justice, either paying him back herself or hiring someone in the Heads to do it. Knowing her, I'd say the former. Still, she has a debt to pay, so she goes to work for the Demons as a courier. And so it goes from there, until the day the Demon leader, Gonzaga, gets tired of her, for whatever reason. But even that has some questions built around it."

Jones pulled out the final photo from the file and handed it over to Ari. It was obviously the most recent of Terry (her arm was in a cast), but for Ari, it was also the scariest. It was a full- front shot of her, striding toward the camera carrying a shotgun in her good arm. That in itself was unnerving. But when you added to it the firm set of the jaw, the eyes that seemed to bore into the lens taking the picture, that took what was merely unnerving into downright frightening. "That's the last surveillance photo taken of her," Jones continued. "The camera placed at the Demon's Head's hideout hasn't recorded her being back since. Not long after this shot was taken of her, a group of gang members were seen going in and out of the clubhouse, including Ernesto Gonzaga, the leader. All were carrying small packages kept in plastic. We didn't make the connection until recently. Gonzaga has two brothers that he uses as bodyguards. A couple of really huge guys, Samoans, I think. Only one of them has been seen around the house since this pic was taken. And since these two brothers are always seen together, it's not hard to read between the bloody lines."

"Terry killed him."

"Bingo. And if you've been keeping count, that's *five* dead bodies that can be traced to Terry. Hell, that may be a conservative estimate. So now you know why I thought it imperative to see you. To let you know what you may be up against. I don't want you being number six, son."

By now the cold in the pit of Ari's stomach had hit absolute zero. "You really think I'm next? Jesus, Detective Jones . . . Barney. . . what the hell am I gonna do?"

Jones placed a hand on the younger man's shoulder. "Easy there, tiger. I'm not saying that anything will happen. I just noticed a disturbing trend. First comes Rusty, then comes Terry."

"But *what do I do?* My dad'll never pay her off to go away. We don't have that kind of money. And what's more, my dad treat nickels like manhole covers."

"Well, as much as it pains me to say this, your dad may be right. If you do pay her off, that's no guarantee she won't come back. Look, son, this is a police matter, no matter how you slice it. This still goes under the jurisdiction of my case, so let me handle it."

"So what're you gonna do? What can you do?"

"Maybe just enough. I think our girl needs to be reminded of what it feels like to be leaned on. By a professional. And I know just the man." Jones gathered up all the contents of his file and replaced the large rubber band around it.

"In the next couple of days," he continued. "I'll take a field trip over to West Virginia myself. I'll have the sheriff's department bring her down. Then, me and Miss Terry will have a nice little talk. Just the two of us. Alone."

"Can you do that?"

Jones gave Ari a strange smile. "Son, you'd be amazed at what the badge can do. Now, see me to the door?"

While passing through the living room, Jones retrieved his badge from the coffee table in front of Mr. Sussman, all the while ignoring the hairiest of eyeballs Ari's father was giving him.

Jones was about to climb into his car when he paused and looked up at Ari, still standing on the landing. "You seem like a good enough kid, Ari," he said. "I'm glad of it. From the address, I was expecting some rich snot who just couldn't be bothered. I'd congratulate your parents, but after meeting them, I'd bluntly say they had very little to do with how you turned out. The best parents can have the worst kids, and vice versa. All in the luck of the draw. Don't worry about a thing, okay? I'll give you a call after my little talk with Terry. In the meantime, stay cool."

The detective was about to slam his car door shut when Ari called out. "Barney?" he called out.

"Yeah?"

"Thank you."

Jones smiled as he drove off, watching the young man's form shrink and disappear in the rear view. Ari, for his part, felt the cold pit of his stomach warm a few degrees.

CHAPTER 34

The knock on the trailer's door caused Terry to wake from a dreamless sleep and flash the handy .45 automatic in its direction, a backup for the shotgun trap she had laid last night. It had just crossed her mind the Nesto and his goons would exactly knock first when the knock came again, followed by a recognizable voice. "Terry!" it called. "You in there? We need to talk to you!"

Terry relaxed, but not all the way. Without a sound, she crept from the bed to the window, poking open the blinds a fraction to see if she'd guessed right.

She had. "Goofus and Gallant", she muttered as she let the blind fall back into place. "Cooper's Gulch's Ain't Hardly Finest."

Goofus, the knocker and speaker, was Cletus Prather, a huge bear of a man that looked every inch the stereotypical small-town deputy sheriff: bright, carrotty-red hair, pale skin spattered with freckles, and as bright as a burnt-out bulb. His one saving grace as a lawman (in Terry's opinion, anyway) was his remarkable kindness. The most anybody seemed to trust him with was writing speeding tickets, and half the time he failed at that, preferring to let violators off with a warning. He just didn't have the heart, as he put it, "to part a hard-working man or woman from their hard-earned cash."

Of course, when sent out on errands with "Gallant", it was a different story. Francis Percy more than made up for his partner's lack of guile and cruelty with his own special brand. When he was on duty, no one, but *no one* got a break. People still talked of the time when he came upon a speeder rushing to get his kid to the hospital after the kid put his hand through a glass door, slicing into an artery. At first, Gallant lived up to his ironic nickname, giving the father a police escort after taking the trouble to pull him over. But when they got to the emergency room, not only did Gallant charge the man with speeding, but with reckless endangerment of a minor. The distraught father was now serving ten years in the state pen for subsequently assaulting a police officer. Naturally, Gallant saw the man prosecuted to the full extent of the law.

Such was the state of law enforcement in Cooper's Gulch.

Yeah, Terry said to herself as she slinked back over to where she'd discarded her clothes the night before. *Ol' Franny boy really likes to swing his deputized dick around. Wonder how long before-* As if on cue, a louder knock came from the door, a knock that could only come from a lifeless object, like a night stick. "Open the hell up, Terry," Gallant called out in a much louder voice. "Or I'm fixin' t' bust the goddamn door down."

Terry non-hurriedly dressed herself with a sneer on her face. *You ain't got the balls to do that, Gallant. Cuz you know I can still kick yer ass. Even after all these years.*

Her mind flashed back to the time when she and the young, pre-deputized Francis Percy were in grade school together, years before the reformatory, and when she only had the domestic form of hell to contend with. She came upon the young sadist-in-training amusing himself during recess by tying some smuggled fire crackers to the tail of a stray cat who had wandered onto school grounds. Terry, who then (as now) took a rather dim view of people who tortured animals for fun (*why the hell would anyone want to pick on something that won't hurt you unless you hurt it first?*, she thought as she pulled on her cut-off jeans), pulled the matches away from young Francis just as he was about to light the fuse.

"Wha-?" was all the little monster was able to get out before little Terry's fist connected with his mouth. Immediately, he started to cry.

"You want somethin' t' cry about, Fran-sissy?" Terry had said to the little boy sprawled out before her. She followed up with a kick to his hind parts. Now the little shit *howled*. "If I ever catch you doin' that to a cat, or *anything,* again, I'll punch you inna teeth so hard, you'll be sittin on yer food t'eat it!"

Little Francis got up and ran, bawling all the way. What happened next, only a young grade-schooler wouldn't predict. The young Gallant told the nearest teacher that 'that mean ol' Terry was trying to blow up a cat with fire crackers, but I stopped her! Then she hit me!"

Terry was sent home immediately, suspended for a week. Her father, who ordinarily didn't need much of an excuse, whaled the tar out of her. He liked to keep in practice. And because he could.

This was Terry's first major indication that the world was against her. It would far from be the last. "Keep it in yer pants, Percy!" she called out loud. "Not that you could find it!"

"I mean it, Scranton!" came the growl from the other side.

"Gimme a minute. I'm puttin' shit on!"

Now dressed, Terry grabbed the shotgun. For a brief, crazy moment after she laid her hands on it and started dismantling the makeshift trap, she saw an image of herself pointing it toward the door and giving the little prick both barrels in the chest. Fortunately, she beat back the impulse; for two reasons, as she saw it. One, she'd also have to blow away Goofus, who didn't really deserve it. And two, once you kill one cop, they'll all keep coming after you, now matter how shitty the son-of-a-bitch you killed was. And Terry wasn't ready yet to open up that particular can of worms. Yet. So instead, she stuffed all the gear (including the .45) in a side closet and went to the door unarmed. She had just placed her hand on the knob when the knock came again. "Scran-", Gallant began.

Terry threw open the door. *"What?!"*

Gallant jumped back about a foot, nearly landing on the squad car he and Goofus had pulled into the driveway. His hand went to his service revolver as he recovered himself. His partner, standing a little to the right and in front of the car, gave out a brief snort. When Terry had time later to reflect on it, she realized Goofus was trying to choke down a laugh.

But now Gallant was speaking. "What in the hell took you

so long?" he demanded, his face flushed under his immaculately groomed blond hair.

He really looks like a fuckin' Ivory boy, Terry reflected to herself before speaking. "I was gettin' dressed, moron," she said. "Didn't think you'd wanna see my scarred-up cooter, Fran-sis. But I guess you'd take what you can get, huh?" Gallant's blue eyes about popped out of their sockets. He was about to speak when Goofus broke in. "That yer ride over there, Terry?," he asked, indicating the bike she had kick-standed near the house. "Goddamn! That is *sweet.*"

"Yeah, it is. Got my old bike trashed over a month ago. Thought I'd take the time to rebuild it, soup it up a little. Like it?"

"Hell, yeah! Let me cruise on it sometime?"

"Goddamn it, Cletus!" Gallant snarled. "We're here to do a job, not beg for pony rides! He turned his attention back to Terry. "Sheriff told us to come get you. Bring you down to the station."

"What the hell for?"

"Fuck if I know! Who do I look like? Tourist Information?"

Terry threw back her head and laughed. "Well, ain't that some shit? Sheriff Tate sends you down here, and you don't even know why? Goddamn, Fran-sis! What if he told you to shove yer pistol up yer ass and pull the trigger? Would ya do that? Shit! Yer so far down on the totem pole, you don't even know it. You ain't nothin' but his white nigger."

Black, Francis most certainly was not, but his red face now showed traces of purple around the edges. Terry was making a mental bet with herself on the color he would turn next when Goofus piped up again. "Aw, give us a break, Terry, will ya? The sheriff wants ya down there to answer a few questions. It ain't like yer under arrest or nothin'."

"Sounds like it to me," she retorted. Then she shook her head and seemed to come to a decision. "Fuck it. Ain't like I got anythin' planned this morning." She brushed by Gallant and opened up the rear door of the squad car herself. She made as if she was climbing in when her arm shot out, placing a vice-like grip Gallant's wrist as he drew back with his night stick.

Gallant jolted back in fear, but Terry held on, tightening her grip. Gallant winced as Terry turned to face him.

"Ya see that, Cletus?" Gallant said, his voice tremoring slightly. "Resisting arrest, plain and simple!" "Cletus just said I wasn't under arrest, idiot," Terry snarled.

"Then you're assaulting an officer."

"Nope. I'm keepin m' back protected, Fran-sissy. I know you. But lemme tell you a little somethin', Percy."

She lent close to his face, intentionally assaulting him with a reeking mixture of whisky, cigarettes, and morning breath. "I ain't no kitty-cat," she said huskily.

Gallant's eyes clouded over in puzzlement, then suddenly widened. In his eyes, Terry got what she was looking for: the spark of fear.

Goofus gave out a big sigh behind her. "Go ahead and get in the car, Terry. No one's gonna hit you from behind."

"What about m' ride back? What about m' bike?"

"If you wanna trust me, gimme the keys. I'll take care of it. It'll be in the lot waiting for ya. I'll come back and get it after we drop you off."

"Careful there, Cletus. You might give the law 'round here a good name."

Never taking her eyes off Gallant, she climbed into the back seat. Gallant slammed the door shut behind her, then sullenly sauntered up to the front seat, a spoiled brat about to throw a temper tantrum. *Good to see some things never change*, she thought. *Gallant looks the same after I beat his ass on the playground.*

She hunkered down in the back seat as Goofus clicked on the ignition and made his way down what passed for the Scranton driveway. And as she watched the scenery float by from the back seat of the police car, the thought came to her again. *Yeah, some shit never changes at all.*

CHAPTER 35

"Push it, Sussman! Push it!"

Ari strained at the effort, his mouth a growing rictus of determination. His entire chest felt as though it was on fire, a blaze that was rapidly spreading outward to his upper abdomen an arms. His stressed muscles seemed to be loosening and tightening at the same time; it was a pain/pleasure sensation that freed as much as constricted him.

And with one last, monumental effort, he straightened his arms, bringing the weight to its resting place suspended over the bench. The sharp *clang* was the most beautiful sound he'd heard all afternoon.

It was the day after his meeting with Detective Jones. He hadn't thought he'd get much sleep that night after all he had learned. Surprisingly though, he'd slept like a stone. *Maybe there's some comfort in knowing who's out to get you and why*, Ari thought.

His parents, of course, demanded to know just what transpired between him and the detective, and Ari gave them a brief overview. Naturally, his father reacted in his usual cool, calm and collected manner, demanding to know when they would be receiving police protection (not yet, since Terry Scranton hadn't actually done anything provable) and that Ari drop out of school immediately and make himself a virtual recluse at home (*And listen to all your paranoid crapola full-time? I don't think so,* Ari thought). It was only after Ari pointed out that it was too late to receive a full refund of the semester's tuition did his father relent. Never let it be said that Maury Sussman wasn't able to see the practical side of things.

After further such pleasantries, Ari went on his way. He caught the tail end of his last class at U of M and went directly to his dorm. As he passed through the hallway, he paused to knock on Graziano's door. "Yo," came the answer.

"It's Sussman, Graziano. You and me getting together tomorrow?"

There was a brief silence, then a rattling of locks. When the door opened, Ari was hardly surprised to find Graziano standing there in his skivvies. "You still up for it?" came Graziano's reply.

"More than ever."

Graziano regard him for a moment, then nodded. "Yeah, I can see that. When's yer last class end?"

"At three."

"Be at the gym at three-thirty. And dress to move, sonny-boy, cuz that's what yer gonna do."

"Good."

Graziano gave him a rather unsettling grin and closed the door, free to pursue whatever evils he entertained himself with during his private time.

And now, one afternoon later, saw that same evil rictus plastered on Graziano's face as he peered down at his victim/trainee. "How do you feel?" Ari's tormentor asked.

"Like someone took a sledgehammer to my chest."

Graziano barked out a laugh. "That's just growing pains, m'boy. You'll get used to 'em."

"How come you ain't workin' out?"

"This is my day off. The amount of rest you get in between is just as important as the working out you do."

And work out he did. Before he even started on the weights, Graziano made Ari ride on the stationary bike for twenty minutes. "Just a little warm-up", he said.

Warm-up, hell. Ari felt beat to shit from pumping his way through. His legs felt like two huge pieces of pulled saltwater taffy. And it felt like his entire crotch had fallen asleep on him when he finally stumbled from the seat.

After that, the weights. Double-handed bicep curls, leg extensions, wrist curls, calf raises, shoulder presses, hamstring curls, ab crunches, bent-over rows. All of this leading up to the center piece of that torturous afternoon. The bench press.

In between sets and gasps for air, Ari told Graziano all he had learned about Terry. For most of it, Graziano listened, not giving anything away. The only time he betrayed any real emotion was when Ari described what had been done to her by the gang of black girls at the reformatory. And even then, he remained fairly inscrutable, choosing just to mutter "Jesus Christ" under his breath and shake his head.

When he was done, Graziano remarked, "Damn, Sussman. You get all the good chicks, dontcha?"

"You're welcome to her," Ari responded. "You two would make a better couple."

"Thank you very little. Now stop wasting energy. Gimme another set."

And so it went. Finally, they got to the bench. "This'll make a man outta ya, Sussman.

How much you weigh?"

"One fifty-five."

"That include nose?"

"Fuck you."

"That's the spirit. Let's give you a hundred thirty-five."

"Holy shit! Are you kidding?""You should be able to lift your own weight. But don't worry. If it's too much, we'll pyramid down."

It wasn't too much, but it was considerable. Body parts Ari never knew he had ached.

Now, in between, he sat up, feeling the weight on his chest ease up a little. "How long you been doing this shit, Graziano?", he asked.

"Since high school. Made me feel better about myself."

"Don't tell me you were a ninety-eight pound weakling."

"More like a hundred ninety-eight. I was a fat kid."

"*What?* The big, bad Vinnie Graziano was a *nerd?*"

Graziano smirked. "There's a lot about me you don't know, Sussman. But there's stuff I know about you."

"What the hell are you talking about?"

"Later. For the time being: *gimme another set.*"

Sighing, Ari flopped backward on the bench. With another monumental strain, he got the barbell in the air again. He had just completed one rep when Graziano yelled out, "C'mon, Jewboy! Show me what you got!"

Ari immediately re-racked the weight. He sat up and turned to face the young man hovering over him. "Don't call me that," he said.

"Call you what?"

"Jewboy. Don't call me Jewboy."

"Why the hell not?"

"Because I don't like it! Because . . .because Terry Scranton calls me that."

Graziano's jaw dropped open, then immediately closed with a snap. "Jesus," he said. Man, I'm sorry, Sussman. Got a lotta Jewish friends back home. We bust back and forth on each other all the time. Just the New York way, I guess. Never thought anything about it."

"It's okay. I just . . .I just don't like it."

"Gotcha. Won't come up again." Then Graziano's face re-hardened. "Well, don't just Stand there. *Gimme another set.*"

When he had a moment to think upon it (after the weight-training had ended and Graziano, the sadistic bastard, made him walk another twenty minutes on a treadmill), Ari wasn't sure what had surprised him more: Graziano giving out an apology? Or the fact that he had found the guts to snap at Graziano in the first place?

CHAPTER 36

Terry was sitting sullenly behind the table in the interrogation room, fingering the edge of her styrofoam cup of coffee. Every now and again, she glanced balefully over at the two-way mirror on the far side of the room, absently wondering if there was anyone on the other side, staring back, not really caring either way.

However, there was. Jones stared out at her with disdain, if not outright hostility, on the other side. He tried to reconcile the history of the wounded child he had compiled over the past few weeks with the figure before him, but was failing miserably. *Maybe the milk of human kindness has already curdled itself into sour cream in me,* Jones said to himself. *Especially where Miss Scranton is concerned.*

The trip into West Virginia had been fairly uneventful. He had phoned the local sheriff's office soon after getting back from the Sussman house yesterday afternoon. The sheriff had been willing enough to help, and promised to send two deputies to pick her up the next morning.

When he did finally meet with Sheriff Tate that morning, he was pleasantly surprised to find that the man was different from the usual small-town cops he had dealt with before. Though his girth and large mustache gave him an uncanny resemblance to a walrus, Tate was pleasant, polite, helpful, and had a good degree of intelligence and common sense to work with.

"Nice to meet you, Detective Jones," Tate said as he rose from behind his desk to greet him. "Sit down. Let's talk a minute."

He did as the man requested, pulling up a chair and taking a moment to politely admire the many fish trophies in his office. "I want to thank you for taking the time to do this, Sheriff."

Tate gave a dry chuckle. "It's not as though we're overwhelmed with work here, Detective. Anything to help."

"Barney, please."

"Then it's 'Jeff'. Anyway, I hope you don't mind my asking why exactly you've come all this way? Terry's more of a localized problem."

"She's gotten a little more ambitious as she's gotten older. She's under investigation as being part of a multi-state drug ring."

"With the Demon Heads?"

"Yeah."

Tate sighed. "Those assholes have been like a pimple on my ass ever since they came to town eight years ago. I keep asking the State Police to help move 'em along, but they keep telling me they can't supply the manpower. Guess we're not 'A#1' on their priority list. But now you tell me they're part of something big, and people are interested. Go figure."

"Sorry, Jeff. But if everything goes well, they'll be outta here soon enough."

"Glad to hear it," Tate responded as he slunk back in his chair. "Terry, on the other hand," he continued. "She's a special case. Sure she's involved?"

"Got her on film and tape. They don't lie."

"No, they don't. But still. . . ." He drifted for a moment, then shook his head. "What do you know about her?"

"Quite a bit. Got a file on her."

"Shit. Then you've probably shown more interest in her than anyone in her miserable life. She was an abused kid, you know. Sexually, even."

"Yeah, got that."

"I'll bet. You know, I was one of the deputies who went to the Scranton house the night her mom died. And I was one of the ones who came to get her and her brother out of that hellhole and into foster care."

Now Jones was surprised. Admittedly, he had not taken much stock of certain names. "No, sir. I did not know that," he replied.

"Yep. I was just a lowly deputy then, brand new to the force. Moved here from North Carolina. Sheriff Herbert Walker was in charge then. Biggest goddamn do-nothing this side of Appalachia. I knew that goddamn drunk Scranton killed his wife, but Walker didn't pursue it. Might've meant actually locking him up in our drunk tank, and he didn't want to smell the place up. So he went with Scranton's view of events, and let it ride. Then Terry started making a nuisance of herself, and finally he had to get off his ass and do something."

Tate leaned forward in his chair. "Y'know," he said. "That's the crazy thing about small town life. It does its best to lull you into inactivity. It's scary, but the longer I spend in this job, the more I begin to see things Walker's way. Things are peaceful for so long that when something comes along to disturb it, to upset that particular apple cart, the more and more you strive to squelch it. That's the consequences of living a small-town life. That's the *real* small-town values, boiled down to its most basic."

"So that day you picked up Terry-"

"I was glad, to be sure. But then things turned bad for her. That poor bitch couldn't catch a break if it fell into her lap with the handle still on it. I'd heard something really bad happened to her when they sent her to the reformatory, but I never knew exactly what. All I know is, she came back worse than ever. But that's the price you pay for letting things go in the first place. It always comes back to bite you on the ass."

"So you feel sorry for her."

Tate shrugged. "For the girl she was, yes. What she's become, no. Now, I just want her to go away. And a lot of that's probably just me, y'know? She's evidence for how I failed, on all levels, on doing my duty as a lawman. But that's just dime-store psychology talking. Doesn't do you any good, Barney, but maybe you can understand where I'm coming from. Are you actually arresting her?"

"No, I'm still hoping to persuade her to turn on the Heads. Maybe by putting a scare into her."

"Good. Need any help, or would you like us away for the little talk?"

"As far away as possible. If it blows up, no need to get any undue stink on you. I'll take full responsibility for what happens."

"Thank you. Me and the deputies'll keep to the front office. There's a buzzer on the side of the door. Ring if you need anything."

Jones had no intention of ringing the buzzer. If anything, it was Terry who he'd have to keep from ringing after he was done. Sighing to himself, Jones took off his suit-jacket and laid it on the chair in the viewing room. Then he put on his game face and made his way to the interrogation room.

Terry blinked in surprise upon seeing Jones enter the room, then turned her face back into the sullen mask she had been practicing alone all afternoon. "Well, well, well," she said in a thick draw as she leaned back nonchalantly in her chair. "They done sent the house nigger. You here to sweep the place up, Mr. Janitor Jones?"

Jones said nothing, just continued to approach her. Before she had time to react, he kicked the chair out from under her, causing her to flip backwards with a surprised yelp.

Then he was on her. *Can't give this bitch time to think,* Jones said to himself as he grabbed up a handful of her ripped t-shirt (causing it rip even more) and her arm.

He threw her up against the cinder block wall of the interrogation room, pinning her against it. She gave out a sharp gasp as the wind was knocked out of her. Jones placed the flat part of his arm against her throat and kept one hand on her shoulder and he drew his face right up to her own. "I hate to break this to ya, Terry, but you ain't cute," he said. "And you ain't funny, either. But, y'know, *this* is pretty funny. Big, bad Terry Scranton, bullier of college kids and half- assed drug courier, pinned to the wall by her worst nightmare. A nigger with a badge."

"Get . . . get the fuck off me!"

"In a minute. I just wanna savor the moment. And tell you a few things. Number One: you're gonna leave the Sussman kid alone."

"What the fuck are you talking about?"

233

Jones pushed his arm against Terry's throat, cutting off her air. She gagged, began to turn red. "If I don't get that promise outta you, Terry, I'm gonna crush your windpipe. And all the police reports are gonna say is that it was self-defense. You can be sure of that. I repeat: you go nowhere near the Sussman kid again, or near his family. And if you even think of going down the same road he takes even a half-hour later, I'll know. And I'll be back."

Terry was changing from red to purple, so Jones eased up a fraction. Now her gasps became more pronounced as she forced the air back into her lungs. "Number Two," Jones continued. "You tell me everything you know about the Demon Heads' operation. You turn for me, and I'll make sure none of them ever do what I'm doing to you right now."

"Fuck you!"

Jones pressed hard again. Terry started clawing at his arm, making deep scratches Jones would only feel later. "I'm running out of patience, Terry," he said.

The back of Jones' mind registered the commotion out in the hallway a fraction of a second before the door flew open. On the heels of the explosion into the room came a voice: a deep, rich alto steeped in Louisiana. "Detective . . . Jones, is it? Would you be so kind as to remove yourself from my client? Perhaps then I'll leave with enough money to live the rest of your days in peace, rather than sue you, your department, this department and the whole goddamn states of Maryland and West Virginia for *violating my client's basic rights!!*"

Keeping one hand on Terry, Jones turned to face his new opponent, readying his retort.

It died in his throat.

Not because of *who* it was; that was hardly a surprise to him. What was the surprise was *what* he saw. Before him stood a middle aged woman with a freckled, florid complexion with red hair streaked with grey. But what really got him were the eyes. Twin orbs of blue fire that pierced him with the shock of a bullet. Those eyes, and the expression in them, were familiar. *Very* familiar.

Jones turned to look back at the woman he'd pinned to the wall. And saw those same eyes staring back at him.

No, not exactly the same. The color was different; Terry's blue being the shade of a barren sky while Rusty's were bordering on violet. But the shape and expression were an exact match.

And now, Jones knew. He *knew*.

Rusty spoke again, her voice betraying the anger that pulsed in her eyes. "Are you deaf, Jones? *Put. . .her . . . down!!!*"

Jones released Terry, who fell into a heap on the floor. He barely noticed as his mind raced. *That's the missing piece*, he thought. *How the hell did everyone miss this?*

He had to pull himself together, to regain focus. "Don't tell me, let me guess," he said. "The famous Rusty Darrow? Can I ask how you happened to show up here? Your girl isn't under arrest, and I wasn't aware she'd requested her lawyer."

"There's very little that goes on in Charles Town, Detective, that I don't know about. Some well-placed sources told me Terry was picked up this morning."

Terry muttered from where she lay sprawled on the floor. "Must not be that good. I been here all fuckin' day."

"Shut up, Terry," Rusty voice whip-snapped.

Terry's mouth closed with an audible snap. *Damn, this day's full of wonders, ain't it?* Jones said to himself.

Rusty turned her attention back to him. "As I was saying, unless you have anything specific to charge her with, we'll be on our way."

"Oh, I don't have anything yet, Ms. Darrow, but I'm working on it. I'm sure your girl here won't disappoint. You know she trashed Ariel Sussman's car a couple of days ago?"

Rusty's eyes flickered just enough for Jones to know that she didn't. "Are you sure?" she said. "I would suspect not, since you haven't formally charged her."

"No. But like I said, give her time."

"Be that as it may, Detective, we're done here. Terry, untangle yourself and get away from Detective Jones. Now!"

Terry gave Jones one last, hateful look as she picked herself up and sauntered out the door. Jones called out to her as she left. "You stay away from the Sussman kid, you hear me, Terry? And his parents, too. You don't and I'll be on your ass even worse."

Rusty stepped right in front of Jones. And even though the detective was a head taller and at least seventy-five pounds heavier, he flinched. *When God made this lady, He was tired,* he thought. *He forgot to give her fear.* "That is enough, Detective, she said. "Another word and I'll slap a writ so big and mean on your department, you'll be shoveling the K-9 Corps' shit for the rest of your natural life."

"Then you better get your own bitch to heel, Ms. Darrow. She's harassing an innocent kid who was just in the wrong place at the wrong time. I don't like that. And neither should you."

Rusty said nothing, just gave Jones a final, baleful stare, turned on her heel, and followed Terry out the door.

Jones watched her go, then sat himself down on the table with a heavy sigh. At least he knew the answer to one part of the question. Did Terry know? On some level, maybe. And it was still to wild an accusation to make without proof. And for that, he would have to probe even further into Terry's past. And Rusty's.

CHAPTER 37

Rusty shoved hard against the safety bar as she exited the police station with Terry hot on her heels behind her. "Thanks fer savin' my hash back there, Rust," the younger woman yapped like a hyperactive puppy. "That big nigger nearly crushed my-"

Rusty said nothing, but cut her eyes at her, giving Terry such a withering look that whatever inanity was coming next out of her mouth up and died there.

After about a hundred yards of walking through the station's lot (and after a quick glance to see if they were well out of sight of any nosy passers-by), Rusty moved. Before the younger woman had time to react, Rusty grabbed Terry by the front of her shirt and slammed her backwards against the side of a parked van.

Terry gasped out loud as the wind was knocked out of her for the second time in less than an hour. The back of her mind noted she'd have some impressive bruises come the morning, but even that thought was cut off once the deadly earnestness of Rusty's gaze and voice reached her.

"If I didn't know better, Terry-girl, I'd swear the doctor who delivered you dropped you on your fuckin' head," Rusty said. "*What* did I *tell* you, girl?"

"Jesus-"

"*What-*"

"Rust-"

"-did-"

"-get-"

"-I-"

"-offa-"

"-*tell*-"

"-me!!!"

"-YOU!!!!??"

Rusty punctuated this final exclamation with another slam against the van. "Did I not tell you to stay away from that kid?!", she roared. "Did you not stand before me in my office and hear me say to you that you were not to harass that kid in any way, shape or form?"

Terry said nothing at first, then gave out a weak, "Yeah."

"So what do you do? You go out immediately and trash his car? Why?"

"I thought he needed persuadin'. To help settle the case. I thought that's why you gave me the file. Like with the judge."

Terry saw Rusty's hand draw back and knew what was coming. She made no effort to stop it. The slap rattled the teeth in her gums. "You stupid girl," Rusty said. "You stupid, stupid, *stupid* girl."

Terry said nothing in response, just sunk her head down low. Rusty released her, but she didn't move from her position slumped against the van.

Rusty felt the pain start in her temples and massaged them. *Another Terry-inspired headache,* she thought. *What a surprise.*

For a time, neither spoke. Then Rusty said, "I can't do this anymore, Terry. I'm dropping the suit."

Terry stiffened in her crouch. "Wh . . .what?!"

"You heard me. I ain't goin' through with it. I'm discontinuing the suit against the Sussmans."

"Goddamnit, Rust! You can't do that! We hadda deal!"

"Dammit, Terry, don't you get it? After what you did, it'd be impossible for me to continue! They start sniffing around what happened to that kid, they start sniffing around *us*. And if they take a hard look at us, what d'ya think they'll find?" Terry lowered her voice. "The judge . . .my dad . . ."

"That's right. And then we'll both be so deep in the shit field, a herd a' cows couldn't pull us out."

"But . . .dammit, Rust! It was my only shot! The only thing I got left!"

"Then here's the choice as I see it, Terry-girl. You can have nothing. . . or you can have less than nothing. Cuz both of us'll be locked up. Me for aiding-and-abetting, you for the whole deal. You wanna go away for life? Cuz that's what you'll be facing. And I won't be around to bail you out . . .even if I wanted to."

She gave out a harsh laugh. "Hell, we might already be fucked. I don't think that cop just came outta nowhere. You're damn lucky Cletus gave me a call as soon as they brought you in, otherwise you'd've had your ass handed to ya."

But Terry was no longer listening. She was instead dealing with a familiar feeling (*betrayal*) and fighting back an unfamiliar emotion: true, deep sadness. She felt the hot sting in her eyes, spreading through her nasal passages to reside in her mouth. She hadn't felt tears like these since she was a little girl. "Dammit, Rust," she said. "I thought you was my friend."

"I am your friend, Terry. But look at the facts of life. I ain't been able to turn up nothin' on this kid. He's cleaner'n a nun's underwear. A couple of speeding tickets, but that's it. Nothin' to build anything on. End of story."

"Rust, I trusted you!"

Rusty's florid face turned an even-deeper shade of crimson. "Don't put this on me, girl!" she said. "I did all I fuckin' could. If you hadn't blown your fuse, maybe I coulda done something. But I ain't gonna try and process a suit that's gonna do us more harm than good!"

Terry could feel the tears forming, but she would not, *would not* cry. "Rust, that was my last shot," she said. "The only thing I had left. And you just throw it away. Goddamnit, I fuckin' trusted you, but you just turned out to be like all the rest."

She turned to run, heard Rusty call out to her, ignored it. Instead, she made a beeline to the back of the lot where the sheriff's office kept the impounded vehicles.

She slammed her ticket against the plexiglass booth where a

rabbit-faced attendant watched a double-header on TV. "Thirteen!" Terry bellowed. "Where is it?"

The attendant, still looking like something out of a cartoon, jolted backwards in his chair. His hands shook as he held out the matching key ring to the apparition before him. It snatched the ring so fiercely that its fingernails tore into the attendant's hands. Terry found her bike easily enough (the only other vehicles in the lot being an old pick-up and a VW Beetle), mounted it, inserted the key, and let the body engines roar into life between her legs. The rumble of it made her feel slightly better. *But what I really need now*, she thought, *is the open road.*

She sped out the lot without a backward glance, letting the power and the fury of her turbo engine carry her away.

Terry drove down the back streets for roughly five minutes before she had to stop. She pulled over to a heavily wooded area with plenty of cover. She parked her bike, killed the motor, and let the emotional wave that had been threatening finally wash over her. She felt her face explode from the hot tears she had been holding back. Her chest heaved with bitter screams and sobs. *Maybe it's my time*, she thought between spasms of grief. *Time to cash it all in.* Her mind turned to the shotgun she had liberated from the Demon Heads' clubhouse; a little maneuvering, and she could probably get both barrels under her chin. Or maybe she'd save herself some trouble and just blow her brains out with her daddy's .45. Press the muzzle to her temple and pull hard on the trigger, if she could. Or maybe she could use her favorite weapon of choice for one last time, slicing open her veins with the straight razor. She'd heard once if someone soaked in a hot tub while they did it, it would be a gentle death, almost like going to sleep. And hadn't she known enough pain in her life?

She wondered vaguely who would find her body. Rusty? Would she actually drop by the house after not hearing from her again? Or maybe she'd be found by one of Nesto's boys, finally coming to finish her off, but then finding he could've saved the trip.

Or would she even be found at all? Would her body just lay in the house or out on the lawn somewhere, rotting, putrefying, being fed on by the flies and picked at by larger scavengers, bit by bit, until only some bones remained, because no one ever thought to look, or cared? She would just molder away, dying as she lived. Alone, and forgotten.

The coldness of that thought formed hard in the pit of her stomach. A hardness stronger than a diamond, as unrelenting as a tsunami. It was the cold, hard prick of pure, unadulterated rage.

That's what they want you to do, Terry, a chillingly familiar voice whispered inside her head. It was a voice that had been speaking to her ever since those cold, lonely nights she had spent in the reformatory's hospital ward. *They want you to kill yourself. They want you to just go away and not bother them anymore. That's what happens to unwanted, unneeded children. They get pushed aside until they can't take being pushed anymore. Till they get pushed off the edge.*

"But sometimes . . .sometimes they get pushed too far," Terry said out loud.

Yes, the voice responded. *And that's when they have to take it upon themselves to start pushing back. Off yourself, you're doing everyone a favor. Stay alive, think, plan . . .and you'll be the coldest, meanest, most merciless in-your-face bitch that ever walked the earth.*

Terry smiled.

CHAPTER 38

Ari jolted awake and immediately wished that he hadn't. His first sensation was pain; pain and stiffness that coursed through his limbs and torso like a living thing.

"Christ," he said out loud to his room. He didn't think he'd ever been this sore, even when he was trying out for baseball back in high school. Those days felt like a love tap compared to how he felt now. It was as if every muscle in his body had been removed, pulled to their limit by some fiendish stretching machine, then replaced. Backwards.

"Yer gonna feel a little sore for awhile," the sadistic Graziano had said with uncharacteristic understatement. "But that's a good thing. The fibers that make up your muscles have been torn up a bit. It takes about forty-eight hours for them to mend themselves, and they come back stronger, coarser, and more dense. And then it'll be time for another session!"

Ari groaned aloud at the thought. The hour-and-a-half he had spent with his tormentor felt like boot camp without the love. How was he going to last the next few days? Weeks?

Months?

Slowly, he was shaken from his reverie and realized why he had been awoken in the first place: the phone was ringing. Everything fell into place for him as he got his bearings. He had come back to his room after the torture session and decided to take a few minutes to rest his weary bones. Those few minutes must have turned into hours if the twilight outside his window was any indication. He blindly groped for the phone, the clouds in his mind still overcasting much of his thoughts as he put the receiver to his ear. "Hello?" he asked thickly, sleep still slurring his words.

"Hell-fuckin'-lo, yerself, Jewboy."

The fog of his mind dissipated instantly. His balls felt as though they had just shriveled into raisins in his sack. "Who is this?" he asked mechanically.

"Man, you really are wiping yer ass with yer daddy's money if'n you don't know the answer to that, college boy."

"What the hell do you want?"

"Now, that's a bit smarter. Not much, but yer learnin'. I want you, Jewboy. We tried to do things the easy way, but I guess some people want it hard."

"What the hell are you talking about?"

"Now yer insulting my intelligence, kid," snarled the voice on the other end. "An' I don't like that. That was quite a stunt you pulled, sending that nigger cop to put a scare into me. But I don't scare, boy. Been through too much to have fear of *anything*."

"Yeah. I know."

There was a silence from the other end. "What do you know, Jewboy?!" the voice roared. You don't know me. You don't know nuthin' about me. All you had to do was settle things like a man, pay off yer debt, gimme what you owed, and that woulda been it. But nooooo! You hadda go and involve the cops in our little argument. Send that nigger to do your dirty work for ya. Typical fucking pussy-ass Jewboy mother fucker!"

"I repeat, Terry, what the fuck do you want!?"

Terry laughed. "That's the spirit, Air-y-el! Don't make this too easy. Show me they dropped sometime. Like I said, I want *you*. I want you to know what it is to have everything taken away from you. Bit by bit, a little at a time. Till your left with nuthin'. Just like me. Just like my whole friggin' life."

Ari said nothing. Years of experience, if nothing else, told him when to keep silent when others had more to say. And some deep instinct told him Terry definitely had more to say. "It's been so fuckin' easy for you, hasn't it, Air-y-el? You had parents who took care of you. You never had to fight for anything. I did. I fought my whole to be something someone would notice. Or even care about. Instead, I got shat on from day one and tossed aside like a used ass-wipe. And no one fuckin' noticed, or cared. Yer life just becomes a wreck. A wreck on the highway that everyone passes by. Maybe they look, but no one stops to help. Nobody." Ari could hear the emotional catch in her voice. Was she on the verge of tears? He couldn't picture it, but that didn't mean it wasn't possible. "But fuck it," Terry continued as her voice evened out. "What d'ya care? You just sit over there in your dorm with all your money and your bright future and laugh at people like me."

"I'm not laughing, Terry."

"Yeah, right. Pull the other leg. It plays fuckin' 'Jingle Bells'."

"Terry . . .we're more alike than you think."

"Bullshit! We ain't nuthin' alike."

"Yes, we are. It started at home. With someone who was supposed to protect us. With our fucking fathers!!"

There was silence for a full thirty seconds on the other end. Then: "Who told you that?" Terry asked hoarsely. "Who the fuck told you that?!"

Ari said nothing.

Terry, on the other hand, had plenty to say. "Oh, Jewboy," she continued. "Yer gonna seriously pay for that one. Bit by bit. Yer gonna wish to Christ you never even breathed the same air as me."

"Is that an actual threat, Terry? Because I can have you arrested for that."

Terry laughed. "Try me, Jewboy. It's only a matter of time."

"Then fuck it!!! Take the goddamn money! You can have everything I got! Just get the fuck out of my life!!!"

"It's too late for that. It used to be business. Now you've gone and made it personal."

"You fucking bitch."

Terry laughed louder. "Goddamn, what a mouth on you, Jewboy! I didn't know you knew words like that."

"Fuck you! Why the fuck do you want to throw your whole life away on just trying to get at me?!"

There was another pause, and Ari had thought that Terry had disconnected the line while he was shouting at her and didn't hear. Then her voice came back, clear as a death knell. "Since ya know so much about me, Jewboy, then maybe you know that sometimes there are worse things than dyin'. Sometimes it's worse when yer left alive."

Then came the click, and Ari was listening to dead air.

He quietly replaced the receiver in its cradle. His hands shook. With fear? Yes, but also with quiet rage. Why did he try to make that connection with her? Didn't he realize that it would just be thrown back into his face? "Yeah, that's what my old man would say," he said out loud to the room. "Just a lot less polite. And he'd tell me I didn't have the balls to tell her to fuck off in the first place."

Get your head out of your ass, Ari, a voice that sounded a lot like Rachel's said inside his head. *You had to try. You were doing something admirable. You were trying to reach out to a person. Don't let that asshole old man's point-of-view color everything.*

"You're right. I shouldn't," Ari responded out loud. "But there's one thing I know I should do."

He fumbled around on his desk for the card Detective Jones left him. Finding it, he punched out the number for his office on the phone.

Jones answered on the third ring. "Jones."

"Barney? It's Ari.

"Ari! I was just about to call."

"I wish I didn't have to save you the trouble. I just heard from our mutual friend. Have you seen her yet?"

"Shit. I was afraid of that. Yeah, I saw her. This morning. But who do you think came and rescued her in the nick of time? Lady Rusty of Darrow, riding her white fucking briefcase."

"Crap. What happened?"

"She came in just as soon as I was getting somewhere with Terry.

In other words, just as I was choking the damn life out of her. But I then proceeded to make it very clear to Ms.

Darrow why I was doing said action. I said that Terry had made threatening actions toward you by trashing your car and that it would be nice if she would consider reigning her in. Either she didn't listen, or maybe there's been some sort of break between them. I suspect the latter, because I happened to see a particularly interesting incident out in the parking lot from the vantage point of a window in the sheriff's office. Aided, of course, by some binoculars the sheriff had so thoughtfully provided. I saw the rather frightening if not wholly unsatisfying scene of Rusty slapping Terry around so hard that *I* was crying."

"Oh, my."

"Yes. Unfortunately, I don't consider it good news. It might mean that whatever control Rusty had over her may be gone. And your phone call clinches it. What did she say?"

"That I was gonna pay for all the things I did. That I would 'wish to Christ that I didn't even breath the same air' as her."

"That's a direct quote?"

"Yeah."

"Well, she has a colorful way of putting things, but that constitutes a legal threat. I can call a friendly judge and have a restraining order slapped on her."

"Thank you."

"Don't thank me yet. Those damn things are notoriously hard to enforce. Until she actually tries something, she remains free."

"Well, shit! What do I do?"

"Sit tight. Let me do my job. Go about your business like you'd normally do. I'll have a squad car put on your house so she won't bother your folks. But most importantly, do what you always do."

"What are you going to do?"

"Me? I need to continue investigating a little something. I think I know what the connection between Terry and Rusty is. It was literally staring me in the face today."

"What? What is it?"

"Can't tell you just yet. It's only supposition, and I don't wanna open my mouth too wide and fall right in. Once I've got all the facts straight, I'll bring you up to speed. More importantly, I'll tell Terry. And Rusty. I guarantee Terry will quickly lose interest in you if what I think pans out."

"Okay. I guess you know what your doing."

Jones chuckled. "Believe me, Ari. It's better this way. If I let you know and turn out to be wrong, I'll be in such deep shit that all I'll see is brown for the next decade."

"All right. I'll sit tight."

"Good. I'll be in touch."

Jones rang off and Ari replaced the phone. He sat back on his bed and stared up at the ceiling. So much was happening in such a short time. What happened to the time when the worst he had to worry about was a failing grade and whether or not there was enough hot water in the dorm's shower? Now, in less than a month after starting school he had Terry-the-killer-biker- queen-from-hell threatening to use his guts for garters. It all seemed so unreal. Should he knock on Graziano's door, tell him about this latest development? No, he probably wasn't even in. Probably out banging his nutso Puerto-Rican girlfriend Janice somewhere. Or worse: he was in there, right now, hammering away at her. Much as he started to like Graziano, he still did not relish seeing that sight.

Phone Rachel? No, it was Wednesday, Law Review meeting night. Wouldn't be home until late. Still, he needed to phone and update her on what was happening, if only to tell her to watch out. After she flipped out on the phone at Terry, she might be a target.

Ari sighed as he looked out his window at the darkening day. *Somewhere out there,* he thought. *There's someone who would prefer to see me dead. And is probably making plans on how best to do it. And the hell of it is, there's very little I can do about it.*

It was at that moment, he knew what it was to be alone. Totally, utterly, cripplingly . . .

Alone.

CHAPTER 39

Terry strained, using all her considerable might. She felt the burst of adrenaline that gave her extra push she needed to work her way upward, ever so slowly upward.

Clang! The twin set of fifty pound weights met together in the air over her torso. *Nineteen,* she thought. *One more.*

The weights came down again, even slower than they went up. She held them to either side of her chest and gradually worked her way upwards again. The strain this time was harder, deeper.

Clang!

Done! She thought as she let the weights drop to the floor. She rose from the bench, the fire in her chest slowly burning itself out. Covered in sweat, she grabbed a nearby towel and mopped herself down. *On to the bag,* she thought. It had been nearly a week since she had called the Jewboy at his dorm, and got one hell of a surprise for her trouble. How the fuck did the little son-of-a-bitch know so much about her?

The spade cop must've had some kinda talk with him or something. Somebody had to learn not to be such a nosy-ass motherfucker and go telling tales out of school, and she was more than happy to be the teacher.

Almost a week, but she hadn't exactly been sitting on her ass. No, sir. Miss Terry had been preparing. Getting ready for the Big Payback. For the Big Get Even. And when she was done, there would be a path of destruction and bodies in her wake that would stretch from the hills of West Virginia to the high-falutin' suburbs of

248

Maryland. *I been preparin' fer this all my life,* she told herself. *Damn if I ain't finally ready for it.*

She gave her wrist a quick once-over. It seemed to be fully healed and rehabilitated. She was at full strength.

She stepped over to the punching bag, a fairly recent addition to her home gym. She slipped another tape in her boom box, Molly Hatchet this time, and cued it up to "Flirtin' with Disaster", a personal favorite of her's. She cranked the bass and volume up to their maximum, shaking the floorboards and rattling the windows.

That task complete, she began to tape her fists up in preparation. She never bothered with gloves; most of her fights were bare-knuckled anyway. Taping offered the happy medium between delivering a real-life punch and keeping some protection on her hands.

Her hands ready, she stood before the bag. A crude drawling of a face had been taped to its upper-half, placed roughly where a head might be. The only distinguishing feature of this face was the over-sized nose drawn upon it. Terry snarled, then followed with a roundhouse blow to the bag.

The first punch opened up a flood in her. Soon she was pummeling the bag with a storm of lefts and rights so devastating the house's frame shook. Her mind flashed back to the first time, and the very first person who got to feel the full extent of her wrath all those years ago.

She had spiked Tammy Brown's lunch with soap flakes from her laundry detail that afternoon. The soap did its job well; the black bitch was sick to her stomach all during her gym period. Terry could see Tammy retching into the toilet, could smell the stench of her vomit as she crept up behind her in the stall.

The first cut from her home-made shiv was a small one, just enough to draw blood and get Tammy's attention. The black bitch howled as Terry sliced across her right achilles tendon. She whipped around to be confronted by the sight of Terry holding a blade the size of a small butcher knife.

"Feelin' a little pukey, Tammy?" Terry had asked with mock

sympathy. "*Now I guess y'know how the resta us feel when we look at ya!*"

"*Whachoo want, cunt? Back for mo'? Didn't yo cracka-ass get enuf las'time?*"

"*Oh, I got plenty, nigger. That's why I'm here. To give it all back!!*"

Tammy paused then, perhaps considering her options. Considering she had none, she charged Terry, giving off a guttural roar as she came. This tactic was far from a surprise, and Terry reacted accordingly, plunging the knife deep into Tammy's considerable belly.

One of Terry's fondest memories was the look in Tammy's eyes at the very moment the knife went into her. All the cock-sure, uppity-spade attitude drained right out of her and she finally became someone who realized it was all over, that the person who was going to kill her was standing right in front of her. That marked an important turning point in their relationship.

Tammy tried to pull away from her, howling this time in pain and fear rather than bravado, but Terry held fast, punching, kicking, biting, crawling, and stabbing, always stabbing.

When the deed was done, she showered quickly, pulled out the change of clothes she kept in the plastic bag she had dragged through the vent system with her, changed, then went back through the ventilator to the laundry room where she was working her unsupervised detail.

Her bloody clothes had just started their Rinse Cycle when the alarm sounded.

"And Ida been home free, too, if'n that other spade bitch hadn't ratted us all out," Terry said out loud in the present. "But I got back at her, too, in the end. Yes-fuckin'-sir!"

Indeed. After her release, already indebted to Nesto for helping to "clean house" before she returned to the old homestead, she had decided to take the further step of asking for his help in getting even with Alisha Green behind prison walls. A few well-placed bribes later found the rat-bitch stabbed to death too.

"Cuz nobody fucks with me, Jewboy! *Nobody!*" she screamed as she gave the bag one final slug right into the crudely drawn face. It crumpled, tore free.

The song ended, and Terry became aware of another sound: a fierce pounding at the front door. Though the more rational part of her brain realized that anyone who presented any real danger to her wouldn't exactly be knocking, she instinctually picked up the .45 she now kept with her at all times.

A quick peak through the spyhole confirmed the former impression. *Goofus?!* she thought. *What the hell does* he *want?*

She tucked the gun down the ass side of her pants and threw back the deadbolt. "Cletus," she announced as she opened the door. "If I knew you was comin'. . . I still prob'ly wouldna done anythin'."

Goofus stood on the remains of the stoop looking like a kid who was about to receive a castor oil enema. "No jokin' here, Terry," he said. "I'm here on official business. To serve ya with this."

He held out a wad of official-looking papers that Terry snatched from his grasp. She quickly skimmed them as an obscene humor grew on her face. "Why, Cletus, this sounds like an official-type restraining order."

"I reckon that's what it is, Terry."

"That Jewboy really think a piece of paper's gonna do anything?"

"It's not my business, Terry, but whatever it is yer doin', I'd advise ya t'stop," he drawled.

He hesitated before going on. "And I think Miss Rusty would want ya to, too. I hand-delivered another copy to her."

That actually took Terry aback. A flood of emotion overwhelmed her, threw her off- balance, made her at a loss for words. A more sophisticated (or less conflicted or violated) person would've recognized these feelings for what they were: love. As it was, Terry could only stammer and flush. "Uh . . .well, well, whatever, Cletus. Do what you gotta do," she allowed finally.

Goofus shrugged and turned away, meandering back to his squad car. Terry watched him until he got to the door, then called out again. "Hey! Cletus!"

Goofus barely turned his head. "Yeah?"

"Thanks."

"Yeah, right, Terry."

"I mean it, Cletus. Thank you."

Now Cletus did turn and regard her fully, with a hint of a smile. "You're welcome, Terry."

Terry nodded, watched as he started up the car and drove off. She then went back inside, shutting the door firmly behind her.

CHAPTER 40

The pain in Ari's legs was excruciating. The fire started from the soles of his feet and spread upwards through his ankles into his calves finally landing in his thighs. A separate fire tore through his lungs, like they were being jabbed by a thousand sharp needles.

And always came the voice. The constant nagging, annoying, fucking pain-in-the-ass voice: "C'mon, Sussman! My grandmother moves faster than you! And she's *dead!*"

"How far . . .have we gone?," wheezed Ari.

"Two miles. Maybe two and a quarter."

"I'm gonna die."

Graziano laughed. "Okay, we'll slow things down to a walk, then. But keep it to a steady pace."

It was a bright, sunshiny day outside and more than a little warm. For all his bravado, Graziano was sweating pretty freely himself in the afternoon sun. *Sadistic fuck's human after all,* Ari thought.

A week had passed since Terry Scranton's threatening phone call, and not a peep out of her since. Ari was supremely worried that this was just the calm before the storm. So was Graziano, though he didn't come right out and say it. He'd listened without comment as Ari related the story, nodding in the right places, but during their next session, he worked Ari twice as hard.

And now this. Running outside on a track instead of walking on the treadmill. Just as he was getting used to it. *Which is probably the point*, Ari thought morosely.

Ari felt his feet getting heavy; his shoulders sagged. How easy it would be for him to just give up. The appeal of it was very seductive. *You always hear about the champ who 'risked insurmountable odds and won',* he thought. *But come on, is that even realistic? Most people fail at what they try, anyway. Why don't you hear about those poor fuckers? Maybe I should just let Terry go ahead and kill me. It's not like I'm actually doing anything with my life anyway. Let her have her goddamn revenge, if it means that much to her. I'm just taking up space here. I'm-*

Ari's thoughts were cut off abruptly by the sharp blow to the side of his head. Jolted back into the here and now, he angrily turned in the direction from which the blow came.

Graziano stared back at him with the familiar smirk on his face. "Sorry, pal," he said. "But as the man on the TV says, you needed that."

"Fuck you, man! I asked you to train me! Not slap me around!"

"You looked like you were fading there, so I thought you needed to be smacked back into reality."

"Go to hell! I don't need this shit anymore! I'll take my chances with the bitch I know that's crazy."

Grazianos' face clouded over. "You think this is the greatest thrill of my life, Sussman? Tryin' to get yer skinny cracked ass into shape? Hell no! I got better things to do with my time than to listen to you bitch, moan and complain."

"Well, pardon me all over the fuckin' place! When was the last fuckin' time someone was out to kill you!?"

Graziano said nothing for a moment, then turned away. Ari knew he had just hit a sore point. There was a long tense silence. When Graziano at last spoke, Ari was surprised by his tone. Gone was the raspy bravado from his voice. He spoke haltingly, uncertainly.

"Wasn't that long ago, Sussman," he said. "I was just out of high school, graduated, on my way here. Y'know, my dad split on me and my mom when I was a kid. Ain't seen him since. I got over it, but I don't think Ma ever did. She'd stick it in the air for every two-bit hustler that showed a goddamn interest. Which gave me a great childhood, let me tell you."

Part of Ari wanted him to stop, to tell him he didn't want to hear this. To tell him he had heard enough atrocities over the past week or so to last him a lifetime, thank you very little. But the better part of him kept silent. *Besides,* he thought. *This may be my only chance to find out what makes this guy tick.*

"Not long after I got my scholarship, my damn 'CAPA', Mom started hanging out with this real prize by the name of Ralphie Vitale. Her words, even. "'He's a real prize, Vinnie, so youse be good t'him,'" Graziano mocked in a high-pitched falsetto. "Ha! 'Real prize', my ass! He was just a gofer for the friggin' Gambinos out in Queens! Guess that's what made him all so goddamned important in her eyes!"

Ari said nothing. By now, the bitterness in Graziano's voice was so thick it could have chewed through the neck of a soda bottle, so Ari thought it best to give his unlikely friend space. "As you might guess," Graziano continued. "Me an' ol'Ralphie didn't see eye-to-eye on a lotta things. When I told him I was into acting and stuff, he asked me point-blank if I was a fag. So I told him to go ask *his* mother, and the fight was on. That was the first time we nearly duked it out. It sure wasn't the last."

"See, Sussman, I hadda take a lotta shit over the years because of what I liked doing. Just I had to learn how to fight, or I'd take a lot of shit. And I don't like takin' shit. Besides, this was the only thing I've ever been good at, y'know? I think God, or whoever, gives us all at least one thing, one special talent that we have to try to hold on to, or we're gonna lose it over the years. The really lucky ones get more than one. For me, being able to be other people has been my only gift. Well, that and my charming personality."

"Do tell."

Graziano laughed. "Well, lemme get to the point, before I bore ya t'death. After a few weeks, Mom and Ralph's situation turned kinda sour. They came home one night, drunk an' arguin' while I was tryin' to sleep. Nothing unusual, but tonight it was loud. Real loud. I started hearin' words I didn't like comin' outta Ralphie's yappin' little mouth. Like 'cunt' and 'whore'. It sorta got my attention."

"I came outta my bedroom in only my boxers. They was standin' in the kitchen, with Ralphie havin' his back to me. Then Mom opens up her little bitch-mouth and Ralphie cracked her one. Hard. With his fist. That got me *pissed.*" "I grabbed the little runt from behind, slamming his head down on our kitchen table. I looked quick-like over at Mom, an' she's slumped against the wall with her hand to her mouth, an' I see she's bleedin'. That's all I needed to see."

"I grabbed the little bastard's arm an' twisted it up behind his back. You shoulda heard him howl, Sussman! Youda thunk the Devil Himself had come outta Hell to personally give him a rectal!"

"Then he starts cussin' me out in that high-pitched monkey-voice of his. 'Kid,' he says, tryin' to sound all tough. 'You don't wanna do this. I'm gonna have yer balls fer cuff links if you don't leggo. Maybe I won't even have yer Mom killed. Just you.'" "Well, when he said that, I didn't just see red, I saw fire-trucks! That's the way I always been. The worst thing you can do is threaten me. Threaten my life? I say, why wait? Let's throw down now!"

"'Listen here, shorty,' I says real low so only he can hear. 'Who said I was lettin' you walk outta here alive?'"

"And so he'd get the point, literally, I grabbed one of the butcher knives we kept on the counter and put the sharp edge to his face. Now Ma was screamin' at me, beatin' on my back, yellin' at me to let him go. I just ignored her. For me, there was just two people in the world at that moment, me and Ralphie-boy."

"I get real close to his face, so close I could smell the whiskey an' garlic on his breath. Things had entered a whole new level with him, you see. I was the one in charge, an' he was terrified. 'You need to learn some manners, Ralphie-boy,' I says to him. 'I don't give a hairy rat's ass who the fuck you are, or who the fuck you think you are. Who'd'ya think's gonna give a fuck if you disappear?'"

"Ralphie didn't . . .*couldn't* say a word. I had him by the short and curlies, and he knew it. I'd be lying to you if I said I didn't enjoy it. Little bastard comes into my home and slaps my mom around? Fuck no!"

Ari was speechless. *Looks like I picked the right son of a bitch to come to with my problems*, he thought. But Graziano had fallen silent. After several seconds of just watching him stare off in the distance, Ari nervously cleared his throat. "Um. . .so . . .what happened then?", he finally managed.

"Eh? Oh. . . . I let him go."

"You what?"

"You heard me. I let Ralph go."

"But he threatened you. He said he was gonna kill you!"

"And believe you me, I wanted to kill him. But, as I started described to him how I was gonna cut him deep in his eyes until he died blind and stupid, something stopped me. And it wasn't my mom. Maybe it was the look in his eyes. Something changed. I'd broken him. I realized I had power over him, and that was all I needed. That realization. Just that."

"So what did you do?"

"Well, first I took his gun off him, a Saturday Night Special he had, then I bum-rushed him head-first out the door. Landed on his ass out on the front stoop. He started pounding on the door as soon as I slammed it shut behind him. Had to keep up appearances, y'know? He kept it up until I reminded him I had his gun and was gonna shoot him through the door if he didn't beat it. After that, he decided to leave."

"And your mom?"

Graziano's voice lowered in pitch, so soft Ari had to strain to hear him. "When I got back to the kitchen," he said. "Ma was still bleedin'. I tried to help her, tried to clean her up, but she pushed me away. 'Go away,' she says. 'You ran off my only chance at bein' happy. You always done that, since you was born.'" Graziano paused. "'I hope he does kill you'".

Ari was thunderstruck. Sure, he and his family had their share of scraps, but not this vicious. A parent actually wishing her kid dead? As far as he knew, he'd been able to avoid *that*, thanks.

Graziano was still speaking. "So I ask you, Sussman. What d'ya say to that? I just went back to bed, slamming the door behind me, carrying the gun. Let her clean up her own friggin' mess. Christ knows I did plenty of that over the years."

"I'm sorry, man," Ari finally said.

"No need. You wasn't there. Anywho, I watched my back for the next week or so, but nothin' happened. I shoulda known: when the mob boys come for ya, they come for ya directly, no fuckin' around. Face first, and on the street."

"So I came home one day to find this big Caddie practically on my doorstep. Two riders Was in it. A big, fat schlub sittin' behind the wheel, and a young guy, barely older'n me, leaning Up against it."

"'Hey, kid!' the younger one yells. I hate it when guys not much older call me 'kid'. 'You Vinnie? Vinnie Graziano?'"

"'Who wants to know?' I ask."

"'Somebody who wants to meet ya.'"

"'I'm busy.'"

"Then the little peckerwood pulls back his coat to show me the .44 in his waistband. 'I ain't askin' kid.', he says."

"I had half a mind to plug him right there. The .38 was in my jacket pocket. But what good would it do? They'd just send more. And they'd also be after Mom, then. Besides, somethin' was off about these guys. For one thing, they didn't bother to search me when I came over. And they didn't plug me when they saw me. So, somethin' was up. Might was well see what it was. Not like I had any choice in the matter."

"The younger guy sat in the back seat with me while the fat guy drove us through Brooklyn. Nobody said much, but it wasn't like all somber or anything. Both of 'em seemed relaxed, so it didn't feel like they was takin' me for a ride. The two of 'em would make some occasional jokes between 'em. I didn't say shit, though."

"I started gettin' a hunch on where we were going when we made the turn-off into Queens. The hunch went into overdrive when we started going into Ozone Park, and when we pulled in front of the Bergin Hunt and Fish Club, I *knew* who the fuck we were going t'see. I just couldn't believe it."

"Who? Who was it?"

"The Man, Sussman. Somebody I'd only seen on the news. Well, no. Actually I did see him once going into a restaurant in Brooklyn."

"Who?! Who did they take you to see?"

"Him, Sussman! Gotti. They was takin' me to see John Gotti."

"Get out!"

"I'm serious, dude! I couldn't make this shit up! The kid got out with me, and the fat guy drove off. When we went inside, it was like the casting call for every bad mob movie you've ever seen. Hell, even for some of the good ones! Place was swimmin' with guineas. Some were playin' cards, some was drinkin' but they all stopped what they was doin' when I came in. Then you coulda heard a rat fart, it got so quiet. Felt like I was breathin' chicken soup. Here I am, at ground zero for the Gambino family, fer chrissake! Then I seen. . .him. Standin' at the end of the bar. He turns around, all suited up, and looks at me."

"Holy shit."

"Yeah, tell me about it. Here he was, standin' in front of me, just like I'm talkin' t'you. Gotti looks me over for a second, all serious-like, and says, 'So youse the kid that slapped Li'l Ralphie around.'"

"So, what am I gonna do? Lie? So I does the only thing I can do, say the only thing I can say. 'That's right', I says. Hell, I even managed to keep my voice steady!"

"He nods at me, still serious, then his face breaks into this huge grin and he says, 'Hey, Sallie! Give this kid anything he wants! The fuckin' stones on him!'"

"Then the whole room busts out laughin', and all the tension drops out of me like a rock. Then all the wiseguys came up, started backslappin' me, huggin' me, shakin' my hand. They all introduced themselves, and I don't remember a single guy's name, man. That's how fuckin' bowled over with relief I felt."

When things got back to normal, Gotti came back again. He put his arm around my shoulders and says, 'When you get your drink, come into the back with me. I wanna talk with you.'"

"He musta felt me stiffen up again, cuz he says, 'Aw, c'mon.

What're ya worried about? If I wanted you hurt, you think I'd go to all this trouble? Ida done it already."

"Point taken. So I got up to the bartender, Sallie, and get myself a Johnny Walker Blue on the rocks. Then I followed Gotti back into his office."

"Christ, I couldn't believe how damn plush it was! Most a' the wiseguys in the neighborhood seem t'be competing for *Better Homes and Garbage*, it's so friggin' loud n' flashy. Not Gotti. Tasteful down to the leather chairs and solid oak and steel desk. Even the gold letter opener had style."

"He motioned for me to sit down while he sat behind his desk. He offered me a cigar; they were Cubans, big ones, and I took one, but for later. Then he got down to business. 'Like I was sayin' back there, kid,' he says. "You got some balls. Y'know, Little Ralphie was responsible for a couple a' hits.'"

"I was surprised, and showed it, so he went on: 'Yeah. Course, he shot 'em both inna back, but still, dead is dead. So when he comes t'me a few days ago, sayin' he wants to take a couple a my crew to take some punk out in Brooklyn. . .' he broke off and shrugged."

"I didn't know what to say, so I kept my mouth shut. 'So I have two reactions t'that,' he went on. 'First, this must be some kid! And number two, what the fuck is goin' on here? What's the real story? Cuz Ralphie's the type a' guy that when he tells me my shit is brown, I'm still gonna look behind me t'see.'"

"He kinda laughed at that, and said, 'Ralphie said you blind-sided him, and threatened to cut his eyes out. That the truth?'"

"'Well, yeah,' I says. 'But he slapped my mom a good one. Hard. Made her bleed.'"

"'Yeah, that's what he said,' Gotti said. 'Afterwards'."

"I wanted to ask him, 'after what?', but didn't think that'd be a good idea just yet. Figgered it was better to let him talk He'd tell me. In due time."

"'I owe ya, kid,' he says finally. 'I knew Ralphie was a piece a'shit, but after this little . . . incident . . .I knew he was a *worthless* piece a'shit. Bad for business. Bottom line? You n' yer mom ain't gotta worry about Ralph Vitale no more.'"

"'Well, I didn't have to call a psychic to tell me what he meant by *that*. But then he said, 'Y'know, there's ain't many good kids these days. Hell, good *people*. Stand-up guys. Guys with heart. And brains. I asked around the neighborhood where you live after you. People say you got both.'"

"And there it was. The real reason he called me in. He wouldn't have disposed of Ralph without thinkin' he had some sorta replacement for him. 'Bad for business', y'know? But what he said next really surprised me. 'They also tell me you got plans. That yer goin' college this fall."

"'That's right,' I says. 'Gotta scholarship to go to University a'Maryland.'"

"'Damn! Long way off!,' Gotti says. 'Tryin' t'get as far way from the old neighborhood as possible, huh?'"

"'Somethin' like that, yeah.'"

"'What're y'takin' up?'"

"I braced myself. 'Acting,' I said. 'Theatre.'"

"Surprisingly, he didn't laugh. One a'the few people I told who didn't. He just nodded.

'That's kinda tough. Guess ya think yer pretty good'."

"'I guess,' I says. 'We'll see'."

"'Well, you ain't gonna know until you try, huh? Anyways, far be it from me t'take a kid outta college if they's set on goin'. I fuckin' hated school, but I hear college is different. Nobody on yer case, fer one. I tried t'get my kids t'go, but y'think they'd listen t'their old man? Hell, no'."

"Then the strangest thing happened. He started t'get all misty-eyed. I've thought about why, and I think it was cuz a' his kid, his favorite, bein' killed on his bike when he was about twelve or so. That mighta been the one he was thinkin' of when he was talkin' t'me about college."

"But then he shook it off, and looked over at me again. 'How much does Maryland cost per year?,' he asked. "'If I wasn't on scholarship,' I said. 'Five grand a semester.'"

"He just sorta nodded, then reached into his desk. He pulled out a big wad a' cash out of a box, and started counting out hundreds and fifties. 'Mr. Gotti,' I says. 'I can't take your money.'"

"He just looked up and burrowed his eyes into me, and I felt this chill come into the room. 'I insist, kid,' he said. 'I owe ya. And John Gotti always pays off his debts.'"

"Gotti counts out ten large and passes it on over. 'Here', he says. 'Use it as emergency money. Even if you lose yer scholarship, you can pay fer another year. Or use it fer expenses. Whatever. Now, we're even.'"

"He hands me a manilla envelope and tells me to keep it hidden. Talk about unnecessary advice, but I just nodded. Then he put an arm around me and walked me to the door. 'Now', he says. 'If'n you change yer mind and decide to come back t'New York after youse graduate, an' yer lookin' fer some work in between acting jobs, come see me. I'll have somethin' fer ya t'do.

Who knows? Maybe it'll even be legit!'"

"Then he laughs, cuffs me on the cheek, and sent me on my way."

"When they dropped me off, just where they left me, out on the street, it just seemed so unreal. Like the ultimate in acid trips. Here I am, this knucklehead from Brooklyn, told by the most powerful mob boss in the country that he's impressed by my *stugazz'*? And gives me money!? Christ, it almost made up for all the shit that went before."

"What about your mom?" Ari asked. "Did you tell her?"

Graziano shook his head. "Oh, hell no. She woulda tried to take it, spend it on some other loser. Besides, with her fuckin' little bitch-mouth, she woulda blabbed to the whole neighborhood about it. And then where would I be? All the assholes and fair-weather friends would come outta the woodwork, kissin' my ass, thinkin' I was Gotti's fair-haired boy now. Or worse, some prick'd try to rob me, or go the cops. Nah, it just wasn't worth it. I kept myself to myself. You're the first person, outside a' Janice, who I told this to."

Graziano paused a second, then went on. "Look, Sussman," he

said. "There are two reasons why I'm doin' this fer ya, helpin' ya out. First, cuz I know what yer up against. You ever read *The Godfather*?"

"No, but I saw the movie."

"Shit, man. Everybody's seen the movie. I'm talkin' about the book. You get some little nuances outta readin' the book you can't get from the movie, good as it is. One part that's not in the movie is when the Don and Tom Hagen, the *consigliere,* are talking about Woltz, the producer who won't give Johnny Fontane the comback movie part he needs. The Don asks Hagen if Woltz had any 'real balls'."

"Now, Hagen takes a moment to consider what the Don is askin'. Is he askin' whether Woltz has a strong will, or character, or that he can't be bluffed? No. What he's askin' is if Woltz has the balls to risk *everything,* to lose it all on a matter of principle, for his honor, for revenge. So far, I myself have only seen two people who've struck me as bein' that type. One was John Gotti. The other is Terry Scranton."

Graziano leaned close to Ari. "To quote another great movie, 'what are ya prepared to do', Sussman? I mean, have you really taken stock of this situation? Have you thought about that just givin' this bitch the big beat down might not stop her? Sussman . . .Ari . . .you might actually have to kill her to get her to stop. Have you considered that, and what it means?"

Ari felt a chill that had nothing to do with the autumn day. As a matter of fact, he had considered it . . .but not on a conscious level. It was more like the proverbial white elephant in the room: there, but not fully addressed. Until now.

"So you see, Sussman," Graziano continued. "I know the sorta person yer up against, 'cause I've been there. And I don't want you to go into this unaware."

"And what's the other reason?"

Graziano considered him for a moment, as if uncertain on how best to go on. "Well," he finally replied. "I'm also doin' it fer yer grandpa."

That knocked Ari for a loop. "My grandfather? What does he have to do about this? He died a long time ago."

"No. No, he didn't. It was only two years ago."

"Man, what fuckin' truck did you fall out of? He died when I was a little kid. I don't hardly remember him."

"Yer dad, he's Maury Sussman, innit he? And your grandfather, he started his clothier business in Bay Ridge? Lived in Brighton Beach?" "Yeah . . ."

"Then yer Gramps is Ariel Sussman, and I heard stories about him all my life. About what kinda man he was. How he'd mend clothes for the neighborhood kids when they needed it, and wouldn't even take their money. How he always gave back to the neighborhood he worked in. How everyone loved his ass, cuz he was the kindest, most big-hearted sonovabitch that ever lived."

"But they also tell me that, back in the neighborhood, it seemed to skip a generation. That yer dad, on the other hand, was as mean as a snake with a hemorrhoid. When he took over the business, all the charity stopped. He turned his back on the regular customers and started caterin 'to a more snooty clientele. But, even before then, he was a pain in the ass. Spoiled rotten, always pushin' people around. A classic bully. Everybody wondered how the hell Old Mr. Sussman could spawn such a rotten kid. They used the call him 'The Orphan' behind his back because they seriously thought he was adopted!"

"My dad . . ." Ari responded haltingly. "He . . .he always said my grandfather died when I was little . . ."

"Then I hate to say this, Sussman," Graziano rejoined. "But yer dad's been lyin' to you. "Why, I don't know. All I know is that as soon as yer dad took over the business, he turned his back on him."

"Oh . . oh my God. . ."

"What's more," Graziano continued. (*Christ, can't you* stop?, Ari thought weakly), "Yer dad wouldn't even pay fer the burial after he died. When the neighborhood heard about that, they took up a collection. All of those people he helped over the years footed the bill for his funeral. And once again, yer dad didn't show up. Or the rest a' the family. I'd always wondered why."

Ari's head swum. Now it felt as though *he* was the one who'd swallowed acid. Graziano had more than just upended his world; it felt as though he had obliterated it. Everything his father had told him over the years was turning out to be a lie (*What? Are you surprised?* a dark voice sneered inside his head.), and the worst part seemed to be how easily he had followed along with it.

But Graziano was still speaking. "Look, Sussman," he said. "For all I know, maybe yer dad had a good reason fer doin' what he did. The neighborhood didn't know everything that went on in yer granddad's house. But still, I'm surprised you didn't know anything about it. Didn't you wanna know? Did you even ask?"

Ari said nothing, only stared. A shadow of doubt crossed his mind. *Maybe Graziano's bullshitting me,* he thought. *Maybe everything he told me is a great big fuckin' joke, and he hasn't gotten to the punchline yet.*

Except that it wasn't. He knew it by looking at Graziano's face that every damned word he said was the God's honest truth. For all his other faults, it was hard for Graziano to lie. Even as a joke.

"Maybe I said too much," Graziano finally allowed. "Obviously, yer dad kept you in the dark fer a reason. After knowin' you a bit, I don't think you woulda let yer granddad die alone if you'd known. But that's what I've been tryin' to get through to ya, man. Ask questions. Find out shit fer yerself, and don't let yer parents point-of-view turn out to be yours. Not just about Springsteen, but *everything.*"

"John Lennon said it best, baby. 'There ain't no guru who can see through your eyes'. Remember that. Now, if you'll excuse me, I gotta get some runnin' of my own in before I go to rehearsal tonight. See ya back at the dorm. We'll do this again in a coupla days."

And, without another word, Graziano dashed off into the woods on the far side of the track, taking the well-beaten cross country path the campus had cut for runners over the years.

Ari just stared after him, silently. Alone. *Well, maybe not as alone as I think*, Ari considered to himself as Graziano disappeared into the woods. *Not as alone as all that.*

CHAPTER 41

Terry shifted her legs under her, feeling the tingle up and down as she switched positions. *Damn,* she thought. *Well, whadya expect? It's been over two and a half hours, fer chissake.*

All in all it was a nice day, by anyone's standards. The air was beginning to cool, losing the humidity that had marked the whole summer. *Still,* she thought as she stretched out on the ground. *There are more exciting things to do in life. Like watching fresh paint dry.*

She stubbed her cigarette out in the dirt beside her. *Anyhow, things'll be gettin' pretty exciting soon enough.*

Terry had placed herself behind some trees at the top of a small hill overlooking the road, a little-used (but still paved) rural lane half a mile distant from the Demon Heads' clubhouse. She had been over this particular roadway several times when making her runs to DC. A few days previous, Terry was pleased to note that the current maker of the rounds also used this stretch to go to and from the clubhouse.

She was less pleased to note just who had taken her route. *Caywood!?* she had thought as she spied the large, hair-covered form as it passed her on its equally-large (*and fucking loud*) chopper. *Christ, Nesto! What, you couldn't get a fuckin' baboon at the zoo?*

Alvin "Ten-Ton" Caywood was probably the largest of the Demon Head roster, and most definitely the stupidest. Standing a good six-foot-seven, he also carried well over three-hundred pounds on his massive frame. He also had the distinction of failing out of school by the eighth grade after a third-times-not-the-charm attempt. Some of the Heads even claimed (behind his back, of course) that he was 99 and 44/100% brain free.

But what Caywood lacked in intelligence he more than made up for in brutality. No "gentle giant" he. Terry remembered one get-together at the clubhouse she had attended at the beginning of summer, (*Christ, was it that fuckin' recent?*, Terry thought. *Damn, feels like an age.*) when a fine example of human being named Ratso started bragging about a fun little sexual assault he had participated in. "An' after alla us wuz done," he said. "Caywood waded in. Goddamn!! When that boy got through with 'er, she wuddint ever breathin' anymore! He done squashed all the air outta her! An' you know what he said? 'I t'ink I broke 'er'. Haw Haw! Fuckin' hell! 'I t'ink I broke 'er'."

Ratso laughed by himself for nearly a full minute before he noticed that no one else had joined in. "Huh? What? What I say?" he gazed around, looking like a retarded kid caught playing with himself. Then he looked over at Terry.

No, not at her. Behind her. "Why the hell you wavin' at me, Doc?" Ratso said, his red, rheumy eyes thickening their gaze.

"Prolly cuz a' me, Rat," Terry said.

Ratso's eyes seemed to gain focus as they fell on Terry and the realization crossed what was left of his mind. "Oh, Terry," he said. "Sometimes I ferget yer a-"

"A woman, Rat? True, I ain't got many a' the parts left, but just enough t'make the cut.

But that's okay. Sometimes I ferget yer a man."

Terry paused, as if considering. "Nah, that ain't true", she finally admitted. "Sometimes I ferget yer a *human*."

She punctuated this last with a full cup of cheap beer in Ratso's face. (*Fuck it,* she thought. *Not like I'm wasting good shit.*) Ratso sputtered for a second, then made a move as if he were about to rush Terry.

He never made it to her; but then, neither did Terry make it to him. The larger, older man standing behind Terry waded in, putting himself between them. "Stand down, Rat," Doc growled into the smaller man's face. "You ain't gonna wanna continue this."

"Fuck you, Doc!" Ratso snarled back. "I ain't lettin' some bitch-!"

"You can an' you will. You fucked up, Rat. Accept it like a man and stand down. Or both me an' Terry here are gonna take turns bashin' yer head in."

Terry didn't know that much about Doc up until that point, and he was something of a mystery to most of the Demon Heads themselves. Rumor had it that he was one of Nesto's oldest acquaintances, running with him in the Hell's Angels before Nesto was kicked out. Rumor also had it that, unlike 95% of the Demon Heads, he had actually completed high school, even going so far as completing a year or two of community college (which put him ahead of all of them). Thus his nickname; no one knew his real one.

Needless to say, Terry was stunned at this turn of events. No one outside of Rusty had ever stood up for her before. Which made the man A-OK in Terry's all-too-short book. Not that she ever had a chance to pay him back. She saw Doc precisely one time after this particular face- off with Ratso. One day, after a run, she entered the clubhouse just as he was leaving. She gave him a friendly nod of affirmation, which he returned, a smile crinkling his clear blue eyes as he saw her. Or maybe it was just gas.

At any rate, that was the sum total of her interactions with him. She never saw him again. Rumor (once again) had it that Doc had split for greener pastures after a beef with Nesto. Terry privately thought what actually happened was that Nesto soon realized Doc was a better leader and forced him out. In other words, too good a man for the Heads, while all the idiot low-lives like the Rat lingered on.

And Caywood, of course, Terry said to herself as she shifted her weight under the trees. *Happy-Ass Ten-Ton Caywood, the ol' Woman Breaker himself.* Oh yeah, she was anticipating some *real* fun this afternoon.

"If he ever gets around to haulin' ass, that is," she said out loud to the day. "Christ, he's so damn fat it probably takes him three trips to haul ass!"

She picked up the magazine she'd been trying to read, skimmed it for a few minutes, then gave up. *Shit, maybe I shoulda brought one a' those books Rusty's always after me to read,* she thought. *Christ, I must be bored.*

Just then came the sound of a low-flying airplane. Or rather, the sound of Caywood's chopper farting down the road. *Thank Christ. Some action.*

She popped up her head and checked the road in both directions. All clear. Luck was with her.

Terry reached into the small burlap sack by her side, pulling out the small home-made objects from within: a set of three pronged spikes made from nails and razors, each edge and point filed to extreme sharpness. Just the perfect thing for shredding tires.

She threw two handfuls, a dozen in all, out into the road as Caywood rounded the bend. The mammoth biker had jacked up the front handlebars so high he looked for all the world like a grand marshal in the world's most pathetic parade.

She braced herself as Caywood's chopper roared by with slightly less sound than a world war. Then over the din came a huge popping sound as sharpened steel dug into hardened rubber.

Caywood almost tipped over from the shock. Once righted he pulled over to the road's dirt shoulder, about a hundred feet away from where Terry hid herself. He thankfully killed the engine, and a hush fell over the day. Terry slowly emerged from her hiding place, the only weapon the omnipresent razor in her pocket.

Caywood was too absorbed in his bike to notice, his thick fingers digging into the tires. He pulled out the spike and stared at it with a puzzled expression on his face, like he was wondering what kind of rock it was.

Terry crept up behind him. "Caywood," she said simply.

Caywood looked over at ther slowly, then rose up and up. "Terry," he grunted back. "What the hell're you doin' here?"

"Waitin' fer you, big boy," she responded as she ticked off mentally points of attack. "Well, waitin' fer that sacka money yer carryin'. Now be a good boy and hand it over, an' maybe I won't hurt ya too bad."

Since Terry's head reached about the center of Caywood's chest, he might have been forgiven for his reaction to Terry's less-than-polite request (even though it took him a moment to actually process it). He looked puzzledly at her, narrowing his tiny eyes (the only real visible part of his face above the bushy beard and beneath the long, greasy hair) in what passed for thought, then threw his head back and started to laugh. Big, booming, it came, matching the offensive volume of his roaring, bellowing bike. "Haw! Haw! Haw!" he laughed. "Haw Haw Haw!"

Yes, his reaction might have been forgiven, if Terry was ever in a forgiving mood (or even the forgiving sort). "Haw Haw Haw Ha-Urk!!!" Caywood choked as Terry planted a side kick straight in the big man's solar plexus.

Caywood was knocked back, but not down. His head, though, was at the proper level from being hunched over, and Terry delivered a swift roundhouse kick to it.

Now Caywood did go down, to his knees, but not for long. He made a grab for his attacker, but was nearly as slow physically as he was mentally. Slower, even, what with two well- placed body kicks to soften him up.

But Terry was ready for this as well. Out came the razor. Down came the slash that split Caywood's palm open.

Now the big biker yelled. The pain, however, served to speed his reactions up. Managing to throw a punch that would have killed a smaller person, Terry nevertheless dodged it easily. *Fuckin' hell, that was close,* she thought. *The damn breeze from it nearly knocked me down. Gotta end this shit. Fast.*

The attempted punch left a certain part of Caywood's anatomy exposed, and Terry took full advantage of it. Steel-tipped boot met jean-clad crotch and Caywood howled, doubling over in pain. Terry followed her kick up with a downward pound from her doubled-up fists, slamming them in the back of Caywood's shaggy head.

Caywood went face-first in the dirt. Terry heard a satisfying pop that could only have been the breaking of his nose. Still, wanting the man to roll over and give her his complete attention, she followed up with a kick to his ribs, rolling him over.

Now Terry was on top of him, the razor inches from his face. "Alvin," she admonished. "See what happens to bad li'l boys who don't do what they're told?"

"Fuck you!" he spat, blood flowing from his mouth.

Terry slowly and deliberately drew the razor down the side of his face. Though it only brought a trickle of blood from his temple, the biker screamed like all of his pubic hairs had been ripped out at once. "That was a warning, hot shot," Terry snarled. "Tell me where you stashed the money, or the next one'll slice off somethin' you *need*."

"All right! All right! It's in the left side! Take it!"

"See? Was that so hard?" she smiled sweetly at him. His little pig eyes stared hatefully, stupidly back at her. The thought popped into Terry's head that those eyes might have been the last thing that poor girl he'd raped and crushed to death had seen before dying, and a fresh, cold rage bloomed within.

Without changing expression, Terry folded the razor with her right hand, keeping Caywood's attention on it, while her left snatched up two of the home-made spikes off the ground. Caywood actually started to relax, thinking he could possibly still get out of this mess, maybe even renew his attack.

Terry began to move off of him, but then stopped. "Oh, by the way, Ten-Ton," she said as she faced him. The puzzled look came back into his face. "I t'ink yer broken!" she snarled as she drove both spikes into his eyes.

Now Caywood *screamed*. Screamed so loud that Terry thought her eardrums would rupture. Quickly, she rolled off of him, not fast enough to miss being hit by the sudden splurt of blood, but certainly fast enough to avoid Caywood's subsequent grab for her.

"AAARRRRRRGGGGHHHHH!!!!!!" he cried as he tried to rise. "You fuckin' *bitch!!!* When I get my hands on you-!"

On a cold, wet day in hell, Terry thought as she crept over to Caywood's bike. She popped open the left carry-on compartment and saw a handle jutting from within. Automatically, she reached in and gave it a hearty tug.

Right away, Terry knew something was wrong. No, not wrong. Just different. The carrying case Caywood had was bigger than what Terry used to bring back. A *lot* bigger.

Fifteen feet away from her, Caywood finally managed to get to his knees and was pulling the spikes from the bloody sockets that were once his eyes. Terry hardly noticed. She was too fixated on the size of the case and what it might mean. *Sweet Jesus*, she thought. *I may have hit the motherlode. The case I used to take was a battered-up briefcase. This is something you take on a trip. A* long *trip.* This case was beat-up and second hand looking, too (the less new, the less notice) but that was where the similarity ended. Breathlessly, she undid the latch, paused, then popped the top open all the way.

The breath she didn't realize she was holding was knocked out of her, and she fell backwards from her squat. Not that she felt it, because there before her lay more money than she had ever seen in her life. *Shit, I wouldn't see this much in ten a' my lives!* she thought.

Inside the case were fresh, clean, and wrapped-in-plastic packages of hundred and fifty dollar bills. Images of Ben Franklin and U.S. Grant stared grimly up at her. *What the fuck is goin' on here?*, Terry thought. *When did Nesto start moving this kinda package?*

She slammed the case shut, fixing its clasp, then checked on Caywood. He was still bleeding, flailing and cursing, but nowhere near her. Good. As a matter of fact, he was wandering even further into the road. Even better.

She watched him for a second, thinking. Then an idea popped into her head so sudden and bright, she knew it had to be the answer.

Caywood taking over her route. The appearance (and disappearance) of Doc, Terry being forced out, not just out of the courier business, but all the way. Of course.

But now wasn't the time for the pondering crap. She had to blow this popsicle stand with her ill-gotten gains before some pain-in-the-ass innocent bystander happened upon this happy little scene.

Quickly, quietly, she stole past Caywood down the road, not even giving him the barest glance as she went by. She reached her bike, stashed away behind some trees, and strapped the case to it. Then, with a final backward glance at the blind man flailing and cursing in the road, she revved up and roared off.

About a hundred yards down the road from her chopper-jacking, a large, blue Ford pickup passed her going the other way. The driver, a fat old man in bib overalls who looked like he shouldn't be riding anything more complicated than a go-cart, sped by at quite a good clip.

Terry slowed her bike to listen. After about ten seconds came the sounds she was waiting for: the squeal of tires from a sudden slamming of the brakes, a hoarse shout, then the unmistakable sound of three tons of metal and glass colliding with three-hundred fifty pounds of flesh and bone.

"Daaaaayyyyyyymmn!" Terry drawled when the sounds subsided. "That's gonna leave a dent."

She allowed herself a brief chuckle as she gunned the motor, her mind wandering back to the prize strapped to the bike. *If this here means what I think it does,* she told herself. *Ol' Nesto's gonna want it back for more than just the amount. More'n happy to be a finger in his eye in more'n one way.*

She dug into her pocket for her smokes, then grimaced as she realized she'd smoked her last one while waiting on the hillside. *Fuck it,* she thought. *Not like I can't afford to get a new pack at the 7-Eleven on my way home. That, and a calculator.*

CHAPTER 42

Please be home, Rache, Ari thought as he heard the electronic ring on the other end. *When I really need you, please be there.*

The sixth ring passed and he was about to hang up when it was finally picked up. "Hello?" came Rachel's voice.

"Rache? It's me."

"Ari? You sound terrible. What's wrong?"

Ari told her. The afternoon spent with Graziano, what he told about himself, then what he told about Ari's family.

Rachel was silent for the majority of it, only asking a few leading questions to keep him on track. But when he was done, there was silence from the other end. Then: "Ho . . .lee . . .Crud!"

Another brief silence. "Jesus," she said finally. "What the . . .?"

Pause. Then: "This guy, Graziano. Do you believe him? Do you trust him?"

Yeah, I think so. You'd be amazed what kinda trust develops when a guy's keeping a hundred-forty-five pound weight from dropping on your head."

"Good point."

"Besides, what would he have to gain by lying? It's too fucking whack not to be the truth."

"But why would your father do something like that? To his own father, no less!"

"I don't know, Rache. I really don't. And what the hell am I gonna do with this? If I didn't hate my old man already, this takes the cake. How can I even look at him knowing this?"

"I wish I could answer that for you, Ari. This is stunning to me, too. This is low. Really fucking low."

There was a brief silence on the phone between them. Then Rachel said, "Well, whatever you decide, I'll be there for you. You know that, don't you?"

"Yeah. Yeah, I do. You always have been." "And I always will be."

"I'm afraid, Rache. Really afraid."

"About your dad? Don't be."

"No, fuck him. I'm afraid of. . . . I'm afraid you're going to get caught in the crossfire, Rache. Not with me and Dad. Between me and Terry. Scranton. I'm afraid she might hurt you."

And then Rachel responded in a way that would haunt Ari for the rest of his days. "Oh, come on, Ari. That'll never happen."

But, at the time, it made him feel good. He smiled, the first honest one in days. "Thanks, Rache. For everything. For always being there."

"No problem, big Ari-on-the-town. Besides, it's not like your parents and I aren't being watched. When I passed your house, the cop car was right in front. So we're in good hands."

"Cool."

"And if that red-neck bitch shows up on my doorstep, I'll tear her fucking head off!"

And I believe you could do it, too, Ari thought. *No question.*

"G'nite, Rache," he said out loud. "Study hard."

"You, too. And get some rest, will you? And remember: even if you don't have your parents, you'll always have me."

Ari hung up the phone slowly. The dark shadow had reached his heart again, and he stared at the phone for a long time. ·

CHAPTER 43

Terry put down the pencil she was using and shut off the cheap calculator. She stretched, reaching towards the ceiling, feeling the knots and cramps pop out of her muscles.

It was a well-lit night; she could see the landscape outside the trailer's window bleached by the full moon. Nesto and his team of numb-nuts had yet to show. Terry truly doubted that they would this night. *Tomorrow's a different story, though,* she told herself. *They'll be here, and probably not in the best of moods.*

She lit a cigarette and smiled. *Let 'em come. I'm ready for 'em. All of 'em. Ain't no way no one gets outta here alive.*

Her eyes drew back towards the pile of money stacked neatly in front of her on the cracked kitchen table. Twice she'd counted it out, and twice she came up with the same figure: $350,000 in unmarked hundreds and fifties. It was truly the mother load. "Three hundred-fifty large," she said out loud as she exhaled. "How d'ya like that?"

She was troubled by just one thing: a nagging voice in her head that was constantly telling her to get out now, to start running, and never stop until she got to her destination, far, far out of the country. She did her best to squash that voice. *Well, I am gonna run,* she thought. *But not til I get back some a' my own. T'show people what it means to fuck with Terry Scranton.*

Nesto and his goons were just the beginning. Then she'd go on to the nigger cop. Then the Jewboy's family. And his girlfriend next door.

Then the Jewboy himself. The motherfucker singularly

276

responsible for this whole downward slide. Terry felt a slight burning sensation in her hand and realized she had just crushed her cigarette. After scraping it into the overflowing ashtray, she looked up at the cracked Budweiser clock her daddy installed on the wall. 10:05 pm, it said. *Man,* she thought. *I ain't been t'bed this early in a long time. Must be gettin' old.*

She considered it. *Nah, I just know that tomorrow's gonna be a hell of a day, no matter how y'look at it.*

Terry switched off the light and tumbled onto her cot. *Prolly be up half the night, though,* she told herself.

She was only half-right. Five minutes after her head hit the pillow, she was sound asleep.

CHAPTER 44

The next morning saw Ari locking the door to his room when he spied a familiar figure down the hall punching the buttons of the elevator. "Hey, Grazzy," Ari called. "Wait up."

When he reached him, Ari said, "I was wondering if you wanted to get together for a quick workout session after class."

Graziano's expression was a mixture of confusion and (rare for him) unease. "Well, sure," he responded. "But don't you wanna rest? We did one yesterday."

"I know," Ari said. "But I got some aggression to work off."

Graziano nodded, but made no comment. The elevator opened, and the two clambered on. There were a few moments of silence before Graziano broke it. "Look, Sussman," he began.

"Don't worry about it. Knowing my old man, you're probably telling the truth."

"I am. Just because I'm an actor. . .well, maybe *because* I'm an actor, I always try to tell the truth. In real life."

"Good to know."

The elevator arrived at the ground floor and opened. Its cargo exited and made their way to the dorm's front door.

Outside, Graziano headed left while Ari split off to the right. "Three o'clock?," Graziano called back.

"I'll be there," Ari responded.

So began the most horrible, terrifying, liberating day of Ari's life.

CHAPTER 45

Blam! Tchink!

"Bullseye."

Terry shifted the gun. The remains of beer bottles littered the ground around the tree in which she had placed them. So far, she was four for four.

Blam! Tchink!

Five.

It was high noon, and Nesto and his slime bags had yet to show themselves. Terry had risen early, fitted in a workout and a run, and still the numb nuts were nowhere to be found. *Maybe they got lost,* Terry thought. *Not like I've had Nesto over for drinks a whole lot.* In the meantime, she decided to amuse herself with a little target practice.

One of the few decent things her daddy had taught her was how to shoot. This skill was not passed on to his daughter out of any benevolent feelings or (God forbid) love, but out of necessity. Since dear old dad was prone to drinking up whatever paychecks he received, the Scranton family often had to forage for food as best they could; the nearby woods happened to be the best source. Terry frequently proved to be a better shot than her brother (*Sheee-it,* Terry thought. *During target practice, the little panty-waste nearly blew himself* and *daddy away. Too bad he missed*) and it was usually up to her to bring down the small birds, squirrels, and occasional deer that made up the family meal.

Blam! Tchink!

Six.

Terry grinned. She rarely missed when she didn't shoot from the hip. She couldn't wait to decorate the old homestead with (the admittedly small amount of) Demon Head brains.

Unfortunately, she was so lost in that pleasant little thought that she failed to notice the shadows gathering around her until it was almost too late. *Sheeee-oot,* Terry swore mildly to herself. *Ain't it just like company to come when yer not-*

The rest of her thought was cut off as she felt a blow to the back of her head. She staggered forward, then fell. When she looked up (not very far), Nesto was standing over her with a look of pure rage on his face. In fact, this was probably the maddest she'd ever seen him. She had to bite her tongue in order to keep from laughing out loud.

"Damn, Nesto," she said evenly. "Who pissed in yer mornin' beer?"

Nesto looked about one second away from throttling her. Behind him stood Pig Meat and the other Samoan brother. Each had an equal amount of rage on their faces and guns stuck prominently in their waistbands. *Least they ain't drawn 'em yet,* Terry thought. *That's good, though I think I'm kinda insulted.*

"Where is it, cunt?" Nesto bellowed.

"If you dunno where a cunt is, Nesto, you got more problems'n I thought."

Nesto responded by slapping her hard enough to draw a bead of blood from her lip. Terry was beginning to get a little ticked, but was smart enough not to show it. Yet.

"Yer about t'get a hellava lot worse, bitch, if'n ya don't tell me where the money's at," Nesto said.

"Money?" Terry asked as she'd started to stand and brush herself off. "What the heller y' talkin' about?"

Nesto advanced on her, shoving her back onto the ground. By now, Terry was furious, but still kept it under control. *Just think about the end result,* she told herself.

"Oh, *that* money," she said out loud as she got up again. "You mean the three-hundred thousand I took offa Lard Ass Caywood? That money?"

Nesto put his hand on his gun, but didn't move otherwise. Obviously he'd decided it was prudent to reel in his own rage, as well. "That's a hellava lotta dough, Nesto," Terry went on. "More'n I'm used t'seein' round the ol' clubhouse. So, I got t'thinkin."

The gang leader said nothing, just continued to watch Terry. The two behind him continued to play follow-the-leader so well she wondered who'd plopped in the community brain that morning.

"Why wuz I suddenly forced out?" Terry asked. "An' why did ya pick Caywood, of all people? He ain't got the brains of a cactus."

Nesto still didn't move. He could have been an ice sculpture for all the heat and energy he was putting out. So Terry tried for a more direct approach. She faced Nesto head on as she spoke her next words. "It was because he had the brains of a cactus, wasn't it, ya fuckin' midget? I woulda noticed how big the case wuz gettin', and woulda started askin' questions. Worst a' all, I mighta seen how much you wuz makin' and demanded a bigger cut, 'steada that coupla hundred ya piss out t'me every week. An' you prolly paid Caywood even less, an' he's too stupid t'know the difference."

She paused. "At least, he *was*," she said with a cackle.

Nesto didn't eve bat an eye. Instead, he said, "He was man enough ta lead me t'you. After ya gouged out his eyes, he got in the way of a fuckin' pickup. Killed the old guy drivin' it instantly. But Caywood? He held on in the hospital until I managed ta get t'him. All I had to do was ask, an' he said 'Terry', plain as day. Not that I couldna figgered it out fer m'self, who was stupid enough to fuck with my money."

Terry's eyes narrowed. "But it ain't yer money, is it, Nesto?" she said. "Yer jest holdin' onto most a' it fer somebody else."

At first, Nesto said nothing, but Terry could see a flicker in his eye. After a beat, he said, "What the fuck're ya talkin' about, Terry? You dunno squat."

"But I think I do, Nesto. I think I know why I was out. An' I think I know why yer buddy Doc was here, then up an' split. I know why yer bringin' tons more cash than ya used to. Who've ya hooked up with, Nesto? It ain't just home-cooked meth anymore, is it? It's big money now. Big drug money that yer sellin' and transferin'. Whose is it? The guineas up in New Yawk? The Columbians? Or the spics like you from Mexico? Doc was here to set you up, to arrange a deal, wannit he? To hook up the pipeline an' make it clear. What're ya into, Nesto? An' are ya sure a little sawed-off runt like you can handle it?"

Nesto pulled the gun from his waistband and pointed it directly at Terry's face. "One more fuckin' word outta ya, cunt, and I'll blow yer ugly head off," he snarled.

Terry laughed. "No, ya won't. Cuz you dunno where it is. Where I hid it. And gettin' that money back is a lot more important to ya than gettin' yer feelins hurt."

Nesto lowered the gun again and regarded Terry with a cold smile. "Mebbe yur right," he said. "Actually, I wuz hopin' you won't tell me too soon. The boys n' I'll have more fun beatin' it outta ya! Piggy! Ron!"

The two bikers behind him moved in. Quickly, Terry reached down and snatched up the gun she had dropped when Nesto first hit her. She pointed it directly into his face. "Here's a little reminder, fellas," she said. "I gotta gun, too."

Pig Meat and the Samoan stopped in their tracks, but Nesto regarded her with such a smug look that Terry was thrilled about what was to happen. "Stupid bitch," Nesto said. "A .45 only holds six shots. And you've already fired off six without reloadin'. I counted."

Terry stared at the gun stupidly, like she had never seen it before. "God damn, Nesto!" she said. "Yer right!"

Without another word, she pistol-whipped Nesto across the face with the .45's barrel, the sudden snap and pop telling her that she had broken his nose. The gang leader went down, howling and clutching at his face. The Samoan went for him as Pig Meat made a grab for Terry, which she easily dodged. She dropped the empty gun and ran for the shed behind her house where she'd home-cooked methamphetamine for years.

Pig Meat tried his best to keep up, but he was hauling nearly three hundred pounds on his frame. Terry ran five miles every other day and was almost half his weight. Needless to say, it wasn't much of a contest, and Terry had to even slow down so Pig Meat could close the distance a bit. Behind them, she half-heard Nesto scream to the Samoan to cut her off around the other side of the house.

Terry made it to the shed and dove face-first through the open window. Pig Meat, as she expected, crashed full-speed through the shed's ajar door right beside it.

Pig Meat sputtered as the contents of the bucket placed over the door fell on his head, soaking him. When the pungent scent of gasoline assailed his nostrils, he knew he was in trouble.

Terry was right upon him, popping her new Zippo open in his face. "Sheeeee-it, Piggy," she gloated. "Oldest trick in the book, an' you fell for it. Couldn't ya just die?"

Pig Meat didn't answer, just stared in wide-eyed terror at the woman brandishing the open flame. "Now, why don't we just back up?" Terry said, thrusting forward.

Pig Meat did as he was told. Terry backed the man to the outside of the shed, in full view of his fellow gang members, then shouted "Roast Pork!" as she threw the lighter at him.

The results were as instantaneous as they were horrifying. Pig Meat howled as he was turned into a man-sized fireball. Terry didn't even bother to look back as she ran off, diving straight into the woods. Out of sight, she climbed a tree to get a good vantage point.

Pig Meat was thrashing himself all over the back yard. "AHHHHHHH," he screamed. "I'm burnin' up!! SWEET JESUS I'M BURNIN' UP!!!!"

By now, the flames had totally engulfed him. She could barely make out the man for the fire. Terry saw the Samoan appear on her left, staring dumbstruck at the scene before him.

Pig Meat had stopped speaking words and was by now just screaming. Terry hadn't thought a human voice could shout so loud; her ears were ringing from yards away.

Then, over the screams came the sound of two quick shots. The fireball stopped thrashing and the yelling ended. The fireball sank a bit, then fell forward continuing to char the grass beneath it. Through the smoke and flames, Terry saw Nesto emerge, quietly, deliberately. Scanning the woods, he passed the flaming remains of Pig Meat without so much as a glance. *Fuckin' cocksucker,* Terry thought. *Piggy was one of his oldest friends. He deserves every bit a' what I'm gonna serve him.*

Nesto searched the woods to Terry's right, gun still drawn. The Samoan was to the left, doing likewise. Terry watched them for a moment, then silently clambered down from the tree. *Time to divide and conquer,* she said to herself as she grabbed a large rock from the tree's base. She tossed it to her right, making sure it landed in the woods. Nesto immediately perked up and chased the sound.

Terry made to the left. Crashing through the outskirts of the woods, she saw the Samoan with his back to her. "Hey, big boy!" she called. "Try'n catch me!"

As she ran, the heard the Samoan's gun go off behind her and felt the dust kick up around her ankles. *Keep it comin', big boy,* she thought. *Right into my little surprise.*

Terry speeded up, placing some distance between her and the Samoan. She crashed through the front door of the house and half-ran, half-dove through the living room and over and behind the broken-down couch.

The Samoan crashed through the door after her, but couldn't immediately locate her; he hesitated and was lost. The question in his mind was answered in spades as Terry popped up from behind the couch, cradling the shotgun she had liberated from the Demon Heads clubhouse two months before. The same shotgun she had used to kill his brother.

"Surprise, sonny boy!" she yelled as she chambered a round.

The blast echoed through the early afternoon air. The Samoan took both barrels directly in the chest, blown back to finally rest half-in, half-out of the doorway. *Two down,* Terry thought. *One-half to go.*

"Hey, Nesto!" she shouted as the echo of the blast died away. "Yer down two Heads! Like I said before, hard t'get good help these days!"

Slowly, carefully she inched her way to the front door, shotgun at the ready. "Now it's jus' you n' me, wetback!" she called. "Ready fer a li'l one-on-one?"

Nesto's answer came in a form that scared Terry shitless: the sound of a motorcycle's engine being started. "Fuck!" Terry screamed as Nesto throttled it into a roar.

Someone who didn't know Nesto as well as Terry did might have been heartened by the sound, but she knew what it really meant. Nesto was making a tactical retreat in order to go back and bring more men. *A lot more men*, Terry thought as she bolted from the door. *They'll be Heads from here to Christmas! I ain't prepared to take on no army!*

Nesto was already halfway down her driveway, barely giving her a backward glance as he speeded up. For the first time in her life, she thanked God she was never able to get the driveway paved. Otherwise, Nesto would've been off like a shot rather than having to gradually speed up. Terry knew that best she'd get was one shot. The problem was, where to put it? Shoot at Nesto? No, too small a target. The gas tank of the bike? Again, too much chance of missing. Then she hit upon it: the front wheel.

All this thought process took less than a second as Terry hauled ass across the front lawn. It took her twice as long to chamber a round and draw a bead.

The blast made the entire front wheel explode, sending shards of rubber and steel flying. Nesto pitched forward, landing face-first on the gravel. She heard a sharp *snap!* and the rest of the bike went flying through the air, crashing into the tall grass on the other side of the road. The engine roared, then sputtered and died.

Terry approached Nesto's body cautiously, shotgun at the ready. She quickly realized that, though still alive, he was no longer a threat. He was screaming, but his head was the only thing that moved, contorted as it was at an unhealthy angle.

"Auuugghhh!!" the head gurgled, its mouth dripping blood and saliva. "I can't feel nuthin'!"

"Tough break, Nesto. Really," Terry cackled. "Looks like yer neck's broken an' yer paralyzed."

The bloodshot eyes focused on her, pulsing with rage. "Well, c'mon, bitch!" Nesto roared. "Finish it!"

Terry stuck the business end of the shotgun in Nesto's face, and Nesto closed his eyes. She regarded him for a minute, then shouldered the shotgun and grinned. "Nah, don't think so, Nesto," she said. "That's what you want. Ain't gonna be that easy, though. I can put ya outta yer misery, sure. But after all you done, t'me an' ev'rybody else, you don't deserve to go out easy." She looked up into the sky at the small, dark forms circling overhead. "See that?" she asked. "Crows. They know sumthin's 'bout t'die. Trouble is, sometimes they don't wait. If the carcass ain't movin', hint hint, they comes down t'investigate. By peckin' at a thing. So they're gonna come down soon and start feedin' on ya, bit by bit."

Terry leaned over and gave Nesto her most savage grin. "That's the kinda death you deserve, spic. A slow one. And all you can do is let 'em peck away."

She stood back up. "Have a nice death, midget. Maybe you'll die when they get to yer brains. Then again, maybe you won't."

Terry turned and walked away, the shotgun resting on one shoulder. She laughed as Nesto hurled curses and insults at her back. But halfway to the house, she heard something amidst the *bitches*, *fucks* and *cunts* that froze her in her tracks.

Something that sounded a lot like the words *daddy* and *still alive*.

"What didja say, motherfucker?" Terry asked, turning back.

The remains of Nesto's face widened into a bloody, gap-toothed grin. "I said," he said. "That when me an' the boys left here, yer daddy was still alive."

"What the fuck're ya talkin' about?"

"Whoever plugged 'im did after we beat the shit outta him an' left. We left his ass on the driveway, an' he wasn't dead. He was still moanin' from the pain. So whoever forced that gun down his throat did at after we hightailed it on outta here."

"Now," Nesto continued. "Y'think about that as I'm lyin' here, rottin' away. Cuz if'n you do, me dyin' slow won't be that bad."

Terry had already been approaching Nesto as he spoke; now that he was done, she chambered another round. "Aw, c'mon, Nesto," she said. "Y' know me better'n that. I hate leavin' anything lyin' around unfinished."

"Yeah, FUCK YOU!!!" Nesto screamed.

One blast from two barrels later, the remains of the gangleader's head spun off to join his cooling bike at the side of the road.

Terry threw down the shotgun and collapsed into herself. It was over. She had won. She had single-handedly taken on the top tier of the Demon Heads and finished them off. Phase One of her plan was complete. *Don't re-break yer arm pattin' yerself on the back just yet, girl,* she told herself. *There's still a lot more t' do.*

Turning, she walked back to the house. *First thing,* she thought. *Gotta put Piggy out. Then I gotta drag what's left a' him inside the house. That's gonna be a fun fuckin' chore.*

Behind her, unseen, swooped down the first crow. Almost silently he started pecking away at Ernesto Gonzaga's remains. Soon came more.

CHAPTER 46

Ari unlocked his room and entered. All was as he'd left it that morning. He looked at his clock. 6:34, it read.

He had just come from dinner. Along with Graziano's physical training had been advice on Ari's diet. "Stop eatin' all that fried shit," Graziano had said. "Eat broiled or baked meats and veggies. And while yer at it, cut back on the amount of red meat you eat." "Doesn't it have a lot of protein?" Ari had asked.

"It does, but it also has a lotta fat." Graziano gave him the once-over. "Maybe it's not as much of an issue with you, ya damn toothpick," he said. "But you'll feel a lot better. Have more energy."

Graziano was right, damn him. Ari did feel a lot better lately. True his outside stressors still weighed heavily on his mind, but his adjusted diet, along with the copious amounts of exercise, made him feel a lot better physically than he ever had in his life.

Ari looked at his mirror's reflection for a second, then thought, *oh, what the hell,* and took off his shirt. *Well, I still look like a "Before" ad,* he told himself as he examined his naked upper torso. *But I look less like one. Actually starting to see some definition, though nobody's gonna confuse me with Schwarzenegger.*

Today's workout was extremely gratifying, if also tiring. He took to the weights with such vim and vigor that Graziano had to keep reminding him to slow down. The run was a revelation, too. True he had huffed and puffed for the last half mile, but considering he'd completed the first three in record time, he felt he had a reason to be proud. *God damn!* he thought as he flexed in the mirror. *Didn't think*

I'd ever say this about myself, but I feel damn near giddy! The ring of the phone intruded upon his thoughts. Ari checked the time again. 6:36. He frowned. *Don't think it's Rachel. She usually doesn't phone till about eight or nine.*

The more disturbing thought came into his head as he placed his hand on the receiver.

Maybe it's my redneck "friend". Knew this evening was too good to last.

But it was neither. "Hello?"

"I just turned into *my* driveway, looked across *my* yard, and saw a cop car sitting across the street. As a matter of fact, it's the last thing I see before I go into *my* house."

"Hi, Dad."

"And it's been that way for over a week now. How much longer am I gonna have to put up with this?"

"I hope for not much longer, Dad. Mr. Jones thought it was best. For you guys protection and all."

"Oh, yeah. *Detective* Jones," Mr. Sussman said in a voice that made Ari want to reach through the phone and slap him. "Your new buddy. Yeah, I'm sure if we leave it in his hands, everything'll just turn out fine."

"What's that supposed to mean?"

"Oh, c'mon, Ari! Can't you tell that guys fulla shit? Didn't I teach you better'n that?" *You didn't teach me shit,* Ari thought. Out loud he said: "How is he 'full of shit', Dad? He's a cop. He's doin' his job."

"Yeah, well, I checked up on him."

"Yeah? And?"

"That your Detective Jones is one of the biggest drunks on the Maryland police force. That he's had the most write-ups from his superiors than any other detective. That he's one of the most useless fuck-ups they have. Do you know that he's an inch away from being let go? That he's been busted for insubordination half-a-dozen times?"

"No, Dad. I didn't."

"Oh, fer chissake, Ari! Wake up! This asshole's pullin' a scam on you! When're you ever gonna realize you can't trust nobody but your family?" *And sometimes, not even them*, Ari thought. Out loud: "Look, Dad, I don't know the full story, but I'm sure Barney's doing the best he can."

Mr. Sussman chuckled with no humor. His voice dripped condescension. "You poor, stupid, naive kid. I try to tell you somethin' and you just go on believing the best. When are you ever gonna grow up and see things for what they are? You're damn lucky to have the old man around."

The red hot anger turned cold. Bitterly, frigidly, clearheadedly cold. "Just like your old man, huh, Dad?"

There was the barest hesitation on the other end, then: "What the hell are you talkin' about? Pop's been dead for years."

"Yeah, musta been rough being an 'Orphan'."

This time the pause was much longer. "Wh . . .What did you say?"

"That's what they called you back in the old neighborhood, didn't they, Dad? You musta left all that out during the times you were 'teaching' me."

"How did you-?"

"You think you're the only one who can check things out, Dad.? You think you're so fuckin' clever? And Pop didn't die a long time ago now, did he?"

Now things got so quiet over the phone that Ari thought they had been disconnected.

Finally, Mr. Sussman said: "You . . .you. . . .", and fell silent.

Ari waded in. "And he died alone. How's that for lookin' after your family?"

"How did. . .how did you . . ."

"Is it true, Dad? Is it true!?"

The silence on the other end was all the answer Ari needed. "Goddamnit, Dad!" he exclaimed, on the verge of tears. "How could you?"

"Oh, like you treat me any better?"

Ari exploded. "Don't you fucking dare turn this back on me! It's not about me, remember? Isn't that what you n' Mom tell me all the time? Now you can have it all back! *In fucking spades!!!*"

"Why, you resentful, ungrateful, spiteful-"

"Aw, go fuck yourself, you sorry excuse for a father!!!"

The line went dead in Ari's ear, leaving only the open hum of the dial tone. Air slammed the receiver back home, cracking the phone's frame down the middle. He looked for something to hit. Seeing his books lying on his study carrel, he swept them off the table. Then he picked them up one by one and threw them against the wall. Pages flew everywhere. Then he slammed his fists as hard as he could down on the study carrel itself. The base of it cracked, but it did not break. He stood against it for a long time, body slumped forward, hands pressed against the wood, feeling twenty years of surpressed rage flow through him. *Motherfucker,* he thought. *I never wanna see you again. I'm ashamed even to be related to you. You can rot in hell, old man. And it's one you made for yourself. What you did to Pop, I'm gonna do to you. Do a slow fucking roast in your own hell, old man.*

He sat down on the bed, spent. *Christ, I wish I could just close my eyes and have all this go away. All over. Everything. My parents. My accident. My life.*

Then he fell back into the threshold of sleep, and thought no more.

CHAPTER 47

Terry tightened the final knot attaching the case full of money to her motorcycle. After one last satisfying yank, she stood and looked at the scene behind her.

Her home looked no different from the countless other times she had seen it, save for the fact that she knew she was now viewing it for the last time. The sun was just beginning to disappear over the horizon; in an hour or so, if she had decided to let things be, the whole place would have been shrouded in darkness. *Can't believe I actually conked out this afternoon,* she thought. *Otherwise, I'da been long gone.*

And conk-out she did. After the messy work of dragging the two bodies of Nesto's henchmen into the house, and the more pleasant task of packing up the money (which, ironically, had sat on the trailer's table all during the resulting battle; it wasn't at if she'd gone to any great lengths to hide it), she felt beat. *Well, I guess it wouldn't hurt to lie down fer awhile,* she told herself as she flopped down on the cot.

But the minutes turned to hours. Finally, Terry jerked herself awake as she regained her conscious bearings. She stole a look at the clock; well over three hours had passed. Somewhat shaken, she emerged from the trailer . . .and walked straight into the horrific scene that presented itself across the late afternoon.

The crows had stopped feeding on Nesto's body, but only because something much larger had taken their place. And the creature that

292

had come from the sky so much resembled the monster bird of her dreams that Terry nearly screamed.

The bird was certainly big and ugly, but lacked both features to the degree that the South American Condor possessed. *Vulture*, Terry thought. *Nesto's stink done brought down a friggin' vulture!*

The great bird was in the process of pulling a long, slender entrail out of Nesto's stomach when it spotted Terry. The dark, beady eyes bore into her as it flapped its great, dark wings and hissed.

That was enough to send Terry back into the trailer. For one brief second, she had no idea what to do. Then she spotted the .45 she had placed on the table after the afternoon tussle. Re- emerging, she made a beeline for the big carrion bird. Once again, it flapped its wings and hissed, but now Terry answered with a single slug into its festering little heart.

There was a brief flurry of wings and a choked-off *squak!* as the creature tumbled forward onto the body it had been feeding on. Terry, however, felt no better. "Sorry, birdie," she murmured. "Don't like killin' animals, 'cept fer food, but you was just too damn ugly t'live."

She tucked the gun into her waistband. "Time t'get a move on," she said to the empty air. "Before someone comes a-lookin' fer these deflated douche bags."

The next two hours were busy ones as she packed up all the things she wanted to take (precious few), packed away the money, and carefully situated all the tanks of kerosene she had bought and stockpiled the week previous. She drenched the inside of the house with one (bodies included) and placed one tank right in the front door. Another she planted in the shed, then left a path with another to the trailer. Inside the trailer, she placed two more, one in the door way and one on her cot.

While loading up the trailer, she felt a pang of regret. In the past, it had often been her only refuge from a shitty world. *Not only that,* she told herself. *From a shitty father. But still, if I'm gonna make m'self a fresh start, an' fer m'plan t'work, everythin's gotta go.*

Now she stood at the yard's edge, leaning on her motorbike, staring at the view under the setting sun. *Place's been like the best n' worst fer me*, she said to herself. *Even so, here's where it all ends, I guess.*

She pulled the .45 from her waistband and drew a bead on the kerosene tank sitting in the front doorway. *Or maybe, this is where it all begins.*

The early evening air was split by a single shot and a much louder, longer explosion. Soon the whole house was consumed in a blazing fireball. Sparks from the house landed on the shed, which quickly carried its own blaze. Then another explosion obliterated it as the fire reached the tanks inside.

Terry watched this conflagration calmly, almost impassively, with a hint of smile on her lips. It took only five minutes for the whole property to become an inferno after which time, Terry decided she'd seen enough. *Bright n' hot enough now fer the neighbor's t'see, half a mile away*, she thought as she mounted the bike. *Prolly callin' the fire department right now. Best I be gone.*

She grinned as the mighty engine roared into life. She popped a tape into its deck, while simultaneously kicking up the kick stand. W.A.S.P.'s "Show No Mercy" soon accompanied the growl of her motor, and she roared off just as there was a final, earsplitting explosion as the fire reached the tanks inside the trailer.

She never looked back as her self-made nova lit up the night.

CHAPTER 48

Jones slapped the file closed and slumped back in his office chair. He rubbed his eyes in an effort to remove the blear from them. *It fits, goddamnit*, he thought. *It fits!*

On his desk lay "The Hobby", the collective files of Terry Scranton and Rusty Darrow. (*Maybe I should be taking up a real hobby*, he admonished himself. *Needlepoint. Paint-by- numbers. Something.*) He had just been reviewing a rather intriguing police report faxed in from the San Francisco police, dated from 1966. Six members of a local biker gang found slain in a basement apartment. All six had had their throats sliced upon from a nearby discarded butcher knife. *Clean of fingerprints, of course*, Jones thought. *No suspects, no leads. Case remains officially unsolved. Tox screen from the autopsy showed that each one had twice the legal limit for alcohol, and enough drugs to make up the entire GNP of South America. It's a wonder they could fuckin' even move!*

Jones shook his head. All in all, it proved nothing. The cops at the time thought they were the victim of a rival gang. *Or maybe not. Maybe they were partying with a certain red-headed biker chick, and someone got it into their feeble little minds to carry the party even further.*

"And after the dirty little deed was done," Jones said out loud. "The bikers went on partying themselves into a stupor. And Rusty, being the clever little gal she is, just lays there. Then a different sort of party started."

Jones sighed heavily. It was all circumstantial and speculative, he knew. One kink was Rusty's admitted time-line/interview that claimed she'd been raped during the Summer of Love, 1967. "That throws the time line-off, maybe," he said to the empty air. "Except that maybe it was intentional, covering her tracks. And not just because of the murder, no. Because after that, she'd disappeared, resurfacing a couple years later in West Virginia. Why West Virginia? Probably because it was the furthest she could get from Frisco, distance-wise and culturally. So why did it take her two or so years to travel cross-country? Because, courtesy of the gang rape, Rusty soon realized she was carrying a little passenger with her."

Jones looked over at the office clock. 9:31, it read. *Fuck it,* he thought. *Need to call it a night. Gotta figure out, for my own ends, just what the next step is here. Cuz how'd'ya hit someone with this, especially a woman like Rusty Darrow?*

"Probably should be soon, though," he said as he rose from the desk. "I need to get Terry offa poor Ari's ass. Not to mention that little peckerwood Reed offa mine."

Jones had just placed his hat on his head when the phone rang. He briefly considered letting the voice mail pick up, but something inside him told him this one was important enough to take. "Jones."

"Barney? It's Sheriff Tate. From West Virginia?"

It took Jones a second to make the connection. *Damn, I'm beat,* he thought. Out loud, he said: "Of course. What can I do you for, Jeff?"

"We have some recent developments down here I think you'd like to know about. Ernesto Gonzaga is dead."

"What!?"

"It gets better. We found him at Terry Scranton's place." Jones felt his knees start to weaken, so he sat down in one of his office chairs. "Start from the beginning, Sheriff. Please."

"Roughly two hours ago, a call went in to the Charles Town Fire Department. Some neighbors saw a bright glow at the Scranton place, half a mile away. It took them ten minutes t'get there, and by then the whole house and yard was lit up like the Devil's back yard. But even before they started in with the equipment, they found the body, lying near the driveway. That's when they called us in."

"The body, or what's left of it, was laying there plain as day. Some scavengers had already been feeding on it and, this is where it gets really odd, a dead vulture was slumped against it."

Wha-? "Go on, Sheriff."

"Cause of death appears to be decapitation by a shotgun that was also lying near the body. We dusted it for fingerprints, but it was clean. The head itself was blown against the remains of a motorcycle that was lying in the bushes about ten feet from the body. We also found two intact motorcycles parked across the road. By the time me an' m'boys got there, the fire was out. And that's when we made an even more horrifying discovery."

"Go on," Jones replied in a surprisingly steady voice.

"There were two more bodies in what remained of the house itself, burned beyond recognition. Can't even tell the sex, much less the identity. A coroner is coming in from Wheeling tomorrow."

Jones let out a breath he hadn't been aware of holding. "You think one a' them mighta been Terry?"

"No idea," Tate responded. "But it could be. But if it is, what in God's holy name went on here?"

"How did you manage to identify Ernesto Gonzaga without his head?"

Tate chuckled drily. "Old fashioned police work, Barney. We checked his wallet."

"Nice work. Where are the bodies now?"

"At the local funeral parlor. Town's too damn small for a morgue."

"Good. Gimme two hours and I'll be there."

"See you then."

Jones pressed the hang-up button on the phone and immediately dialed another number. "Connors," answered a voice at the other end.

"Dave, we gotta problem. Get the task force together. We're hittin' the Demon Heads first thing tomorrow morning."

"Why? What's up?"

Jones told him the whole story, from the beginning of Tate's call to his packing up to head to West Virginia. "Christ," was Connors reply. "What a fuckin' clusterfuck!"

"Well said. The excrement has definitely hit the air conditioning. And we need to make a move before word gets back to the rest of the Heads that their fearless leader is no more, and they start destroying evidence. Like I said, I'm on my way to Charles Town right now to access the situation. See you at, what, 8 a.m.?" "Will do. Hang in there, boss man."

"You, too."

Jones placed the receiver back in its cradle and paused for a moment, thinking. Should he call Ari and tell him his troubles might be over? *Nah, don't have time,* Jones thought. *Besides, I'm not sure of anything right now, much less who did what to who.*

He eyed the file on the desk. "Better take you with me," he murmured to himself.

Something tells me I'll be running into Ms. Darrow tonight. Whether or not it's the right time to bring up the past to her, I dunno. Guess I'll figure it out when I get there." He scooped up the file and went out the door, tucking it under his arm. No one inside made note of him as he exited the building.

Rather nice night, Jones thought as he stepped out of the station. *Won't last, but it's good to enjoy the Indian Summer while it lasts.*

Unseen by him, a pair of predatory eyes watched and moved.

Jones found his car, got in, and rolled down the window as he started it. *Might as well enjoy the night air as I take this scenic route,* he thought. *Oughta keep me awake.*

Unheard by him, a motorcycle started and had its engine muffled by the flick of a switch.

Jones pulled out of the station lot and made a left on Montrose Road. The road was quiet, empty, and Jones was completely alone as he stopped at the light.

Inside the car, its occupant was lost in thought, flashing forward to the million things he had to do once he'd gotten to Charles Town. *A million-and-one, if I run into Rusty Darrow,* he thought. Unseen and unheard, a shadowy figure approached the car, all lights off, with only a tell- tale *putt-putt* sound to mark its passage. *Unbelievable how she managed to cover her tracks all these years,* Jones pondered as he waited, the fatigue and the woolgathering masking the sound from his conscious mind. *If nothing else I have to give her credit for-*

"Hey, nigger."

The rasping voice battered its way into his thoughts. Even before he turned his head, he knew who he'd see. And that he was a dead man.

Jones last thought as he turned to look at the gun pointed him was two-fold, meant for both Ari and his own child: *I'm sorry, son. It looks like I failed you.*

There was only one shot. One shot to enter his forehead and blast out the back of his head, blood spraying all over the unopened window on the other side.

When the last echo died, Terry muttered softly: "Told ya, nigger. Told ya what happens to coons who don't let go."

Hurrying now, Terry replaced the kick stand on the bike and dismounted. Reaching in, she grabbed what she wanted through the window. Achieving that, she remounted the bike and peeled out into the night. She paid no mind to the blood-and-brain spattered pages sitting next to Jones's body. If she had, perhaps she may have stopped right there. Or perhaps not.

The entire execution of Bernard Jones took only two-and-a-half minutes. It took twice that long before anyone stumbled across the scene.

CHAPTER 49

Patrolman Jason Thompson had one hand on his cock and the other on his copy of *Big Buttz* magazine when call came through on the scrambler. "Officer down, on Montrose!" the broadcaster fairly screamed. "We've got an officer down! All units in the area, report immediately to the main house!"

"Goddamn!" Thompson yelled in response. "That ain't too far away! Finally, some fuckin' action!"

He tossed the magazine on his squad car's floor, tucked his business away, and took a final look at the Sussman house threw the windshield. "Anything's better'n babysittin' these rich fucks," he said as he started the ignition.

Thompson sped off, cranking up the siren as he left gravel and hit solid road. His face had the expression of a kid on his way to open Christmas presents.

His erection stayed for the entire trip.

Terry barely glanced up as she saw the squad car whiz by, siren wailing. Once it passed, she turned back to the pay phone in the lot of the closed-for-the-night convience store and continued to dial the number she'd thought she'd never call again. "Hello?" came Rusty's voice after the first ring. Terry noted how out-of-breath she sounded, frantic.

"Rust, it's me," she responded. "Terry."

"Oh, thank God!" came the reply in a voice so loaded with relief it made Terry's heart hurt to hear it. *Steady, girl,* she said to herself. *Ya gotta keep hard n' tough if you wanna continue on.*

300

Rusty was still talking. "Where are you?"

"Can't tell ya that, Rust," she replied. "Don't wanna get ya in any more trouble on account a' me. I'm takin' care a' business."

Rusty said nothing for a second, then: "They told me you were dead. Your house-"

"Did that m'self, after I took out Nesto and his goons."

"Why?"

Terry steeled herself for what she had to say next. "Cuz I had to, Rust," she said. "Believe me, its been a long time comin'. I think it was meant to happen this way. I sure as hell weren't good fer anythin' else."

"Terry-"

"Please, Rust. Lemme finish. I done thought about this a long time. I just wanted to call an' let ya know we're square. And t'thank ya. Yer the only one who ever fought fer me. Yer the only real friend I ever had. I know it's been tough sometimes. And I know ya did all y'could. But it wasn't enough. It was prolly too much fer anybody. Fer any one person t'handle."

Terry's voice started to crack on that last word. Her eyes had started to water, and she felt a sting in her sinuses. Wiping her eyes, she fought to keep her voice steady. She had to end this, and soon. "What I mean t'say, Rust," she continued. "I love you. I didn't think I'd ever live t'say that t'somebody, but there's a first time fer ev'rythin', y'know? But now I gotta go. This night ain't over yet fer me. Still gotta lot t'do."

"Terry, wait!"

"Y'know what I wish, Rust? This'll kill ya," Terry said as the tears ran down her cheeks. "I wish you woulda been my mama, 'stead a' that stupid drunk cow I got stuck with. I know ya never wanted kids an' all that, but there ya go. Maybe things woulda turned out diff'rent. Who knows?"

"Terry, I have-"

"G'bye, Rust. An' thanks fer ev'rythin'. I mean it. I love you."

"Goddamn it, Terry-!"

Perhaps if Terry had been an instant slower in hanging up the

301

phone, things would have turned out differently for everyone that night. If she had not been in such a hurry to remount her motorcycle and ride off into what she thought was her destiny, she would have heard the deepest secret of Rusty Darrow's heart, a secret to turn her own heart around. As it was, the confession was lost to the electronic snap and hum of phone cables, echoing uselessly, gone forever. "Goddamn it, Terry!" Rusty had said. *"I AM your mother!!"*

CHAPTER 50

Maury Sussman flung his papers across the desk in frustration, unable to concentrate for the past several hours.

He looked at the clock in his study. 10:05 p.m. Three-and-a-half hours since he'd had his fight with his worthless piece-of-shit of a son. "How?" he shouted to the walls. "How did he find out!?"

Maury Sussman had always lived his life carefully, expediently, leaving nothing to chance. And (above all) keeping things under control. Under *his* control. Of the situation. Of his emotions. Of himself.

It was the only way he knew. It was what got him out of that slum full of ignorant kikes who still covered the mirrors in their houses when anyone died. Where old, bearded idiots rambled on non-stop about a past that never existed, except in the minds of senile old fools who disproved the adage that age is accompanied by wisdom. Where they blabbered on endlessly about their beloved old *shtetls* where life was simple, plain, and where they were only surrounded by people like them. Not this *goyim* "melting pot" that tried to weed out all that was different, all that gave them (the Jews) their identity. This hostile land that was only the latest in a series of nations antagonistic to the Jews and the Jewish way of life.

The Jews, the Jews. That's all Maury Sussman heard about growing up were "The Jews". "The Jews" and how things affected them. How everyone was against them. How that the only people Jews could trust were other Jews.

Maury Sussman had had enough of "The Jews". "The Jews"

had kept his family in poverty, had kept him slaving away in the back room of his own father's shop for pennies (and sometimes not even that if his father was feeling "charitable" to some old hymie or guinea, all to keep the Sussman name pure in their little enclave). *Charity begins at home, old man*, Maury Sussman wanted to say many a time out loud to his father, but couldn't quite dare. *Start by making sure I get paid for my time in this shit hole.*

But he never did; instead, he bided his time. And when that day came for his father to step down and give the reigns to his only son, Maury seized upon it like a half-starved dog on a splintered bone. Gone were the acts of "charity" his father was known for; gone was anything at all done for free. Maury even went so far as to ask certain long time "customers" (whom he'd long since marked as deadbeats) to show him the money to pay for his services. Most of these hangers-on left in a huff, and good riddance. All the better to weed out the dead(beat) wood.

Instead, he courted a more well-heeled clientele. He ended up alienating many of his father's long-time customers (ones who actually paid), but so what? Business was business, and what did they ever do for him? One store became two, two became four, and Maury Sussman made his first million by the time he was thirty. He had turned a little, half-assed, mom-and-pop operation into a cheap suit empire that stretched up and down the East Coast.

Fuck the old neighborhood. Up with being the man he wanted to be.

At first, his father was impressed. But, gradually, word began to get back to him about some of his son's business practices. "Vhat are you doink, Maury?" his father had scolded him in his thick Yid accent. "Ju haf chased away all our people!"

"What did 'our people' ever do for me, Pop? They're the reasons you were such a failure!"

His father had exploded then, crying all the way. Maury just gave him a cold smile, banished him from the stores, and broke off all contact. He especially wanted him away from his grandson, lest he fill him with his Old World foolishness and ways. The ideas of weaklings.

But now, this. Someone had opened their big mouth and told tales out of school. It had somehow gotten out of the box he had so carefully placed it in. And now the little snot-nose thought he had the moral authority to judge *him?*

"Boy's gotta learn who's boss," Sussman said out loud in the study. "And as long as I'm the Dad, that's me. No exceptions."

He shook his head in disgust. Try as he might, there was no getting over it: his son was a weakling. Maybe the grandson of Ariel Sussman the First was doomed genetically to be so, he didn't know. Maybe it was that, against his better judgement, he had married a weak woman. *But the dumb bitch got herself pregnant,* he told himself. *What was I supposed to do? But she gave that damn kid everything he wanted. And what did it get her? Drunk and drugged out on the couch every night. No wonder we never go anywhere. I'd be too damn embarrassed.*

"Weaklings, both of 'em," Sussman said out loud. "How the hell did I get stuck with such a family? How? Why?"

He shook his head. He must be becoming *meshugganah*, a crazy person, talking to himself like that. Only crazy people did that, and Maury Sussman was not one of those.

"Fuckin' kids these days," he continued out loud. "No nerve, guts or balls. Just a nation of whining, spoiled wimps. No backbone at all."

Then what passed for an idea came to him. *If that kid thinks himself some kid of moral example,* he thought. *Let's see him go it alone for awhile. See how he handles that!*

First thing he would do, come the morning, was call the financial office at University of Maryland and tell him he wanted a full refund on the tuition and dorm deposit money. *Best of all, I don't even bother to tell that little shit. Just wait till the administration comes to him and tells him what happened and how he's getting thrown out on his ass! And when he calls me up to whine about it, I'll just say, "Well, you wanted to be done with me? So we're done. Have a nice life."* *We'll see how far he gets after that! Hell, I never got a chance to go to college. Why should he? Let him go out and earn a living, like I had to!*

Pleased with himself now that he had decided on a course of action, Sussman sauntered Out of his private study with a stride reserved for those who were born winners. He went into the family room and heaved is bulk into the big, brown chair situated in front of the TV.

As he had passed his soon-to-be-ex-son's room, a breeze blew through the open window, narrowly missing him as he strode by.

The weakling was passed out on the couch again, no surprise there. She had even pulled the afghan up to her chin. Sussman shook his head in disgust and settled back into his chair, his eyes glued to the TV. Five minutes passed. Nothing moved. Maury stole a glance from the screen just long enough to once again take in the prone form of his wife. She hadn't moved an inch from the last time he looked.

Seeing her face, and that unusually peaceful expression on it, made him uneasy. When was the last time she had fallen asleep with that sort-of-a-smile on it? Angry, he barked, "For Chrissake, Deb! Get to bed! I don't wanna hear you snore while I'm tryin' to watch!"

Nothing. Not even a grunt. He fairly leapt out of his chair and grabbed his wife's arm to shake it. It came loose from its perch and fell to the floor, the knuckles making a sickening *clack* on the floor.

It was then he saw the blood, dribbling down her front. Aghast, he pulled down the afghan. A huge, bloody gash had been opened along her throat. And despite the evidence of violence, Debbie Sussman's countenance showed no signs of resistance or torment. Just the fixed, dreamy grin of someone finally at peace.

Behind him came a sound: the dull thud of boot leather stepping on hardwood floor.

Directly afterwards came the metal-on-metal *clink* of a gun's safety being released. "She went easy, old man," a hoarse, raspy voice said behind him. "How easy you go is up t' you."

Maury Sussman felt his bladder go, the warm spray of urine drenching his groin.

CHAPTER 51

Rachel yawned and stretched, peeling her eyes away from the pages of her five-hundred page-plus law book for the first time in an hour. She rubbed her eyes, certain that they were becoming crossed. *Oh, well,* she told herself. *Only fifty more pages to go. And only ten-thirty. Whoopee.*

She stood up from the bed she was lying on and gave a more complete stretch, reaching for the ceiling. She stole a look at herself in the bedroom mirror, half-expecting to see bags forming under her eyes. Grabbing her coffee cup from the night stand, she exited her bedroom and started down the stairs. The house was quiet, her parents away on one of her father's business trips. *Toronto,* she shook her head ruefully. *Just in time to start freezing their asses off up there.* Then she smiled to herself. *And maybe when they get back next week, they'll find they have a new house guest. Unexpected, but welcome just the same.*

A deep frown crossed her features as she reflected upon her last conversation with Ari. *That fucking hypocrite dad of his,* she thought. *I knew he was a pain-in-the-ass, but I didn't know he was such a* malignant *pain-in-the-ass. Hope to God he's able to stand up to that asshole this time. Knowing what a lousy piece-of-shit Maury Sussman is, he'll probably disown him. But fuck it; Ari can stay here. The parental units like him, and when I tell them the reason, Maury Sussman will become persona non grata.*

Rachel sighed. *Probably won't bother him, though. The Sussman's aren't exactly number one on anyone's invite list around here. But*

*then again, neither are the Brannans. Guess it's because we both had
to work for a living.*

By now she had entered the kitchen and appraised the beckoning
coffee maker. She poured out the grounds (half-and-half, all good).
Measuring out the scoops, her mind turned to that *other* problem of
Ari's. The one that rode a motorcycle and probably chawed "tabacky"
to boot (always a habit that nauseated her). *Literally a bitch-on-
wheels*, she mused to herself. *Almost hoping she does try something,
so they can put her down a deep, dark hole where she belongs.*

She was measuring out eight cups of water when she saw movement
out of the corner of her eye. Looking over, she saw the
curtain that draped in front of the sliding glass door billowing in the
night breeze.

The realization of what it meant coincided exactly with the
creak on the kitchen tiles behind her. Not missing a beat, Rachel
spun around and doused the creature stalking her with the coffee
pot's contents. The apparition was taken by surprise and gave out
a startled *glug!* Something the thing was holding clattered to the
ground; Rachel didn't bother to see what it was. Instead, she bolted
as fast as she could for the front door.

Unfortunately, the being behind her recovered quickly, tackling
her around the waist as they both crashed down in the foyer. Rachel
and the intruder wrestled for a moment, the former punched and
kicking at the latter with all her might, but to no avail. It simply
would not let go.

With one desperate move, Rachel grabbed the base of the coat
tree next to the door and sent it crashing down on her assailant's head.
It grunted in pain and was still.

Rachel scrambled to her feet, pausing a moment to pull back one
of the coats to see who her uninvited guest was. She gasped to see
the intruder was female. *Terry,* she thought. *This can only be Terry
Scranton.*

Then Rachel Brannan made the bravest, stupidest decision of her
short life: *I have a chance to end this. Right now.*

She ran over to the ornamental desk her father kept in the living room for mail and other minor family business and grabbed the large letter opener. Then she rushed back over to the prone form in the foyer.

Terry, only stunned, saw her coming and reacted, lashing out at her would-be killer with a side kick that sent Rachel hurling backwards into the living room and over the nearby couch.

Terry picked up the letter opener that had clattered to the floor. "Yer gonna kill me, Barbie doll!?", she snarled. "It's gonna take more'n you t'do that!"

She then tried to vault over the couch herself, but just as she rested her boot on the back end, Rachel lifted from its base. The combination of Terry's weight and Rachel's move made the couch tip backwards, making Terry lose her balance and go sprawling.

Rachel half-ran, half-crawled out of the living room and into the kitchen again. Seeing the rack of carving knives on the counter, she chose the largest and spun around just in time to nearly impale Terry in her chest.

When she came face-to-face with Rachel and her knife, Terry stopped short and jumped backwards, nearly colliding with the wall and brandishing the letter opener before her. They froze, two Valkyries dueling over the treasure of Odin, staring each other down, not saying a word.

Terry finally broke the silence, her face splitting into a nasty, death's head grin. "I'll give it to ya, sugah," she said. "Y'got spunk. Gonna be a shame t'kill ya."

"Try it, you red neck bitch," came the reply.

Terry took a step, and her foot landed on what she'd dropped earlier. Without thinking, she pushed the object underneath her foot toward Rachel.

It slid across the floor, her trusty straight-razor. Rachel's guard dropped for a second as her eyes went to it.

It was brief, but it was all the opening Terry needed. She ducked down away from the knife's point, then jabbed upwards, plunging the letter opener deep underneath Rachel breastbone. Rachel cried out as she dropped the knife and collapsed forward.

In the next second, Terry had grabbed the opened straight-razor with one hand and Rachel's long, dark hair with the other. "Like I said, girl," Terry remarked. "Y'got spunk in ya. So I'm almost sorry to haveta do this. But here's somethin' that'll make ya feel better."

Terry leaned close, putting her mouth almost to Rachel's ear as she put the razor to her throat. "Yer boyfriend's gonna get it worse," Terry snarled.

Rachel's last thought screamed through her head as Terry raked the blade across her throat. *Oh Ari I'm so sorry I couldn't save you this time-*

CHAPTER 52

-oh god I've failed you OH GOD!!!!!

Ari jolted awake, Rachel's scream dying in his head as an echo of it threatened to burst forth from his own mouth. "Oh, Jesus, Oh God," he said over and over as he tried to get his bearings. "What a terrible dream!"

But was it a dream? Ari couldn't remember anything up until the point the voice blew through his head. It was one moment, he had been in deepest slumber; the next, the scream.

He looked over at the clock. 10:40, it read. He had been asleep for roughly four hours. Time flies when your dead to the world, Ari thought. But Rachel's probably still up. He snatched the phone out of its cradle and dialed.

After five rings, the answering machine picked up. Rachel's dad's dulcet tones for oncefailed to sooth him. Hanging up, he stared out the window into the night, thinking. *It could mean nothing. She could be asleep herself. Maybe if I called again.*

The phone rang. Ari grabbed for the receiver like a drowning man. "Hello?"

"Red rover, red rover, send Ari on over!" the voice at the other end cackled.

The low level panic Ari had been feeling jacked up five hundred points. "You," he said, surprisingly evenly.

"Yeah, me, Jewboy. Ready to play?"

"What?"

"You ain't never gonna guess where I'm callin' from," Terry said. "Aw, fuck guessin' games! I'm at yer home sweet home, sugar pie!"

"Bullshit."

"It ain't bullshit, asshole. Me n' yer folk's're havin' a helluva time! Daddy's all tied up in his big, brown leather chair, and Mommy's getting that nice white couch dirty from wettin' her pants! Now. . . .how would I know that?"

Before Ari had a chance to answer, he heard a scraping sound come through the receiver. "Here that?" the voice on the other end said. "That's my blade. Be here in an hour, or I'll start cuttin' up. Oh, and no cops! Or they're both dead."

Then Terry clicked off, and was gone.

Ari let the receiver drop to the floor. His mind raced. *What the fuck am I gonna do?*, he thought as he paced. *Even if I go, Terry's gonna kill us!* Then it hit him. "Graziano," he said out loud. "Graziano!" he repeated as he bolted out the door and down the hall.

Please God, let him be in, he thought as he pounded on Graziano's door. *Dear God, let something go right in this whole bloody mess.*

Behind the door, he heard movement. Then came the sound of the lock rattling, and Vinnie Graziano stood before him, resplendent in a pair of boxing shorts. Ari was briefly thankful for the small favor of not seeing him nude, but then the weight of the situation hit him again. "God damn!" Graziano exclaimed. "Can't a guy get any beauty-"

He stopped himself short upon seeing the expression on Ari's face. "Sussman?" he said. "Whassa matter?"

Ari told him: the phone call, that Terry was holding his parents hostage, that she demanded that he himself show up. And no cops. "Aw, Christ," Graziano managed when Ari finished. "Come in."

When the door closed, Graziano asked, "An hour, you say? Let's synchronize watches. She called about five minutes ago. How long will it take you to get home?"

"Thirty to forty minutes," Ari responded.

"Then there's no time to spare. C'mere."

Graziano knelt down to get something from under his bed, a small, wooden box. Ari gasped when it was opened. "A gun!" he exclaimed.

"Shush!" Graziano admonished. "Canada don't need t'know!"

"What's it doing here?"

"Protection, obviously. It's the gun I took offa Ralphie. No serial number, and the stock is taped over for no fingerprints. Add to that the fact it's a Saturday Night Special, and it's as cold as they come."

"But I can't-"

"Yes, you can. Yer gonna have to. To survive."

"But I don't know anything about-"

"Then I'll show you. C'mere."

Ari did as he was told. Graziano made him hold it by the stock. "Safety's on right now, he explained. "Keep it on until yer almost ready to start shootin'. Even then, don't put yer finger on the trigger until yer ready t'let one fly. Keep yer finger on the guard, like this."

"Which is the safety?"

"Little button on the side. But like I says, don't release it yet."

Ari stared at the gun in his hand with a dazed expression. *How the fuck did I get here?* he asked himself. Out loud, he said, "How many shots?"

"Yer fully loaded at six," Graziano replied. "I've got a small box of bullets right here. But still, be conservative."

"I can't do this, Vinnie. I'm not-"

Graziano grabbed his arm, hard, and shook him. "You can and you will! Now, listen up. I'm thinkin' you gotta keep it hid. Don't go in with yer gun blazin' immediately. Yer best bet is to surprise her. Let 'er underestimate you, then you spring it on 'er! Here, lemee get ya somthin'."

Graziano went into his closet and started rummaging through it, finally pulling out a flannel, button-down shirt top. "Here, put this on," he said. "But first, tuck the gun down yer belt, ass-end."

Ari did as he was told, feeling the cold chill of gun-metal swipe against his butt-crack.

"Now," Graziano continued. "Put the shirt on and pull the back over yer ass, and the gun is hid."

"What if she searches me?"

"She won't. She'll be in too much of a hurry, if I'm guessin' right. She won't be spendin' too much time on being careful."

"What if she out-and-out shoots me?"

"Well, keep yer eyes open and yer head down. And shoot back."

"Graziano, I don't know if I can-"

"Then get blown away!" Graziano snapped. "What's it gonna take to get yer head outta yer ass an' realize the seriousness of the situation!? She ain't playin' by rules! She'll kill you and the resta yer family if you give 'er half a chance! So don't be givin' 'er no quarter, cuz sure as hell she ain't gonna be givin' you none! Now, come on." Graziano was silent on the elevator ride down, giving nothing away. Finally, Ari said, "Graziano, if I don't come back-"

"Her name is Terrencia Ann Scranton, she lives in Cooper's Gulch, West Virginia, a few miles away from Charles Town. An' I know what she looks like. Don't worry, man. I'll make sure that, one way or another, she gets got."

"No, no. I wanted to say thank you, for everything. All you've done."

"Ain't done much, pal. Yer the one's gotta do the heavy liftin' from here on in."

The elevator door opened on the empty dorm lobby. Exiting the building the cool night air assaulted their faces. "This is as far as I go," Graziano said when they got into the courtyard in front of the building. "If I don't hear from you, how long should I wait? Two hours? Three?"

"Go with two-and-a half, though that may be too late. You may just be calling a clean-up crew."

"Don't underestimate yerself. You'll psyche yerself out, and you don't need that."

Ari was about to walk away when he did something that surprised him: he held out his hand. "Thanks, Vinnie," he said.

After the barest hesitation, Graziano took it, giving him a firm shake in return. "Good luck, Ari," he responded.

Ari turned and walked away. He had all the courage of a death-row inmate, but he didn't look back. But when he swung back around in his car, he was surprised to see Graziano still standing there, waving as he went by. It was the last Ari ever saw of him.

CHAPTER 53

Ari's drive home was anxious and tense, but largely uneventful. He kept fondling the gun as it sat in the passenger seat. His only lifeline, it was the only thing that didn't make him pull over and curl up and die on the side of the road. It was cold, solid and no-nonsense, just what he needed to get himself through. But all bets were off when he pulled into his driveway and saw the front door standing wide open.

Throwing aside caution, he killed the engine, grabbed the gun and burst from the car, in such a hurry he left his own door open. Studiously ignoring Graziano's advice (for the moment), he brandished the gun before him (just as he had seen it done on a multitude of cop shows), and leapt up the front stoop's steps.

The first thing that hit him when he entered wasn't the sight, but the smell: a putrid stench of sour copper mixed with rapidly spoiling meat. The first sight the greeted him was his mother lying slumped half-on, half-off the couch, a pool of congealing blood underneath her. Calling "Mom!" over and over, he set the gun down on the coffee table and went to her, fulling resting her body back to its usual place on the couch.

Her face looked peaceful, more than he'd ever seen it, the deep slash in her neck the only evidence of violence against her. Dazed, not even sure of what he was doing, he pulled the quilt up over her. "Oh, mommy," he cried. "I'm so sorry. I'm so sorry."

Something registered in the corner of his eye, and he looked over at the bloody leg jutting out from the hallway. Slowly Ari approached, knowing what he would find, but still hoping he was wrong.

He wasn't; it was his father. What little violence that was done to his mother was more than made up for here. Dried steaks of blood tore down the hardwood floor like angry scars, pointing the way to a body that looked it had been cut in a hundred places. But the worst was the face: the brilliant purple of it in stark contrast to all the scarlet elsewhere. The bruises and massive swelling evidenced a brutal beating; one eye was swollen shut and the other bulged out of its socket, staring up accusingly at Ari. *You did this to me,* it seemed to say. *You and your damned careless ways. You killed me. Not you personally, of course. You were too much of a pussy. But you were the one who sentenced me to this, sure as I'm lying here.*

"Shut up," Ari said out loud. "Shut your dead fucking mouth!!"

But even as he turned away, he still saw it: his father's rotten, puffy visage burning in his mind's eye, there to remain, always.

Just as that thought died in his head, the phone rang. Stumbling, unsteady, shaking, he answered it. "Hello?"

"Sorry 'bout the mess. Me'n yer folks got a little impatient, so we started early."

"God damn you-!"

"He already has, kiddo. It ain't obvious? But I wouldn't be cryin' too hard, if I was you. I done you a favor, at least as far as yer old man is concerned. Yer moms was easy. She took one looka me and practically offered herself up. But yer old man . . . he *offered* you up. Most fucked-up thing I ever seen. Takes one looka me an' wets his pants. Then he starts pleadin', offerin' me money an' shit. Told 'im it was too late, that he shoulda settled when he had the chance. Then, get this, he says, 'You want my son, don't you? It's really him you got the quarrel with, not me. Let me call him, and you can settle it all between yourselves.' Damn!"

Ari's mind reeled. Was what Terry saying the truth? He looked over at his father's body, but saw no answers there, just the pulped mass of face and its one staring eyeball.

"Well, after that," Terry went on. "I knew I hadda kill 'im. Snivelin' fucker like that deserves t'die. Smashed him one upside his head with my gun. Tired to run, but I was on 'im like stink on shit. And, man! Did he scream! Specially when he stopped tryin' t'run and I started in with the blade. You gonna scream I get t'you, Jewboy? We're gonna find out, ain't we? But before we do, y'gotta make one more stop."

"Fuck you."

"No, fuck you. You need to head on over next door. There's a little lady there who's just dyin' t'see ya!"

He heard the scream from his dream. "Oh, God!" he cried. "Rachel!!!"

He ran out of the house, the receiver clattering to the floor as the grate of Terry's laugh beat a relentless tattoo in the room where only the dead heard.

CHAPTER 54

Ari bolted through the small clump of woods separating the Sussman and Brannan houses, barely noting the sliding glass door opening unto Rachel's back patio as he burst through. Entering the house through the glass door, he found himself tangled up in its curtain. He only managed to disentangle himself by finally pulling the whole drape down on top of him, rail and all.

The living room was a shambles, with furniture over turned everywhere, but deserted. Then Ari looked over into the kitchen. A small moan escaped from his lips as he viewed the prone form of his best friend lying on its tiled floor. Not even aware that he was moving, he approached her. As he took in the full scene, her slumped body, the letter opener plunged deep in her chest, the large, angry slash across her neck draining into a pool of blood beneath, Ari just stared. Then he screamed.

If there was one single moment of this hellish night where it could be pinpointed that Ariel David Sussman's mind snapped, then this was it: the realization that everything good in his life was no more as he stood over the corpse of Rachel Marie Brannan, his oldest friend and soul mate. The eggshell holding his mind together fractured in a dozen places, and he let out a howl of one who knows he's truly been damned. In sheer volume and intensity of hate, pain, rage, fear and loneliness, it nearly eclipsed the one given off by Terry at the start of this whole sorry series of events: the one singular moment when Ari Sussman carelessly made a left turn when he shouldn't have, and now was paying for it beyond the limits of any rational mind or sense.

He held Rachel's head in his lap, cradling her, his tears from his eyes washing away the blood streaks on her face. Thanking God for (extremely small) favors, Ari was glad that Rachel's eyes were closed so he could not imagine them staring back at him with any hint of accusation. He might have stayed there all night, the next morning, and many days afterward in time for Rachel's parents to return home to view the pathetic scene of Ari weeping over their murdered daughter, but the phone rang.

It took two rings before it cut through the clouds of Ari's mind. When it did, he carefully laid Rachel on the floor and dashed into the living room where the intruding buzz was coming from.

At first, he couldn't find it. Then he noted that the sound, slightly muffled, was coming from a nearby credenza, ringing from underneath a torn and slightly tacky piece of cloth draped over it. Ari shoved aside this cloth and snatched up the phone, snarling, "You fucking BITCH!!!"

Terry laughed like it was the funniest thing she'd heard all week. Hell, probably in her whole stinking, filthy life. "Surprise!" she said between guffaws.

"I'm gonna kill you for this."

"Funny you should mention that," she responded. "I was gonna suggest we have ourselves a li'l one-on-one now, just the two of us, now that all the extras are outta the way."

"What makes you think I won't go to the cops now, let them fucking deal with you?"

"Three reasons," Terry answered. "One, you done worked up enough steam now you wanna chance at me yerself. Two, when I left the mess behind, I used gloves. Did you?"

Ari felt his stomach clench as he digested the implications. "Yeah," Terry said, giving voice to his thoughts. "Y'call the cops now, yer suspect number one. And they're gonna believe that before some cockamamie story about some killer biker chick, specially if she left no trace."

"One cop knows."

"Which leads me to reason number three," Terry said. "See that thing you had to take off the phone t'find it?"

Ari looked over at the scrap of cloth and noticed for the first time that it was a hat, shredded, and that the tacky substance on it was blood. Just as quickly came the realization of whom the hat had belonged to. "A'fore me'n yer folks had our fun," Terry continued. "I paid a visit to yer nigger cop. Or ex-cop, I should say. I blowed his brains out all over the front seat a' his car."

Ari felt faint, but he squelched it by tightly closing his eyes until it passed. "Thought of everything, haven't you?", he found himself saying.

"You betcha, Jewboy. I wouldn't want anybody comin' between us."

"Get to the point. Time and place?"

"Time is another hour. I think y'know the place. Where we had our first date."

"And if I don't show up?"

"Then I call the cops m'self and send 'em on over. But you'll show."

Ari winced at the sound of telephone slamming in his ear. He was left alone with his thoughts and the wreckage of his life.

He silently hung up the phone and noticed for the first time that the gun was missing. Silently, he cursed himself for a fool. *Gotta keep it together, man,* he told himself. *Another slip like that could kill you. And not let you get back at Terry. Now, where-?*

Then it came to him. Of course. He'd left it on the table next to his mom. *Your late mom,* a voice whispered inside his head, and for some reason, that thought make him feel . . . relieved?

But then he looked over into the kitchen, and all relief vanished. Rachel was still dead. *Gotta put her someplace better than the kitchen floor,* he told himself. *Maybe cover her up. Best .hell, only, thing I can do for her.*

No, that cold voice interjected again. *There is something you can do, and you know it. You have to take that monster down. Make her pay for all the hurt she's caused. And not just yours, either.*

And, as he stepped into light from the kitchen to start straightening up, the casual observer would have noticed the change in him. Especially in his face. It was a man's face.

PART FOUR

GO!

CHAPTER 55

Ari pulled over at the intersection of Route 355 and Shady Grove Road, parking his car against the median strip on his left. Above him, the flashing red and yellow light of the resting traffic signal made the night and its surroundings look alternatively bloodshot and anemic.

The clock on the car's dashboard read 12:20 AM. Only a minute to spare.

He spent what was maybe his last hour alive cleaning up. He had placed Rachel's body on her now-righted living room couch, covering her with a bed sheet from the linen closet. It was the same with his mom, but let his dad lay where he was, only covering him with another bed sheet. *More than he deserves*, he thought at the time. *Especially if Terry's telling the truth.*

That happy task done, he retrieved the gun from the coffee table, checked the ammo for the umpteenth time, and then left in his car for the appointed rendevous. On the way there, he continued to stroke and fondle the gun, its cool solidity eased his tortured mind. *God, please*, he said silently. *For once in my life, let me do something right, even if it's murder.*

All things considered, it was a pleasant night, neither too hot or cold. Waiting, Ari wound down the sunroof for the combined advantage of getting more air and being able to hear Terry coming.

The night was quiet. Five minutes passed. Ari was just synchronizing his clock to his watch and checked his bullets again when the sound came: a low buzzing he could not identify.

Unrecognizable, yet somehow familiar.

He looked toward the front at the two sections of road before him. Nothing. Looked over his shoulder out the rear window. Still nothing. Just that thick-sounding buzz.

He had just leaned halfway out his side window to check again when he realized the sound wasn't just closer, it was actually *behind* him.

He jerked back into his car just as he felt a tear at his sleeve and something large go by. When he looked at Graziano's borrowed shirt, there was a long, gaping rip right through it. Then he saw a dark rider and its bike go by through the windshield. And as she pulled away, he knew why he hadn't seen her: he was checking the street and the clever, crafty bitch *had ridden her bike along the median strip.*

Terry spun her bike around, facing him, and stopped. The flashing light alternately lit up and darkened her. "Damn!" her raspy voice cut into the night. "Ah missed! Mus' be gettin' old!"

The most hideous sense of deja vu engulfed Ari. Not only did she look the same from their first encounter at these crossroads (minus the sunglasses, instead being replaced by a pair of oversized goggles, and the fact that she now rode the biggest meanest motorcycle he had seen outside *The Road Warrior,* but Ari was also reminded of his dream as he unconsciously fingered the tear in his shirt. *There she is,* he thought. *The world's biggest wasp, come to sting me to death.*

That thought made him see red even without the help of the flashing traffic signal. He gunned his car's engine and lunged at Terry, accelerating as he went.

Terry dodged casually the oncoming car with her bike, smirking all the way. Ari blew past her, then made a sharp U-turn, squealing wheels 180-degrees to face her. "We can do this all night, Jewboy," Terry called out to him. "But I's too fast fer ya! Now why don't ya just step outta that car like a good little boy an' lemme cut yer damn throat! Jus' like I done t'all yer family!"

Ari fumed, but said nothing. Then he looked past Terry at the ramp to the highway, and the makings of a plan flashed in his head.

Draw her in, Graziano had said. *Make her think yer vulnerable. Then take her out.*

He floored the gas pedal, rushing at Terry, and, once again, she easily dodged. But then he kept going, blowing past her and making a beeline for the on-ramp.

Terry was stunned for a second as she watched her prey's escape. Then she chuckled as she replaced the straight-razor back in her pocket. Pulling out the .45 and chambering a round, she said, "Shee-it, Jewboy. Thought you'd make it easy. Guess I gotta work fer it a bit."

Then she gunned her own engine and sped to the on-ramp herself, opening the throttle in pursuit of her runaway quarry.

CHAPTER 56

Ari sped his way onto Route 370, then had to make a split-second decision between the Washington or Frederick turn-offs. *Frederick*, he told himself. *Less people, less chance of anyone getting hurt by this maniac.*

He considered it. *Us* two *maniacs*, he amended.

As he rode down the Frederick ramp, he checked his rear-view. Nothing. No sign of a pursuer. *Don't tell me I lost her already*, he thought.

Suddenly, the giant cyclopean eye of a powerful headlight winked on roughly twenty or so feet behind him, accompanied by a mighty engine roar. Saying nothing, thinking nothing, Ari reacted, pushing the accelerator down further.

When he hit the main highway, he floored it, watching the speedometer needle creep upwards to 70 . . 80 . . 90 . . .95. Still the light stayed the same distance behind; if anything, it was getting closer. *She was always good on a bike,* the voice of the late, lamented Detective Jones whispered in his head. *Took to it like it was a part of her.*

But then other sounds entered the fray: a loud, sharp report and the crack of breaking glass. Ari nearly swerved off the road in shock as he felt the cool air at his back. *She's shooting at me,* he told himself. *The bitch has a gun and she's shooting at me!!*

He reached over to grab his own entry in the firearms sweepstakes.

Clicking off the safety, he readied his trap. "This better work," he mumbled out loud. He knew he'd only have one chance to get her; after that, it was anyone's guess.

Another shot rang out, and he felt the car swerve slightly as it landed in his rear. *There goes a tail light,* he told himself. *Better slow up before she hits the gas tank.*

He let up on the accelerator slightly and watched the speedometer crawl back downward. *This'll' make her think I'm hit, maybe. Or too sacred to go on. Knowing her, she'll wanna take a look for her own sick little kick,* he thought.

At 75 MPH, he saw the motorcycle headlight shift to his right. "It's working," he murmured. "Come on, Terry. Come and get a good look."

He kept his left arm on the wheel as he hid his gun hand under the sight of the passenger window. Gradually, he saw the light coming closer up to his right side. "Steady," he told himself. "Steady."

Terry didn't disappoint. The light brightened further. Then he saw her bike's handle bars. Then Terry's own grinning gargoyle face was framed in the passenger window. "Hold it . . .hold it," he whispered as she drew even further alongside.

Now they were riding virtually side-by-side, looking straight into each other's eyes. He saw her arm move as she reached around with her gun . . .

The last thing Ari saw before Terry disappeared from his view was her face twisting in surprise as he brought the gun up to the window and fired.

His own shot was deafeningly loud, followed by the crack of the shattered passenger window. Ari heard a snarl from the bike and Terry was gone.

"Sorry 'bout the window, Dad," Ari said out loud, a strange giddiness in his voice. "But hey, since you don't care, I don't care!"

Then he got into a giggle fit that dissolved into hysterical laughter.

Unfortunately, Ari was celebrating (if that's what it could be called) prematurely. Terry saw the Jewboy's gun at virtually the last possible moment and tapped the brakes, more out of instinct than conscious thought.

Her reflexes saved her life. The bullet whizzed by heard head so close she felt it pass through her hair.

She slowed the bike to fifty and let the silver Honda pull ahead. "A gun," she said to the night air. "Somebody gave the little sonovabitch a gun!"

An all-too-familiar rage blossomed within her, tempered with something else. Fear? She had almost bought the farm back there. The little Jew-bastard nearly got one over on her. "On me!" she reiterated out loud. "Little fuckwad nearly took out *me!*"

Her lips drawn back in a snarl, she gunned the engine and engined the gun. "Time t'stop pussy-footin' around," she murmured as she raced to catch up.

CHAPTER 57

Ari's heart sank as he heard the revving of the engine and the growth of the headlight in his rear view mirror. *Christ!!* he screamed inside. *What the fuck do I do now?*

Then the headlight veered to his left and Terry was on the move. She pulled up closely to the driver's side.

Ari tried to bring the gun around for another shot, steering with his right hand while aiming with his left, but didn't get that far. Before he could draw a bead, Terry made her move. Giving Ari her sweetest smile, she fired her own gun directly into his left rear wheel.

Ari heard the tire blow and felt the car go out of control under him. "Blowout!" he screamed as he began to fishtail.

Terry slowed to forty-five, staying out of the way as Ari's car did its little dance on the highway, rocking back and forth before spinning a full 360 degrees around and around until it skidded into the shoulder. Ari furiously stomped on his brakes, but that only made him skid more. Then he began to scream, a high, piercing scream that didn't stop until the right side of his car slammed into the jersey barrier cutting off the median and his head whipsawed into the steering wheel, knocking him unconscious.

When the car finally stopped (engine still running), Terry pulled up behind him on the shoulder. She pushed down the kick stand and dismounted, still holding the gun, smirking all the way. She was trying decide whether to put a final bullet in the Jewboy's head or to get up close and personal with the straight razor when she heard a squeal of brakes and saw the world around her turn alternating fields of red and blue. "Freeze!" a voice commanded.

Shit!! she swore inwardly. *Always around when ya don't want 'em!*

"Drop your weapon and step away from the vehicle!!" the voice commanded, punctuated by the *clack* of a shotgun chambering a round.

Still holding here own piece, she stole a look over her shoulder. The brown and tan Maryland State Trooper's car stared back at her with its lights. When her eyes adjusted, she saw the cop himself, cradling his shotgun in the crook of the car's open door. He was a young kid, with all the snot-nosed arrogance of someone fresh out of the academy, drunk with his own importance. She saw babyish blue eyes trying to look hard under a blond crewcut, and the wispy mustache of a kid barely out of his teens. "I mean it, lady!" the baby trooper said. "Put it down, or I open fire!"

Though the shotgun was aimed directly at Terry's mid-section, she had no illusions that she couldn't get off a round faster than this pudgy little peckerwood could even think. Just one half- drop to the ground with one bullet fired into his spreading waistline, and it would be all over.

But what fun would that be?

Terry dropped her gun on the gravel and smiled at the kiddie-cop. "Pretty big gun fer ya there, li'l boy. Sure ya can handle it?"

"Shut up, turn around, and keep your hands where I can see 'em!" =

He could be rattled. Good.

Terry did as she was told, putting her hands in the air and turning on her boot heel. Her razor was in her pocket, but she didn't think she'd need it. Nope, this little puke was gonna give her all she needed. "Ya gonna cop a feel on me, kiddo?" Terry taunted. "That how ya get yer li'l pecker up?"

"I said, shut up, lady! And get down on your knees!"

"Oooooooooo, are ya gonna take advantage a' li'l ol' me!? Thas the way ya like it, dontcha? Gimme a dollar an' I'll suck the chrome offa yer fender!"

"Lady, I'm warning you-!"

Terry got down on her knees, feeling gravel dig into her flesh. She barely felt it as she strained her ears for the kid cop's approach.

He was walking slowly, with a slight saunter in his step. Terry grinned to herself. The taunts had done their job, and she knew he'd be aiming for a little payback. But she had to be sure. "Whassa matter?," she said. "Hit a nerve? You even like women, or are y'one a' those flamin' faggots who join the poh-lice to *hang out* with all the boys?"

"Shut up!!!!"

Now Terry heard him directly behind her, and could also make out the tell-tale sounds of metal and wood shifting on flesh. The stupid fuck had taken the bait, preparing to give her a little tune-up.

The exact move Terry was waiting for.

For in the brief instant the kiddie cop pulled back on the shotgun in order to deliver a blow with the stock, Terry made her move. Pushing herself backwards, her back and head collided with the trooper's legs. Unable to stop his momentum, the cop swung the shotgun, but now it was just above Terry, within her reach and vision.

She grabbed it with both hands, but the cop gripped it tighter. Terry was prepared, swinging upward with her legs, catching his jaw with the toe of her boot. The cop jumped back more in surprise than pain, but the result was the same: he let go. And Terry had it.

She rolled onto her feet just as the kiddie cop went for his side arm. One blast from the shotgun turned the kid's right hand into a shattered, pulpy mass.

The trooper screamed, his gun clattering uselessly to the ground. "My hand!!" he bellowed, clutching at the bloody stump. "You blew off my hand!" Then he started to bawl.

Terry cut his screams off with a blow from the gun barrel directly into his ample gut. He let out a *woof!*, and fell to his knees. "Y'know," Terry said. "You friggin' cops kill me!"

Behind her, unseen, Ari began to stir in the car, awoken by the deafening roar of the shot gun. He shook his head to clear it, to try and shake himself awake.

"Please," the trooper sniveled. "Don't kill me!!"

Terry responded with a sweeping kick to his ass, sending him sprawling. "Y'all strut around all high n' mighty," Terry continued as the cop burst into another round of heaving sobs. "That is, when yer dealin' with reg'lar people. But when somebody gets the drop on ya, ya fold like the pussies y'are!"

"Please," the cop tried again.

Terry pointed the barrel directly at his face and commanded: "Move it! Other side a' th' road!"

The cop did as he was told, but Terry was still talking. "You motherfuckers got no problem with pushin' people around. Hell, most a' ya are school bullies who growed up and wanted t' push people around fer a livin'! Easy t'pick on people when they got nuthin' but when they do and complain, y'all pull out that old saw about how tough a job y'got', and how y'put yer life on the line ev'ry time ya go out, an' you citizens dunno what it's like. Well, boo-fuckin'-hoo. If'n it's so fuckin' tough, find a new line a' work, I say." She winked. "Betcha wish you were anythin' *but* a cop now, doncha?"

Terry had forced the trooper to the other side of the road and against the cement jersey barrier blocking off the street from the grass. The barrier came up to their waists, and Terry forced the man down on his knees. In the car, Ari was still try to get his bearings. He heard Terry's voice, but couldn't make out her words. For now, all he heard were sharp, angry sounds, growing ever clearer. He would soon regret that they were.

The cop's knees were flush with the barrier's base. Terry basked in his groveling for a moment, then gave a command that made the kid's eyes grow wide.

"Open yer mouth and bite down on that edge."

"NO! No-!"

Terry delivered the same blow to the cop's head that he had tried to use on her earlier. "Do it," she snarled. "Or I'll bash yer head in here."

332

Ari was now fully awake, transfixed by the horror playing before him. He scrambled around in his car, trying desperately to find his gun. He looked on the passenger seat, beneath it, then to his own side. Nothing. It was only now he realized that his engine was still running. He could hear the young trooper's screams, coming across garbled as he bit down on the barrier's cement edge. "Please," Ari thought he could hear him say. "I gotta wife! I gotta family!"

Terry's response was a simple as it was chilling. "I don't." Then she slammed the butt of the shotgun with all her might onto the back of the cop's head.

There was a loud, sharp crack, followed by a wet popping sound that reminded Ari of a freshly-cooked turkey leg being pulled out of its socket. A splurt of blood fanned out beneath the cop's head, and his limp body slid to the ground noiselessly. Terry followed the body's collapse with a finishing round from the shotgun; the smell of blood and cordite wafted through the air.

Ari nearly heaved, Terry's final blast waking him out of his stupor. He grabbed the wheel and pressed on the accelerator instinctually.

At first, he didn't think the car would move. But then there was the creaking of metal and it pulled free. The right side was trashed and the left rear wheel almost completely flat, but the silver Honda moved. Not very quickly, though; along with the creaking of crushed metal came the relentless beat of flattening tire, the *lubba-dub, lubba-dub* sound echoing in his ears nearly as loud as his heartbeat.

Terry saw him escaping and fired another round from the shotgun in response. The blast blew apart his rear window, but he was still moving, heedless to the shards hitting the back of his head.

Ari pressed even further on the accelerator out of shock. The engine gave off an unnerving howl as he looked down at the speedometer. For all its roar, the car was hovering at a disquieting forty-five.

In his rear view mirror, Ari saw the rapidly diminishing form of Terry throw aside the shotgun and make for the bike. Ari knew the chances of his getaway were about as slim as monkeys flying out the sky to snatch Terry away, so he slowed a bit. *Think, goddammit,* he told himself. *There's gotta be a way outta this!*

But there was really only one option, and he knew it. Only one way to finish this mess and maybe get out alive. Maybe. All he needed was a bit of luck.

He said a silent prayer as he slowed the car further and began the laborious process of turning it around. Once he did, he fastened his seat belt.

Terry opened the throttle on her bike and lurched forward, smiling to herself. Jewboy was only prolonging things, and he knew it. In her right hand, she held the cop's discarded handgun, the easiest one to pick up as she ran for her bike. Time to make things short and sweet, though nothing would have pleased her more at this point then being able to stick its barrel down the kid's throat and watching his pussy brains get blown out the back of his head. But she wasn't fussy; a quick pop and his pussy brains decorating the inside of his wrecked car would do.

But something was wrong. Instead of the red of taillight, she saw the unfiltered glow of a single uncrushed headlight. Then came the sound, the thud of a dying heart, slowly reviving itself as the headlight pinned her. "Sheeee-iiiit!" she said gleefully. "He wants t'play chicken with me!

Well, time t'put 'im outta his misery. An' mine."

She aimed the pistol at the driver's side and fired. Ari saw it, and moved just as the muzzle flash came.

It was close; he saw the window pockmark, and felt the bullet whiz by his ear, burying itself in the seat's headrest. Then he righted himself and pressed on.

Terry was nonplused, to say the least. Half the kid's car was totaled and the tire flat, but he kept on.

So did Terry. Fifty yards, then forty. Thirty.

They got to ten before Terry realized Ari wasn't going to stop, but it was too late. She swerved, but the car hit her head on just as she veered rightward. Two tons of car hit one-half ton of bike and caused the bike's owner to go flying head over heels. *Go limp! Go limp!* Terry screamed inwardly as she sailed through the air. Luckily for her, the momentum caused her to fly over the road to the soft grass and ground of the center median. She went as limp as she could, but the impact was enough to stun her into unconsciousness.

Ari wasn't so lucky; once he collided with Terry's motorbike, his vision was cut off as it flipped and smashed in the rest of his windshield. He blindedly drove over the grassy center of the highway and into the opposite lane, barely in control. He slammed on the brakes, causing a squeal that was even louder than the engine's roar. Through a gap in his windshield, he saw what he feared most: the growing vision of cement wall. He braced himself, but the collision was greatenough to destroy the bike's remains and crush in the whole front of his car. Ari himself, restrained by the seatbelt, knocked his head into the steering wheel and lost consciousness for the second time in less than ten minutes.

CHAPTER 58

The automatic doors of the all-night convience store opened with a *whoosh*. Earl Kelly emerged, sipping a cup of coffee and hoping the smell of it alone would light a fire under him. Or at least pull him out of his haze.

He had been on the road ten hours, and it was all looking alike to him since he left Pittsburgh. Especially now. *God damn Maryland,* he mused to himself. *Ain't even shaped like a real state. Looks like a goddamn cock n' balls.*

Earl hailed from Alabama, a real state if there ever was one. And Alabamy-bound he was. *First I gotta get through this shit hole. Wanna put goddamn DC behind me a' fore I call it a night.*

He chanced an out-and-out swig as he made his way through the parking lot. It burned his tongue, but the pain mixed with caffeine woke him up, a little. *Well, shit,* he told himself. *Only a coupla miles left til Virginia. Let's make it quick and painless. Know a good rest stop there where I can catch some Zs.*

Giving out one last mighty yawn, he climbed into his rig, popped the clutch, and started steering his 18-Wheel gasoline tanker toward the turn-off on south-bound Route 270.

Terry woke first. She gingerly made a mental inventory of the body parts she hoped were still intact. Relatively certain she was still alive, she sat up. *Aw, man! Head rush!* she told herself as the wave of dizziness overtook her.

When her head cleared, she dully wondered why her vision was still hazy and her head felt tight. Then she realized the cause: the damn goggles she had placed on her head when she and the Jewboy decided to re-enact the Indy-500 on the freeway.

Flinging them off, she felt much better. Until, that is, she chanced to look over at the opposite lane and saw the sorry sight of her bike crushed against the far wall by what remained of Jewboy's car. For a moment, she panicked; then she spotted what really concerned her: the big, mud-colored case containing the money sitting underneath the whole demolition-derby sculpture. Battered, yes, but still in one piece.

Terry slowly picked herself up, wincing slightly as she tried to put weight on her left foot. *Damn!* she thought. *Musta hurt it when we crashed. That's another limb I owe ya fer, Jewboy.*

Still thinking of Ari, she looked around her for a weapon. Nothing. The cop's service revolver must have been lost in the crash too. *Looks like the decisions been made fer me,* Terry told herself as she dug into her pocket.

A flick of the wrist and the blade was out. *Time t' finish cleanin' house,* she thought as she limped to where her prey lay unconscious. *'Bout fifty yards away. Hope he's still alive. Be a damn shame if'n he offed himself already.*

Inside, Ari awoke. He groaned aloud as he took stock of his own pains; they mostly seemed centered on his head. It throbbed like a rotten tooth. *Or like somebody's been using it for an ashtray,* he mused to himself.

Even that thought seemed too much, as the grey in his head dipped toward the black end of the color-spectrum, threatening to go total.

Then the feeling passed, and his inner vision went back to a shade of grey. *Maybe I should just pass out again,* he told himself. *Just keep on sleeping . . .* Forty yards away, Terry stumbled. She let out a quiet moan as pain shot up her leg. *Damn! Maybe it's worse'n I thought,* she mused to herself. *Feel m'ankle swellin'. Gotta make this shit quick . . .* Ari slumped backwards in his seat, forcing himself awake, his eyes open. By now the blackouts had mutated into black spots before his eyes; he supposed it was progress. Also progressing was his sense of time and place. Little by little, it came back. The chase, the crash, the cop. The death. *Gotta get it together, man,* he told himself. *That maniac might still be out there.* Twenty-five yards away, Terry could see the Jewboy moving. *Don't look like he's goin' anywhere,* she told herself. *Maybe he'll scream a little.* Ari felt around the gash in his forehead; his hand came away wet. *Bleeding pretty good,* he told himself. *But I think head wounds usually do.* Better yet, the pain he received as he probed cleared his head further, cutting through the haze.

The haze and pain subsided enough for him to chance taking off his seatbelt. It took him several tries, but he got it. And now his vision improved enough so he could see his surroundings more clearly. . . Fifteen yards away, she hit the asphalt. It was a little rougher on her ankle, but by now she barely felt it. Her eyes were focused on the sluggishly moving form seated in the wreck. She glanced at the case full of money under Honda/bike's remains. *Grab the cash, or cut his throat?* she considered. *Hmmmm. Pleasure before business . . .* Ari was surprised (and not a little creeped out) to find the motorbike's handle bars pointed directly at his face. The windshield had completely shattered. Piles of glass littered the dashboard, the front seats, him. Some of it carried streaks blood. His blood. Through the windshield's remains, he saw his crumpled hood. Hell, his whole *front end* was jammed accordion-like against the base of one of the highway's street lights. Ten yards. Now Terry was close enough to see the bleeding gash in her victim's head. *Gonna be a lot more blood when I get done,* she told herself. Unconsciously, she was salivating. A night breeze blew through the car, its cool balm waking him completely now. *Maybe it's time I got out. See what's what,* he thought.

Five yards. Ari reached for the door handle. Two yards. A voice tore through Ari's head. If he'd had time to reflect, he'd have recognized it as Rachel's. *Ari!* it screamed. *LOOK OUT!!!*

338

From the jolt backwards in his seat, Ari's eyes lit upon the cracked side-mirror. In it shone the gleam of a straight-razor.

More out of instinct than thought, he reacted. He seized the side-door handle, tugging it with all his might while he pushed against the door, slamming it with all the force that sudden shock gave him into Terry's mid-section.

Terry let out a startled *woof* and was knocked off-balance, her razor clattering to the ground. Then Ari did something that would have been inconceivable to him a mere day ago. But all the anger and hatred that had accumulated over the past few hours (and the past twenty years) by now had reached its critical mass. Seeing the killer of his family and best friend sprawled before him, only one thing entered his mind. And it wasn't running away.

"You killed *Rachel!!!*" he screamed as he kicked with all his might into Terry's side.

Terry gasped as the breath was forced from her and she fell over on her back. She made one more desperate grab with the razor, but Ari was on her, screaming obscenities and grabbing double handfuls of her shirt in order to lift her up. Then she fell backwards again as Ari planted a haymaker upside her head.

The blow wasn't the worst Terry had received over the years, but it was enough to cross her eyes for a moment. Falling uncushioned on the gravel hurt more. But then Ari delivered another kick to her side that flipped her off her back and face-first, on hands and knees, into the ground.

Ari was about to kick her again, a square blow he'd intended on planting up her ass, when he heard her sob out: "How could ya? I'm a *woman!!*"

Ari paused for a second, but it was enough. Too late, he'd noticed the half-smile on her face; it was the last thing he saw as Terry launched a side kick that landed right in his mid-section, knocking him backwards into the cement of the jersey barrier.

She jumped up in a flash. Despite the blood leaking from her mouth, she was laughing. "You damn city boys," she chortled. "Fall fer the same shit ev'ry time!"

339

Now it was her turn to grab hold of Ari by the shirt and pull him close. "Ya wanna duke it out with me, boy?" she snarled. "Glad t'oblige!"

She followed up this statement with a *real* punch, one that knocked out a tooth. But Terry was far from finished. She went berserk on him, pummeling him with so many lefts and rights that he lost track of how many landed, lost track of even how to defend himself. "Fuckin'pussy!!" she cursed him as she attacked. "Yer fuckin' girlfriend put up a better fight than you! Ya think ya c'n take me on? Fuckin' pussy-ass, cocksucker Jewboy!!!"

Ari fell to his knees, spent. But Terry would not stop. She kept raining blows on him left and right as he slumped further and further to the ground. But the torment in his brain was worse than any physical abuse Terry could unleash upon him. *Get up, goddamnit!!* a voice that sounded a lot like Graziano's bellowed in his head. *Don't be such a fucking stereotype!! She just one person. Get up and fight!!*

But it was no use. He went to his hands and knees, ready to curl up and die, ready to face the inevitable, the killing stroke.

Terry grinned as the Jewboy fell over. Turning from her victim, she grabbed the straight-razor.

Ari, lost within his own misery, dimly aware of Terry's momentary distraction, at last heard the one voice in his head he needed, finally recognizing it as Rachel's.

Ari, get up.

And hot on the heels of that, Graziano's: *Draw her in,* it said. *Let her underestimate you. Then* Boom! *You got 'er!*

Terry approached Ari, razor in hand. She grabbed him by the back of his shirt and forced him up.

Just as his head rose to her waist, he dove, wrapping his arms around her mid-section in a death-grip, knocking her off-balance.

She was thrown backwards, but not down. As long as the Jewboy had her in this position the razor was useless, so she continued to pummel him on the back, trying to force him loose. It was no use; his arms were like a pair of vices, refusing to be thrown off.

Terry pushed with all her might against him, ramming him up

against the cement barrier, then his car. Then Ari countered with his own push, and he and Terry fell into the car itself, thrashing about like Siamese twins trying to fight off nature.

The shock of being pushed in the car caused Terry to drop the razor. Ari reached for it, but Terry responded by biting deep into his hand. Ari screamed and let go, and now Terry was on *him*, slamming him backwards into the backseat while dislocating the gear shift.

The car began roll backwards, flung in "Neutral" and pushed by the force of the fight. Not that either of them noticed; for the moment, all they knew was each other.

Terry fought for a grip on Ari, but he was slippery (*slimy?*). He punched and kicked out at her, and at such close range, it was hard to fight back. One wayward kick of Ari's collided with the radio; "Tainted Love" started blaring through the stereo system.

While it made Terry flinch, it completely distracted Ari, and she saw her chance. She punched him one in the stomach for softening, then followed up by grabbing him one-handed around the throat.

The jolt of the steel-grip around his neck caused Ari to fall all the way into the backseat. Then Terry's other hand followed, and his vision wavered. With both hands occupied on trying to break her grip, he tried to lash out with his feet. Terry grunted in pain as one foot connected with her bad ankle, but she held on.

Her grip loosened for a moment, and it was enough to let precious oxygen back into Ari's brain for him to think. *Her left ankle's hurt,* he thought. *She was limping.*

But it seemed no use. Terry kept dodging his kicks, and it was taking more and more energy to lash out. He was being choked to death, on the verge of passing out. And the fucking radio played on. "Friday I'm in Love", by The Cure.

Wait, the radio, Ari gasped to himself. *The battery's still on.* Opening up his eyes (which were starting to glass over), he saw Terry's face, grinning as she cursed him. Then he looked beyond her. To the open sunroof.

Maybe . . . a chance, he thought brokenly. *Only one . . . I got.*

To strangle him, Terry hovered over him, propped against the two front seats. Now Ari reached, inch by inch, to find the seat releases.

He reached it just as he was about to black out. Terry gave a startled yelp as she landed on top of Ari. More importantly, she loosened her grip. Taking advantage of her distraction, he sat up (*head rush!*)

Terry tried to gain purchase with her feet. She tried placing them against the roof, but slipped and her legs went out the sunroof's hatch. It was what Ari was waiting for. Falling forwards, he jammed his fingers on the "Close" button.

Terry saw what he was doing too late. She got her right foot out, but the left was a hair slower, and soon the hatch closed on her injured ankle.

Terry howled, more out of anger and frustration than pain. Ari fell out of the car, sprawled onto the street. With a herculean effort, he rose, only to fall again against the crumpled front of his car. He reached in and tore out the wires connecting the battery.

The blaring radio fell silent. More importantly, the sunroof's "Open" button was killed the instant after Terry pressed it. It moved a fraction of an inch, then died.

Terry tried to get her foot out, yanking hard, but only hurt her ankle further. She was trapped. And Ari was out of reach.

Now Ari did collapse in the road, oblivious to the curses Terry threw at him. He gulped hungrily at precious air, oxygen his only concern.

Until the headlights appeared. Earl Kelly was dozing off, the coffee being unable to revive a man who had been up eighteen hours straight. He dimly heard the Roy Acuff tune playing on his radio, and was starting to drift off.

His conscious mind alerted him, and he jolted himself awake. But not soon enough to avoid the wreck on the highway. The powerful headlights emanating on the far side of the wrecked Honda pinned Ari in their glare. Ari didn't know what was bearing down on them, but it was huge. Probably a truck.

A *very big* truck.

Without thinking, he went back into the car for Terry. He got as far as placing his hand on her arm when he was rewarded with a slash across his scabbing-over forehead. Apparently Terry found her razor.

If Ari hadn't reacted quickly, the slash would have cut his throat instead. Realizing this (and seeing the hateful grin on his adversary's face), a cold voice spoke up in his head. *Leave her,* it said. *No way in hell she'd help* you. *You knew that you'd probably have to kill her to get her to stop.* Now *would be a good time to start running.*

So Ari did. He ran off the road and onto the central median strip, hoping to find a place to dodge flying debris. It was only as the truck passed him speeding the other way that he realized it was a gasoline tanker. He ran faster.

Terry only noticed her world getting brighter as the Jewboy ran off. Sickened, she turned to look, knowing what she'd see. She was right: a huge, eighteen-wheel rig bearing down on her.

In her last coherent thought before the impact, she realized why the kid had suddenly appeared at the car when common sense told him to turn and run. *He was trying to save me,* Terry thought as the razor slipped limply from her grasp. *After all I put 'im through, the kid's first instinct was to try and save me. And I tried to kill him for it. You win, Ari. You WIN.*

Terry screamed, a heart-breaking mixture of pain, loss and fear that was cut off when the truck hit. Earl saw the car too late, but instinct made him slam on the brakes and yank the wheel to the right. All for nothing. The truck hit the car off-center, but it was more than enough.

Earl was flung from the wheel as the rig started to tip over. The last sight he saw haunted him into his very early end. Upon impact, something landed on his windshield. Something barely recognizable as human. Bloody, battered and broken though, it still lived.

The sight of this creature was bad enough; what started him on his death scream was its still-living eyes, focused on him.

And its grin.

His scream was the loudest thing in his head; then his world turned bright orange before finally fading into the blackness of eternal night. Ari ran faster than he would have done pre-exercise, but it still wasn't enough. His eyes searched for a refuge from the coming explosion, settling on a grass-covered ditch in the center of the median.

Behind him, he could hear it all: Terry's scream, abruptly cut off by impact. The squeal of brakes applied too late. The mechanical howl of ten tons of truck tipping over. The slosh and crack of a thousand gallons of flammable liquid as the rig fell over and the tank cracked open.

Then, the explosion. The explosion from sparks of metal scraping hardened tar landing in spilled gas. Ari heard it beginning behind him and dove for the ditch. The force of the blast blew him the rest of the way, head over heels, landing on his back.

The night sky above him brightened into man-made day. All Ari could do was watch. He felt himself drifting, slipping finally into the darkness that had threatened to overtake him since his and Terry's game of chicken, the second and last time she and he would collide.

Something landed on the ground next to his head. Letting his head fall, he looked over.

The straight-razor lay inches from him, still glowing from the flame licking at it.

Then darkness overtook him, and he knew no more.

EPILOGUE

THE PHOTO FINISH

Sometimes I sit up in the darkness
And I watch my baby as she sleeps
Then I climb into bed and hold her tight
I just lay there awake in the middle of the night
Thinking 'bout the wreck on the highway

-Bruce Springsteen

The Maryland hills were turning brown; the long-delayed autumn was beginning. Another day ended, the sun going down.

Inside, Rachel was visiting Ari in another dream. He was standing on a bleached-out empty beach while she stood waist-deep in the black water. He held his breath and closed his eyes as he himself waded in. Up to his heart the water rose, and he felt her warm embrace as they both sank beneath the waves.

He and Rachel were drifting deep, but he never felt like he was drowning; indeed, it was the most peace he'd felt in his life. He reached out and felt her hair, and was rewarded with her warm scent that the water could not fade. He wanted to join her. He so desperately wanted to join her. Instead, he felt her stiffen and try to pull away.

He looked into her eyes, trying to find peace there. But he saw nothing, no sign of love behind her tears. They were as empty as everything else in his life. *You have to go, Ari,* she said in his head. *It's not your time.*

I don't want to wait, Rache. There's nothing for me on the other side. I can't wait forever for you.

In life, he had never seen such a sad expression on her face. *It won't be as long as you think. Be careful. They're coming. They're coming for you.*

Who? Who's coming?

And, Ari, set her free.

I don't wanna set you free, Rachel! I love you!

But Rachel slipped deeper into the cold waters while Ari felt himself be lifted up. *Set her free,* he heard her say in his mind again, but fainter. He tried to buck the tide, to no avail. He felt himself break above the waves and the sun upon his face. It was getting brighter, ever so brighter . . .

"Rachel."

One word, spoken aloud. The world around him came into focus. It wasn't the sun; it was an overhead light. Through his blurry vision, he saw the outlines of a room. A room with white industrial tiles on the wall. A shadowy figure was seated there. Dimly he saw the figure rise and poke his head out the door in front of him, heard the rumblings of a conversation.

Ari closed his eyes again. He went to rub them, but his arm wouldn't move. Looking over to his right, he saw it suspended in the air, encased in plaster. *Hospital,* he thought. *I must be in the hospital. Man, what happened when I landed?*

Next he tried to move his legs; only one responded. Looking down, he thought, *My left leg, too? What the fuck did I do to myself?*

Something moved to his left. He looked over and saw a young guy in his twenties, dressed in what must be his Sunday's best. Doled out in a seersucker suit, his blondish hair was slicked back by an unidentifiable substance that looked like Vaseline. His cologne was cheap and overpowering in its sweetness, and Ari figured he'd bathed in it before he came. Staring at him with a vapid grin that could only be described as "shit-eating", Ari felt an immediate distaste, shortly followed by self-loathing for being too judgmental. "Mr. Sussman?" the apparition inquired.

"Yeah . . .yeah, I am."

The guy shook his good hand like he was expecting to get water or butter out of Ari's mouth. "Blake Scranton," he said.

It took a moment for the name to register. "Terry's brother," Ari said.

The man visibly winced and let go of Ari's hand. "Yes. Yes. I am," he allowed. "I just wanted to be the first to apologize for all this . . .unpleasantness."

"Where am I? How long have I been out?"

"You're at Shady Grove Hospital, and the doctors told me you've been out about a week."

"Holy shit."

"Yes, you gave them all quite a scare!" Blake said in a way-too-friendly voice.

"Yeah."

There was an uncomfortable silence, then: "Could you hand me the call-button? I need the nurse."

"Oh, before I do that, Mr. Sussman, I was wondering. Could you do something for me?"

"Huh? . . .Oh. Sure. What?"

A slip of paper magically appeared in Blake's hand. "Could I trouble you to put your signature on this?" he asked. Then a pen just as mysteriously was put in Ari's good hand.

Ari tried to read the document, but his vision kept blurring, going in-and-out of focus so quickly Ari thought there was a monkey inside his head turning a switch. "What is this?" he finally asked.

"Oh, just a little agreement."

"Huh?"

"Just a document that says you don't hold me financially responsible for anything my sister did."

This was just sinking into his confused cranium when there was a commotion outside. The door to his room opened and a rich alto voice split the air. "Blake," it said. "What the holy hellfire are you doing here?"

The plastered-on grin on Blake's face disappeared faster than a crowd of swimmers after someone yells *Shark!* "Rusty," was all he could manage in response.

The woman moved fast, grabbing the paper out of Blake's hand before he could think to move. "What the fuck is this?" the woman known as Rusty asked as she skimmed it.

As she did, Ari saw Blake's face transform from surprise to sick, sweaty fear. With good reason. In a horrifying sense of deja vu, Ari saw the rage build up in the woman from the back. *Just like Terry,* he told himself. *She's going to start screaming and split the rest of my skull.*

But she didn't. Instead of exploding, she lowered the paper and fixed a stare on Blake that must have been pretty impressive, at least from what Ari could deduce from the latter's expression. "You sniveling little . . . son . . .of. . .a . . .*bitch!!!*", she said hoarsely.

Blake tried to reply with a snarl of his own, but only managed to look more ridiculous. "Like you wouldn't do the same thing?" he rejoined.

"I wouldn't be waitin' by the man's bedside fer 'im to wake up!!" Rusty replied. Her voice had taken on a familiar cadence that made Ari wince.

Rusty tore up the document in front of Blake's face. "Get out," she said. "Get the fuck out of here before I kick yer ass so hard you'll be fartin' out yer shoulder blades!"

"You know, all this wouldn't have happened if you'd been a better lawyer."

The room went silent for a moment. Then Rusty grabbed both lapels of his cheap seersucker and threw him against the door. "You were her family, Blake," she said in a hoarse whisper. "All this wouldn't have happened if you'd been a better *brother.* Now get the fuck out!"

Blake slunk his way out the door, not even giving Ari a parting glance.

Another silence, filled with . . .what? Ari wasn't sure. But now he was alone with this very tough (and possibly dangerous) woman. Ari darted a glance toward his side-table, praying he'd find the call button there. Then the woman spoke, and her voice was in such a marked contrast to his first impression, he had to blink twice to make sure she was even the same person. "I'm sorry for that, Mr. Sussman," she said in a soft, almost musical voice. "But if you had read that . . .piece of *shit* . . . you'd know why."

"I can guess. He made my skin crawl."

The woman gave out a dry chuckle just as it clicked with Ari why she seemed so familiar. "You're Rusty Darrow," he remarked flatly.

Rusty turned toward him, and Ari noticed for the first time how painfully drawn and tired she looked. *What the hell, I probably look worse,* he thought. Out loud, he said: "You're Terry's lawyer."

Now the woman visibly flinched, and Ari saw the haunt in her eyes. "Yes," she replied. "Yes, I was. But I'm not just her lawyer." A pause. "She was my daughter."

Ari was glad his jaw wasn't broken; it would have hurt from falling on the floor. *What kind of hold does Terry have on Rusty?* Ari remembered Detective Jones musing out loud in his room a century ago. *What's the missing piece?*

Well, Barney, he thought. *Don't know if you lived to find out. Or maybe you did, and that's what got you killed.*

But Rusty was still speaking. "I'm going to tell you a story, Mr. Sussman," she said as she positioned a chair at his bedside. "And when I'm done, it's up to you to decide what must be done. I'll abide by whatever you want. It's the least I owe you after all the pain I've caused."

Ari didn't know what to say, so he kept quiet. Instead, he fumbled until he found the call button. It was only an inch away in case this woman . . .what? *Starts acting like her daughter,* Ari finished unhappily.

If Rusty noticed him situating the call button, she made no sign of it. Instead she moved closer so her (somewhat captive) audience could hear. "My real name," she began, "is Clara Deureaux. I changed it because when you've got a father that terrorizes you every day, you always want to make a clean break. I couldn't take livin' at home anymore, so I made tracks when I turned sixteen. Hitch-hiked my way west to San Francisco. The newspapers I was reading kept talking about this 'youth movement' that was starting out there. New music, new fashions. 'Cept they always made it sound scary. Not t'me. I thought something incredible was about to happen, and I wanted to be there when it did."

"Got there in the spring of 1966. The whole hippie thing was startin' then, and I was smack dab in the middle of it. Haight-Ashbury, all of it! You've probably read about it in the history books, it's been so long now."

"Made a lot of friends while I was out there. Also hooked up with some bikers. Hell's Angels were comin' around then in Oakland, and I knew a few of their off-shoots 'round Frisco. They taught me how to ride, and all that good shit. They also taught me how to party! Oh, man, were those some good months!"

Rusty sort of drifted off for a second, and Ari began to get uncomfortable. He was about to say something when she continued. "I think now I was just tryin' to drink and drug away my childhood. Blot out all the bad memories with good ones, or even none at all. There were quite a few floors I woke up the next day on, hung over and not knowing how I got there."

Rusty gave out a cynical laugh. "But all that fun had a price. One night I did somethin' stupid, as only a teenage farm girl could. Started partyin' with a group of bikers in this basement apartment. Just me n' those six guys. Maybe I shoulda been concerned bein' the only girl there, but I was too young, dumb and trashed to see it as anything but an honor. Hell, I thought they was m' friends, but I guess sometimes lessons are learned the hard way."

"We had just seen a concert by this group that was makin' a name fer itself in the Bay area called Jefferson Airplane. We came totally trashed and left the same way. And in that apartment, the party continued."

"Wasn't long before things turned ugly. I had a little confrontation with one of them about somethin', and the next thing I know, it was like they all had one mind. And that mind was to rape me."

Tears welled up in Rusty's bright blue eyes, and she determinedly wiped them away. "I was starting to sober up and wanted to leave. They had other ideas. They grabbed me and threw me on that filthy floor. Then all six of them took they're turns dippin' their wets."

"After they were done, they left me there like a sack a' garbage and continued their own party. Drinkin' and gettin' high until, one by one, they all passed out. All that time I waited. Gettin' more and more sober. Thinkin'. Plannin'. And when they were all helpless, I knew what I had to do."

The tears were gone now, replaced by twin beacons of blue fire. "While they slept it off, I went into that germ factory they called a kitchen, and got the biggest knife I could find. And then I cut their throats."

Ari went pale, but Rusty didn't seem to notice. She was lost in time and memory. "The first two were easy," she said in a voice that had dropped an octave. "Number Three knew what I was there for, but too late to help himself. Four and Five tried t'get away, but I got them. Only Six, whose name was Chris, I remember, he tried to fight. But he was so tanked it was like fightin' someone drenched in molasses."

"After I was done, I left. Wiped the knife free of prints and dropped it down the sewer. Far as I know, they never found it. Then I went to the hospital. Told the nurse on duty that I'd been raped in order to get a shot for the clap. That's what I was most scared of. Then I beat it before they called the cops. Split from Frisco that night, liftin' one a' my 'friends' bikes."

"I drifted for a month and two hundred miles, stealin' what I could from here and there, wonderin' what my next move was. It was made for me. My missed period told me that I'd just been given something that was harder to deal with then the clap."

"Terry?" Ari asked.

Rusty nodded. "But that's gettin' ahead of ourselves," she scolded mildly. "Don't make an old woman lose her train of thought."

"Sorry."

Rusty smiled sadly at him and continued. "Yeah, it was Terry. And I was scared to death now. Knew I couldn't just drift forever. Couldn't go somewhere to get an abortion; there weren't that many clinics around then. Besides, old Catholic habits die hard. So I decided to keep her for the time being. Maybe this was God's way a' tellin' me t'slow down. So I made my way to Youngstown, Ohio and hooked up with Catholic Charities there."

"Now, I know better than anyone that there's big problems with the Catholic Church and their stands on certain issues, but I saw none of that there. The sisters were kind to me, especially after I told them of my rape and my decision to keep the baby. An' even though I had t'work fer my daily bread, I felt more at peace there than any other time in my life. Or even since."

"I gave birth to a healthy baby girl on April 20th of 1967. But I knew I couldn't stay with the Charity forever. Especially since the nuns kept pushin' at me t' give her up for adoption. So, one night, I lit out. Packed up little Evangeline on my stolen bike an' didn't look back."

"You named her Evangeline?"

"Yeah, after the poem. Popular name in Louisiana. Anyway, after about two weeks of riding around with her perched on the back, I did somethin' awful."

"She'd been fussy that whole day, and I hadn't slept much. Pulled over to change her, but she wouldn't stop cryin'. And I took my frustration out on her by slappin' her."

Rusty's eyes began to tear over again. "I was ashamed a' myself. Eventually, after holding and rocking her by the side a' the road for awhile, she calmed down. But by then, I knew I was licked. The nuns were right: I was in way over my head, and had no business being a mother. And taking it out on a child who's only crime was bein' born was the last thing I wanted t' do."

"I gotta map of the USA and blindly put my finger on it. When I opened my eyes, it was on West Virginia. So that's where I went. Some planning, huh?"

"I don't know," Ari allowed. "I might've done the same thing in your shoes."

"Still, there I went. I hit Wheeling, 'cuz it seemed half-way civilized, and I left little Eva in the emergency room on the largest hospital I could find there. It was the only thing I knew t' do. I thought it was the best chance a' her gettin' with a good family, one that would look after her a lot better than I could. But I was wrong."

Rusty paused. "Do you mind if I get a glass of water, Mr. Sussman? This part's a little . . ." she trailed off, leaving the thought unfinished.

She didn't have to. "Please do," Ari said.

Rusty went into the bathroom, leaving Ari alone with his thoughts. *I can't believe I ever thought this woman could be a monster,* he admonished himself. *Life dealt me a winning hand compared to her. And Terry. All the times I wallowed in self-pity . . .*

Rusty emerged from the bathroom a little more dry-eyed and composed. She tossed her Dixie cup into the thrash and re-positioned herself next to Ari's bed. "Thank you, Mr. Sussman," she said.

"Look, call me Ari, please," he replied. "Don't think this is the time to be so formal."

She offered him a weak smile. "No, I suppose not. So. After leaving the baby behind, I made my way east to the other side of the state, Charles Town. I didn't want t' be that far from her. I always had the notion . . .fantasy, really . . .that we'd see each other some day and I could explain to her why I did that. Hopefully when she was a teen herself. But it didn't turn out that way."

"I got a waitressing job, and studied for my GED. Aced it, then I decided to go to college, night school. That's when I figured out what to do. I was always a pretty good talker, so I thought the law might be the way to go. And that I needed to give back all that I took over the years. I didn't want as many hard-luck stories walking out there."

"And you were good at it," Ari replied.

Rusty smiled the first genuinely happy smile he'd seen from her since she arrived. "Damn right I was. Signed up with a big firm after passin' the bar. Wasn't happy there. Too many people were gettin' run over, and I didn't like it. Got enough of a rep to go into private practice, and I never looked back."

"When . . .all this . . . started happening," Ari said. "A police detective was compiling a file on you and Terry. He showed me a lot of the things you did over the years."

"Was it Jones?"

"Yeah, he was trying to find the connection between you and Terry. Is he really dead?"

"Yes, they found him shot to death in his car just outside the station."

Ari sighed. "Terry?"

"As far as I know. They're still investigating. Didn't find any finger prints, but it's probably a safe bet. My girl left quite a mess behind her."

"You read the file?"

"Yes."

"So you know what was done to her during the time I was involved in my own petty concerns."

Ari grimaced. "You were only doing what you thought was right. You couldn't have known. So how did you find out?"

"Time passes; it can always be counted on to do that. Shortly after what I calculated to be her sixteenth birthday, I did some searching. I have a private investigator I sometimes use to dig up some dirt. He's a good friend. I offered to pay him, but he refused. Said it was a gift, not a job he was doing."

"It took him a month, but he found her. He called me up and asked me if I wanted the bad or good news first. My heart sank. I asked for the good news first, and he told me she was still alive. The bad news was that she was locked up in a reformatory and facing a murder charge."

"Tammy Brown."

"Yeah, her. I asked him for all the details, and he listed them off for me: her abominable childhood, her being sent to the reformatory on some trumped-up charge of theft, her rape, and her taking her revenge. When I finally got off the phone with him, it was like black hole had just opened up in my office and was tryin' t' suck me through. Can you understand that, Mr. . . . Ari?

I thought I was doin' right by her by givin' her away, and instead she had a carbon copy of my own life! Who the fuck is runnin' this show, anyway?"

Rusty looked on the verge of tears again. "Sorry," she said. "I've been turnin' this over in my mind for years."

"Ms. Darrow . . .Rusty, you couldn't have known."

"Maybe not, but that's no excuse fer bein' a selfish, self-centered bitch."

Ari said nothing. And when Rusty next spoke, her voice was much softer. "Since Terry was now in need of a lawyer, it was nothing to pull a few strings and get myself assigned the case, pro bono. I got her case file and made myself read every horrifying picture and word of it. It was like when my own mama made me take castor oil; horrible, hard to stomach, but necessary."

"Finally, after knowing everything back-and-forth, I was ready to see her for the first time since she was a baby. I'd known what she'd looked like from her mug shot, but a pic doesn't tell the whole story. And when I saw her sitting there, slumped over in her chair in the reformatory's common room, bleeding attitude from every pore, it was all I could do from breaking down then and there."

"Instead, I put on my best poker face and took the seat across from the table in front of her. 'Ms. Scranton?' I said."

"'Who wants t' know?' she said."

"'I'm Rusty Darrow. The court appointed me as your lawyer.'"

"'Zat a fact?'"

"I thought to shake hands, but knew she'd just ignore it. So I got down to business. I pulled out her file and started going through it. I said, 'You're to be arraigned next week, so that doesn't give us much time. Still, the evidence is largely circumstantial. Shouldn't be too hard to mount a defense.'"

"'Why're y' doin' this?'" she asked.

"'Pardon me?'"

"She was looking directly at me, sizing me up. That's when I

355

noticed how much she looked like Chris, the last biker I killed that night, down to the hateful expression. 'You heard me,' she said. 'Why the hell you doin' this? Make y'feel better? Nice fancy lawyer like yerself, gettin' yer hands dirty fer some shiftless, no-account piece a' trash like me? What the hell d'ya get outta it? Brag t' yer lawyer buddies what a great gal y'are?'"

"'Is that how you see yourself? A shiftless, no-account piece of trash?'"

"'Mebbe. Mebbe not.'"

"'Well, the way I see it, we're all equal under the law. That's why you're getting a defense.'"

"Terry laughed at me. 'Yeah, I heard that shit in social studies. Too bad I don't believe it.'"

"'Why not? You are a person, after all.'"

"'Never stopped anybody from steppin' on me before. So why you?'"

"'Because I think you deserve it.'"

"'Deserve ain't got nuthin' t'do with it.'"

"'So what does?'"

"'Where the fuck were you people when I needed you? When m' dad was stickin' his cock up my ass? When me an' my brother was starvin'? It's too fuckin' late fer y'all t' start carin' now!'"

"She said more, a whole lot more, and I just let her rip. Every word was like a needle in my heart, but figured it was the least I owed her for all her pain. And when she was done, she stared at me like this was the first time she'd even noticed me. 'What the hell're ya starin' at, lady? What the hell do you get outta this? Why the hell are ya here?'"

"'Because I also grew up in a bass-ackwards shithole.' I said. 'I also got fucked by my dad while mom just looked on. And when I was your age, I was gang-raped by six men.'"

"Well, that stopped her. Then it was like someone pulled a plug in her, like the levee inside broke and flooded her heart. I've seen plenty of clients' tears and frustration in my life, but this girl was so hurtin' inside you'd have thought she was a century older'n her years.

And then I held her, gave her the first real affection she'd had since she was a baby. And why not? I'd ruined her life, and now it was time for the chickens to come home to roost."

"When she calmed down, I gave her my plan of action and we settled upon it. As I was about to leave, she called out to me: 'What happened to those guys? The fuckers who raped ya?'"

"I just gave her a sideways glance over my shoulder. 'They died,' I said. Then I made a beeline for the can, because it was time to attend to some tears of my own."

"The next day, I went out to the Scranton place. It wasn't as bad as I thought; it was worse. 'Cesspool' was too kind a word for it. I went with my detective, ostensibly to gather information, but in truth, I wanted to see the monster who'd violated my daughter for most of her childhood."

"He was drunk, of course, and I couldn't get much outta him, but that was okay. I'd only gone for my own satisfaction, to mark him, because his days were now numbered."

"Terry's trial was actually the easiest part. Did she do it? I don't delude myself into thinkin' she was innocent. Far from it. But I also know that if I had been in the same situation . . . hell, I *had* been in the same situation . . .that I would've done the same thing."

"Maybe me too," Ari allowed. "I've asked myself the same question a lot lately."

"Yeah, but I took it a step further, Ari. I was the one who made the right bribes to the wrong people to get that reformatory snitch killed. And I was the one who went to the Demon Heads to arrange their raid on the Scranton place right before Terry got out."

Ari's eyes widened in surprise. "Oh, yes," Rusty continued. "I knew Nesto Gonzaga back when he was a little Hell's Angels wanna-be in Oakland. I told them to take what ever they wanted, but to leave the old fuck alive. Beaten half-to-death, but alive."

"I watched from my car the night the Heads raided the Scranton place. They trashed everything and took what wasn't nailed down. Not that there was much. The old fuck'd drunk up most of it. It was a

357

damnation that he didn't off himself sooner. Guess it's the truth about God watching out for fools and drunks."

"The Heads roared off and then it was my turn. I got out of my car and walked the hundred yards down the driveway to that hell hole. Scranton was lying on his back in front of the house, moaning in pain. 'Lady, help me,' he says when he spotted me. 'Help me inside.'"

"'Sure, I'll help ya, old man,' I said. 'Do you know who I am, Mr. Scranton?'"

"He looked at me with the eye that wasn't blackened and swollen. 'Yeah. Yer that lawyer lady. The one fer Terry,' he mumbled."

"'Oh, I'm a little more'n that, Mr. Scranton. Y'see, I also happen t'be Terry's mother.'"

"I leaned close, close enough to smell the rot of his teeth. 'Her *real* mother.'"

"His whole face shifted as he took that in. 'Oh . . .' he said. 'Lady, I'm sorry-'"

"'How does it feel, Mr. Scranton? How does it feel bein' helpless? With no way t'fight back? Sorta like a kid when yer violatin' them?'"

"'Lady, I had no idea she was anybody's daughter. She was just an orphan kid we took in t'get state cash. Y'know, a foster child! Got us an extra $200 a month! Who's gonna turn that down?'"

"'You never told her she wasn't yours?'"

"'My wife wanted a girl, not a boy. She made me get 'er! That's the only reason I took 'er!'"

"I pulled the .38 out of my purse and pointed it at his pathetic face. 'Too bad,' was all I said."

"That's when he started cryin'. 'Please, lady, ya gotta unnerstan'! A man has needs! Mah wife died on me. 'Sides, it's not like she was *my* kid-!'"

"I couldn't take anymore, so I stepped on his broken hand and ground into the remains of his fingers. His scream was the best thing I'd ever heard come outta his mouth."

"And when that mouth opened, I shoved the barrel of my gun in it. I said, 'Save a seat for me in hell,' and pulled the trigger."

It wasn't the words themselves that caused the chill in Ari's soul.

358

Rather, it was the *way* the middle-aged woman before him said them. The way she *looked* as she said them: her face a solid mask, her eyes the only living thing within, and even those cloudy with feeling. The eyes of a predator contemplating fresh, bleeding flesh.

Then it was gone, and Rusty only looked miserable again. "I called the police afterwards, left an anonymous tip. Then I tossed the gun. Next day, I told Terry the news. Her father was dead, and now she could return home in peace."

"But there was still some unfinished business. The judge who sentenced her to that hell hole was still on the bench. I tried removing him legally, filing suit to have him disbarred, but the old bastard was so deeply rooted in the WVA power structure it was impossible. So, against my better judgement, I got justice the only way there seemed to be left: by letting Terry know where the son of a bitch lived and worked. She handled the rest."

Ari shuddered. *He got a taste of the private part of himself,* he thought darkly.

"After that," she said. "I was hoping things would go back to a sort-of normal. But I made a mistake, because there was *nothing* normal about what had happened to Terry. I don't know why I suddenly expected her to have any life even approaching that. Even though I was content to settle into a somewhat regular life after I did what felt I had to do, Terry wanted more. Not just from the people who wronged her, but the entire world, it seemed. She started working for Gonzaga and the Heads, dealing drugs for them. I tried to straighten her out. Dear God, how I tried! But you develop blind spots sometimes toward the people you love, or want to. The last thing any parent wants to believe about their child is that they've gone bad."

"I'm sorry, Ari," Rusty said. "I didn't know how bad things were getting. If I had . . .hell, if I'd done one thing differently through the years, all your family might still be alive. That weighs on me, being willfully stupid while my daughter turned the world into a bloodbath."

Rusty looked out the window at the darkening sky. "I buried her, y'know? Took what was left of her and buried her in a plot marked

'Evangeline Deureaux' in Charles Town. There's been quite a bit of media attention going on during the time you've been unconcious. Reporters asking questions. Hell, they're casing my house right now, probably. Terry's become an infamous boogey-person, like Charles Manson, or that poor woman they've arrested down in Florida recently. Aileen Somebody. She'd probably like it, Terry would. For now though, I want her left in peace. Give her the peace in death she never had in life."

She reached into the briefcase she had brought in with her, digging out a large manila envelope. Placing it on the small side table next to Ari's bed, she said, "That's all the evidence you need to nail me to the wall, Ari. It's part of the file Jones had assembled, linking us. Right now, the police are outside, probably waiting to take your statement. It's up to you whether or not you wanna share this info with them."

"How did you get ahold of it, Ms. Darrow?" Ari asked.

Rusty smiled grimly. "It pays to be well connected, Ari. But all that's about to change. I'm tired of secrets. I'm tired of living on the run from everything. I want to live honestly, even if it means I have to go to jail."

She closed her briefcase and prepared to leave. "I'll abide by whatever you decide, Ari. I'm going back to my hotel down the street. I'll wait for the police there, if that's what you want. Or you can call them in now. Whatever you want."

Ari stared at the envelope before him. It was so plain, so ordinary. The perfect mask for the emotional landmine within. *Do something right by us, for once in your life,* his father's voice whispered in his head. *Make this woman pay!*

And then, the voice of Rachel. Cool, logical, warm-hearted Rachel: *Set her free.*

"I'm not you, Dad," he muttered. "And you're dead. So shut up."

The voice of his father went silent. It would never trouble him again. "Ms. Darrow? Rusty? Stay here, please. This is my answer."

He picked up the envelope by one end and put the other in his mouth. Pulling on it, he tore it in half, and let both pieces fall to the floor. "We could wait for the cleaning crew to come pick that up, but that might be dangerous," he said. "Perhaps you could burn it?"

The look of relief on the older woman's face was heartbreaking. "Ari? Are you sure? Why-?"

"Ma'am, you've already been punished. You made mistakes, but you tried. That's more than a lot of people." *Including me*, he wanted to add, but didn't. "Besides, I'm tired of payback. You said so yourself, that's all that Terry lived for. And I don't want to go down that road if I can help it. So it starts here."

"But, if it hadn't been for me-"

"If it hadn't been for you, a lot of other people would've been a lot worse off. Like I said, I read the articles Barney collected. You've probably saved more lives than you ever *wanted* to take. I gotta believe that means something. So any revenge sorta has to go by the wayside compared to that."

Rusty knelt to gather up the file, placing it back in her briefcase. "How can I ever repay you?" she asked.

"Just by doing what you're doing. Help people. Make this world less shitty so that people like Terry won't exist anymore, because they'll actually get a fair shake out of life."

"You've gotta deal, Ari."

Ari was distracted by the sound of determined footsteps outside his door. The door burst open and three men entered the room, two of them dressed in police uniforms. The man in the center wore a cheap suit and a condescending smirk on his face. Studiously ignoring Rusty, he focused all his attention on the young man on the bed. "Ariel Sussman?" he inquired, his beady, too-close together eyes fixed in a stare.

"Yeah, that's me," Ari responded, a sinking feeling in his chest. "Are you here to take my statement, Mr.-?"

"Lieutenant Reed, Maryland Police. And I suggest you don't make any statement for now."

He pulled a pair of handcuffs from his pocket and fastened one end on Ari's wrist and the other on the arm support of Ari's bed. "Ariel Sussman, you are under arrest for the murder of Maury and

Deborah Sussman, Rachel Marie Brannan, and the manslaughter of State Trooper Thomas E. Jones and Earl Kelly."

"Excuse me," Ari heard Rusty say behind Reed.

"You have the right to remain silent," he continued. "If you give up that right, anything you say-"

"Excuse me!"

"-may be taken down and used in a court of law. You have the right to an attorney."

"Excuse *me!*"

Rusty grabbed ahold of the man's arm. Reed pivoted away from her, throwing the hand off. "You do not wanna do that, lady!" he said. "That's assaulting a police officer!"

"Then know this, officer," she said acidly. "I don't like being ignored when I'm trying to get your attention."

"Who the hell are you?"

"I'm that attorney my client has a right to. You remember that part of Miranda, or is it all just words to you?"

Ari could see Reed's jaw muscles working, grinding away as he tried to keep his composure. "Well then, your client here, ma'am," he retorted. "He's in a lotta trouble. The D.A. has issued a warrant for his arrest on those murder and manslaughter charges. His parents, his next door neighbor, the state trooper and that truck driver."

"Terry Scranton did those murders," Rusty rejoined. "Don't you read the papers?"

"Well, you'll have plenty of opportunity to convince him otherwise. The D.A. found no evidence linking Terry Scranton with the murder of Ariel Sussman's family. But we did find his fingerprints and the murder weapon used on them lying next to him when we picked him up."

Ari blanched as he remembered the still-flaming blade as it landed on the grass as he blacked out. Rusty, however, didn't even flinch. "You also found him in a 'field of grass'," she cracked. "While you're at it, why didn't you bring him up on a drug charge too?"

"Be that as it may, lady," Reed answered. "The D.A. has sent in his indictment, and your client is officially under arrest. He's to be arraigned in a week, whether he's mobile or not. We'll be keeping him here under police surveillance until that time."

"Then I will follow you down to the station house and have him officially released on his own recognizance."

"Whatever you want. It's your dime."

"And take off these ridiculous handcuffs."

Reed gave her a smug look that could only be cured by a good slap. "Uh-uh," he stated. "The cuffs stay. Rules are rules."

"He's gotta broken arm and a leg! What's he gonna do? Hop outta here?"

"The cuffs stay."

"Fine. Then get the hell outta here while I confer with my client."

The two uniforms left the room first, with Reed trailing after. Just as he was about to leave, Ari piped up. "Why are you doing this?" he cried. "I didn't do anything! Why me!?"

"Ari, hush!" Rusty snapped.

Reed barely even looked over his shoulder. "I don't care, kid," he said. "Somebody's gotta go down for it, and you're the only one left. Tough break." And out he went, closing the door behind him.

Rusty gathered up her briefcase, her face flushed crimson. "Arrogant sonuvabitch," she muttered. "Gonna be a pleasure nailing him to the wall."

"Rusty, thank you," Ari said. "But I can't pay you. I can't afford you!"

Rusty gave him a strange smile. "You can, honey. But that doesn't matter now. This is a freebie. I think I owe you, no?"

Ari dropped his eyes, and Rusty gave a reassuring squeeze on his hand, minding the manacles. "Hang on, Ari," she said. "We'll get through this. Show a little faith. I'll be back soon."

And now Rusty left the room, closing the door behind her. Ari was alone. Again.

He stared dully at his handcuffed wrist, wondering (not for the first time) how he got there. Had it really been two months since this madness started? Since he had driven down the highway to school, so full of hope for the future?

He flashed back to a time, years ago, when all this seemed impossible. He was sitting in Rachel's house, not long after graduation, and was flipping cable channels as he waited for her to get ready to go out. Eventually, he landed on MTV and, as luck would have it, they were about the premiere the new Springsteen video. "Brilliant Disguise", this new song was called.

Eagerly he waited for it, but came away from the experience a bit shook up. Because this video was different from what he was used to from the Boss. Gone were the bright colors and enthusiasm that had marked *Born in the USA*. Filmed in stark back and white, the whole video consisted of Bruce sitting in a kitchen that had seen better days, strumming a guitar. Gradually, the camera moved in until all you could see was Bruce's face. It was this that unnerved Ari the most. He wasn't exuding energy anymore; instead, he was subdued to the point of . . . . what? Disappointment?

At the very end, the close-up made Bruce seem tired, haunted even. His eyes burrowed into the back of Ari's head. "*Tonight our bed is cold,*" he sang/rasped (it took Ari a moment to realize that Bruce's vocals were live). "*Lost in the darkness of our love. God have mercy on the man . . . who doubts what he's sure of.*"

That's all I've got left, Bruce, he told himself as he stared into the night.

Then came Terry's voice. *Dyin' ain't always the worst thing,* it said. *Sometimes it's worse when yer left alive.*

Alive, he cried.

Printed in the United States
by Baker & Taylor Publisher Services